Praise for *Transformation*

"Plenty of action, some interesting magic, and a
pair of unlikely heroes keep this first novel
powerfully entertaining."
—*Locus*

"Superby textured, splendidly characterized, this
spellbinding tale provides myriad delights."
—*Romantic Times*

"[A] wonderful debut novel. Her heroes come
alive on the page . . . [and] the magic is
fresh and full of purpose."
—Lynn Flewelling, author of *Traitor's Moon*

DON'T MISS CAROL BERG'S
BREAKTHTAKING FIRST NOVEL

TRANSFORMATION

"Vivid characters and intricate
magic combined with a fascinating
world—luscious work!"
—Melanie Rawn

REVELATION

Carol Berg

A ROC BOOK

ROC
Published by New American Library, a division of
Penguin Putnam Inc., 375 Hudson Street,
New York, New York 10014, U.S.A.
Penguin Books Ltd, 27 Wrights Lane,
London W8 5TZ, England
Penguin Books Australia Ltd, Ringwood,
Victoria, Australia
Penguin Books Canada Ltd, 10 Alcorn Avenue,
Toronto, Ontario, Canada M4V 3B2
Penguin Books (N.Z.) Ltd, 182–190 Wairau Road,
Auckland 10, New Zealand

Penguin Books Ltd, Registered Offices:
Harmondsworth, Middlesex, England

First published by Roc, an imprint of New American Library,
a division of Penguin Putnam Inc.

First Printing, August 2001
10 9 8 7 6 5 4 3 2 1

Cover art by Matt Stawicki
Cover design by Ray Lundgren

 REGISTERED TRADEMARK—MARCA REGISTRADA

Printed in the United States of America

PUBLISHER'S NOTE
This is a work of fiction. Names, characters, places, and incidents either are
the product of the author's imagination or are used fictitiously, and any
resemblance to actual persons, living or dead, business establishments, events,
or locales is entirely coincidental.

BOOKS ARE AVAILABLE AT QUANTITY DISCOUNTS WHEN USED TO PROMOTE
PRODUCTS OR SERVICES. FOR INFORMATION PLEASE WRITE TO PREMIUM
MARKETING DIVISION, PENGUIN PUTNAM INC., 375 HUDSON STREET, NEW YORK,
NEW YORK 10014.

For Ginny, Jane, and Shirley—
friends and craftswomen all—
my eyes and conscience.

And for Andrew, first fan and true believer.

CHAPTER 1

Verdonne was a beauteous woodland maid, a mortal who caught the eye and heart of the god who ruled the forest lands of earth. The lord of the forest took Verdonne to wife, and she bore him a child, a fair and healthy son named Valdis. And the mortals who lived in the lands of trees rejoiced at the alliance between their own kind and the gods.
—The story of Verdonne and Valdis as told to the First of the Ezzarians when they came to the lands of trees

I am not a Seer. What lies ahead, now that I have done the unthinkable, I cannot say. I believe . . . I hope . . . it will be wholeness. For sixteen long years I had assumed I would go mad—when I was a slave and believed the life I loved forever lost to me. But I've come to think the gods play tricks on us. Only when I had reclaimed sanity and surety did my world begin to come apart, and once on the path to my own disintegration, I could find no way to stop.

"Hold still," said the slight, prim young woman who was dressing my bleeding shoulder. She dabbed at the deep gash with a cloth soaked in teravine, an acrid medicament surely concocted by some Derzhi torturer. Her hand was surprisingly heavy for one with her waiflike body, but then I already knew Fiona's frail appearance was as painfully deceptive as an iron splinter.

"All I want right now is a drink of water and my own bed," I said, pushing away her unsatisfactory ministrations and reaching for the gray cloak that lay on the floor. The orange light from the dying fire glowed warm in the polished stone. "The bleeding has stopped. Ysanne will see to healing it."

"It is irresponsible to expect the Queen to care for an unbandaged wound from demon combat. Certainly until her child is born."

"Then, I'll do it myself. I would not endanger the child— *our* child."

Spending every waking moment with someone who considers you an abomination is not at all comfortable. Perhaps it would have been easier to ignore Fiona if she had not been so good at everything she did. She exhibited precision and intelligence in the weaving of her enchantments, and perfection in her adherence to law and custom. Every movement of her hand, every glance, every word she deigned to speak was a reproach for my own lack of virtue, so that I found myself feeling guilty for my constant state of anger and frustration.

"But it should be bandaged before you leave the temple. The law says—"

"No poison will get into it, Fiona. You've cleaned it well, and I thank you, as always. But it's the middle of the night, I've fought three battles in three days, and if I hurry, I might get to sleep on something other than this rock of a floor before I have to fight another. You need to rest, too. We can't afford to slip."

I fastened the cloak about my shoulders. Although the night was pleasantly warm, the rain that whispered through the oak trees surrounding the open-sided temple would cool me off too quickly, a risk for cramps. I was still overheated from a ferocious fight in a landscape that made the furnace-like heart of the Azhaki desert feel like a spring garden.

"As you wish, Master Seyonne," said the young woman, her narrow nose flared in distaste and her slightly overlarge mouth pressed into a familiar disapproval. She gathered up her bags of herbs and medicines, the roll of clean linen, and the slim wooden box in which I had placed the silver knife and the oval mirror I used to battle demons. "I'll complete the cleaning and the invocations."

She almost made me feel guilty enough to stay and help with those things Ezzarian custom required of the Warden and the Aife to ensure that no trace of demon lingered in the temple, and I could well imagine her jotting down this latest transgression in her growing list of my faults. But the prospect of being out of Fiona's sight even for a few moments would have made me abandon a great deal more than a few meaningless rituals. There comes a point when you can't pretend anymore, even when you know your choices are going to make your life miserable. I was very tired.

With a self-righteous flourish Fiona threw a handful of jasnyr leaves on the smoldering ashes of the temple fire, and the sweet-pungent smoke trailed after me into the rainy night.

Despite the constant drizzle, the late hour, and my fervent wish to be in bed with my wife, I walked slowly along the well-trodden path through the open woodland. I inhaled deeply, the fresh scent of the night a balm for aches and bruises and a troubled heart. Rain . . . new-sprung grass . . . rich black earth . . . moldering oak leaves. Melydda—true power, sorcery—in every leaf and stem. Ezzaria. Our blessed land. As I did every time I walked its forest paths or sat atop its green velvet hillsides, I sent my gratitude to the Derzhi Emperor-in-waiting.

I had not spoken with Aleksander since the night of his anointing. While my days had been consumed with the resettlement of Ezzaria and the resumption of the demon war, his life had taken him to the farthest reaches of his sprawling empire. Almost two years had passed since we had joined my strength with my power to defeat the Gai Kyallet, the Lord of Demons, and ruin the Khelid plot to place a demon-infested emperor on the Lion Throne. I never failed to smile when I thought of the wild and arrogant prince, which was perhaps the strangest outcome of all from our strange adventure. How often does a slave come to love his master like a brother, and the master return his love with gifts of a renewed heart and the most marvelously beautiful land on earth?

The path crested a hill, and I looked down into a tree-lined vale where lamplight shone like tiny jewels nestled in a fold of black velvet. I could have run down the path and within a quarter of an hour drowned myself in firelight and dry blankets, slender, loving arms and dark hair tinged with red-gold light. But as I always did when I walked that particular path, I climbed up the limestone bluff that crowned the hill like a white tooth in the jawbone of the earth, and I sat for a while. Though I would never again believe I could fight any battle unaided—my ordeal inside Aleksander's soul had taught me that, at least—I still needed time alone once the fighting was done. Time to let the fire of enchantment in my blood cool. Time for the intense concentration that it took to pursue demons to subside into more normal perceptions of the peaceful world. Time to ease the toll a life of violence—no matter how worthy its goals—took upon the soul. And after sixteen years of life in bondage, when I could not afford to live beyond the present moment lest I founder in the pain of my existence, it was an exquisite pleasure to sit, gaze down at those lights, and savor the expectation of joy.

As had been the case for several months, this brief interval was also the time I forced my anger, frustration, and indignation aside before going home to Ysanne. For half my life I had been a slave to the Derzhi, taken at eighteen when the sprawling Derzhi Empire had at last engulfed Ezzaria. In those years of pain and degradation, my existence was everything my people deemed corrupt. Ezzarian law viewed my impurity as a sure channel for demon vengeance, and so even after Aleksander had granted me my freedom, I was supposed to be shunned . . . dead, in effect. No Ezzarian was to speak to me, to acknowledge my existence, to hear any word that came from my tongue lest I infect them with my corruption and put our secret war at risk. Only the persuasive power of my dead mentor's granddaughter and that of my wife, the Queen of Ezzaria, had convinced my countrymen that the circumstances of my battle with the Lord of Demons were so extraordinary as to merit an exception to our law.

In the autumn of the year of my freedom and homecoming, we had moved back to the remote, southern land Aleksander had returned to us and resumed the vigil that few people beyond our borders even suspected. I had once again become a Warden of Ezzaria, who walked into tormented souls on the paths of enchantment woven by my partner Aife, there to face the demon beings who drove human victims to madness or grew strong by feeding upon their wickedness. And so at thirty-five I had taken up my life again where it had ended when I was eighteen.

As I expected, some among my people were not reconciled to my reinstatement and swore I would bring disaster upon Ezzaria. But I never imagined their voices would be so strong that they could set a watcher to follow me every moment of every day, examining my works, judging my words, waiting for me to slip, to err, to demonstrate subtle signs of demon infestation. In the year just past, I had fought over two hundred demon combats. There were days when I stepped through the Aife's portal still bleeding from the last encounter, days like the past three, when I snatched sleep rolled in my cloak on the temple floor, because word had come that another combat was set, another soul in torment who needed our help. How long would it take to prove that I was only what I claimed—a man no better, no worse, than any other, trying to make sense out of the strangest life anyone could live? Until then, there was Fiona.

As if I had conjured my nemesis from the stuff of night, determined footsteps intruded on the quiet, and a glaring yellow light flickered through the trees, disrupting the soft darkness. The footsteps stopped just at the base of my hill, though she could not possibly see me from the path. "The rites are complete, Master Seyonne. I'll be at the bridge at first light."

Of course she would. I needed no reminders. After a moment's silence, the footsteps resumed their cadence and quickly faded into the night. I sighed and hunched my cloak about my shoulders against the rain.

The intense young Aife had been appointed by the Mentors Council to be my shadow. Bad enough to have her watching and listening as I taught our student Wardens, to see her diligently taking notes when I skipped rituals I found hollow or spoke of how my beliefs had changed in my years of bondage, though my commitment had grown deeper and my faith stronger as a result. I could not hide how I had come to see that matters of good and evil, purity and corruption were far more complex than the precise

definitions of Ezzarian tradition. But there had come a day
when my wife could no longer be my partner, the peerless
day when I learned we were to have a child. A woman
carrying a child could not risk demon infestation—the child
had no defenses—and so the partnership that had begun
when we were fifteen would have to end until the birth.
But that day so ripe with promise had soured quickly when
I was told I could not choose Ysanne's replacement.

A Warden's life depended entirely on his partner Aife—
on her skill at weaving the enchantment that created physical reality from the substance of a human soul, on her understanding of what techniques worked best for him, on
her endurance at holding the portal until he could withdraw
victorious or escape defeat. And not only had the Council
forbidden me the power to choose, but they had paired me
with Fiona. I was beside myself with fury. Yet I could not
refuse to fight without proving the very ill that was said
of me.

"Fiona is the most skilled of Aifes," Ysanne said to
me every time the call came, and I had to leave her for
the temple and Fiona. "I would have no one else weave
for you. Only a little while longer."

And, of course, as I looked down on the lights winking at
me from the quiet forest midnight, that consideration ban-
ished everything but joy. Some night soon, when I walked
down this hill into the vale where our house stood safely
nestled in the trees, I would find the proof that I had indeed
been graced with every gift a man could hope for. Our
child would be born in Ezzaria. There was no room for
anger when I thought of that.

I jumped up from my rocky perch and started down the
hill. Halfway down I stopped to reposition Fiona's wadded
cloth against the gash in my shoulder. The wound had
started bleeding again, and I could feel the trickling warmth
soaking my shirt. No need to worry Ysanne over nothing.

During this pause I heard a faint cry in the distance,
scarcely audible against the rain that was drumming harder
on the path, cascading from the thick leaves overhead,
splashing and pooling in the hollows. I passed the back of
my hand across my eyes, shifting into my more acute
senses, tuned to see and hear at great distances and beyond

barriers and enchantments. But all I heard was a horse galloping away far beyond our house.

Uneasy, I picked up the pace. Abandoning the muddy track that wound gracefully around the vale, I headed straight down the steep hillside through the thick, wet leaves. The nervous pricking between my shoulder blades grew insistent. The winking lamplight taunted me as I dodged trees and my boots slid in the mud. Bypassing the longer route across a wooden bridge, I leaped the stream at the bottom of the gully, whispered open the barriers of enchantment, and ran up a flight of wooden steps. Breathlessly I burst through the door into the large comfortable room that was our private part of the rambling Queen's Residence. No one was there.

The chair cushions of russet and dark green, the woven rug, the loaf-shaped mourning stone, the simple furnishings of oak and pine, the weavings on the walls that told the stories of Ezzaria, the precious books of history and lore that had been carried into exile and back again—all were as they had been three days before when I had last seen them. The lamp of rose-colored glass beside the window was lit as it always was when I was away. Nothing was wrong. Ysanne would be in bed. She tired easily in these last weeks, and she knew I would not stay away longer than necessity bade me.

Yet my uneasiness did not vanish. The house was not asleep. Sparks popped quietly in the hearth from coals that pulsed glowing orange. Someone had been there not an hour since. A walking stick of ash stood beside the front door. The scent of unfamiliar bodies lingered. And other smells—the pungent tang of juniper berries and the dark earth smell of black snakeroot, used for healing. *Ysanne* . . .

I blew out the lamp and tiptoed into our bedchamber. It was dark, the windows open to the soft sound of the rain. Ysanne lay on her side, and I exhaled when I laid my hand on her cheek and felt it warm and soft. But she was not asleep. Her breathing was shallow, tight. I knelt on the floor by her side, brushed the dark hair from her face, and kissed her. "Is all well with you, beloved?" She made no answer, and when I stroked her arm and kissed the palm of her hand, I felt a tight quivering just beneath her skin.

"Let me get out of these wet things and get you warm," I said. She still said nothing. I left my soggy clothes in a heap, and made a halfhearted effort at wiping off mud spatters and tying a clean strip of linen about my wounded shoulder. Then I climbed in beside my wife and wrapped my arms around her . . . and discovered that she no longer carried a child. "Sweet Verdonne!"

Believing I understood everything, and preparing myself for tears and grief and the slow journeying from pain to acceptance, I whispered a word of enchantment and cast a soft silver light. Ysanne blinked her violet eyes at me as if she had been sleeping, then brushed her hand on my cheek and smiled. "You're home at last! I've missed you so. When Garen told me they'd set a third battle and you'd not have time to come home, I almost bundled our blankets and pillows and brought them to the temple so we could at least sleep together in between."

"Ysanne—"

"What's this?" She sat up and pulled away my hasty bandage. "You didn't let Fiona work on this. You should, you know. Not for any fear of demon poison, but to set it healing quicker . . . and here it's raining and you're so cold."

"Ysanne, tell me what happened. Someone should have come for me. How could they have left you alone?"

She jumped out of the bed, lit the lamp, and brought the box where she kept her medicines. I tried to stop her, to make her talk to me, but she insisted on dressing the wound, reciting every word of the invocations and cleansing prayers. When she was done, she started to get up again to clean up the mess, but I took her bloody hands and held her there. "Tell me what happened to our child, Ysanne. Born . . . dead? You must tell me."

But she widened her violet eyes and stared at me as if I'd lost my mind. "Was your head injured, too, my love? What child?"

"She won't speak of it, Catrin. She pushed me away, telling me I was so tired I was dreaming, that I was thinking of Garen and Gwen and their new little one. Then she refused to discuss it anymore. I'm afraid for her reason." I shoved aside the cup of wine that sat untasted on the table in front of me. "Tell me what to do. This is beyond anything I know."

The dark-haired young woman in a white nightdress tapped her fingers on her mouth. "Have you spoken to anyone else about it?"

"I tried Nevya. She claimed that she had delivered no child these three days. Aleksander once told me that I was the world's worst liar, that I turned yellow and my eyelids twitched. But these women are far worse. Daavi said she wasn't permitted to speak of the Queen's health to anyone. Anyone? Catrin, I'm her husband. Why won't they tell me? They act as if she never conceived." I rubbed my head viciously, trying desperately to cut through a suffocating fog of uncertainty.

Catrin stood up, folded her arms in front of her, and stared out of her window at the watery gray of dawn. "So what do you think is the truth?"

"I think the child was born dead, of course . . . or born alive and died. I don't know. What am I supposed to think?"

"Perhaps that's the question you need to answer first."

My head was a muddle. I had not slept at all, but given it up and come to Catrin when Ysanne fell asleep an hour before dawn without answering even one of my questions. And now Catrin, whom I'd counted on for straight answers, was dancing around the subject, too.

"Come, my old friend, stretch out by the hearth and sleep for a while. You're going to collapse in a puddle if you don't get some rest. The answers will come if you stop trying to create them on your own."

"Catrin, was my wife with child or not? Answer me."

Her dark eyes were clear, though filled with sympathy. "I cannot answer that, Seyonne. But I will tell you this. She is not mad. Now sleep for a while, then go home and tell her how dearly you love her." She laid a hand on my forehead, and a wave of exhaustion sapped the last strength from my limbs.

And of course Catrin was right, as she so often was. As soon as I let go of my fear and my grief enough to sleep, I knew what had happened. The infant was dead whether or not it yet breathed. Our child had been born a demon.

CHAPTER 2

We Ezzarians knew very little of our origins. Oddly enough, for a people so steeped in arcane lore and practices, we had almost no tradition of our beginnings, only the myth of our gods and two scrolls written a mere thousand years in the past at the inception of the demon war. Somehow in the lost years before the time of those writings, we had found our way to Ezzaria, a warm, green land of deep forests and open hillsides that seemed to nurture the extraordinary power we called melydda. And somehow in those years we had discovered the way to free a human soul from the ravages of demon possession.

The Scroll of the Rai-kirah taught us of demons—soulless, bodiless creatures, not evil in themselves, but who satisfied their hunger with human terror and madness and unholy death. The writing said that demons lived in the frozen northlands and would return there to regenerate when we cast them out of their human hosts. If they refused to go, we killed them—reluctantly, because we felt the world diminished, thrown out of balance, by the explosive power of their dying.

The Scroll of Prophecy warned us of corruption and the need for vigilance lest the rai-kirah follow the path of our weaknesses to infest our own souls. In this scroll a Seer named Eddaus had written of the war to end the world, and the battle where the Warrior of Two Souls would face the Lord of Demons. Eddaus never mentioned that the Warrior of Two Souls was really two men, a Derzhi prince and a sorcerer slave—Aleksander and myself. Together we had fought the battle and won it. After foretelling this combat, the prophecy ended. Abruptly. Whatever further seeing had been granted to our ancestors had been lost or destroyed with their other writings.

Other than the scrolls only two artifacts remained from that ancient time: the originals of the silver knives that could be transformed into any kind of weapon when carried beyond the portal, and the Luthen mirrors, the oval glasses that could paralyze a demon by showing the creature its own reflection. Everything else we knew had been learned from hard experience. Though we could explain so little of our history, the evidence of our eyes taught us why we had to do it—the terrible consequences of demon possession left unopposed. Only a few other people in the world had power for true sorcery, and none of them seemed to know anything of rai-kirah. We buried our questions because we saw no alternatives.

No scroll or writing or experience explained this dreadful thing that happened to our children—the one in every few hundred births that was born possessed. An infant had no barriers to the demon within it, and so the child and the demon were inseparable. And even if we had known how to untangle the child's being from the demon, it was impossible to create a stable portal into an infant's soul—so small, so inexperienced, so chaotic. Yet we dared not have a demon living in our midst, and thus our law required us to be rid of them. I had never given the dilemma much thought. Not until it was my own.

"She killed our child." I sat on Catrin's hearth rug, the afternoon sun pouring in through the open front door. I had slept for a few hours before waking with the understanding I would have fought fifty demons at once to avoid. My body was numb. My soul was desolation. A sword could have sliced off my arm, and I would not have felt it. Catrin pressed a cup into my hand and forced me to drink from it, but I could not have said whether the drink was hot or cold, bitter or sweet. I was as lost and adrift as the dust motes floating in the angled sunbeams. "She left him naked on a rock for the wolves to find, and now everyone pretends he never existed. They shun even the memory of him because they don't know what else to do. How could she do it? We say self-murder is abhorrent to the gods. What of infant murder? A child can do no evil."

As she took the cup away, Catrin pressed a finger to her mouth and shook her head slightly. But the seed of anger, planted in me when Fiona took up her watch, began to grow as if watered by Catrin's tea.

"And she tries to play this game with me. Am I to convince myself that I didn't use my power to see that we had made a son? Am I to go through the rest of my life pretending I didn't feel his heart beating? I can't do it, Catrin. We gloried in the wonder of a life created from love and faithfulness, and now she says I can't even grieve. My wife has murdered my son, and I am not to take note of the fact?"

Catrin sat on the floor in front of me. In the corner behind her was the plain gray block of her mourning stone, its nine candles lit to warm the spirits of her grandfather and her long dead parents. I had interrupted her afternoon meditation. My friend and mentor took my hands in her own. "You've been asleep, Seyonne. Dreaming terrible dreams. As I told you earlier, I can do nothing for dreams."

So Catrin, too, had decided to live the lie. But she placed a finger on my lips before I could protest. "Now you must think of something else for a while," she said. "A message has come in from a Searcher in Capharna. They'll be ready three hours from now. Can you fight? Have you rested enough?"

It took me a moment to comprehend. The rest of the world had faded into insignificance beside the devastation of my family. "Fight?" A demon battle. The net of enchantment that Ezzaria strung through the world had snagged another demon. I stared at her in disbelief. How could anyone think I could fight on this day?

"Fiona says it's a wicked situation, a slave merchant. If you can't do it . . . "

Why this one of all days? I closed my eyes and tried to draw myself together. There was no one else. "No. No, of course I'll do it." Three hours. Barely enough time to prepare. Dismal life would have to wait. "If you could just help me with this. . . ." I removed one sleeve of my shirt and had her loosen the tight bandage Ysanne had put on my shoulder. Better to risk a little bleeding than restrict my movements.

After she had rebandaged my shoulder and made me eat a plateful of cold meat, Catrin laid her small, strong hand on my head. "You'll have help soon. Three months and we'll have Tegyr and Drych ready for their testing. And Gryffin sends word from the east that Emrys and Nestayo will be ready soon after. You've done marvels with them, Seyonne. You're an exceptional teacher." But her kindness rang hollow.

"It's not enough, is it? After this no one will believe I'm uncorrupted. They'll say I've brought a demon into the Queen's house. Into the Queen's body."

Catrin sighed in exasperation and shook my head with a handful of my hair. "Be careful in this battle, my first and most prized pupil." I looked up at her and realized she was not referring only to the combat of the next few hours. The sentiment made more sense when I kissed her cheek and stepped out of her door to find Fiona sitting on the steps. My watchdog would have heard every word we'd said.

I did not trust myself to speak to Fiona, so I strode out through the woods toward the temple, trying to decide what I might do when the battle was over. It was no use attempting to settle my mind about things. That was going to be a longer ordeal than the time I had available at the moment. All I could hope for was to come up with some step I could take that would begin to set life back in order. I couldn't think of a single one.

Ezzarian temples were simple stone structures built in deep forests whose richness seemed to strengthen our power. They were scattered throughout Ezzaria, always similar in appearance: a roofed circle of five pairs of white fluted columns, rising from a floor of polished stone. In the center were a few small, enclosed rooms, but most of the place was open to the wind and weather. The temple floor was inlaid with mosaics depicting events in our history, and in its open expanse were a fire pit and a low stone platform where we would place the victim on the rare occasion the person was brought to us. Most often the victim was in some distant city or village in the care of an Ezzarian Com-

forter. The Comforter was a channel; he would lay hands
upon the victim and spin out a simple line of strong enchantment that would reach all the way to the Aife in the
temple.

Since I was the only Warden who had survived the Derzhi conquest and the Khelid conspiracy, this particular temple was the only one in use. A temple aide had made the
place ready for our coming venture. Beside the fire where
Fiona and I would join our magic and make the attempt,
the aide had laid out a white robe for Fiona and a brass
jar filled with jasnyr leaves. Accompanied by a proper enchantment, jasnyr would make the neatly laid fire in the pit
burn long and true, and prevent its smoke from stinging
the eyes. Too, the Scroll of the Rai-kirah said that jasnyr
was abhorrent to demons. In the preparation room—an
empty, unadorned room in the center of the stone building—the aide would have set out a pitcher of water for
drinking, a basin of water for washing, a clean drying cloth,
a set of clean clothes made to fit me, my dark blue Warden's cloak, and the wooden box with the knife and the
mirror.

I had to wait for Fiona before beginning my preparation.
She needed to tell me more about the victim, and I would
be unable to speak to her once I was prepared. So I sat on
the temple steps and watched the sun settle beyond the
trees. I almost laughed. If Ysanne had never been with
child, then why was Fiona my partner for this battle?

"Are you ready to fight again so soon, Master Seyonne?"
Fiona arrived more quickly than I had expected. She stood
in front of me, her whole posture a reproach, as if my
sitting down were just another of my crimes.

She was not unpleasant to look on, small, slim, her dark,
straight hair kept short—unusual for Ezzarian women, who
favored single braids or long falls of hair caught with flowers or woven ribbons. She disdained skirts and dresses in
favor of full-sleeved shirts and breeches, but one could not
say she dressed like a man, for there was no mistaking the
womanly aspect to her slender figure. The costume looked
natural on her. Ysanne had told me that many of the young
women who had spent the years of Derzhi occupation hiding in the forest preferred to dress in that fashion. They'd

had no materials to make clothes, and so they had taken what they could find on the fallen bodies of our countrymen and in the abandoned cottages they passed as they fell back deep into the trees. They had become accustomed to the freedom of movement men's clothes afforded them.

"Catrin told me this is a slave merchant," I said.

"Yes. He's recently begun specializing in young girls, selling them to Derzhi nobles . . ."

The disgust in her voice when she spoke of the Derzhi was a continuing indictment of me, who dared call one of the despised conquerors my friend. She proceeded to tell me of the horrors the merchant had committed, and of what the Searcher had found out about his life. Clearly he was no innocent taken by a hungering demon to be devoured quickly, but rather one who was a source of long-time sustenance for his resident rai-kirah. Such long-nurtured demons were the most difficult to root out.

"You seem distracted, Master Seyonne. Perhaps we should call this off."

"And leave this rai-kirah to its work?"

"We cannot right every wrong in the world."

"If you had lived in the world, you could not say that so easily. Let's get on with it."

She nodded, gazing reproachfully at the scar on my face—the royal falcon and lion that had been burned into my left cheekbone on the day I was sold to Aleksander. "As you say. You'll not forget the purification in your preparation?"

I forced myself patient. "I have never forgotten the purification, Fiona."

"Hammard found the towel dry yesterday. If you had washed—"

"I need no teaching in how to wash myself, nor do I have to justify the weather. If you remember, the afternoon was hot. I did not use the towel. Has Hammard nothing better to do than examine my towels?"

Fiona glared at me. "You skip steps in the rites. They are there for a reason. If you were sincere in your intent, you'd do things correctly."

I would not get into an argument with her over my sincerity. If two hundred demon encounters in a year were not sincere enough, then no words were going to convince her. I needed to be at peace. "If there's nothing else. . . ."

"I had to clean the knife again after you left last night."

My irritation bristled into true anger. "You have no business touching the knife. You overstep yourself, Fiona." The enchantments on the Warden's knife were very precise and not completely understood. We had learned how to duplicate them through the years, but we did not know what might affect their peculiar magic. The knife was the only weapon a Warden could take beyond the Aife's portal. Every other would disintegrate in your hand. We dared not tamper with it.

"But you had—"

"It was perfectly clean. If you touch it again, I will insist on your replacement."

Though she set her jaw defiantly, she knew she had gone too far, for she didn't take time to list the other hundred things she had planned to accuse me of.

"We'd best make ready," I said. "I'll need an hour and a half, as usual." I had a feeling that a hundred hours weren't going to put me in the proper state of calm readiness I needed. I left her there, holding her robe and glaring after me in the waning light.

As always, I worked for an hour at the kyanar, the martial exercises that helped center my thoughts and prepare my body for the coming confrontation. On that night, for the first time in my career as a Warden of Ezzaria, I thought that the combat beyond the portal might be a relief.

By the time Fiona came for me, robed in plain, shapeless white as ritual specified, I had washed myself, drunk most of the clean water in the pitcher, donned the clothes, the Warden's cloak, and the weapons, and used Ioreth's Chant to put myself into a state halfway between the world we walked and the one the Aife would create for me. The rite was immensely calming, and despite my distress, I felt quite capable of the focus necessary to do my job. Fiona led me to the temple fire, and when I nodded that I was ready, she took my hands and worked her awesome magic.

To anyone who watched, it would seem that I had vanished from the temple, yet I could see it behind me, a pale outline against the bright stars of the Ezzarian night. Before me was another place . . . of rocks, earth, water, and air to breathe . . . and a rai-kirah waiting—a demon, who might appear in any of a million different shapes.

When I stepped through the misty gray rectangle that was Fiona's portal there were no whispered words of comfort or well-wishing. And once I was through and the house-sized man-thing with four arms and daggerlike fangs dropped instantly on my back, I had no time to think of Ysanne or Fiona or anything else. I could not see the landscape, could not assess the possibilities for disposing of the leather-hided creature, could not do anything but keep my vital parts away from the fangs and keep moving fast enough that it could not grab me with its multiple limbs. I had only enough breath to get out half the words of the warning I was required to give. "I am the Warden, sent by . . . Aife . . . the scourge . . . demons . . . challenge you . . . this vessel. Hyssad! Begone. Not yours." It did not deign to answer me, only devoted itself more devoutly to removing my head.

Twist the upper left arm. It's already damaged. Tearing the ligaments will leave it useless. Transform the knife into a short sword . . . long enough to keep the fangs at bay while you wrap your legs around . . . No. No thinking. Just do it.

And so I fought. Untold hours. Whenever I would gain the advantage, it pulled away and I had to give chase, losing it in a murky wasteland until it pounced again. The place was dreadfully cold. I hated the hot places, but the cold ones were more dangerous. Cramps and stiffening muscles that could tear easily. Numbness, so you felt the touch of claw or steel too late. Sluggish senses. I was slathered in green blood that ate into my skin like cold fire, and the wound in my shoulder was bleeding again. Then my eyes began playing tricks on me.

As I plunged my blade into a gaping orifice that was spewing venom, I caught the glint of metal. Steel bands appeared about my wrists. I jerked my hands away from the monster, but the flat rings did not disappear . . .

. . . slave rings . . . and my hands were not my own. They were slender young hands . . . a girl's hands . . . and

*the monster was not a misshapen manifestation of demon
life, but a slack-jawed man with eyes that devoured me with
imaginings of unholy pleasure. He licked his lips . . . and
his tongue came toward my face . . .*

With disgust and fury I lashed out, trying to banish the
images of the evil this soul had wrought. But one after
another they came upon me in all their terror, pain, shame,
and degradation. I lived those children's horror as I fought,
unable to see the monstrous limbs or sharpened fangs because of the visions that clouded my sight. I had to fight
with senses that were not sight, to guide my hands and feet
with the remembrance of the bestial form, not allowing
myself to be misled by the evidence of my eyes. And when
I at last plunged my dagger into the living center of the
demon shape, I was so outraged at the violation of those
children, that I made a terrible mistake.

When its physical manifestation dies, the rai-kirah is set
loose. The Warden must discern the position of the demon
as it leaves the dead hulk, and use the Luthen mirror to
paralyze it, giving it the choice to leave the host or die.
But on that day, once I had the demon trapped, I gave it
no choice. I killed it, not in sober judgment, but in rage,
and I killed it so violently and so viciously that I killed the
victim, too.

Whatever land and sky had existed around me dissolved
instantly into chaos. A whirlwind of darkness streaked with
garish colorings, a nauseating disorientation as up and
down, left and right, lost all meaning. I struggled to keep
my own body from being ripped apart in the tumult, and I
lunged for the gray portal, shimmering, wavering at my
back . . .

"Do you know what you've done?" Fiona's harsh accusation was the first thing to penetrate the momentary confusion of my return to the real world. The Aife could not see
into the landscape she created, only sense the shape of it
and the outcome of the battle as it progressed. But she
would not mistake the death of the victim.

"I struck too hard," I said—in explanation, not justifica-
tion. A Warden did not have to justify the outcome of a
battle save to another Warden. No one but another Warden

understood how difficult demon combat could be. "He did not deserve to live." I believed that. I had walked his soul and I knew. But I had never intended to kill him.

I got slowly to my feet, taking stock of limbs and senses, of bruises and aches, making sure that the blood that soaked my clothing and covered my hands was not my own. A red clay jar and mug sat on the stone platform, and I filled the cup over and over until the cool, clean water was gone. I felt as if I'd been trampled by a herd of maddened chastou. Every bone ached. My skin felt stretched tight and was raw from venom and scraping claws.

"What happened? Explain it."

"I don't have to explain it." Every breath grated like skin on ground glass.

· I cleaned and put away my weapons, washed my hands and face, and retrieved my cloak from the preparation room.

"You're not leaving? We've not sung the chants or wiped the floor or—"

"Do them if you wish. I need to sleep."

"This is a violation. The law says—"

"Gods of night, Fiona. I've just fought a monster for half the night. I can scarcely stand. The demon is dead. The victim is dead. Wiping the floor and singing will change nothing."

I did not look back as I strode into the forest. The raging in my blood masked the too long hours of combat and the too short hours of sleep. I didn't know when I would ever be able to sleep again. How could I have done it? I was not fool enough to believe I could fight as I did and never make mistakes. We had to take the risk, and my old mentor Galadon had made sure I understood that I would have to live with failure. Sometimes the victims died. Sometimes they went mad. Sometimes we lost and had to leave them to their fate. I had done my best, and I could not fault the outcome.

Yet the event was immensely troubling. I had lost control. Because I was tired. Because I was angry. Because the victim had raped and enslaved children. And most worrisome of all was that the demon knew to use those things against me. *Damned, cursed fool. What's wrong with you?*

The Council had the bow strung and ready, and I had given them the arrow.

I paused at the top of the hill, faced with yet another dilemma—where to go for the rest of the night. Catrin would have me back, but as I began to cool off, I heard the favor she had asked of me while Fiona was listening. Only a few months until she would complete the training of two new Wardens. Until they were ready, she needed to be my mentor, not my friend, lest she be tainted with whatever suspicions attached to me. And so she had asked me to hold back. To be careful. Too late for that, but I could at least leave her unburdened with my presence. I could not embroil her in my trouble until she had ensured our future.

I had other friends . . . friends who would know by now of Ysanne and the child. Some would agree with me that shunning a dead infant was useless, that slaughtering a demon-possessed child was murder, and that murder was no solution for ignorance. Others would pretend there had been no child. All of them would be sorry for Ysanne and me. None of them could do anything. I could stomach neither pity nor hypocrisy, so the only place to go was home—what was left of it.

The lamp was in the window when I arrived. I stepped back out the door and threw it into the stream that danced under the wooden bridge in the moonlight. When the glass shattered against rock, the oil flared up, then went out. I pulled off my bloody, stinking clothes, found a blanket in the chest, and curled up in a chair by the cold hearth.

CHAPTER 3

For one year of my time in bondage I had been owned by a vile Suzaini ivory merchant named Fouret. An innately cruel man, Fouret had always taken pleasure in the pain of others: luring innocent lovers into the depths of depravity and driving his business rivals into such financial ruin that they took their own lives. He would sell his rivals' children into slavery and bed their wives before destroying them, and before casting off a young mistress for some new innocent, he would reveal to her family and friends the degradations he had required of her. To his slaves, whom he valued far less than his women or his rivals, he was worse.

I was fortunate to leave Fouret's service with all of my limbs. One could say I made my own luck, of course, for there came a day when I loosened the railing on the balcony where he stood to watch his slaves being whipped to death, and I made sure that he drank enough marazile in his breakfast tea that he would be groggy for the entire day and need to lean heavily on the rail. As it was my own flogging that was interrupted by his plunge to his death upon a spiked fence, I thought I managed things very well. I was not proud of killing him, but neither did I feel guilty. It was the same now. I did not feel guilty for killing the demon-possessed slave merchant.

I thought of Fouret for another reason on the morning I woke cramped and stiff from sleeping in a chair. I had once seen the mad Suzaini open the chest of a living man and lift the heart from his body. And I had seen the victim's face in the instant before he drowned in his own blood. I feared my face would look the same when I had to confront my wife and name her a murderer. How could a man live without his heart?

So I didn't face her. The morning was warm—no need for a fire in the hearth. We had a quiet·young man named Pym who took care of our house and cooked for us, but there was no evidence of him that morning, save a neatly folded stack of clean clothes—shirt, breeches, leggings, boots—and a plate of bread, cold chicken, and sugared cherries left on a nearby table beside a blue teapot. I was hungry—absurd, but I had lived long enough to expect it— yet I could not eat until I had talked with Ysanne. I donned the clothes and stayed where I was, in my chair with my back to the room, and when she came at last, I did not turn around.

The breath of morning air from the opening door behind me gave her away. I could not mistake the sweet smell of her skin or the rain-washed fragrance of her hair. She had damp earth on her shoes. I heard the soft shuffling on the rug as she took them off and walked three steps toward me. Not even halfway across the room.

"Trust me, Seyonne."

Absurd was too generous a word for what she asked of me. "As you trusted me?" I sat staring into the cold ashes of the brick hearth. "Did you arrange for the third battle so I wouldn't be here before you finished cleaning up?"

"I warned you two years ago that you were marrying the Queen of Ezzaria, and not just a woman who loved you beyond reason. I told you there might come a time when I had to choose."

"And so you have done." I closed my eyes and ignored the emptiness in my chest where my heart had once lived. "If it were only about me, I could not fault you. But you murdered our son and gave me no chance to save him, and I don't know how I'll ever be able to forgive you."

She stood there without speaking for a very long time. Only a sorcerer could have detected her stony presence. Only a lover could have felt the doors closing on the passionate heart that so few had ever been privileged to know. Then the oaken floorboards creaked, and she was gone.

I started eating then, commanding my stomach not to revolt. I could not afford weakness. At the rate the Searchers were unearthing demons, I could be fighting again before nightfall. I ate until I could not look at another tasteless bite, then I got up and left the house. Fiona was waiting on the wooden bridge. I walked past her as if she didn't exist.

It was almost midday. On most mornings, I would work at the kyanar for an hour, go running for another hour, and then go to Catrin's practice arena to help in training her student Wardens and hone my own still returning skills. Catrin was a tremendously talented mentor, having grown up watching her grandfather and possessing the sorcerous ability and strength of mind to make use of what she had learned from him. Though it was unusual for a woman to mentor Wardens, who were all men, she was already held in such high esteem that she sat on the Mentor's Council, the five men and women who oversaw the training, pairings, and assignments of those who fought the demon war.

Ezzarian society was very different from that of the other lands of the Empire. Among ourselves we did not trade or compete, but settled into our assigned roles to support our single purpose. Nor was there any rank or nobility among us, save what fell out from our natural gifts. All children were tested at age five. Those found to have the strongest melydda—true power for sorcery—were designated from their earliest days to assume a role in the demon war according to their particular talents. They were freed from all other responsibilities to devote their lives to training mind and body until they passed rigorous testing and took up their assignment. Honor and renown often accompanied such a life, as did danger and death and frequent nightmares. We called them valyddar—power-born. One of the valyddar—always a woman of immensely powerful gifts—served as our Queen. As she grew into middle age, she would, with the aid of her closest advisers, select her kafydda—a young woman to be trained to succeed her.

Those children found to have modest amounts of melydda—the eiliddar or skill-born—grew up to serve in other ways: warding our borders; building homes and temples; keeping our water clean, our fields protected from blights, and our homes clear of vermin; even teaching our children and doing craft work such as pottery or metalsmithing. To shape anything of permanence, whether a pot or a buckle or a child's mind could not be left to those without melydda, lest their lack of power might leave their shaping flawed and thus a danger to us all.

The tenyddar or service-born—those who had no power for sorcery—did whatever tasks they were assigned: hunting, farming, animal husbandry. We had a duty to guard an unknowing world from the horrors of demons. Even those who shoveled manure in the fields knew that their work was valued and necessary.

This is not to say there were not jealousies and rivalries. The results of a child's testing—the sole determinant of his or her future—were a matter of grave import in many families and had caused not a few disputes. Many tenyddar like my father had talents or loves for some occupation but, because they had no melydda, were assigned menial tasks instead. Some had not his grace to find the beauty and satisfaction in the life he was given—working in the fields. He had wished to be a teacher, and I had always grieved for the students who never knew his wisdom or his gentle hand. Only since my return had the consideration of that made me angry. Fiona had faithfully recorded my opinions on the matter.

Catrin was an excellent teacher, and she could have taken her charges ahead well enough without my help, but there could never be too much preparation for what they would find when they stepped through a real portal. To have an experienced opponent to practice with was a helpful addition to the very real visions Catrin conjured for them.

I was not as proficient at training students in ritual. In my years with the Derzhi, I had longed for the order and beauty and purpose of Ezzarian life. But once I was immersed in it again, it was very easy to see the flaws, the places where ritual had replaced purpose, and tradition was valued for its own sake. I had dared suggest that it might serve us better to take our young students into the world to broaden their perspectives. But I had been roundly chastised for that idea, as if I had suggested that they could learn to bathe by rolling in the mud. Though we spent our lives working to protect them, Ezzarians had little use for the people who lived outside our forest boundaries. Outsiders brought corruption.

"Seyonne!" Catrin seemed surprised to see me walk into the long whitewashed building. "What are you doing here?" Sun poured steeply through the tall open windows, drenching a narrow strip of the dirt floor where nine youths, ranging in age from eight to twenty, were engaged in various activities from sword practice to acrobatics to sitting absolutely motionless with legs crossed and eyes closed in the image of sleep. They were all so very young.

"This is what I do, I believe," I said. "What else should I be about?"

"I just thought . . ."

"No call has come this morning, and Fiona has informed me that using enchantments to repair the rotten crossmember of the bridge beside our house is an unconscionable waste of a Warden's melydda. So rather than teetering on the verge of such corruption, I am at your service. A nice eight-hour practice session . . . maybe Ezzaria's ten best students at once might be a pleasant diversion." I offered her a smile, but neither of us believed it.

"We need to talk, my friend," she said, "after we've done with these boys." She nodded curtly to Fiona, who had followed me into the practice arena and settled herself on the floor to watch and listen.

Two sturdily built young men were moving strangely in one corner of the room surrounded by a silvery curtain of light. Contained in a space twenty paces square, they passed within a hair's breadth of each other in violent activity, yet apparently unaware of each other's existence. Tegyr and Drych, Catrin's two most advanced students, were buried deep in her illusions. They believed they were fighting demons, taunting predators who disappeared and reappeared in landscapes of madness. They had likely been fighting for several hours. The morning was heavy and damp, and their skin was dripping with sweat, though in their minds they were probably bleeding and slimed with nastiness spewed from their opponents. As we watched, the shorter one, Drych, dropped his sword and held his stomach, letting out a groan of agony as he sank to his knees.

Three younger boys stopped their sword practice to gape.

Catrin snapped at them to get back to their business or they would never make it so far as Drych. Then she gave me a shove with her hand on my back. "Go pull him out. Make him believe he's not as worthless as he thinks. His practice was much harder than Tegyr's. I'll bring this one down to earth."

Tegyr, blond, wiry, and the taller of the two, carried an oval glass in one hand—an imitation of the Luthen mirror. He appeared to have vanquished his invisible foe, for the mirror was raised as if to show the demon its own reflection, and the young man's knife was ready to send the demon to its death. While I went and dragged the gasping, moaning Drych back to reality, giving him a moment to feel his abdomen and realize that he was not watering some alien landscape with his blood, Catrin stood beside the silver curtain and drew her fist through the air, leaving a silvered pattern hanging like the trail of a falling star.

"Brynnidda!" Tegyr cried out, then leaped backward and fell on his backside, dropping the mirror. He began to struggle desperately. Apparently his illusory opponent was not quite defeated. You had to be certain that the physical manifestation was dead before attacking the demon itself. Always a hard lesson. And Catrin would have no mercy on the boy. He had called out his paired Aife's name—a slip so grave it could set him back three months. Names are the channel to the soul. Demons tried every maneuver to elicit the names of Wardens or Aifes.

Drych bowed to me without greeting. For him to speak unbidden in the middle of a training session was improper. He was still quivering, either with relief that his ordeal had been only illusion, or perhaps in terror that he would be found wanting and never make use of all his hard lessons. In the next two hours I required him to review every move of his fight for me, so that we could find his mistakes, and we practiced until he had the needed corrections so imprinted on his mind and body that he would still be repeating them when he slept that night.

At one point in the middle of the session, I glimpsed Catrin and Fiona talking to a tall, formidably constructed gray-haired woman. Talar. As ever when I saw Fiona's mentor, the First of the Mentor's Council, annoyance and resentment seethed beneath my skin. Talar was the instigator of the humiliating watch on me, seemingly determined that I should be proved corrupt because I dared disagree with her. She had dragged it out for almost a year already, with six endless months to go.

Ysanne could have stopped it at any time, of course. My wife was the Queen, chosen to rule our land and people as our goddess Verdonne ruled the forests of the earth. But she had insisted that it would be better to let it go on. "Let them see. Let them be satisfied. If I suspend the watch, Talar will claim we're hiding something, and you'll never be free of suspicion."

On this day my resentment of the gray-haired Aife was worse than usual. Talar leaned upon an ash walking stick—the same I'd seen in my home on the night my son was laid out to die. Of course the self-appointed guardian of Ezzarian purity would have been there to make sure all was done correctly.

I worked alongside Drych and the other older students through the rest of the afternoon until they were wilting like scalded lilies. And then I made them begin again, and I did two moves for every one of theirs until I felt the same. Maybe they would begin to understand that there would be no end to it. Not if they wanted to stay alive.

In the past months the demon battles had become more frequent, more complicated, and more ferocious. We had expected it. The Demon Lord's attempt to take power in the human world by controlling Aleksander had signaled a departure from everything we knew of rai-kirah. In the past they had concentrated on individual domination. Now they seemed to have learned more of human ways and human evils, and wished to use their power over us for larger aims. I was trying to convince Ysanne that we needed to keep closer watch on the affairs of the world, lest they try again to insinuate themselves into human troubles. Though I had no evidence of new plots, I had seen the reflection of the change in my battles—increased cunning, viciousness, distractions, and surprises, as on the previous night when the demon seemed to be waiting at the portal. Expecting me. Knowing me.

"Again," I said when Tegyr sank to his knees in the dirt,

shaking his head as we started another set of movements. "You claim that you can stand against the worst that demons can do. Don't think they'll give you their worst when you're fresh." And as they began again, I conjured for them an image of the monster I had fought the previous day, and I laid before them the horror I had lived during that battle. I forced them to see, and I tried to teach them how to convert anger into strength and endurance. It was a lesson I needed to review.

"What perversion is this?" said Fiona, staring at the image of the monster fading into the angled sunlight. She snapped her gaze to my face. "This is yesterday?"

"This is what's out there," I said.

Drych, shaken by what he'd seen, asked permission to speak. "Mistress Talar says that too much thinking about the victim can taint a Warden," he said. "Is that what caused you to fail yesterday?"

"Mistress Talar has never fought a demon," I said. "It is the victim who gives you strength and purpose; they give meaning to everything you do. You can't let them distract you, but you must never forget them. Never. I made a mistake yesterday. That's all. Now, begin again."

Ordinarily I spent at least one hour with the youngest boys. They were awkward and clumsy and in awe of me, but I took pleasure in giving them each some reason to stand up straighter in a time when they could do so little right. On that day, though, I could not bear the sight of wiry young limbs or excited dark eyes, oversized in eager faces, alight with melydda.

I told Catrin that I would await her outside until she dismissed her gaggle to go stuff themselves with supper. When she came out, I was sitting on the damp ground leaning on a tree, watching the fish rings spread on a still pond. The trees crowded close about the pond, the brilliant new-green leaves motionless in the sunset glow, as if held in breathless anticipation of night. Fiona sat on the steps of the practice arena, far enough away that normal hearing would not catch what was said. I wasn't fooled. She could hear a beetle's clicking at three leagues.

"And how did Drych progress?" Catrin stood in front of me, her arms folded across her breast.

"Work him through a similar test tomorrow and see," I said, crushing a sprig of clover between my fingers. "He learns quickly. You've pushed him hard."

"We don't have a lot of time."

I looked up at her quickly. "What do you mean?"

"I mean you're tired. You can't fight every day. In this past year you've spent more time beyond the portal than in the real world. You can't carry this entire war on your shoulders."

"I can do what I need to do. Give them the time they need to be ready."

I wanted her to sit down beside me, to let me put my head on her shoulder and weep. But instead she remained standing, unblinking as she looked down at me. "You need to stop for a while, Seyonne. A few weeks. A month. You're going to die if you don't. Or something worse."

"So you heard about yesterday."

"Of course I heard. I am your mentor. You should have been the one to tell me."

I could have made excuses such as "it was the middle of the night" or "I had to confront my wife, the murderer," but instead I confessed that I hadn't even thought of the requirement to report such a grievous mistake to my mentor without delay. Of all the protocols surrounding demon battles, it was one I agreed with wholeheartedly. Though always tempting to overlook one's own shortcomings, it was good to share them with someone, to lay them out piece by piece, to analyze them without emotion or blame, looking forward, even while speaking of deeds already done. It made you better. More honest. More understanding. "It was a damned wretched day, Catrin. I'm sorry."

"You will come to me at dawn tomorrow, and we'll review it."

I bowed my head to her as was proper from a student to a mentor. A Warden was a student until he was retired or dead.

"Now, go home." She laid her hand briefly atop my head, then went off to drag her students from their plates and cups and set them to work again at books and pens. Throughout Ezzaria mentors were doing the same, pushing

their young charges to be ready. The Searchers already bypassed half the calls they could have sent us.

I never made it home that night. A runner caught up
with me just before I crossed the wooden bridge to the
house. "Master Warden! A call . . ."

I waved to Fiona to hurry so the panting girl would not
have to repeat the news. My watchdog was rarely more
than ten paces behind.

In the next ten days Fiona and I took on twelve combats.
In the short hours between them we never left the temple.
Fiona had no opportunity to nag at me for flaws in my
preparation, for we would sag into our blankets as soon as
we were done. Pallets were brought for us, though cold
stone and bare ground were comfortable enough when one
was as tired as we were. Catrin kept us supplied with food
and wine. She probably guessed that when presented with
the choice of using our time sleeping or going somewhere
to find a meal, we would always choose sleep. Twice she
came herself to make sure we were not pushing too hard.

"You know you can refuse a call," she said one evening
as we sat on the steps of the temple, watching a flock of
sparrows fluttering about the trees. "No ill judgment will
come from it."

"This last one was a Derzhi baron who burned three
villages and his own house with his wife and children still
inside it. The one before was a ship captain who abandoned
a sinking vessel with slaves still chained to the oars. Which
ones do we refuse?"

"What of Fiona? She's young for this." The aforemen-
tioned young woman scowled at us from her place by the
fire. It was her own fault for eavesdropping.

"She does well," I said, staring at a leg of roast fowl in
my hand, trying to decide if it was worth the effort to lift
it to my mouth. "But you'll have to ask her for yourself.
She's not about to admit any weakness to me."

"Or you to her?"

I glanced at Catrin and grinned. "Not in this life."

She did not return my attempt at humor, instead repeating what she had told me at her practice arena. "You
need to stop for a while, Seyonne."

"I'll be careful," I said. "But I can't say I mind being busy. Less time to think about things I'd as soon forget."

Like a twittering cloud, the sparrows rose from the trees, circled, and settled back again, just where they had already been.

In nine of those twelve battles the demon chose to abandon its host and return to its frozen realm to live again. In two I had to kill it. One battle I lost, the second venture in a single day. Stupid to try it, but it was another case where the victim's madness was of such a cruel nature that I could not stomach letting it pass. Fiona agreed to go ahead, and I told myself she was a grown woman who knew her own capacities. But I was the more experienced partner, and I knew she would not refuse to weave if I was willing to fight. I should never have allowed her to weave.

I stepped into a landscape of absolute darkness and bitter cold—signs of a drained Aife and always a terrible risk. *Light, Aife!* But the blackness did not ease, and I could not muster the concentration I needed for my other senses to compensate. I needed to move. To find light enough to see what I was doing. *Run. Fly . . .*

I had one talent that no Warden in the living memory of Ezzaria had possessed. While beyond the portal I could trigger a self-transformation that gave me wings. No one understood how it was possible, and there had been a number of skeptics when I was eighteen and told of my first experience. But to me it had become a natural extension of my melydda, just as my sword had become a natural extension of my arm. Wings brought me power and mobility that made the difference in many demon confrontations.

Fighting to discover what might be lurking in the darkness, I triggered the necessary enchantment, but just before the wings took shape, when I was the most vulnerable as the burning in my shoulders consumed my conscious mind, the demon attacked. I had no time to discern its shape. No time to shift my senses or regain my composure. I was too slow and too tired. I had to get out or I was going to die.

"Aife!" I screamed as claws raked my flesh from three directions at once. The portal appeared, but the beast had dragged me farther away from it than I had expected. I wrestled loose and ran, the ground beneath my feet drumming with the monster's steps. The darkness quivered with its stinking breath. Raw evil surged on every side, hatred that froze the blood and turned limbs to lead, sapping the will and drowning the soul in despair. My weakness was affecting Fiona, too, for the portal wavered, fading in and out of the darkness. "Hold, Aífe!" I cried as the rectangular borders fragmented. I leaped for the dim grayness and landed facedown on the floor of the temple. One leg was on fire, ripped by the demon's claws, but I could do nothing about it. I wasn't sure I would ever be able to move again.

"Stupid, stupid," I said, shaking the darkness from my head as I lay there limp and exhausted, my heaving breath burning my lungs, the pall of grotesque horror not yet withdrawn from my spirit. "I'm sorry. Are you all right?"

Fiona's only answer was a quiet choking, and I raised my head enough to see. She was collapsed on her back beside the fire pit, as deathly pale as her white robes. I crawled over to her and rolled her onto her side, where she proceeded to vomit up the remains of our last hastily eaten meal. She looked very frail and vulnerable.

I lifted her up out of the pool of vomit and carried her to the eastern steps of the temple where the morning sun shone hot and clean, then fetched water and bathed her face and dripped some on her lips. She would likely be incensed at my ill use of drinking water for washing, yet it brought the color back to her thin face. An enjoyable irony.

"A nasty one," I said when her eyelids flicked open. "You may write it down that I freely admit my damned foolishness in attempting it." Which she would likely do, even though it would be her own admission of excessive pride in not refusing to weave.

"Are you all right?" she said, sitting up under her own power and squeezing her eyes shut against the glare, even while trying to examine me.

"Thanks to you." When a Warden was in shambles, it was wickedly hard for an Aífe to hold a portal. The alternative, of course, was to close the portal and leave the Warden behind in the abyss of a demon-possessed soul—every Warden's soul-gnawing dread. "Whoa. Stay there. You don't need to get up. I'll take care of the cleaning . . . and I promise I'll do it right. Rest for a while." I owed her a great deal more than an hour's ritual.

For once she didn't argue, though she didn't sleep, either. She watched my every move as I spent an hour cleaning my weapons, the floor, myself, and even the firepit, carefully reciting each word of the invocations designed to close off any remaining links to the still-active demon.

"So you do know them," she said as I finished the last words of the endless closing chant used after a lost battle.

"And they don't burn my tongue or cause my eyes to burn demon-blue. But I would really prefer to be asleep." I did not retreat to the pallet laid out for me in one of the inner rooms, but stretched out in the shade of the western steps and slept for twelve hours straight. I dreamed of killing.

We refused two calls on the next day, though we still did not leave the temple. We slept. Food appeared beside us. We ate and went back to sleep. On the second morning from the lost battle, Ysanne came to talk to Fiona of portals and shaping strategies and other Aife's business. I did not join them, but sat on the western steps and ate the meat and biscuits and fruit that had been left there for me. When their voices fell silent, I glanced over my shoulder. Ysanne was looking at me through the shady expanse of the temple, her face as expressionless as the stone columns that framed her. I turned back to my breakfast. I didn't see her again before she left.

"The Queen says there's another runner on the way," Fiona said from behind me. "I told her we were well rested. Was I right?"

I worked hard to make sure my voice was composed. "I'm ready." I wondered if I would ever partner with Ysanne again. I could not imagine it.

"She says the Searcher is in Karn'Hegeth and reports that there is strife among the Derzhi." Fiona gloated in the report, as if our safety and security were not dependent on the strength of Aleksander's empire. Whatever people had to say of the Derzhi—and I had as good a reason to hate them as any—it had been the stability of their empire that had allowed us to work successfully for hundreds of years. Aleksander's guarantee of protection would keep us safe for as long as his family ruled. I had spent more than enough time arguing those points with Fiona months before. But, in fairness, Fiona and the others knew only that the Prince had allowed us to return to Ezzaria in thanks for our help with the Khelid. Ysanne and Catrin alone knew that Ezzaria had been Aleksander's personal gift to me. None of them could understand the ties that bound the Prince and me.

The runner came shortly. This was a strange case, she said, before going into her trancelike state and relaying the message from our distant countrywoman. The Searcher's message was garbled, but it seemed quite urgent. All we could gather was that the victim had gone mad and abandoned his wife and children abruptly. With only that much, Fiona and I made our preparations, and as the sun reached the zenith, leaving the temple floor in shadow, I touched the Aife's hands and began the strangest journey in my experience.

CHAPTER 4

"I am the Warden, sent by the Aife, the scourge of demons, to challenge you for this vessel. Hyssad! Begone, it is not yours." The demon did not reveal itself, so I had to go hunting.

Such an odd place. Beneath a spinning sky of pale blue and white lay a garden. Every variety of flower, herb, and shrub was growing in it, lush, green, thick-leafed, splashed with every color nature could produce. Growing, fading, dying, then growing again until I was slightly nauseated by the speed of the changes. I strode through the flowers toward the trees—a forest of impossible variety: tall, massive ashes and oaks, flowering fruit trees, spike-leafed nagera trees, like those that grew near the deep wells and springs of the Azhaki desert, pines and firs and spruce of varieties familiar only to those hardy enough to live in the highest mountains beyond Capharna. Leaves of bright yellow and red mixed in with the liveliest spring greens. And all of it changing as I walked, the fire-red maple leaves falling alongside drifting pear blossoms.

I could discover nothing but this bizarre forest-scape for quite a long time. A brook gurgled alongside the path. Hoping it was the thread that would lead me to my quarry, I followed it, pushing through increasingly dense underbrush, hacking at the thick growth with the silver knife I had changed into a scythe . . . and came near toppling off the edge of a cliff. The forest stopped abruptly at the edge of a fifty-story drop to a forested valley. As I paused to let my transforming enchantment give me wings to explore beyond the cliff edge, a path shaped itself from the steep rock wall like a sand-snake shaking off its gritty coating. I thought the path might be Fiona's doing. An Aife could feel obstacles and could attempt to remedy them through some shaping of the landscape she held in her mind. A tricky business, as she could not see the Warden and risked dropping him over a cliff or into a pit or impaling him on a tree. Ysanne could do such things because she could sense from my mind what I needed. *Oh, my love* . . .

The wave of piercing grief came unbidden . . . unwanted. This was not the place. I marshaled my concentration and started down the path. Into a fertile valley, still of confused season. Trees taller than Derzhi palaces . . . ferns the size of houses . . . black-centered red flowers with a thick, cloying scent that made me dizzy.

"Hyssad! Begone!" I yelled it out when I detected a movement from ahead of me, across the bend of a wide, sluggish river. I whirled about at the sound of a footstep behind me. Sweat beaded on my brow. Where was the demon? I could get no sense of it. Yet something was close. What was wrong with my perceptions?

A gust of hot, humid wind stirred the brooding trees and raised up a cloud of insects. The cry of a bird echoed in the distance. A trailing vine tickled my neck, and I slashed at it with my sword, furling my wings tighter as the trees grew thicker. I could have sworn I heard a laugh. "Hyssad!"

"Are you a bird or one of these nattering creatures that annoys my ears?" The voice came from above me, somewhere atop a pair of shiny black boots. "And you keep saying that vile word. I do wish you'd stop."

I moved backward and promptly tripped over a protruding root that had not been across the path when I had passed a moment before. My sword was ready as I scrambled to my feet, sure the beast would pounce upon my clumsiness.

"Put it away. I have no argument with you." The boots dropped from the tree in a shower of red and gold leaves, bringing with them the image of a slender, fair-haired man of middle age with a cocky smile. His blond beard was neatly trimmed, his hands well formed and clean. He wore a shirt and trousers of deep-hued blue and purple, and a gray-green cloak that shimmered like water in the dappled sunlight. He carried no weapons that I could see. "So which are you, bird or flea? Surely you can't be the one I was

warned of." He twirled a finger, and the trees shifted back
far enough that he could walk around me. I turned with
him, my knife, now a sword, at the ready. "Now, stop that.
How am I to learn of you if you'll not be still and let me
look?" He set his hands on his hips and laughed, yet the
sound of it did not eat away at my ears and my soul as
demon laughter always did.

Verbal bantering with a demon, no matter how monstrous or commonplace its form was never wise. Nothing
would come of it. Words were only a distraction. So I
waited. The demon watched me, leaning his back against a
moss-covered tree trunk and chewing on a long blade of
grass. He didn't seem in any hurry. I waved my sword tip
at him in tight circles, trying to tease his eye as I stepped
closer, but I felt ridiculous when he reached out and
stopped the movement of the blade with his hand, then
jerked backward.

"Ouch!" He stuck his finger in his mouth. "That's
wicked. Are you really intending to poke that into me?"
He looked down at his flat stomach and laid his other hand
on it. "Wouldn't feel pleasant at all. Can't we just skip it?"

"We can certainly skip it, but only if you leave this vessel." *Patience. Don't be drawn in.*

"Ah, he does say something other than the words that
burn the ear. But the sentiment is the same. Leave, begone,
hyssad." He cringed and shuddered dramatically when he
said the last, the word in his own demon tongue that those
of his kind could not ignore. "But I don't want to go. I
like it here, I'm learning a lot, and this"—He waved his
hand to encompass land and sky and trees—"this 'vessel,'
as you call it—quite rudely I might add—doesn't seem to
mind me being here. Why would I want to leave?"

"It is not your choice to stay. Only to leave or die."
Don't argue. He's trying to lure you into distraction.

"No. Not acceptable at all. You must give me some
other choice."

"There is no other. Leave or die." I stood ready, but,
before I could blink, we were in an entirely different place.
A city . . . deserted, a mournful wind nosing a battered,
empty pot through the dirt streets and whining through
burned-out buildings. Bones littered a crumbling market-

place, and a tattered flag fluttered defiantly from a pole
held by a skeletal hand. My skin shriveled, especially the
scar on my face that was the same print of falcon and lion
as the emblem on the flag. Aleksander's flag—the lion of
the Derzhi and the falcon of his Denischkar house.

"What is this?" In my surprise I violated my so recently
professed maxim.

"I thought it might suit you better. You were so grim in
the other place. 'Leave or die.' So unfriendly. This is where
such sentiments take you . . . into the realm of one . . .
Unnamed." A whisper of frost brushed across my soul.
"Not a nice place at all. No, indeed."

"I am not here to be friends with you."

"Then, kill me if you must. We're getting nowhere." He
sat down cross-legged between the wheels of an overturned
cart and ripped open the filmy purple shirt to bare a most
humanlike chest. But he looked down at it and ran his long
fingers over the skin. "On second thought . . ."

My stomach heaved as the landscape changed again. This
time it was Catrin's practice arena, with the same strip of
bright sunshine along one side that I had seen two weeks
earlier. The slender demon had a sword in his hand and
brandished it wildly, much in the way of one of Catrin's
newer students. "All right. Come at me!"

He was pulling things out of my own head. I backed
away, trying to forge new mental barriers, while coming up
with something to explain how he was doing it. No luck at
either task. Most unsettling.

"Not so bold now, eh? I can give you more of a fight
than you think." And in a flurry of blows so quick I missed
seeing them, he nicked the top of my right ear, my left
shoulder, and my right knee, and left a five-mezzit slash in
the toe of one boot. Before I could strike back, he sat down
in the middle of the arena thirty paces away from me and
laid his sword down crossways in front of him. "Why don't
we talk?"

"You must leave this vessel. This is not your place.
Whatever you are, you don't belong here."

"Doubts are terrible things. They twist your gut in a
knot. Surprised that I know of them? My own, not just
yours. Surprised that I have them? Doubt is the enemy of

the . . . Warden . . . that's what you call yourself. I've been told of Wardens and the Aife, the scourge . . . warned to watch out for them . . . for you in particular. The Warden who changes himself. The one who is different from all who have come before. I thought I would come see for myself. A number of my cohorts have no use for you."

I was not going mad. The demon was toying with me . . . or perhaps I had already fought and was injured. What to do? Retreat? Kill it? It wouldn't leave, therefore I was required to kill it. But it was inordinately strange. Every sense I used to search out demons must be dead. No demon music, no creeping dread, no smell of rot, of corruption, of secret foulness that could be detected behind the fair appearance. No wonder he could get inside my head; he displayed nothing that would trigger my defenses. Yet he was a demon. There was no other possibility. The Searcher had detected it through the signs of possession. Twenty-six tests they used to judge. And what else could he be?

"Contemplation. Surely that's a good sign. Shall I tell you how I come to be here? If you would sheathe that ugly weapon, or lay it out as I've done, then we could share a tale or two. I want to know why the scourge of demons wants to send me back with my mind shredded, when I've only just come and have done no harm."

Only one way to be sure. Dangerous to expose one's own soul when beyond the portal. The protective barriers one built through long training were already precariously thin when walking the landscape of another's soul. But I needed something to bring me back to my purpose. An anchor. Surety. And so I crouched down in the dirt in front of the slender figure, and I looked in its eyes . . . and with every scrap of melydda I could gather, I saw true. The fair and pleasant gentleman who sat in front of me with his head cocked and his brow drawn up in puzzled curiosity was indeed the manifestation of a rai-kirah. But in all the truth of my seeing, there was no evil in him.

Impossible! Now surely I ought to kill it. Any rai-kirah that could so confuse a Warden's senses signified such a change . . . such danger that I could not even calculate it. Yet I had come upon other impossibilities in my life. What

could be more unlikely than the mark of the gods I had
found in Aleksander?

"Why are you here?" I said, sitting down in front of him.
"What are you?"

The bearded man, who was not a man, smiled in delight.
"Much better. Those you send back are always so dull.
Gastai brutes. Never quite get over it. Not that they don't
deserve whatever you deal them. They're useful, but I truly
don't want to be like that. But, of course, it's better than
having you poke that nasty slicer into me. And I have no
desire to chop off any of your parts or have you screaming
at me for mercy or any of that sort of thing. I just want to
learn of you and see a bit more of this world. My own is
a bit frosty, though it improves."

"Just want to see . . . ?" My head was swimming with
his prattling. What was a Gastai?

"Gracious, you are hard to convince. Yes, I came hunting
just like a regular Gastai, and I found this fellow who was
so crunched up . . . squeezed, as to say, with his woman
partner and all these screaming little creatures around him,
and all he wants to do is slather colored messes on
papers . . . canvas, he calls it. So I came along and gave
him the wherewithal . . . the 'manhood,' he says . . . to do
it. I'm only here for the fun, and I'm not going to have
him do terrible things, as you seem to believe. He does
indeed have a good eye for interesting sights. We've had a
fine romp, and I'm not quite ready to end it, but someone—
one of your cohorts, not mine—came poking around. My
friend here, my host, my vessel, is mightily afraid you're
going to get rid of me, because then he won't have the
manhood anymore. I don't quite understand it, because I
never learned that a human could change from manhood
to womanhood or anything else, and I don't quite see that it
has anything to do with this splattering on canvas business,
anyway, but whatever . . . I don't want to leave quite yet,
and I certainly don't want to leave with my own head ruined, if you know what I mean."

I had no words. Rather, to my uttermost astonishment,
I found myself laughing. If this was madness, then it was
not half so fearsome as I had always believed. And if it
was not . . . stars of night, what had I come upon?

He shifted the scene in his unsettling way, so that we were outdoors again. Outdoors in some poor man's soul. An artist's soul. We walked side by side through the flowered fields, the blooming and dying profusion of color and life. Sunlight warmed my cold hands. My weapons were sheathed and I felt no danger. How was it possible?

"This is extraordinary," I said. "I have faced hundreds . . . hundreds of your kind, and never . . ."

"You must not judge all of us for some unpleasantness. You've not looked, you know. Do you judge the forest by the unhealthy, wind-stripped trees at its edge? Do you judge the pulp of the fruit by the bitter skin? And, truly, when you go hunting with such things as those"—he jerked his head at the knife sheath and mirror pouch at my belt— "what do you expect to find? The nervous birds are not likely to flock around when you cast out those particular seeds."

"So there are others like you?"

He took a deep breath and sighed ponderously. "Well, I won't go that far. My Gastai cousins are fairly brutish, most of them. But there are many Rudai worth knowing, and a few of the rest of us that are quite sensible and would very much like to get to know you. You need to look. To learn. We can show you a great deal."

"If you think to turn me, to have me do your bidding—"

"Like the other Warden who played a game far above his head? No, not at all." He pulled a handful of flowers and held them to his nose, inhaling deeply and sighing in pleasure. "My friends and I had no dealings with the Naghidda, and rejoiced when you . . . I do believe it was you . . . took the villain down. No, this is . . . Blast and all, what's that?"

The sky turned purple and bulged out toward us like a swelling bruise, and the dirt path beneath us cracked and slithered. Fiona . . . the portal. In the name of the gods, where was the portal? And the demon was still standing. Still in possession of the victim.

"I've got to go." My hand was on my knife. I had sworn an oath that was the cornerstone of my life. What was I thinking?

The demon grinned at me. "So what is it to be? I suppose

I could fight you, but I'd rather not. I won't leave. Can we pretend that you couldn't find me?"

The ground where we were standing slumped down into a hole. I grabbed the wind with my wings and soared upward, looking down on him. His fair hair was whipping about his face as the flowers continued to bloom and fade, more rapidly than ever. I could take him. He was fast and cocky, but I had watched him, and he thought too much.

Well, so did I. I circled and called down to him. "Do you have a name?"

He laughed and used his hand to cup his words so they could be heard over the rising gale. "You could not pronounce it. And it may be different the next time you meet me. But I'll remember you, Warden. We could see a bit of the world together, I think, you and I. Have some adventures. Find some common ground. There may come a time when it serves your purposes."

As the sky fell in and the fields of flowers began to disintegrate, I streaked for the portal. I glanced back once and I still saw him, standing in the black void where flowers had once bloomed. He waved and disappeared into darkness. I passed through the portal and landed feet first upon the temple floor.

By the time my head was unfogged from my return, Fiona was nowhere to be seen. She had abandoned the rites: the cleaning, the duties, the prayers and chanting that were of such importance to her. For a brief moment, as I wiped the unused knife and mirror and laid them in their wooden case, I wondered if she were ill. But as I went about the rituals and considered the unbelievable encounter, I began to feel queasy. I came to the verse in the closing chant where you changed the words depending on the outcome of the battle. One phrase if you had emerged victorious. One phrase if you had suffered defeat. One phrase if the Warden had died. One phrase if he had been abandoned, alive in the abyss. For me on that night, there were no words. What had I done?

Fiona would know that I had not killed the demon. The Aife could feel it in her weaving, just as she could sense when the demon left the victim . . . or did not. My guess was Fiona had gone to report the outcome of the encounter to the Mentors Council. To think that she was speaking my name in the same breath with the word treason was unnerving.

Yet, as I stowed the weapon case in the preparation room, drew water from the well near the temple, and washed myself, my moment's panic was submerged in my wonder at the day's meeting. How I wished that I could talk to Ysanne about it, or that she could have been the one to experience it with me. Her senses were so keen. A demon who was not drawn to pain and horror, but to art, color, learning, and adventure. A rai-kirah with a sense of humor. I had looked into its depths with my Warden's sight, and I could not be mistaken. Incomparably strange. I needed to follow Fiona, to tell my mentor and the rest of them, not of treason, but of something extraordinary. Something we had never imagined.

I had violated my oath, yet I could not feel guilty. It would have been wrong to kill him. Wrong to banish him. We had learned that forcing a demon from a human soul damaged the creature, at least for a time. Ezzarian mentors taught that hunger for evil was the nature of all demons, but if the hunger was not there, then how could I justify harming him? Of course it was possible, likely even, that this demon was only an aberration. But whatever he was, we needed to learn more.

And, of course, as the afternoon waned and I pondered these things, yearning for Ysanne, my mind returned to the matter of our dead child. My heart twisted in my breast, and I wanted to push my fist through the stone columns of the temple. But instead I slumped against a fluted pillar, pressed my hands to my aching head, and cried out in an agony of grief that would no longer be denied. What if his demon had been one like this? In a thousand years we had never even considered such possibilities.

CHAPTER 5

Each of the five well-respected men and women on the Council represented one of the special talents used in fighting demons. Catrin represented those who trained Wardens, and at thirty, was by far the youngest. Maire represented the Weavers, those who held the safety of Ezzarian settlements in their care. Talar represented those who trained Aifes, Caddoc the Searchers, and Kenehyr the Comforters.

Seventy-year-old Maire was a wise, sharp-eyed Weaver who had been my mother's dearest friend. She had known me since I was born and had administered the testing that named me among the valyddar—the power-born. Though she would never do anything to compromise her integrity, she would not doubt me without incontrovertible proof. I trusted Maire's judgment of me beyond my own.

Kenehyr was a round, cheerful man who had once been a Comforter. His melydda was so strong that he could fell trees with a glance . . . but only if no one distracted him. He had always needed a Searcher partner who was a powerful fighter to keep him safe, for he could never do more than one thing at a time and was so gentle a spirit that he could not see danger were it sitting on his toes. Kenehyr had also known me for most of my life in Ezzaria. As much as Ysanne or Catrin, he had convinced my people that my life was a fulfillment of prophecy and thus no corruption, allowing me to come home. He was also the most liberal-minded of all Ezzarians, and would likely not doubt my word even if he saw demon fire in my eyes.

Talar and Caddoc were a different story. On the last day of Ezzarian independence, the third day of the Derzhi war of conquest, it was the Wardens and Searchers and Comforters, those of us with fighting skills or experience of the world, who led the Ezzarian resistance. We had known it was futile. Our strategy was to hold long enough that the Queen and the strongest of the valyddar could get out of Ezzaria, along with all of the precious books and manuscripts, and the weapons we used to fight the demons. Then we would try to save the rest. We succeeded in saving the Queen and the books and a few mentors, but in everything else we failed. Only a few managed to follow the Queen and rebuild their lives in the mountains north of Capharna. Some, like me, were enslaved. I saw so many dead, it was hard to imagine there was anyone left. But hundreds of Ezzarians had retreated into the forest as the ring of Derzhi occupation closed around them.

They had been left with nothing. Our centuries of secrecy and isolation meant that we had no allies to give us refuge. The Derzhi occupied the lands nearest the northern borders, and sent hunting and logging parties deep into the trees. The Ezzarians dared not be seen, so they had to live on what they could hunt or collect. They had no books, none of our magical weapons, and few mentors to train others. They lived without hope of resuming the tasks that we had believed our sacred duties, for no Wardens had survived in their midst, and they had no idea whether the Queen or anyone else had made it away safely. They began to fight among themselves and disregard our customs that seemed impossible to follow in the face of such disaster.

But Talar, an Aife of modest gifts, had taken matters in hand. She refused to allow hardship or despair as an excuse for failed discipline, railing at the others that such weakness would give the demons a foothold among them. She told the tales of Verdonne and her long struggle to protect the peoples of the earth from the jealous raging of her immortal husband, and said that if a mortal woman could hold strong against the assaults of a god, could not embattled Ezzarians do the same? Though near starvation, she refused to drink anything but rainwater or to eat any food that had not been grown, caught, or cleaned in the ways laid down by our ancestors. She led rites of purification and found a few young women with skills enough to attempt Weaver's enchantments to protect their camps. She had the tenyddar teach everyone, even the valyddar, their business of hunting and gleaning, and chastised those who used their melydda for commonplace tasks to make life easier rather than saving their power for the demon war. Her resolve humbled others into following her lead and drew the tattered refugees together again. They came out of exile with immense pride that they had been faithful to the laws and customs they believed given us by the gods.

Those of us who survived other horrors and other kinds of exile rejoiced in their strength and admired their determination. But when Talar and her followers discovered how I had been welcomed back from certain corruption, they were infuriated. And when I said that I had come to new ways of thinking about impurity and corruption . . . that perhaps it had less to do with what water you drank than with the character of your soul . . . I did not make friends of them.

I knew I would be called before the Council to answer Fiona's charges of treason, but with Kenehyr and Catrin solidly behind me, and Maire almost the same, I had no concerns. The Mentors Council could only assert an adverse ruling with a vote of four of the five. More than worrying about politics, I needed to talk to Catrin of what I had seen, a demon outside the boundaries of our experience.

By moonrise, I had regained my composure and made my way to my mentor's home to tell her of my extraordinary encounter. Catrin lived in the house her grandfather had built when he was young and the most powerful Warden in Ezzaria. He had set it on the top of a hill, though still under the trees, for the Weaver laid her enchantments of protection in the trees, and no Ezzarian would think of building a house unsheltered. But from Catrin's porch, you could look out over the rolling rooftop of the forest, glimpsing the trails of smoke from scattered settlements and lights that flickered through the leaves like luminous fish in a dark ocean.

"Is Mistress Catrin here?" I asked the drowsy-eyed young student who answered her door. A pile of books, scrolls, and blotted papers on Catrin's worktable behind the boy gave evidence of a long evening of study.

"She's been summoned away," said the boy, yawning hugely. "Not sure where. Said she'd be back before too late. You're welcome in, as always, Master."

"Thank you, Howel, but I think not, unless . . . is Hoffyd in?" Catrin's husband, a quiet scholar, was a good friend.

"He's not been home nigh on three weeks now."

"His sister's not ill?" His demanding, ailing sister Ennit, who lived in a nearby village, was the only thing I knew that could draw Hoffyd from home now we had come back to Ezzaria.

"No, sir. Mistress Catrin won't say where he's gone, not even to Mistress Ennit, and Mistress Ennit is about to pester all of us to death with her asking."

Unusual. Hoffyd was the least likely man in Ezzaria to be involved in a mystery. "Perhaps he's hiding from Ennit, do you think?"

The boy grinned. "Likely."

Seeing Howel's books made me reconsider, and I did go in to wait for Catrin, taking the opportunity to poke through a few journals where Galadon had recorded his demon encounters. Howel seemed to be impressed that I would sit and study without Catrin's direct orders, so he got back to his own work with diligence.

I flipped through three thick cloth-bound books that covered some fifteen years of Galadon's career as a Warden, but all of the entries, so meticulously recorded in my old mentor's bold hand, were familiar. None spoke of demons who were not as we expected. There were several more journals on the shelf; Galadon had fought as a Warden for some thirty years. But instead of these I lifted out the large folio where Catrin kept copies of the Scroll of the Raikirah and the Scroll of Prophecy. The originals were in Ysanne's care, kept in stiff paper cylinders in a stone box, but Catrin's copies were exactly scribed and illustrated to match the originals.

I read for an hour, forcing my eyes to stay on the spidery script, trying to decipher the archaic language anew from the page rather than speak the words in my head as I had learned them in my schooling. Perhaps a word had been dropped or altered by constant repetition. But I found no change. The story of the demons, the warnings against cor-

ruption, the chants and rituals, and the florid language of
the prophecy of the Warrior of Two Souls were exactly as
I remembered them. I marveled again at the brevity of the
manuscripts, scarcely twenty pages between the two. Not
much to chart the course of a race, much less that of the
entire world.

As I traced my finger over the carefully reproduced
sketch of the winged warrior in one margin, I felt the familiar prickling in my shoulders so like the return of warmth
to numbed flesh. Always it was there, just below the surface
of my senses. Why could I feel it so vividly when it was
only beyond the portal that I could change into my winged
form? Nothing in any Ezzarian writing even mentioned the
change, much less explained it. Until I had first experienced
it when I was eighteen, we'd only had the drawing and the
rumor of such a possibility.

There in Catrin's quiet room, with life at its lowest midnight ebb, I closed my eyes, held myself still, and focused
on the sensation, blowing on it gently with the breath of
my awareness as a freezing man blows on his last hope of
fire. My throat ached. My heart swelled with profound longing, a craving so deep my eyes watered. My veins pulsed
with melydda, yet the transformation remained just beyond
my reach. Just beyond my control. No burst of fire in my
body. No explosion of glory in my mind.

I expelled my held breath, jerked my head, and felt
shamed at my greed, seeking some kind of perverse personal pleasure from a gift dedicated to the defeat of
demons. I forced my eyes back to the page, but the lamp
was failing, and I couldn't concentrate. Young Howel had
blotted his writing with his cheek, and when I nudged him,
he slipped off his chair and onto the striped rug in front of
the cold hearth. I threw a blanket over him, then pulled
off my boots and sprawled out in a chair in the farthest
corner of the room by an open window, lulled by the night
smells of damp clover and mint.

I had just drifted off to sleep, when I heard the door
open. "Just about gave up on you," I said drowsily, sitting
up and trying to clear the thickness from my head and my
tongue. "Came to report, as my mentor commands. Let me
get my wits about me—a cup of something hot might

help—then I'll tell you the most astounding story you've ever heard."

"You will tell me nothing tonight, Seyonne." Catrin stepped out of the shadowed doorway. Her voice carried no warmth, no welcome. "There will be adequate time for you to explain yourself." Fiona followed her into the room, and then another woman and three men. One of the men was Caddoc: tall, spare, grim, long wisps of gray hair falling down in his face. The white-haired woman, deceptively plump and motherly for one of the most powerful sorcerers in Ezzaria, was Maire. The other two men were temple guards, eiliddar of various callings who had some fighting skills. We had very little of what anyone would call crime in Ezzaria, but the temple guards took care of such matters as intruders, or Ezzarians who got drunk or picked fights with others.

I woke up very quickly when I saw them. "What's all this?"

Caddoc stepped forward. "It has been reported that you have violated your oath by permitting a demon to retain possession of a victim without challenge." He came near spitting out the words. "How do you answer?"

I looked to Catrin, but her expression was unreadable, her best mentor's face—no anger, no fear, no concern. Only intense listening.

"It's not as simple as that."

"We're not trying to trick you, Seyonne," said Maire softly. "Only to hear your response before deciding how to proceed."

"Are these men here to arrest me?" Arrest. I could not fathom it. Perhaps one arrest occurred per decade in Ezzaria. And a Warden . . . It was unthinkable.

"How do you answer?" Caddoc's voice was as gray as his hair, his skin, and his cloak. "You did not kill the demon. You did not banish it. The only remaining possibilities are that you lost in true combat or that you failed to challenge."

"Catrin . . ."

"You are not under arrest, Seyonne. But with charges so serious, you cannot be allowed to speak with anyone until the case is heard. You must understand that."

"Not even with my mentor?"

"No." It was Caddoc who answered.

"Then, it makes no difference what I say." I sat down in the chair, and while they watched, I methodically put on my boots and most determinedly did not answer. "I'll be at home."

I headed for the door, ignoring the others who stood about like the stone columns of the temple. But when I passed Fiona, hovering beside the door, I paused. She glared at me, as if daring me to strike her. "Consider well what happened today, Fiona," I said. "Think and feel and remember. When the time comes to speak, tell me what evil you felt when you opened that portal. Tell me what madness you found to pull into your weaving. Find out from the Searchers the things they didn't tell us. I want to understand it as much as anyone, and I trust you to be scrupulous in your telling."

Though it was near midnight, Ysanne was not home when I arrived. No doubt she had heard of my trouble. Perhaps she had decided to sleep elsewhere. She had a number of places to go: the homes of friends or her women attendants, guest quarters in other parts of the Residence. I lit the nine candles of our mourning stone and sat beside it for a while, inhaling the sweet smoke and thinking of my beloved parents and sister, hoping that perhaps they could find my child wandering in the forests of the afterlife and give him the tender comfort they had always given me. Then I pinched out the flames and fell into bed, ignoring the two men who sat just inside the door to make sure that no one, not even their queen, spoke to me. I sank into sleep, wondering what they would do to young Howel, who had not known he might be corrupted by speech with the only Warden in Ezzaria.

The Council convened three days after my encounter, as soon as Kenehyr could arrive from his home in southern Ezzaria. Such charges could not wait. I spent the days training as usual, though on my own, not with Catrin and her students. In the other hours I read everything in the Queen's library on demon lore. There was perishingly little.

Nothing that hinted of demons who only desired to learn of the world.

Young Drych brought me word of the Council meeting as I sat poring over a manuscript that was telling me yet again that a demon's only hunger was for death and evil. The young man was nervous and agitated, and spoke softly as if the guards could not hear. "What's happening, Master? Is it a usual thing to have to explain yourself to the Council? I'm not good at talking in front of so many. And they've said none of us should hold speech with you until they say. I don't understand it, when you are the finest ... the strongest Warden we've ever had."

I was touched that his faith in me was not shaken by what he had heard. "Don't worry about it. You must always review extraordinary encounters with your mentor," I said. "And sometimes the Council wants to hear of them, too, so that we all may learn. Especially now, as things are changing from what we've experienced in the past. You must always be ready to learn something new, to stay alert, to listen to your own reason and judgment. Sometimes we forget that. You can only do your best, and that's all I've done. When your day comes, you'll do very well."

I wished I'd been allowed to review the case with Catrin, but her position on the Council precluded any contact with me until the hearing, even had I been permitted to speak freely. But she was intelligent and clever. She would know how to manage things to get it over with quickly.

The five sat in a half circle in a modest, high-ceilinged room with large windows and a softly shining floor of oaken planks. I was motioned to a straight-backed chair facing the Council. The room had no other furnishings. No hangings, no tapestries, no rugs or tables or footstools. Just warm sunlight. The scraping of the wooden chair legs echoed faintly in the emptiness, until all were settled and only the droning of bees and the occasional screech of a jay from the woodland beyond the window intruded on the silence.

Talar began the proceedings. Her iron-gray hair was twisted into a knot on top of her head, her smooth bronze skin taut over high cheekbones, and her jaw well-

proportioned, but exceedingly rigid. "Seyonne, Warden of
Ezzaria, you are summoned before this Council to answer
the most serious of charges . . . "

She took quite a while to recount them all. The first was,
of course, that I had allowed a demon to retain possession
of a victim unchallenged. The next was the killing of the
slave merchant victim. Then followed Fiona's list of slighted
rituals, suspect teachings, and minor errors. The only real
surprise was the inclusion of the lost battle.

A frowning Catrin, seated at Talar's far left, interrupted
the recitation at that point. "I thought we agreed that this
particular event would not be mentioned. It is no crime to
lose in demon combat. On the contrary, it is imperative that
a Warden withdraw when facing an unwinnable conflict. He
must put his safety and that of the Aife above pride."

Kenehyr nodded in agreement, his wrinkled face troubled. The round-cheeked Maire answered. "We know all
this, Catrin, and will certainly not hold a withdrawal as
evidence of treason. Yet I see value in hearing the pattern
of these past days. The complete view of events helps us
see everything in proper perspective. But truly the loss
should not have been listed as a charge." This last was
directed at Talar, who nodded formally to Maire and made
a notation on the paper.

At this point I resigned myself to a very long day. No
hope of a quick review of the battle in question, a quick
vote, and a reprimand warning me to be more careful in
rituals when our understanding of our own traditions was
so limited. I had hoped to spend the afternoon and evening
talking with Kenehyr. The old man had worked closely with
our best scholars through the years, and knew as much as
any Ezzarian about demon-possession.

Instead, I would spend the day explaining why I thought
wiping the floor of the temple was not necessary after a
battle, and why, since one recitation of the closing chant
was soothing and healing, did I not see that three recitations were even better? And I would have to be on my
best behavior and not insinuate that the innate hostility I
detected in Fiona prevented her from giving a fair appraisal
of my actions. Although her observations were scrupulously

honest, her interpretation of my motives was always the worst it could be.

Indeed, it was mid-afternoon before we got to the crux of the matter. We had been brought food and wine at midday. I had gone to stand beside one of the windows while I ate. Several times I caught Catrin watching me. Of course she could not come and talk to me, but I expected some sign, some gesture of reassurance. Yet she remained expressionless and didn't eat. I felt more than a little uneasy.

After only a quarter of an hour, we resumed. The Council members moved to the edge of their chairs as Talar uttered the most important command of the day. "Tell us of your last demon encounter, Warden."

I had to ignore my growing disturbance and bring all of my senses to bear on my telling. I tried to recall every detail, every word, every sensation, every smell and taste and sound, and relay it to the five who sat in judgment, so they could experience it as truly as I had done. I wanted to make them hear and see and wonder at it as I did. Every passing moment led me to believe that my experience was, in many ways, as significant as my battle with the Lord of Demons, a portent that we could not ignore.

"No evil!" Caddoc had a harsh dry laugh that grated on the ear. "You deemed yourself fit to judge such a thing. Interesting that it was after the creature had shown you its prowess with a sword that you made this determination."

"I have no shame in losing a battle," I said. "Since you included the one I lost in this telling, then take it as evidence of that, at least. I deemed this rai-kirah not attracted to evil, and that it was not to our benefit to destroy him. Bring other evidence of my cowardice, if that's your claim."

"Not cowardice," said Talar. "No one accuses you of cowardice."

Maire leaned forward, her long braid stark white against the dark red of her shapeless dress. "You make it sound as if this demon was expecting you personally. It knew that you transformed beyond the portal. It claimed that it would very much like to get to know you, and that it would remember you. Was this not a concern?"

"Demons always say such things . . ." But even as I made the claim, I heard the voice again.

. . . *Next time we meet* . . . "It was not a threat. He had no malice in him, Maire. Curiosity, yes. Knowledge, yes. He knew me as the Warden; after so many encounters in such a short time, so many demons sent back and no other Wardens, I suppose it was inevitable."

"He knew you as the slayer of the Lord of Demons?"

"Yes." He had known quite clearly, in fact. Known that I was not Rhys, my boyhood friend who had sold his soul to the Lord of Demons. Expressed satisfaction that I had killed the . . . what had he called it? "The Naghidda."

"What's that?"

"It was his name for the Lord of Demons—Naghidda." Only then, as I said it before the Council, did the meaning of the demon word come to me. The Precursor. Why did he use that name . . . and why did it sound an alarm bell in my mind?

"Why were you not afraid, Seyonne? Explain it to me." The kind-faced Weaver was pleading to understand. "This was a demon who said it knew you and expected to see you again. Expected to find 'common ground' with you. Is this not what we have tried to avoid for a thousand years? Tell me why it didn't worry you."

Caddoc did not allow me time for further explanation, even if I could have given it. "Could there be any more blatant sign of corruption?" he said. "Must we see him bring down the host on our heads before we heed the warning? Even if he blinds himself . . ."

Maire sat back in exasperation and murmured to Kenehyr as Caddoc vented his feelings yet again.

They had not heard me. I sagged back in my chair and leaned my mouth on my hand. What would it take to convince them?

"How many battles have you fought in the past month, Seyonne?" Catrin asked her first question of the long afternoon. The others fell silent at her soft intrusion.

"Uncountable," I said without thinking. "Twenty-five, at least."

"And in the month before that?"

"I don't know. Ten. Fifteen."

"Twenty-three to be exact. And twenty before that. More than two hundred and fifty in thirteen months. An unheard of number for any Warden in our history, who have considered five in a month an ominous burden." She leaned forward a bit in her chair. "And how many battles have you lost in that time?"

"One. Only the one." I couldn't understand her. Everyone on the Council knew these things. Because of the war and the lack of Wardens, there was no choice. I didn't want her to make more of it, to make them think it bothered me.

"And in how many have you lost the victim—caused death?"

"Just the one."

"And in how many—in this or in any combat of your warding—have you come upon a demon you would not fight?"

"Only this, but—"

"Tell us, Seyonne, my dear friend, what happened with your wife three weeks ago."

"Catrin . . ." What was she doing?

"You've sworn to answer truthfully and completely, to do whatever we ask of you to clarify these charges and your actions. And so I ask you to tell this Council what happened in your home these past days."

She knew what I would answer—and what I could not answer. The child was a demon. Law and tradition insisted that even his memory must be shunned lest his corrupted innocence taint us. But I was no good at pretending, and I had sworn to tell the truth, whether they wanted to hear it or not. "Our child was born demon-possessed," I said, my soul cold and still. The words fell harshly on the waiting silence. Then I compounded my crime by refusing to blame the gods for the dilemma or its terrible resolution. "And my wife did as Ezzarian law demands and killed him."

My friend did not relent. She was not speaking to the Council, but to me. Though I could feel the shock and dismay from the others in the room, I had eyes only for Catrin.

"And now, Seyonne . . . I know this will be difficult, and I do not ask it lightly . . ." As if anything could be more difficult than the words she had just forced me to say. ". . . I ask you to remove your shirt."

"I will not!" I jumped up from my chair, appalled, disbelieving. "It has no bearing—"

"You will do as you are bid, Warden, or this hearing will
be closed." Talar stood and faced me down, though she,
too, looked at Catrin for clarification.

If the hearing were closed without resolution, I would
be left in a half life of suspicion. Surely Catrin had some
plan. But what plan could require such appalling invasion
of my privacy? To bring up Ysanne and the child . . . and
to force me to expose the legacy of my years in bondage.
I could not believe she would think that some maudlin
sympathy was going to change Talar or Caddoc's mind.
They would only be reminded of the very reason they believed me unfit—that such punishment could only have
come down on me because I was irredeemably corrupt. She
was digging my grave.

"I ask you again, Seyonne. Remove your shirt and turn
around. Only for a moment."

Gritting my teeth and inventing five hundred ways to tell
Catrin how despicable I thought her tactics, I pulled off my
dark red shirt and allowed the others to see what ugliness
could result from a strap of Derzhi leather. Every finger's
breadth of my back and arms was ridged with scars, and
the crossed circle burned into my shoulder—the mark of
bondage—glared like a red sun in the golden light of that
room, a companion piece to the royal mark burned into
my face.

I closed my eyes and tried to control my rage, such a
fierce combat that I almost could not hear the soft command. "You may put it back on and step out of the room."
Sorrow permeated Catrin's words, but it would take more
than sorrow to repair such betrayal.

Yet even as I thrust my arms back into the soft linen
and slammed the door behind me, I did not comprehend
what was happening. As soon as the five had imposed whatever reprimand Talar and Caddoc would insist upon, I
planned to take aside Catrin and Kenehyr, at least, and try
again to explain. I glared at Fiona as she entered the room
after me. Then I paced the long hall, cursing myself, cursing
the women in my life who all seemed to have gone mad,
wanting to put my head through a wall for not being more

articulate, revising words and phrases that I deceived myself into thinking would have made a difference in my explanation. I yearned for them to understand what I had felt from this demon.

Half an hour later Fiona came out of the room, so her story was now told on top of mine. She stayed well away from me, sitting in a window seat at the far end of the hallway. Perhaps she felt my earnest desire to throttle her stiff neck. Only when we were called back inside after an interminable hour did she approach me and attempt to speak, her face cold as always. "Master Seyonne, I—"

"We are summoned. No time for pleasantry," I said, motioning her to precede me into the room. I detested it when she called me "Master."

The five were in their chairs as before, no sign of their conflicts or deliberations on their faces. Talar always looked sour, so I could not count that as good news. Maire had her eyes closed. Catrin sat like stone. And this time, Ysanne was present, sitting in a high-backed chair to the right of the Council circle. She was not there as my wife. As Queen she was required to confirm any judgment of the Council. She met my glance with a steady unsmiling face. I might have been a stranger.

Talar, of course, pronounced the verdict. "Seyonne, son of Joelle and Gareth, you are judged not guilty of treason . . ."

Talar paused only to take a breath, which meant I could not, because she was clearly not done, and there was no relief or happiness or satisfaction among any of the five.

". . . yet you have clearly violated your Warden's oath by permitting a demon to retain possession of a human soul unchallenged. How are we to judge you, save that you are disturbed in mind, whether from corruption or from the excessive burden of your calling or from other things which we cannot name?"

"No," I said. "I'm not—"

"And so we have determined. Therefore, from this day forward, the Temple of Verdonne is closed to you. You are forbidden to engage in demon combat, either in this world or beyond the portal of an Aife, or to teach, mentor, counsel, or advise any student until this Council deems you recovered."

The chill in my soul turned to ice. Forbidden? Impossible. Even beyond my own dismay . . . what of Ezzaria? What of the victims who would be left helpless? "You can't do this."

But she did not stop. "Because no able-bodied man of Ezzaria can live idle, you will report to Pedr for daily work assignments, and because of your . . . unique . . . circumstances, which even those of us who hold you more accountable than this verdict reflects must recognize, you are to submit yourself to Caddoc for counsel. We sincerely hope that with proper care you will someday be judged fit enough to take up your calling again."

I sat numb. Disbelieving. So I was to be grateful that I was not driven out of Ezzaria or shunned again—the living death I had experienced on my first return from slavery. Yet my life was to be destroyed just as surely as the Derzhi had done it. I was not to be allowed to do the one thing I could do better than anyone in history. Never to take that terrible, glorious, difficult step beyond a portal. Never to feel the burning in my shoulders or the ecstasy as my wings filled and bore me upward on the winds of sorcery. Talar said that I might fight again, but I was not deceived. Caddoc would never say I was fit. What god was so cruel as to give me back my life for two short years, then take it all away again?

And what was I to do instead? Report to Pedr. They were going to have me work in the fields as did the tenyddar, those with no melydda . . . as my dear and honorable father had done so that those like me could eat as we did the work we were called to do. I could swallow that. I felt no shame in working with dirt and plows rather than swords and mirrors. But to allow Caddoc to probe my mind . . . to counsel me, to seek the causes of my deviance, to put me under spells and expose my thoughts, my fears, my desires . . . hunting for corruption. That I could not . . . would not . . . do.

"Have you no response to this sentencing, my son?" said Kenehyr. "If what you've said is truth, then you cannot allow these people to silence you."

I looked up at him like an idiot . . . and then I looked at Catrin. She did not drop her eyes. Four out of five.

Kenehyr had not voted against me. Catrin, my friend and mentor, had been the fourth.

Only one blow had not yet been struck. I turned to Ysanne. "And you, madam? Is there any use in an appeal to your wisdom?"

My wife sat straight in her chair, as if she were carved from the same oak, and she did not blink or flinch or hesitate as she spoke. "I see no reason to contradict the saying of the Council. Your Warden's commission is revoked. Your oath is void."

Satisfaction settled on Talar's angular face, a trace of a smile on her colorless lips.

I walked out of the room. Out of the Residence. Out of the settlement. The afternoon light played hide-and-seek through the green roof of the forest. The larkstongue was just burst into blooming, brilliant blue spikes as tall as my knees. The yellow rainflowers were dotted through the grass like stars in a green sky. Spring had yielded to golden summer, yet all was darkness to me on that bright afternoon. Always I had carried my Warden's oath in my heart, a lodestone to chart my course through horror, a talisman to cling to in the depths of pain and ruin. Now it was gone, and I felt the weight of years and injury and grief caving in the bulwarks of my soul.

"Seyonne! Wait!" Catrin called from behind me, but I did not answer to my name. How could I, when all that made it mine was unraveling around me like the landscape beyond a failing portal? "You must listen!" But I did not listen, and I did not wait. At some time I started running, and I was very far from my old life before I stopped.

CHAPTER 6

The rabbit squatted nervously in the spot of shade. The
creature was as still as the rock pile behind it, yet I could
feel its quivering anxiety, just as it could feel my breathing
alter the texture of the air and the stink of my body intrude
upon the smells of hot rocks and dirt and succulent sprigs
of dayflax. It waited and twitched its whiskers. I lay still on
my belly and watched. Two spiders darted past my nose,
like scavengers leaving a battlefield when they see the op-
posing armies forming ranks again. My hand lay beside my
face, the noose of rotten twine prepared to drop upon the
hapless creature. All was ready. Victory at hand. But a
sudden crack of summer thunder split the stillness of the
darkening afternoon, and my quarry bolted, his neck intact
for one more day. My belly empty for one more day.

I rolled onto my back and laughed as the first chilly drops
of rain pelted my face. A fitting result. The only opponent
left to me, and I could not prevail. In a long summer of
tormented dreams I had fought every one of my demon
encounters three times over. Once again, I had destroyed
the Lord of Demons in his every manifestation. I had
slaughtered demons, gutted Derzhi, and strangled Ezzarians
until I had expended every scrap of anger, hatred, and violence in my soul. My sleep had left me exhausted. Only in
the silent days spent sitting in my rocky eyrie and staring
into empty sky had I been able to rest.

Col'Dyath was a ruined tower left by a race of ancient
builders who had scattered their lovely, graceful stonework
throughout all of the lands of Azhakstan, Manganar, Ezzaria, and Basran. No one knew who these builders were or
how it was that all their works had been left in ruins. Our
scholars had taken an interest, because so many of the ruins

sat in places rich with melydda, but neither they nor historians of other races had learned anything of substance about
the builders. This particular tower sat on a bald knob of
wind and stone and treeless sky near the northeastern borders of Ezzaria, and had been my refuge in my youth, when
I was troubled or tired from constant schooling, when I felt
the mysterious changes in my body that would one day give
me wings, when I doubted my calling or my skills, when I
needed to find peace.

Thickening clouds swirled dizzily above me, and the rain
came harder, breaking the drought that had settled over
Ezzaria for the summer. The tiny spring that had filled my
need of water had been little but a mud hole for uncountable days. Thick, cold rivulets ran down my face and into
my mouth. Talar would disapprove; the water that washed
away the sweat and dust would also ease my raging thirst.
But I was not ready to go down from my tower. Not yet.

In the two months since my sentencing, I had found no
peace. Once I had expended all my anger in bloody dreams
and grew tired of staring at nothing, I had damned myself
for not thinking sooner of using sorcery to ease my loss. I
spent a few frenzied days and nights conjuring an image of
my son, taking Ysanne's fine bones and straight nose and
my own wiry build, bronze skin, and deep-set eyes, merging
them to discover how he would look . . . as a babe . . . as
a child . . . as a strong, fair youth. For unending hours I
cast my enchantments. But when I tried to embrace him
and tell him how much I wished I could have saved him,
the image faded, and I cursed the gods and my hands that
could not create life. Only death. I was very good at death.

I had passed through that time, too. Afraid . . . wondering if my reason was intact. I began to sleep again—long
hours in both day and night. At first I dreamed of flying,
through sunlight and ravaged cloud, through red morning
and silvered night, past the moon and the stars to realms
unknown, all sorrow left behind, all love forgotten, all care
and grief subsumed in wind and spreading wing. I began
to think that perhaps I was done with my harshest grieving,
and that I could begin to consider the future. But then my
visions changed, and a new dream crept into my nights. It
consumed me, so overpowering that I huddled in my tower

steeped in dread, yet so insistent that I could not eat or walk or think, save of how soon I could sleep again and go back to it. The dream always began in a land of ice and snow . . .

. . . outside a towered castle carved of ice that glowed blue-gray in sunless gloom. I crouched in the snowy darkness beyond the castle's gleaming light, my limbs frozen, my fingers and feet dead. Bitter wind, sharp-edged with sleet and frost, cut through my flapping garments. Though I could not say why, I was desperate to get inside that frozen citadel, as if I might find sustenance that would keep me living. Not warmth. Nothing would make me warm ever again.

I was not alone. A steady stream of riders and walkers passed into the castle across a bridge of rainbow luminescence, shimmering, wraithlike figures that I could sense more than see, glancing light as when a crystal catches a passing sunbeam. Only when they turned at just the correct angle did their humanlike forms have substance. Such beauty . . . and I wanted to be with them. I cried out from the frigid darkness, but no matter how I hunted, I could not find the path that would take me to the bridge. A gust of wind took my breath, and I started coughing, a racking, agonized stridor that burned my chest and left a spray of blood on the snow. Soon I was crawling, my hands and knees so numb I could not feel the ground.

The stream of riders dwindled. A few stragglers hurried across. Yet I still was not alone. Someone . . . something . . . was in the darkness with me. A horror without a name. It brushed my skin like the fingers of the wind, leaving long, bloody streaks, hunting for the way to get inside me. Again, I cried out for help, and one of the shimmering wraiths on the bridge stopped for a moment, peered out into the gloom, then hurried on its way. I crawled a few more steps before collapsing into the snow. Then came the devouring darkness. The nameless horror crept into my pores, into my eyes and ears and mouth, filling me, blinding me, suffocating me just before it began to gnaw its way out again . . .

Only after uncounted days and uncounted repetitions of this dream was I able to force myself back to some semblance of life. I had not eaten for much too long and scarcely had the strength to lift my hand. The consuming dread and the empty, lonely craving to find my way out of the darkness and into the frozen citadel lingered in a corner of my mind, as vivid as the echo of Talar's judgment or the memory of my arms around Ysanne's empty belly. Yet the urgency to probe the meaning of the dream in daylight was quickly set aside by the abject condition of my body.

When I had first come to Col'Dyath after the Council's judgment, I'd found a cache of hard biscuits and dried meat, tucked in a leather bag and hung up high where animals could not get it, left, no doubt, by some Ezzarian straggler in the days of hiding. Though a meager larder, it had kept me living through the dismal summer. But it had run out before my dreaming, and now that I was awake again, I had to hunt or starve.

Today—my rabbit quarry disappeared—it would be starve. But I planned to drink my fill of the blessed rain as I lay unmoving on my back, as if a giant hand held me down to the rock. Or perhaps it was that I was too tired to move, for I lay there through a storm-wracked night and into the next day until I believed the unending rain might dissolve me into the very soil of Ezzaria. Perhaps that's what I wanted.

"Master Seyonne, can you hear me? Did you fall? Are you injured?" Icy fingers poked at my arms and legs and other parts too confusing to remember. "Idiot. What am I doing here?" I wasn't asking these things of myself, unless my voice had taken on a disturbing female pitch.

I had every intention of batting the cold fingers away to make them leave me alone, but was disconcerted when my hand did not obey. Then an earthquake made my head explode and left me upside down, rain running into my nose as I was dragged across a mountain range. "Please don't," I mumbled to whatever beast was hauling me away. I must have been dreaming.

"Why didn't you come for me a month ago?"
"It was not my place."
The argumentative voices were very soft, but I thought

they might complete the fracture that seemed to go right between my eyebrows.

"Verdonne's child! Is it your place to let a man die?"

"He wasn't going to die. I was watching. This fever is a new thing."

I couldn't place the voices. Probably more dreams. I had dreamed enough for five lifetimes and wanted no more of it; I was afraid of my dreams. But at least it wasn't raining anymore.

"Seyonne? Open your eyes. I saw them move. It's high time you woke up."

Dark eyes with fine-woven lines about them peering into my face. A long braid of thick black hair, three renegade strands of it tickling my nose. A very worried, oval face.

"Catrin."

"I should have known you would come back to Col'Dyath. We searched for you for weeks, but never thought to come this far. We assumed you'd gone to Aleksander."

I closed my eyes and wished she would immediately take back all the memories she had just laid at my feet. "Go away." Only the scraping rawness of my throat that accompanied each syllable convinced me that the harsh croak was my own voice.

"When you're well, I will. I can't imagine you would welcome me. Or any of us."

I rolled over and pulled the blanket over my head, though before burying myself, I managed to budge my eyelids open enough to note that I was inside the tower ruin, spread out on a blanket, my head pillowed on a rolled-up something. Then I asserted, very foolishly considering the anvil that was shifting around inside my head with every movement, "I'm perfectly well. I just stink a bit. Go away."

She pulled away the blanket, laid her cool fingers on my head, and made the anvil be still. "Then, tell me how many days it's been since I came. Or how many days since you were found half drowned on a sliver of a ledge where one move could have sent you falling to your death. Or how many days since you've had a decent meal."

I lay immobile lest she be tempted to move her marvelous hand and let loose the anvil. But I wouldn't give her any easy welcome. "You're not my mentor anymore. I don't have to answer your questions. Go away."

"And you will lie here and die of this fever as you please, leaving me to live forever unforgiven?"

"I'm not a madman, Catrin." I wanted the cool hand to stay. It was the pain I wanted to go away. "I've considered madness here. I've dabbled in it. But I'm not. It wasn't grief over Ysanne and the child. Yes, I was tired, but it was not the two hundred and fifty battles, either. And I survived my years as a slave as well as anyone could. I've spent a great deal of time reviewing it in these weeks. I saw what I saw, and I was not wrong to let him go."

"I believe you. I was wrong to do what I did to you. You were in a terrible state, and I thought I knew what was best. And in case you didn't hear it, I'm asking your forgiveness."

She started to move her hand, but I caught it and put it back on my head. "So how long have you been here?"

In her best schoolmistress fashion, she made me sit up, eat soup, and drink willow-bark tea before she would tell me anything. And when she began telling me, I didn't like it.

"Fiona brought me here?" I tried to bury my head in the blanket again. The last thing in the world I wanted was to owe favors to Fiona.

"She's been camped just beyond that square boulder all summer."

"Watching me."

"She believes her duty was not removed by our judgment. If she hadn't been here, you would still be lying out on those rocks, your bones being picked at by vultures. She saved your life."

"She destroyed my life. What was left of it after Ysanne took her portion."

The worst part about sensible Catrin's care and feeding was that I came all too well to my senses. I was a wretched mess. Dirty. Ragged. Little better than when I was a slave, save my chains were less visible. I had always despised people who got stretched a little thin and took their troubles so much to heart that they abandoned decency and eating

and reasonable pursuits until they became filthy, pitiful
scarecrows. It was an insufferable indulgence. Too many
people had no choice about such things. So, as one has to
do after so many lessons learned as we stumble through
the world, I humbly cleaned myself up and tried to reclaim
some dignity.

Catrin refused to talk business until I was up and about,
which took several days. I had evidently lain out in the
drought-breaking downpour sick and half-starved for three
days before Fiona found me and dragged me back to the
tower. She had little skill at healing and no medicines, so
she went for Catrin. I did appreciate her choice of healer.

So my first excursion away from my sickbed was to Fiona's campsite behind the square boulder, not a thousand
paces from my tower. She was hunched over a tiny fire,
stitching a patch on one of her boots. She'd built a shelter
woven of sticks hauled up from the forest far below us, and
alongside a well-used bow and newly fletched arrows, there
was considerable bony evidence that she was far more successful at hunting than I had been. She jumped up when I
came, standing awkwardly with her stockinged foot held off
the damp ground, her chin stuck out belligerently.

"I've come to thank you for hauling me back to the
tower. And for bringing Catrin."

"Couldn't let you die out there, could I?"

Though sorely tempted to speak the answer that came
immediately to mind, I kept my sarcasm mild. Thunder
grumbled on the horizon, and a damp wind swirled smoke
and ash in our eyes. "It's foolish for you to be out here in
the rain now I know you're here. So if you feel bound to
stay, at least come inside the tower. There's plenty of room,
and Catrin's there to protect you from my unsavory
influences."

I thought she was going to refuse. I hoped she would be
insulted and take her all-seeing eyes back to her home. But
her pitiful campsite was clue enough to her persistence, and
my discomfort had never prevented her from staying
around. She moved in.

By the next day, Catrin allowed me to converse at length,
and I had enough voice to do so. "So Hoffyd has no quarrel

with you spending a week on a mountaintop with me?" I said to my dark-haired physician as we drank chamomile tea and listened to the rain.

Catrin smiled and filled my mug again. "Hoffyd is the most patient and understanding of men."

"So where was he hiding those three weeks? Howel said Ennit was driving you crazy trying to find him."

Catrin pursed her lips in warning, and her eyes flicked to Fiona, who was doing her best to ignore us. "Howel was mistaken. Hoffyd was with his sister for over a month. Poor Ennit's never quite gotten over her flux. But I do need to get back to the dear fellow now you're better."

"How do your students progress?" It was hard to ask. Harder to hear. But if I was to continue breathing, I could not ignore it.

"Drych passed his testing just before I came. I'll take Tegyr through next week. I'll let them begin true combat soon after. I've sent word to the Searchers to bring in a few easier cases to start."

"Take care of them, Catrin. There is so much . . ." I felt like I needed to warn Catrin, but I couldn't come up with words to describe a danger I believed was looming somewhere just beyond the distance I could see. My worries were vague, ill formed, like an interrupted dream. "Tell me, in all your study, in all your grandfather's talk, did you ever come across any mention of one called 'the Precursor'?"

"Precursor of what?"

"Well, that's the question, isn't it? I don't know." We went over the demon's words yet again.

"I don't remember anything about such a name. Are you sure the word was *naghidda*?"

"Absolutely sure. The only thing I can connect with it is something the Lord of Demons said just before I killed him." The memory had come to me in my summer's dreaming. "He said, 'Do not think this battle is over. There is another yet to come. . . .' I thought he meant another battle, and I dismissed it because I got rid of the villain. But now I wonder." Only as I spoke them did the words give shape to my disquiet. "I've done a lot of thinking up here these months. All of this"—I waved my hand to encompass everything of the life we knew—"there's something fundamentally wrong. If I'd not been away for so long, I might never have recognized it. I couldn't see it when I was a slave, because being back in Ezzaria, doing what I was meant to do, was everything I wanted. I could not question, because I had to survive. But since I came back . . . My problem has not been just my discomfort with discipline or my impatience with self-righteous fools. It's not just newly clever demons and harder fighting."

The ideas came tumbling out of me like the rain after my own long drought. "We're missing something. Think of how little we know. Even after so many years, so much study, we can't explain the demon I met. We can't explain why I can grow wings. We can't explain why we can't just kill the demons and be done with it. We can't explain how it is we came to be doing all this. Why are the scrolls so short and so few? Those who wrote them were not savages, but literate men and women, comfortable with words. There must have been more writings. We've no evidence that anyone has ever known enough about us to destroy our history. It's like someone has opened a door a crack, and I can look through it and see the vastness of our ignorance. Your young Wardens must be careful . . . and they must listen, so you'll know how to prepare."

I wanted to say more. Somehow the watch fires of my mind had been lit. I believed I had been given a warning, but I could not say how or why or what about. I just could not get around the fact that if the Lord of Demons, the terrible, powerful being Aleksander and I had fought for three days, was only a precursor, we had damned well better find out what came after.

Catrin did not dismiss my ramblings out of hand. Rather she frowned uncomfortably, saying only, "I'll need to think about this. Do some more reading. Talk to some people. And I thought I was bringing news to you." Then she shook off her thoughtful worry and laid her hand on my knee. "You've never asked why I changed my mind about your story before I came here."

An undertone of excitement drew me out of the tangle of my unnamed fears.

"It wasn't just our long acquaintance and your realization of your own stupidity in doubting me?"

"I don't know how this fits with what you've told me, but we've found something in Grandfather's journals."

"And what was that?"

"There was another Warden who found a demon like yours."

"Damn! I knew it."

His name was Pendyrral, and he had been a Warden when Galadon was a young man. Pendyrral had been called to help a woman who had gone mad and ruined her husband's business. The Searcher had given the woman the required tests and verified demon-possession, but reported that she had never seen a victim so calm and convinced of the rightness of her deeds. Pendyrral had returned from the portal in a daze, insisting that he could not find the demon. After long questioning, he admitted that the only demon manifestation that had appeared at his challenge was a golden-haired woman of dazzling beauty and great good humor. She had teased him and danced with him under a glorious moon. According to the journal, Pendyrral had never fought again.

Galadon, curious at the strange story, had waited until the Searcher and the Comforter had come home to Ezzaria, and inquired after the victim. The Searcher was disturbed and said there must have been a mistake in their testing. The woman—the victim—was considered a generous heroine in her town. It had been discovered that her husband had been stealing boys from nearby villages and putting them to work in his silver mines. The wife had been sneaking the children away one by one and returning them to their families. Her husband could not accuse her publicly, as it would reveal his own crime, so he had proclaimed her mad.

"Pendyrral was dead before I went into training," I said. "But perhaps the Searcher or even the Aife is still alive. If I could talk to one of them . . ."

Catrin shook her head.

"What of the Comforter?"

She sighed ruefully. "Lost in the Derzhi war. There's no

one left who could tell you anything, except for one scholar who spent a goodly time investigating the occurrence."

"Well, I'll talk to that one, then."

"I don't think that's possible."

"Why not?"

"Because it's Balthar."

My soul shriveled at the name. Balthar the renegade. Balthar the traitor. Balthar who had created the soul-destroying rites the Derzhi used to strip Ezzarian slaves of melydda. I still woke suffocating from nightmares of my three days buried in Balthar's coffin. I shook my head. "No. Not even for this could I breathe the same air as that man."

"I'll keep looking. See if there are any more stories."

Two more days Catrin stayed, dosing me with her medicines and trying to unravel the meaning of my fears. But once my cough was gone and I had promised to take better care of myself, she packed up her blankets and bundles, ready to go home to her husband and her students. I cooked her a farewell pot of rabbit stew as proof that I would not starve without her care.

Fiona had not participated in any of our discussions of demons or history. As she had done since coming to the tower—since I had known her—she wore her hostility like a second skin. Yet she was the nearest thing I had to a witness. I still had no idea what she had experienced during my encounter with the strange demon. As Catrin and I pondered philosophy yet again, she sat reading a small shabby book and eating her portion of the day's feast. When the conversation lagged, I broached the subject. "I once asked you to think about that day's weaving," I said, knowing full well she had been listening. "I'd be interested in your interpretation of our experience. Would you tell me about it?"

I had tried to ask in a civil tone, but she slammed her wooden bowl to the floor of broken stone, then jumped to her feet as if I'd poked her with a dagger. "It was a demon. Demons bring corruption and madness and death, and I am sworn to aid a Warden in killing them or sending them back where they belong. I will not discuss this with a madman." She stormed out of the tower into the sunny afternoon.

As the last echoes of her ill humor faded, I demolished the remainder of my stew, watching Catrin scrub out the bronze cooking pot with sand. "I don't suppose you'd tell me what she said to the Council."

"I cannot. We're sworn to privacy, as you well know."

"Sorry. I shouldn't have asked."

"Well, I'm glad she's gone for a bit," said Catrin abruptly, setting the pot aside. "There's another matter I need to speak to you about before I go. A more personal one. Though I was commanded not, it must be said."

For five days I had been waiting for it. "Ysanne?" I doubted my wife had sent any message asking forgiveness. I had already given her my answer to that.

"She grieves for you."

I scooped up the last drops of savory brown juice from the bottom of my bowl, then let them drip slowly off the spoon one by one. "I grieve for her . . . and for our son."

"She had no choice."

"No choice!" I dropped the spoon into the bowl. "Of course she had a choice. Even when I was a slave, I had choices. Sometimes they brought pain beyond enduring, sometimes risk, but I still had a mind and a soul and a conscience I had to live with."

"But your risk and your pain were just that. Yours. Ysanne's risk is for all of us. Only her pain is her own . . . and yours."

"She didn't trust me enough to let me see him. She didn't allow me any choice in the matter."

"She couldn't risk it. You are Ezzaria's only Warden. She believed you would try to save the child, and she believed you would be destroyed by it. She is Queen—"

"She had no right to choose for me. And she has destroyed me after all, hasn't she? You and the others of the Council were convinced I had lost my reason, if not my soul. Ysanne herself believed it, else she'd never have allowed this judgment to stand. Together you've come near making it happen. This danger I feel . . . I can't explain it . . . but we are facing something terrible. And just when we need to look beyond ourselves and find out what it is,

Ysanne has made herself a murderer. If she doesn't see it yet, she will. I know her, Catrin. I love her more than life, and it will destroy her as surely as it has ruined me. And with all of my skill, all of my training, all of this melydda bound into my body and mind, there's nothing I can do about any of it."

Catrin threw her hands in the air and then clamped them on my shoulders. "Valdis' children, you two are the most stubborn, hardheaded Ezzarians ever born. How can you love one another so dearly, yet believe such ill of each other?" She shook me until my bones rattled, then dropped her voice low. "She did not kill him, Seyonne. Though law and custom demand it, especially of the Queen who must bear every grief her subjects endure, she could not bring herself to kill your child. She allowed him to be sent away. The midwives know of a place . . . a hermitage . . . holy men who take children without question. She hopes he will survive until he's old enough that you can save him."

"Hoffyd took him," I said, the words falling from my tongue unbidden, for suddenly I had no mind to control them.

"He was told to go to the market at Teryna and ask for 'Dolgar's Hand,' saying he was sent by the 'guardians.' He says the young priest was gentle and caring and promised to see the babe safely nurtured. Hoffyd could not have left him otherwise, despite Ysanne's command."

"Then, I have to go."

She shook her head. "You can't. You know it. We need you here. It's why I had to get you well before I told you, so you wouldn't do something rash. Think—"

"There's no thinking required. What am I to stay for? So Ysanne can pretend that everything is as before? So Caddoc can pry out of me that I'm terrified of snakes or that I can't walk the southwestern hills without weeping for all who died there eighteen years ago? This is our child, Catrin. I can't abandon him in this world. I know too much of it."

Catrin stood up and folded her arms as if to hold in her temper, as if her stern mentor's words spoken in a calm and serious manner might bring me to my senses. "Wardens cannot leave Ezzaria without permission, Seyonne. It means abandoning your oath."

"My oath is void. The Queen of Ezzaria has informed me."

"You know better. Wardens are sworn to oppose the works of demons whether they can fight or not. And for you . . . your oath is as much a part of you as your head and your hands. You cannot abandon the war."

"I know nothing anymore."

"I thought you rash, Seyonne. I thought you hasty in your words and deeds, pronouncing these ideas before you thought them through. But right or wrong I never believed ill of you. I never thought you would desert a battlefield. Stay here if you want to change the law. If you leave—"

"I'll be back, Catrin. You know me better than anyone in Ezzaria, including my wife, I think, and you know I'd not do this unless I had to. I would rather go with your blessing . . . or at least your understanding."

But she would not relent. "Consider well . . . very well . . . what you choose to do. Ysanne will not have him here. She'll wield the knife herself before she permits it. And prophecies will not shield you from the law if you come back tainted this time."

"If holding my son in my arms corrupts me, then I want nothing to do with our law."

She sighed, her mouth tight with anger. "Have you any message for Ysanne?"

"No." The scar about the empty place my heart once lived had grown thick and hard. "If my wife could ever deem it necessary to murder our child, then I want nothing to do with my wife."

CHAPTER 7

*The forest god grew jealous of the love the woodland
people bore for Valdis, angry at the thought that this
boy—half mortal—might someday steal his throne, and
the god plotted to kill the child and all the mortals
who loved him so. The grieving Verdonne, unable to
persuade her husband of Valdis' guileless nature, sent
the boy into the sheltering trees to save him, and she
took up a sword and set herself between the god and
the world of mortal men.*
*—The story of Verdonne and Valdis as told to the First
of the Ezzarians when they came to the lands of trees*

The narrow street of baked-mud shops was crammed with
people. Already late for my appointment after dealing with
suspicious gate guards, I was trapped behind a Suzaini merchant family that spread itself across the entire street as it
lumbered toward the more prosperous districts of Vayapol.
The merchant himself was in striped robes with colored
beads woven into his hair and beard. His woman followed
after him, draped head to toe in plain white, decked with
a hundredweight of gold bangles and silver necklaces. She
was leading a train of dark-eyed children, goats, dogs, and
fenzai-clad slaves hauling carts and carrying impossible
bundles on bent, scarred shoulders.

Though it seemed impossible to get around the Suzaini
procession, round-faced Manganar women in embroidered
tunics and colored skirts managed to slide smoothly
through the congestion, smiling and calling to each other
despite heavy water jars or linen baskets on their shoulders.
Dusty children with thin legs and bare feet raced under a
red and blue awning, stealing apples from a tall basket and

knocking over makeshift shelves laden with bronze pots
and tools, leather belts and purses, and wooden racks of
colored ribbons.

I followed their lead and squeezed past the Suzainis,
threading my way through a flock of goats and the pawing
hands of the beggars who hovered near the bronze gates
of a shrine to Dolgar, the one-eyed Manganar god. Wondering how anyone ever did business in such confusion and
noise, I dodged the waving hands of two dark-skinned
Thrid women with painted eyes and long necks, who were
haggling with a butcher over three scrawny chickens. I
hated cities.

I could not help but flinch at the sharp snap of a lash
behind me. The Suzaini merchant's overseer must have decided that one of the slaves was lagging. And when a tall
horse came straight toward me, bearing a haughty Derzhi
warrior, his braid long and his sword reflecting the noonday
sun, I pressed my back against the nearest doorway and
cast my eyes down. I could not risk his being offended by
an impertinent look or noting the Derzhi royal mark on
my face. When he was safely past, I stuffed my hand into
my shirt and felt for the leather packet somewhere in the
vicinity of my pounding heart, reassuring myself that Aleksander's paper was still tucked safely away. Twice already
on this journey I'd had to use it. Without that precious
document to prove I was a free man, I could find myself
in chains again with one foot cut off to teach me the consequences of a slave's running. Astonishing how old fear re-
turns like a well-worn garment, still fitting perfectly well,
though you believe yourself grown long past its use.

Once I breathed again, I turned my mind to important
business. Somewhere just beyond Dolgar's shrine was an
alley where my informant had said I would find an ale
shop marked with a white dagger. There, after two weeks'
journeying from Ezzaria and three days being passed from
one contact to the next and waiting for my request to be
relayed and responded to, I would meet the man who had
taken custody of my son.

The air was stifling. Nothing brought my dislike of cities
so much to life as the broiling noonday stink of dung and
butchered animals, cheap perfumes and scented lamp oils,

rotted vegetables and thousands of animals and unwashed bodies in so close a space. Though the stench was no less in the alley, at least there were fewer people: a few beggars, a brawny tradesman hauling a broken cart, and a young woman dressed in a servant's apron hurrying past. Just ahead of me the houses were built right over the alleyway, casting the narrow lane in deep shadow. The first thing I saw, as my eyes adjusted to the dimness of the overhang, was a splash of white paint on the mud-colored wall. The white dagger.

I hesitated before entering the dark opening, as pointlessly nervous as a Hollenni youth setting out to meet the bride chosen for him at birth. I was a warrior who had faced down hundreds of demons, including the most powerful of their kind. I had stood nose to nose with the heir to the Derzhi Empire and dared him to kill me. How could a three-month-old infant and a priest have me in such a pitiful state?

Before I could steel myself and step inside the doorway, a hunchbacked old man in grease-splattered rags bumped into me, trampling my foot. He wobbled and flailed his arms, threatening to smear his pustule-covered face against my own. I recoiled in disgust from his stink and disease, while grabbing his arm to keep him from falling.

"Dolgar's grace, your worship," he mumbled. "Pardons. Pardons." Touching one hand to his head, he bent over and tried to back away, but I didn't let go. "Please, master . . ." With none too gentle a movement, I twisted his other arm into a knot and snatched my leather packet from the surprisingly strong hand that had been stuffing it into the deep folds of his filthy robe. Fortunately, I had not lost my reflexes completely in my summer's madness. When I glimpsed the glint of steel beneath his robe, I whirled about, and kicked the knife into the air, hearing it clatter against a mud-brick wall. To my astonishment the beggar growled in fury and came after me. But I caught his hand in my free one and spun him about until I had him wrapped in my arm like a stinking caterpillar in its bundled web.

"Do not," I said, glaring into his black eyes that were not at all so decrepit as the rest of him. Then I shoved him away, retrieved his knife, and stuck it in the waistband of my breeches. Only as he scrabbled away into the shadows cursing did I flatten my back against the wall and take a few shaking breaths, replacing the precious packet under my shirt yet again. Too close. Already nervous, I almost swallowed my tongue when a large bird of brown and white, some kind of hawk or vulture, swooped down from a nearby rooftop, passing not three handspans from my nose before soaring into the sunlight at the end of the alleyway.

I shook off the disconcerting encounters and stepped into the doorway of the ale shop. The place was dark and airless, scarcely large enough to hold the three small tables and the rickety crates and barrels pulled up to serve for seats. A large man sat on a barrel in one corner, slumped against the wall. From the sound of his snores he was deep in ale-fed dreams, but no sooner did I move past the plane of the door than he growled and gurgled and cleared his throat. "A hot day, traveler," he mumbled. "Have ye a thirst needs easing?"

"Aye," I said. "A mug of your best."

He disappeared through a back door, and before I could find a seat that looked sturdy enough to hold a man safely, he slammed a brimming tankard on the battered table. I pulled a coin from my pocket and spun it upward over my head, and as I expected, his movements reflected no ale-drowned dullness. He plucked it from the air like a lizard's tongue nabs a mosquito.

"Where have you come from, traveler?"

"Karesh," I said. Near enough. Karesh was a Manganar town just over the border from Ezzaria. I knew it as well as I knew any town, and chances were this man had never been more than two streets from the lane where he was born. "I've come to meet a man. I've been told he frequents your shop and picks up packages here. Says it has the finest ale this side of Zhagad, though the brewers in Karesh disagree. Have you seen him?"

Those were the words I'd been told to say by the last of the three contacts in the web of misdirection begun by Catrin's information.

"And who is it has told you that?"

"I was sent by the guardians."

How I could have missed the other man sitting in that dark room, I could not imagine, but no sooner had I said the words than I felt him there, just to my right, sitting at the third table and leaning his chin on his hand. I spun quickly on my seat, almost toppling the tankard in my surprise. *Watch your back, fool. You've let yourself get careless.*

"I see no package, sir," said the quiet voice from the shadows.

"Perhaps I wanted to see what manner of man it was before I entrusted him with my business."

"Good Feydor, a light, if you please. Your shop is like the mine pit of the Nurad, where blessed Dolgar was held prisoner."

The portly landlord produced an earthenware oil lamp and set it on the grimed, knife-gouged table between the soft-spoken man and myself. He kindly transferred my ale as well, then set a barrel—and himself on it—in the doorway of his shop and promptly set to snoring again.

The man revealed by the lamplight wore the wrappings of a priest of Dolgar—shabby, threadbare swathes of dingy cloth wrapped about his chest and his waist—and, like all his brother priests, he had shaved his head. The dark circle on his forehead would be ashes—to remind him of the fire that burned the hero Dolgar into ash—and the burn scars on the backs of both his hands would complete the tale, for the fire had transformed the human man's ashes into a god. But signs and symbols were not the whole story of this priest. I could not fix him anywhere in the span of people I had known. He was a younger man than I expected, no more than twenty-five, and his face was coarse, all angles and bones and deep hollows, his lower lip protruding and malformed. Though his sagging lip and awkward features spoke of peasant ancestry, as was common for the poor priests of the Manganar low gods like Dolgar, his dark, deep-set eyes were as keen as a Warden's knife blade. His long fingers had worked the land. They were cracked and had dirt ground in that no amount of washing could remove. Yet he wore an air of stillness that I had seldom found in those whose lives were defined by hardship and poverty. Peasants, even priests, had little leisure for studied quiet.

"You may skin my looks as you will," he said in the fluid dialect of the Manganar countryside. "There's little enough to see, as my mam always told me, and nothing fair about it. But I don't know you'll be able to tell what manner of man I am by your looking. It's the history of deeds must speak for me."

"Then speak," I said.

"I am but a poor priest of mighty Dolgar. My brothers and I serve our holy master, giving refuge to innocents left without family, whether from war or disease or whatever reason. We ask nothing in return but to be left to our work. Is that introduction enough?"

Both his speech and his gaze were open and frank, no trace of slyness or hidden meaning. I almost felt guilty when I shifted my senses and looked deeper. Perhaps he had been examined in that way before. I didn't know what other Ezzarians had come to this place laying their torn hearts in this man's bony hands. But I would see . . . and he did not look away. It was very strange . . . I saw a good and simple man, one with no great aspirations, a man at peace. Nothing to make me wary or fearful. Yet as I pulled away, I felt a momentary dizziness, as sometimes happens when you are just at the point of slipping into sleep and suddenly feel as if you're falling, though your back is solidly on the ground . . . or as I did when I jumped from a cliff in an alien soul and grew wings to break my fall. I thought it was only me, and the strain of being in the city, for it was glimpses of the city that shot through my head like flickering light beams. Colors, faces, Derzhi warriors with swords drawn, the bird that had flown past my face, beggars, white daggers smeared on walls and flags and faces.

"Introduction enough," I said, taking a drink of my ale to cover my jumpiness. The room was very hot. "You know who we are. I mean, you've seen those like me before." Ezzarians were the easiest to recognize of all races in the Empire, save the dark-skinned Thrid. We had worked for years without success to devise enchantments to mask our features, but to our eternal annoyance could maintain such an illusion no more than a few moments at a time.

"Aye," he said. "But I know naught of your secrets nor do I care to know." He leaned forward. "And now will you tell me exactly why you're here? You're not at all the usual messenger from those of your blood. You've brought no little one with you, have you?"

"No."

He wrinkled his gangly face into a knot. "You don't think to put a stop to our service?"

"No. Nothing like that." Now that the time had come, I wasn't sure what to say. "Tell me . . . you have seen . . . these that my people bring you . . ." Damned awkward.

"Children. Dolgar's eye, they're naught but children."

"The children . . . They grow well? Healthy? Happy?" Or did they cut the wings off of birds or set fire to their cradles or kill each other before they could walk?

"We tend them as we do every child in our care. We give them everything within our power to give: food, medicine, someone to be glad they're alive."

"You didn't answer me." I found it hard to look at him.

"Why should I answer? Will you not keep bringing them? Is what I offer not better than what you offer? What difference to you is the outcome of what we give? We don't sell them into slavery. We don't trade or bargain them. Our god commands us to do our best, and that's what we do."

His calm response held no antagonism, only simple reason. Yet I felt . . . I knew . . . that there was more than he was saying. He just gave me no hook upon which to hang my conviction.

"What is it you want?" Clearly he had no intention of answering my question unless I gave him a reason. And so I proceeded.

"There was a child came to you a few months ago. An infant. Brought by a scholarly man with only one eye . . ."

"I remember him. A kind man. Not easy with infants, or cities either, as I recall. But I honored him and took his charge. To a priest of my order, a supplicant with one eye cannot be refused."

After a moment I remembered that Dolgar's enemies had taken out one of the poor man's eyes before burning him. Lucky for his priests that the ashes and the burns were the only symbols of their god they were required to mimic.

I sipped my ale. I shifted on my barrel seat. I looked him over again, but he was so still he almost faded into the shadows. I could see no way to dance around the subject. What could I do but trust him and try to gain his trust in return?

"That child is my son. I've come to see him and . . ." And what? Take him with me? Where? What did I know of children? I had put aside these troublesome questions in my journeying, delighting in the thought that there was one death fewer to my tally, believing I would know what to do when the time came. But as the dark-eyed young man gazed on me in quiet waiting, I still didn't know what I should do. "He should be with his family," I blurted out at last.

"His family didn't want him."

"I was beyond—" I bit my tongue in annoyance. I couldn't tell him that I had been in a place no ordinary human could walk, battling monsters that he could not imagine in his dreams, that I had been flying on wings of gossamer in airs woven of madness and horror. An illiterate Manganar priest would never understand it. "I've never even seen him. My wife sent him away before I knew. I thought he was dead."

His speech was still calm and soft, yet I heard the rumble of righteous anger buried deep within him, imperfectly masked. "If you had spoken fairly to this one-eyed man who brought the child, then he could have told you of our agreement. We make it clear before we touch the child. We ask no questions, and we answer none. Once the bargain is struck, there is no turning back. You are free of your unwanted burden. The child is free of his." He stood up abruptly and shoved a heavy barrel aside so he could get out of his corner. "If what you say is true, then I'm sorry. But you're too late. May I offer a blessing for you before I go?"

I stood up, too, and forced myself calm. Killing him would do me no good, nor would strangling or pounding or any of the other forms of coercion that came instantly to mind. My fingers were making dents in the dark pine table. "He is my son. Please. I'll do anything you ask. You must—"

"I must not." He leaned forward over the table, so that the force of his words buffeted my face. "I vowed to keep

him safe. I have no way of knowing what you did to the
man who brought him or to your wife, if indeed the child
was yours. It may be your intent to carry out your barbaric
customs. You are not a simple man, my friend. Even an
ignorant priest can see it. Your very posture is violence. So
in order to keep the vows my god demands, I must be wary
and assume the worst."

"I'd never hurt him. Nor you. That's the last thing—"

"The children we take are rescued from their fates, and
we will not send them back. You may do with me as you
wish, my friend, though you must realize that none of my
brothers will ever again answer this call if I do not return."
He held out his hand in a gesture of peace. "If you care
for this child, then leave him be."

I did not take his hand. I was trying to conjure words—
some reason that would appeal to him, some way to convince him that I was not a threat. But I could come up
with nothing. Everything he said was true.

The priest started toward the doorway, where the landlord had suddenly awakened and was gesturing three
shabby customers into the suddenly crowded shop. The
only connection, and he was leaving. I shoved the drinkers
aside and hurried after. "Is there nothing I can do to convince you?"

He spoke over his shoulder. "Nothing."

"Then I thank you," I called after him.

He stopped just outside the doorway and stared back
at me.

"I don't agree with you. I am not what you believe. But
I thank you . . . for taking your duty so seriously. I could
ask nothing better."

He accepted my words as if they were a gift that he
didn't quite recognize, and he took the time to consider
them as if turning the gift over and over in his hand to
discover its nature. After a moment he gave the gift back
again. "You needn't fear. He will grow well."

I followed him into the alley and waited until he joined
the crowds in the broad street beyond the corner. I had
meant it when I thanked him. He had no reason to know
I was not what he feared. But even though my conscience

would not permit me to force him to speak, I wasn't going to give up so easily. As soon as the river of people took him out of sight, I ran down the alley and merged into the street traffic just behind him.

CHAPTER 8

I was a superior tracker. Though I had not yet regained the complete mastery of my sensory abilities since my return from slavery, I could again trace the disturbance in an ocean where a fish had swum past an hour earlier. I could distinguish which branch a bird had used for its perch on the previous day. I could hear the ripple in the air made by a woman's passing, and know it was a woman, not a man. Though I was depressingly average at many aspects of sorcery, I worked at such skills as these. They were necessary in my profession. Yet I lost the priest before we'd traveled two hundred paces through the streets of Vayapol.

I stood like an ox in the teeming throngs of the busiest market town in the eastern Empire. *Lost him. You should be hanged for incompetence.* After a few moments scratching my head and trying to think what to do next, I decided I'd best keep moving. A parting of the crowd and darting furtive movements among many buyers and sellers signified the approach of a redyikka, the Derzhi magistrate who oversaw public markets. From the direction of the disturbance came a loud whack and a gut-twisting scream that quieted the throngs for a moment. The redyikka had likely caught himself a thief or a cheat and executed summary judgment—cutting off the hand or nose of the accused. Such was justice for those who were not Derzhi. Before a moment's passing, life took up again . . . for all but the unlucky victim. *Blundering idiot.* I needed no encounters with Derzhi.

I pushed aimlessly through the crowds for a while, then bought a roasted chicken from a Thrid woman who was sweating over a small brazier and a slab of hot bread from a ragged Manganar boy with only one arm.

"Dolgar defend you," said the boy, when I gave him the copper coin from my tiny hoard, the remnants of those given me when Aleksander had sent me home from Zhagad.

"Tell me," I said, sitting down on the warm stone next the boy to eat my meal. "Do you know of a place where Dolgar's priests live, a hermitage perhaps—somewhere near the city?" It wouldn't be far, for word of the meeting passed between the priest and Vayapol and my Teryna contact in only three days, and Teryna was a day's journey.

"Priests live at the shrine," said the boy, jerking his head back the way I'd come. "Don't know of nothing else."

The shrine. Of course. I gave the astonished lad one leg of my chicken, stowed the rest of it in my pack, and set off for the shrine of the hero god.

The place was little more than a mud hovel, but was interestingly wrought inside. Walls and ceilings were completely covered with bits of metal. Every scrap of copper, steel, tin, or bronze that the god's devotees could scrounge together was cut into a square or a triangle and stuck to the interior with mud. The worshipers who had no metal brought candles or simple clay oil lamps, which illuminated the metal mosaic like the inside of a star. Devotees believed that Dolgar—a poor and humble hero god—would come someday and forge himself new armor to wear in the battles of the gods.

I found a brown-robed priest tending the lamps and asked him if his order had a nearby hermitage.

"Is your life to be given to holy Dolgar, then?"

"I am in between lives," I said. "I've always been solitary, so perhaps the hermit's life might suit me. I've lately become interested in Dolgar, and I've heard of his brotherhood and the good works they do."

The man was old, his skin like folded leather, his bald head mottled. "There's hardship in a hermit's life. Service. No easy pleasure. Young lads like you . . . educated as I hear by your speech . . . like as how you've known only soft days. Don't know what it is to lift your hand in real work." Clearly his eyesight was none too good.

For the first hour of his warnings, lecturing, and five hundred questions about my ancestors and their choice of gods,

I was patient. His shrine didn't seem to get much business. After two hours, I yearned to work some enchantment that could silence his holy snobbery and loose his secrets, yet I still refused to use my skills to coerce him. But as the third hour passed with no hint of how to find his brothers, and only more questions about the exact location, day, hour, and minute of my birth so he could begin some astrological query as to my fitness to forego meat, women, bathing, and literacy to join his brotherhood, I overcame my scruples. I invited him to visit an ale shop with me to talk more deeply about these things. We stayed away from the good Feydor's alleyway shop, but found a jolly place with barrels full enough to quench the prodigious thirst of a man who could talk for seven hours straight without saying anything. I learned what I wanted to know.

After a night in a wheat field, sleeping off far too many mugs of ale of my own and most of two days' walking, I hiked up a steep rocky track toward the hermitage. The bleak edifice of gray stone was perched atop a hill of terraced gardens. Though a few of the plots held a recognizable tangle of onions and potatoes, most were thick with briars and coarse grass. The building was imposing in size, three floors of massive stone blocks built in a U-shape, with a thick outer wall, an iron gate, and corner towers, but it was no fortress. The stonework of the outer wall was in poor repair, tough vines and weeds eating away at the stone, and crumbling mortar leaving long spans of the curving wall sagged or slumped into heaps.

No one answered the gate bell. After a brief wait, I pushed open the rusty ironwork and walked into a shabby courtyard that had once been paved with bricks. Weeds grew freely through the broken paving. A few nausicca vines flowered on the inner walls, but the herb beds laid out in rows between the main expanse of the court, and the cloisters were sadly neglected, the herbs overgrown in weedy clumps.

"Hello," I called out, standing beside a stone well ring in the middle of the courtyard. No one came.

Seeing and feeling no eyes from the windows around the courtyard, I strolled through the shady cloisters, pushed open the front door, and walked into the ancient pile of rock. Though plain and simple, as such places tend to be, the windows were generous, open to the air and blue skies of southern Manganar. Heavy wooden shutters, in somewhat better repair than the outer walls, could be closed and barred to keep out the winter wind that would blow cold off the plains and the river. One room had two long plank tables with stools pulled up beside and wooden mugs and bowls stacked on shelves on the wall. But spiderwebs hung heavy from the lamp hooks, and my steps echoed from the stone floor without answer. The place was deserted.

The double doors in the far end of the refectory went to the kitchen, its ovens cold, its scarred tables bare. Beyond the refectory I found a room where candles had been made and another where leather work was done. Scraps of wax and leather, glue and twine were all that was left scattered on the worktables amid dead flies and rodent droppings. Another room held a long table stained dark, and shelves with a few broken jars. At first I thought it was a writing room, but when I ran my fingers over the dark stains, it was not words I felt, but blood and pain and death. A physician's room, perhaps. Uneasy, I abandoned the first floor and went up the central stair.

On the second level of the central wing I found fifty small rooms, a few with thin straw pallets laid on the floor. Most of the rooms were empty. On the third floor I found the children's dormitory. Two long rooms on either side of the central passageway. Large, airy spaces open to the morning. A few small, ragged mattresses remained. Straw was scattered on the wooden floor, and against the wall stood a rickety table where a washing bowl and pitcher might have been kept. In one corner I found a mouse-chewed doll, made of cloth and stuffed with straw, a smiling face painted on the cloth. And on the walls . . . my heart, tight with grief, smiled when I saw. On the long inner walls were drawings made with coals or burned sticks: faces and stick figures, suns and trees and awkward horses, with a hundred smeared fingerprints mixed in. The old priest had fooled me completely. Years had passed, not days, since priests of Dolgar had cared for children here.

Tired and empty from the futile journey, I stood for a

while by one of the windows that looked out over the green
vastness of Manganar, letting the warm afternoon wind cool
my dusty sweat. The view from the hermits' vantage was
astonishing. The wide bends of the Dursk River were a flat
shimmer in the noonday. Broad block-shaped fields of
wheat stretched all the way to Vayapol on either side of
the river. And just beneath the ridge to the west lay the
Emperor's Road, the wide smooth way that led from Zhagad, in the desert heart of Azhakstan, to the fertile trading
centers of the east. If the children who had lived in this
room were not *in* the world, they could have at least
watched it passing by.

I had lost him. No children were coming back to this
place.

Three days later I sat alone at a crossroads spring in the
shade of a long-leafed nagera tree, drinking cool sweet
water and wrestling with the dilemmas of money, purpose,
and homesickness.

Money, because my few zenars were almost gone, and it
seemed foolish to use them up when I had so little idea of
where to go next. When I had returned to the shrine, no
priest had been there. The old woman I found tending the
lamps said they'd had no priest at the shrine for ten years;
Dolgar wasn't as popular as the newer Derzhi gods. By the
time I returned to the alleyway and found no white dagger
and an entirely different landlord at the ale shop and queried every person in Vayapol who knew anything of Dolgar
and his followers with no result, I decided that my only
course was to go back to Teryna and try to pick up the
trail. And so I had started out. But now, after only a few
leagues, I found my steps slowing. I was certain that I
would find none of those who had directed me to the priest.

As for my purpose, even if I were to find my son, what
life had I to offer him? The priest had seen it. I had studied
war. I lived it. Breathed it. Every day of my life I worked
at the art of killing. What nurturing was that for a babe?
Better the child stay with an ignorant priest of good heart,
than with a man who walked with demons.

, And with no money and no purpose, it was difficult to
fight the homesickness. Despite the penalties of my dis-

grace, I longed for trees and green and rain and quiet days. I had never planned to leave my homeland again. Ezzarian Wardens seldom passed the boundaries of our land, even in past years when there were more than one of us. Our lives and our power were bound up in the trees and the hills and the work we carried on there. I needed to be home, to help my people find out what was to come, whether they wanted to learn it or not. Though I had not dreamed since leaving Col'Dyath, memories of devouring darkness plagued me. I became convinced that I needed to study, to investigate, to look inside myself, even if I had to submit to Caddoc's prying for a time. Yet it was exceedingly disturbing that I could not envision myself back in Ezzaria, working in the fields, being counseled by Caddoc, living in a house with a woman I no longer knew. Stalemate.

So I sat at the spring and drank my water, watching a shabby, hollow-eyed family of three brothers, their wives, and their children pile back in their wagon, on their way to a new life in the borderlands. I wished for the ordinary hopes and fears they carried with them.

Inspiration is often likened to a bolt of lightning in the mind, but never had an answer to a dilemma struck me in quite so graphic a way. As I leaned over to refill my cup from the mossy basin, my head was invaded by the image of a monster—one with a long neck, leathery wings, and a snout that breathed fire. The monster was neither living nor fearful, but only an image from Derzhi legend. A smile came to my lips as I whispered words that anyone hearing would have counted strange. "So where are you, my lord? And why, after so long, do you seek me out?"

A few months after my return to Ezzaria I had heard news of the Derzhi heir's marriage to the fiery noblewoman who had helped me save his life. I had sent Aleksander a gift for his wedding day—a small jade figure of a gyrbeast, a mythical monster of Derzhi legend. Though I put no name and no message with the gift, I was sure he would know who sent it, and that he had but to touch it and say the proper word to know where to find me. I had taught him of such spells when we escaped from Capharna, and that particular enchantment had been attached to the figure of a gyrbeast. I had no idea how long it would take him to reach the meeting place that I had buried in the enchantment, but I had nowhere else to go. So, happy at an event that staved off harder decisions, within half an hour I set out to meet the man who had once bought me for a pitiful twenty zenars.

The spot I had chosen for the gyrbeast enchantment was in the wild barrens of southwestern Manganar, just across the steep mountain border of Ezzaria, only a two-day journey from my home. There was no way to know where Aleksander might be if he ever triggered the spell, but I had not wanted to make the meeting place too far from my work. I had tried to select a place untraveled, where the meeting of a Derzhi prince and an Ezzarian sorcerer could not be remarked. And so I had chosen the lonely ruin we called Dasiet Homol, the "Place of the Pillars."

Dasiet Homol was another of the sites left by the ancient builders. In the treeless wasteland, too rocky for growing things, too dry for herdsmen, too barren and too empty of natural riches to attract men of wealth or enterprise, these mysterious people had built a straight row of paired pillars spanning a quarter of a league. The pillars were plain cylinders of white stone, slightly tapered toward the top, undecorated save by a ring of markings at the eye level of an average man. Each marking was at exactly the same height on every pillar. All the measurements at the site were similarly exact. The pairs of pillars were each a thousand mezzits—about thirty paces—apart, each pillar in a row exactly two thousand mezzits beyond its predecessor, and each pillar seven hundred mezzits high. The row was oriented precisely north and south, crossing the low hills and shallow valleys without a break save by the few pillars that had toppled from some shifting in the land. The place was strange, built for some unfathomable purpose. Ezzarian scholars had tried for years to unravel the mysteries of Dasiet Homol, spending months at a time digging, measuring, and studying the markings. They had gathered the histories and legends of the Derzhi and the Basranni and other desert people who no longer existed. But no one had found evidence of any city or other structure nearby. No one had found any key to the markings, which were different on every pillar.

Every day as I waited for Aleksander, I ran up and down the hills and across the barrens to keep my wind and strength and speed, and I would set my course between the rows of pillars, wondering about them and about the people who made them. To create, transport, and erect such massive structures and to orient them so precisely could have been no easy task. What had driven them to do it? Had they sensed the power that thrummed in that bit of land, as it did in the forests of Ezzaria? As with all of the ruins, the place was brimming with melydda. I could feel it in the shadows that crept across the hillside as the sun moved across the sky. I could feel it in the solid warmth of the stone when I rested my back against it after my hours of running. I could feel it in the still, majestic shapes outlined against the stars when I lay awake in the night, and in the sigh of the wind as it wound its way through the long passage. I traced my fingers through the markings and tried to unravel their meaning, knowing that historians had puzzled over them for hundreds of years and made no headway. Dasiet Homol was a place of profound mystery.

For eight days I waited—running, sleeping, hunting rabbits and birds enough to keep from exhausting my supplies, practicing chants and exercises to clear my mind. Returning to long-neglected practices of my youth, I built a ring of holy fire and knelt within it as Verdonne had done in her long siege between the heavens and earth. I prayed for the wisdom to discern my course and the strength to follow it, and I asked her son Valdis, who had stepped aside to allow his mortal mother to take her rightful place on the throne of heaven, for a small share of his grace. This was not a time of despair or madness or searching grief as were the months at Col'Dyath. It was a "between" time. Between lives. Between fears. Between griefs. Perhaps I *was* called to be a hermit. In those days of running and dreaming, I came to feel that I had no connection to anyone. I lived only for the air and the sky, the stars and the dreams.

Oh, yes, when night fell, I dreamed again of the frozen castle and the wraiths of light who dwelt there, and of the deepening darkness creeping across that gloomy land. This

time I had no fever. I willed myself to dream of it. I needed
to understand. In the quiet of that wilderness I laid myself
open, and as I listened, a voice began to take shape from
the dream—a voice filled with good humor. *The storm
comes*, it whispered. *The days grow short. Shall we see
something of the world, you and I, before it falls?* I did not
know how to speak to him in return, or what I would have
said had I known.

I was almost sorry to hear the drumming of hooves on
my eighth evening just after sunset. Yet the thought of
Aleksander and the explosion of life he carried within him
warmed my frozen blood, and the closer the hooves, the
more willing I was to leave the time of reflection behind
and discover what had brought him to me.

CHAPTER 9

I sat on a hilltop near the center-most pair of pillars and watched the horsemen set up camp near a spring flowing by a grove of stunted willows. Dark shapes passed in front of campfires that sprang up on the hillside, and the low voices of soldiers settling for the night carried across the grassland. There were perhaps ten riders. I would not expect a prince of the Derzhi to travel alone.

The bloated moon hung low on the eastern horizon when I heard footsteps approaching the crest of the hill. One man. He said nothing, and the pillars shadowed his face, but I recognized his shape—tall, lean, as graceful, powerful, and dangerous as a shengar. To prepare the Prince to host the Lord of Demons, the Khelid had set a vile enchantment on Aleksander. At times—sometimes triggered, sometimes random—he had transformed into a beast, a shengar as it happened. He was nearly destroyed by it. The Khelid and their demons had chosen his transforming curse well. Though he was long rid of the enchantment, he was more like that wild mountain cat than any larger or more visibly ferocious creature. He stopped for a moment, perhaps to marvel at the dark ranks of stone stretching to either side, perhaps counting so as to know where to find me. He was not one to hesitate. Not one to hold back for fear of what might lie in such strange shadows, or to be awed by the magnificence of such a monument. Yet as the moon slid upward behind me, I saw the glint of steel caution in his hand. It surprised me.

"Who did you think to find at the end of the gyrbeast's tether, my lord?" I stepped out where he could see me silhouetted against the rising moon, and I spread my empty hands wide apart.

"Is caution the most difficult lesson of kingship or only the most painful?" he said.

"I think there are lessons both more difficult and more painful than caution, though it is a worthwhile study that must not be omitted."

He stepped closer, but remained outside the lane of pillars and moved to the side, forcing me to turn to face him and thus have moonlight reflected on my face. I had not expected such wariness. "You are alone?"

"Indeed. I've brought no horde of vengeful Ezzarians to greet you, nor even a single demon," I said.

"Of course not." He laughed and sheathed his sword, but it was not the same easy laugh that had defied the Lord of Demons. Like his posture, it was cautious.

He came forward to meet me between the pillars, and when he was but a few paces away, I sank to one knee. "It is an honor and a pleasure to see you again, my lord." I could not thank him for the return of Ezzaria. There were no words adequate even to begin. Besides, I didn't think he would want it. We owed each other so much, it was beyond sorting out.

He laid a hand on my shoulder and nudged me to get up, and, with a more familiar twist to his smile, raked me up and down with the razor of his attention. "Druya's horns, you look like your life is in the same wretched state as mine. I thought that next time we met we would look something better than a prince who had come a knife's edge from having his head removed, and an ex-slave who had just been freed of the most atrociously prideful and rock-headed master in the Empire."

Aleksander had always been perceptive, and his judgments of himself were as accurate as any. But it is always disconcerting to find one's private business so obvious to one without even a smattering of melydda. I'd had no intention of telling him of my troubles. As for Aleksander, the moonlight confirmed what his words had suggested. He had seen a great deal of death, and he had not been sleeping enough.

"I see no blood and no missing limbs," I said. "Things could be worse." Only after eight days of clarity could I believe it.

The Prince jerked his head. "Let's walk. I need to stretch my legs. I'm off to Kuvai tomorrow." He had never been one to be still. He strode through the bands of moonlight that pierced the night between the pillars. Silence hung between us like a heavy curtain, and I wondered what was troubling him.

"I hope your lady Princess is well, my lord."

"The dragon woman? As stubborn as ever. Last time I saw her, she smashed three lamps and came near setting the room afire because I refused to listen to a plan for opening up tax-hold lands to tenant farmers. I'd been on horseback for six weeks straight, not a single night with a woman, nor a single day without being in the middle of some stupid, senseless, bloody dispute, and she greets me with an hour's babbling about 'using idle land for something worthwhile' and 'allowing the poor to feed the people when the landlords wouldn't bother.' "

"Sounds like a well-thought-out plan."

"The cursed scheme is brilliant . . . of course it is." Aleksander shook his head, laughing wearily. "She is the most magnificent woman in the Empire. And, yes, I told her so, and she's probably got five crops planted and harvested already, it's been so damned long since I've seen her. The gossip in Zhagad is that I'm going to take another wife, as we've not yet made an heir, but I've not lain with her three nights running in these two years. Lydia says she could as soon conceive with the wind."

I could make no answer to that one.

"And what of your Queen . . . did you get things sorted out between you?"

"I can't . . ."

"Ah, your shy Ezzarian ways. You should veil your face if you don't want to reveal the truth. I'd say things are not going as you hoped."

As we passed another pillar, he fell silent again, and I decided not to dissemble any further. "Why have you called me here, my lord? As glad as I am to see you, I don't think it was for the purpose of exchanging family news . . . no matter how engaging."

He stopped and faced me, and one would have thought his amber eyes had a Warden's sight, he examined me so thoroughly. "I needed to see you and hear you. To judge. To see if what I remembered was truth or only the remnants of some drunken dream from my benighted youth. To see if I had been misled."

An uneasy wind whined through the line of pillars. "And what do you see?"

"You are the man I know. Which means I have no simple answer to my problem."

"Will you explain?"

He started walking again. "Once we had the Khelid cleaned out, I thought we would get back to the usual way of things. That I'd have some time to get my head around what I need and want to do . . . in the future. When my time comes. But my father was affected . . . sorely affected . . . by all that happened two years ago. How he was duped by Kastavan. How close we came to disaster. He has no heart for ruling anymore. Good enough. I am not a child. I know how to keep the appearance and hold my tongue, and no one dares question when I say 'my father told me thus' or 'the Emperor commanded me so.' For a while things went well. I traveled the Empire and made sure all knew that I was indeed my father's voice, as was proclaimed at my anointing."

The Prince walked faster as he talked. "But soon it was as if every noble in the Empire got wind of Father's weakness and decided to strike out on his own. They began encroaching on each other's land, fighting over borders that were settled years ago, violating trading agreements that profited everyone in favor of trade wars that profit no one, stealing horses, kidnapping children to exchange for concessions. Stupid bickering. Senseless bloodshed. Every dispute became a blood feud. You'd think we'd gone back five hundred years. At the summer Dar Heged, three nobles were killed dueling, and one baron defied me so brazenly, I had to exile him. At the winter Dar Heged, five families refused to come at all."

So it was the weight of the Empire that had settled on his light heart and strong shoulders. "They're not letting the Emperor—or you—settle their differences anymore."

"Only when I come with soldiers and swords. I have to pull them apart and make them talk to each other and see their stupidity. Sometimes they won't listen even then, and I have to force them to it." Aleksander stopped and leaned his back against one of the stone pillars. "But I can manage that. Most of them come to their senses once I show them I'm not afraid to shed a little blood. Theirs or mine, either one. Some amount of disturbance is only to be expected with the uncertainty—an invisible emperor, a young heir. If it doesn't get any worse, and if I keep moving fast enough, I can keep it under control . . ."

"Except for what?"

"Another factor has entered into the problem." He fixed his eyes on me again. "Tell me, Seyonne, what do you know of the Yvor Lukash?"

"Nothing. What is it?" The words were some obscure dialect of Manganar.

"Means 'sword of light' or something like that, so I'm told." After a last glance, he started walking again. "The one so named and his followers are the thorns in my side. He has taken it upon himself to right every wrong in this Empire overnight. He wants to share out grain to those who can't pay for it, take the power of judgment away from the Derzhi hegeds and give it to locals, change laws he doesn't like, change the terms of indentures . . . free slaves. My father's advisers scream at me to wipe him out. The bastard has a great deal of support among the people—as one might expect. But for a long time he wasn't worth my trouble. I've no objection to most of his goals, and his methods were mild. Stealing a few cattle and sheep, releasing a few prisoners, trespassing, irritations to landlords who behaved badly. Despite what you and my wife think, I've no wish to have people starve. But in the past months it's gotten out of hand. He's going after tax-levy wagons. Burning houses. Kidnapping my nobles. Hijacking merchant caravans. There are roads that are no longer safe." The Prince stopped at the crest of a rugged hill, just beyond the last pair of pillars on the north end of Dasiet Homol. His arms were folded, and his face was angry, ruddy in the moonlight. "I won't have it." The Derzhi prided themselves on their roads and the peaceful trade that extended to the farthest reaches of the Empire—even if such prosperity never touched their subjects.

But even then Aleksander was not done. "And it's as if they know the sorest bruises in the Empire to poke at. Every time I get one of these annoying problems settled among the hegeds, this Yvor Lukash comes and stirs it up again. I know there are ills that should be righted—I feel your eyes on me every day of my life—but how can I convince my barons I'm in control when I can't keep these pests from disrupting peaceful trade and travel? I can do nothing about these things they want if the Empire is in chaos."

"Is it true Karn'Hegeth and Basran are lost?"

"Three provinces including Karn'Hegeth and half of Basran are ruled by barons who declare they are no longer subject to the Empire. Their fields have been burned. Their caravans raided. Traders are bypassing their lands for fear of these bandits. They're being strangled, but if I can't stop the attacks of this Yvor Lukash and his raiders, I'll have to bring them back by force. Make war on my own people. Civil war. And these are some of the oldest, most loyal houses—families that have been allied with mine for hundreds of years. If I can't hold them . . ."

I still didn't understand. Aleksander knew that my aim had never been to preserve the dominance of the Derzhi. "Why have you come to me, my lord? Matters like these are far beyond—"

"Because I thought it was you."

A chill prickled my skin, though the wind that raced through the pillars and blustered over the hilltop yet held the day's warmth. I started to protest, but the Prince held up his hand.

"Hear the description of the Yvor Lukash as I've heard it from prisoners and witnesses. He is slightly above average in height and slender, but strong enough to wrestle an ox, and he moves faster than lightning. He has dark straight hair, red-gold skin, dark eyes set deep and angled differently than those of other men. His look can paralyze a man. His sword is everywhere. He sees things before they happen. Hears a heartbeat in the silence. He listens to the cries of the poor and knows the hearts of men. He takes ruthlessly and gives generously. He can disappear before

your eyes and travel great distances in impossible times as
if he had wings."

"I swear to you, my lord . . ."

"You see why I had to come. To judge." He shook his
head, his gold earring and the gold windings in his warrior's
braid glinting in the moonlight. "I hoped not. Yet the simple answer was for it to be you, and for me to persuade
you to stop. I couldn't believe you wanted to destroy me.
But if it's not you, then I'm left—"

"My lord Prince! Beware! Spies!" Three dark shapes
came running up the hill, swords drawn. Derzhi warriors.
Two placed themselves between Aleksander and me, just
as the third warrior pulled me away from him and shoved
me onto the ground, clamping a boot firmly on my neck. I
managed to twist my head to the side enough to see two
more of Aleksander's men throw someone to the scrubby
grass and rocks at his feet. "It's an Ezzarian, my lord.
Found him lurking just down the hill. Let fly an arrow in
this direction just as we found him. We think it's one of
the cursed outlaws."

The prisoner spat. "If I'd been aiming at him, you can
be sure I would have taken him. I'd think my life well spent
to draw Derzhi royal blood."

I hammered my forehead into the dirt and cursed so
violently and so colorfully that it silenced every one of
them. How could the world be so absurd? The prisoner
was Fiona.

"They've set a woman . . . this stick of a girl . . . to
watch *you*? To judge your actions as if you were some
squire, some acolyte at Athos' temple who can't be trusted
to wipe his ass properly? I don't believe it."

Aleksander's indignation was flattering, but always dangerous. I didn't think it wise to remind him of his own
doubts so recently dismissed. No doubt they had been quite
vividly revived for the few moments until I managed to
calm my wayward tongue and explain that Fiona was no
threat to him, only to me. I had told him that there were
those among my people who still mistrusted me, that I had
made some mistakes in my demon encounters, and that I
had been forbidden to fight anymore. I said only enough

to explain why I hadn't known the girl was there, and why she saw fit to follow me to a private meeting.

"You need not concern yourself, my lord."

I might as well have been trying to calm a shengar with a biscuit. Clearly he had not grown out of his hasty temper. He paced in front of his troopers' watch fire as if ready to set out to battle my unfathomable compatriots who had judged me unfit to face a demon.

"Have they seen what you are? Do they know what you did inside me, how you fought the Lord of Demons for days on end when you had no blood left inside you? Athos' balls . . . I should go tell them what it was like." He stopped and glared down at the fuming Fiona, who lay bound hand and foot in the circle of firelight. "Or shall I hang the wench and get her out of your way? You could say she was eaten by a shengar."

"No, my lord. This is a tale that must spin out among my own people. Much as I value your offer." I suppressed a smile. His virulence was gratifying.

"She should already be dead. Sovari will flog his men for allowing an assassin to take a single breath after shooting at me."

"She wasn't shooting at you. For all her faults, Fiona is scrupulously honest." She had claimed she was aiming at a rabbit, and two of the soldiers had gone to look for evidence. They would find it, not because her aim was as true as she claimed, but because a whole Kuvai town had once been burned when one of its residents let fly an arrow at a Derzhi prince. I had no intention of such a thing happening to Ezzaria. "Have her swear it to you, and you can let her go. I'll vouch for her good behavior. Please, my lord."

"I would you had not asked it. Not when I can see what these people have done to you." Aleksander gave a last indignant harumph and left us alone then, saying he was going to see what was taking his soldiers so long.

Once he was out of earshot, Fiona broke her angry silence. "How dare you defend me to this murdering barbarian?"

"Interesting that the Derzhi call *us* barbarians." I crouched down beside her and loosened the ropes that were cutting cruelly into her thin arms. She would not deign to waste melydda on making herself more comfortable. "What he said is right. You're lucky they didn't slit your belly and hang you up by your bowels for your stupidity. Probably because there wasn't a tree tall enough to make it interesting."

"Yet you name him your friend and call him 'my lord.' You disgust me."

"Since you insist on listening to things that are not your business, I would recommend that you open your eyes and ears a little wider. You might learn something. There are wonders in this world that neither you nor your mentors understand."

"The wonder is an Ezzarian groveling before a Derzhi murderer."

"You know nothing of groveling, Fiona. You also know nothing of respect. I would advise you to show a bit of it. The Prince will not harm you . . . because I've asked him not . . . but his men will not be so understanding if they hear these insults. You demean yourself and all Ezzarians by your childish behavior. What do you think to accomplish?"

"You might as well have him kill me, for I've enough violations to report that the Council will judge you more than mad."

"A madman. Is that what they've named you?" Aleksander had come up behind me, and I damned myself and Fiona for our loose tongues. The Prince threw a large rabbit, an arrow pierced cleanly through its breast, onto the ground in front of Fiona. She shot a glance at me, and I hoped she was clever enough to keep her mouth shut. It had not been easy to work the illusion while holding a conversation. I trusted Aleksander's word, but not his temper. Not when he was under such strain as he was showing.

"I—as all madmen—claim that judgment is in error."

Aleksander motioned one of his men to undo Fiona's bonds, but I waved the soldier away and did it myself. Ezzarians are uneasy about being touched by outsiders. I left the illusory rabbit in her hands, and she tossed it into the darkness. I hoped none of the men would go looking for it again. I didn't want to have to keep up the enchantment long enough for them to cook and eat it.

Once free, Fiona made a move to leave, but she got a

slight taste of Aleksander's disapproval. He grabbed her arm and shoved her back to the ground. "If you so much as twitch a finger, I'll have you trussed like a goose, my lady. Don't think because I've done as Seyonne asked that I'll not hold you to account for your insolence. And until I do, you will sit here where I can see you. You may be able to do some of this sorcerous foolery, but I've a strong arm, quick feet, and a nasty temper."

I didn't bother to tell him that she wasn't about to go far. Not as long as I was in the vicinity.

"You've not told me everything, have you?" said the Prince, after making enough princely handwavings to have us sitting at his fire with roast partridge and wine, dates and figs and bread in our stomachs. His men had taken themselves out of earshot again, rolling up in their blankets or taking up silent guardposts in the moonlit wasteland.

"No."

He sighed and stretched out on the ground on his back. "Why should I expect it? If you didn't when you were my slave, you're not likely to when you're a free man." He rolled to his side; his head propped on his hand. "But perhaps it will make it easier to ask what I was going to ask when we were so annoyingly interrupted. If your own people have no use for you, then perhaps you'll consider my proposition."

"Which is?"

"I want you to help me stop this Yvor Lukash."

"Despite what you think, he could not be Ezzarian." I felt Fiona's disapproving glare beating on my back like desert noonday. "We don't work that way. Righting ills of the mind and soul, yes. But to interfere in the ways of the world—bloodshed, kidnapping, all these things you've described—it would be seen as corruption. Remember that I was treated as dead because I was taken as a slave, something that was none of my own doing. You can't imagine that the same people who condemned me would condone such actions as this man's, no matter how worthy the cause. Ezzarians have given of themselves for a thousand years, but not in this kind of battle."

"But he's a sorcerer. There's no doubt of it."

"He's a clever, talented brigand. It's not the same."

"But the tales—"

"Were told to you by those who want to believe in him. Those who yearn to think that his promises can come true. They'll speak of you in the same fashion when you do what you are capable of doing in this world."

Aleksander rolled onto his back again, laughing. A better laugh this time. "Ah, light of Athos, Seyonne. Would there were one other man in the Empire who had such faith in me. Lydia calls me the most stubborn man ever to ride the sands of Azhakstan, but I can't begin to match you. Do you still run?"

"I've needed to keep fit."

"Last time we raced, I was only two weeks from a spear in the gut."

"And I had been starved by the Derzhi for sixteen years."

"I will see both ends of this ruin before your sorry Ezzarian bones can get off the ground."

"I respectfully disagree."

Fiona likely thought we had gone mad. Aleksander pulled off his boots and threw them at her, and we took off running, heading first for the south end of the line of pillars, then over the easy rise and fall of the land between them. His long graceful strides were a match for my lightness and speed as we raced through the blurring gateway to the south, step for step until we reached the northern end and started back toward the camp. Then I pulled away and was sitting by the fire unwinded when he flopped on the ground beside me. "Light of Athos. I've been too much in the saddle."

"It is fine to see you again, my lord," I said. "And to hear your sorry excuses."

He grinned, slapped me on the back, and stumbled off to his tent.

I, without so much as a glance at the shocked Fiona, rolled up in the blanket laid out for me and slept better than I had in three months.

CHAPTER 10

The narrow, mist-hung valley was a fine hiding place for bandits. Four shabby dwellings were tucked in between the brisk little river, the trees that bordered it, and the steep slopes. The primary access was flanked by cliffs, making it easy to guard, and the place was well hidden in the maze of interconnecting valleys that webbed the Kuvai hills. A second, more difficult access, a steep track leading from the north end, provided a back way out through the rocky heart of the highland, so convoluted one would need an eagle to guide him through it. The whole place was well below the ridge tops to either side and obscured by the drifting trailers of mist. Safe from prying eyes . . . unless the eyes happened to belong to a sorcerer who had been trained since age five to discern what others could not.

"No more than twenty of them," I whispered to Aleksander, who lay beside me on a knob of rock, peering down into the uneven grayness. "Five archers hidden in those outcroppings just inside the valley mouth—three on the left, two on the right. With the outer guards that makes eight. The six who just arrived are still with the horses, deep in the trees in the northernmost corner of the valley. Three riders injured." I could smell the blood and pain in the heavy air. "Two have come out of the largest house to meet them. They . . ."

I started to say that one of these two was the man we'd come to find, the Yvor Lukash, this "sword of light," the leader of the outlaws. But I could not explain why I thought it, save that I felt a stronger presence where the man stood. My senses did not tell me this. Was it experience? Expectation? I should know better than to assume that appearance or expectation was the truth. In demon battles, the appear-

ance of things as you understood them and the expectation
of where things ought to be were rarely truth. But this was a
human encounter, so perhaps human instinct was more
useful.

"There's another man off in the trees to the southwest—
relieving himself I'd say. There might be sleepers in the
second house. The two smaller houses are definitely
empty."

"Damn! I should have you with me on every expedition,"
whispered the Prince. "We could have all their nests
cleaned out in a month."

"My lord, you promised."

"Yes, yes. I'm here to talk. Minimal bloodshed. Are you
sure you won't come in with us?"

I shook my head. "I cannot." I had my own battles to
fight, and involvement in such matters would just make
them more complicated. "Only when you're ready to talk
to him."

We had talked it out thoroughly as we traveled eastward,
skirting Vayapol and meeting up with Aleksander's larger
traveling force, some fifty Derzhi warriors sitting at the foot
of this range of rugged green hills. Aleksander had information from a prisoner that the Yvor Lukash was headquar-
tered in these folded lands of the Kuvai. It was an unlikely
spot, so far from any major city, among a people better
known for lute-making and minstrelsy than any skill at
arms.

I had told the Prince that those setting out to free slaves
and right injustice were no enemies of mine. I would neither lift a sword against them nor shed their blood. But I
had agreed to help Aleksander confront those who were
undermining his efforts to bring a wider peace . . . and my
hopes that he was destined to be a ruler such as the world
had never known in its sorry history. He had promised
to talk before killing, a major concession on the part of
any Derzhi.

Fiona had spent the entire journey fuming. Aleksander
had commanded that her hands be tied to her saddle, and
her horse tethered to that of a guard. I didn't know whether
Fiona understood the Derzhi insult intended—only danger-

ous prisoners or the lowest, most despised of persons were
not allowed to control their own mounts. But she certainly
understood the soldiers' smirking stares at her man's clothing and their sneering laughs at her humiliation. She could
have snapped her bonds with melydda, but she would not
deign to do so. Melydda was meant for the demon war.
Her frost could have blighted the jungles of Thrid.

After the first day I asked Aleksander to allow her to
ride with us, at least, rather than surrounded by leering
guards. "I appreciate your attempts to help, my lord, but
at some time I hope to get my problems put right, and
having a witness that I've not gone out to negotiate with
rai-kirah could be an advantage."

"You would have her overhear our conversations?"

I felt my cheeks flame. "It's likely she is anyway."

"She can do that?" He glanced over his shoulder
uneasily.

"She is skilled at many things, and listening is one of
them. It's one reason they chose her." I still hadn't figured
out all the reasons. Or why she took to her watch so
ferociously.

Fiona lay beside me on the bald ridge top, squinting into
the mist. If she saw or heard anything different than I did,
she wasn't saying it. Two of Aleksander's warriors stood
just inside the line of trees behind us, guarding our backs.

"We're going in while they're still scattered, distracted
with the new arrivals. This mist hides us as well as them.
A quick demonstration of our superior numbers, and we
can have what conversation we please." Aleksander gestured with one hand, and one of the soldiers in the trees
sounded the call of a wild gorse-hen. It was well-done. No
reason why it should be remarked. Beyond it came the
squawk of a rivinjay. Again well-done. The call was passed
in varying forms until I sensed the Derzhi, who stood waiting in the forest beyond the valley mouth, begin to move
silently, stealthily toward the outlaws' camp. The Prince
eased back from me, ready to go down and join his men
as soon as they had the outer guards in custody.

But the birdcalls were indeed noticed, or the movement,
or something, for I heard a sharp cry of warning, and from

somewhere in that valley there came a pulse of enchantment that almost blinded my inner sight. Sorcerers! The
morning sunlight began to burn through the mist, revealing
men scrambling to shelter under the trees.

"Your Highness, pull them back!" I called out over my
shoulder, but Aleksander was already disappearing down
the path into the trees, and I dared not call louder. "Fiona!
Go tell him! Hurry! They're going to be slaughtered." The
archers would take care of the first wave of Derzhi
horsemen, and when they discovered they were so far outnumbered, enchanters of such power could bring the cliffs
down on the rest of them.

She hesitated, and I grabbed her shoulder. "I don't care
about your feelings for me or for Derzhi. People are going
to be dead if we don't stop it. True corruption can begin
with silence as well as deeds. Now, go. I need to stay
ready here."

She shoved my hand away. "I don't need you to lecture
me, Master Seyonne." She slipped backward and got to her
feet, staying in a crouch until she reached the trees.

I turned back to the edge and peered over again, bringing
all my senses to bear, for in that first moment of clarity I
had glimpsed the two men standing in front of the house,
waiting to greet their comrades. Something was odd, yet
familiar, about them. Something I needed to see beyond
being able to describe them for Aleksander.

Before long I felt the Derzhi warriors in the forest slip
backward, the sounds of their hearts and breathing blend-
ing once more into the life of the trees. Shortly afterward
Aleksander crept up beside me and looked over the edge.
"This had better be important. We had them."

"No you didn't. See how the haze is clearing."

"They wouldn't have seen us."

"They heard you. Somehow they knew you were there,
and they were ready for you. You were right that they were
sorcerers. See . . ."

Warned of the waiting Derzhi, the outlaws were going
to vanish into the hills. Men slipped out of the trees, but
only enough to move up the valley toward the horses,
toward the back passage. An orderly retreat. First the outer
guards, the ones beyond the valley mouth pulled in. Then

the inner guards, the archers in the rocks, came down, drew back, and took up positions in the center of the camp. The outer guards shifted back, then the others, alternating, calm, careful. Silent. The man who had been in the trees had raced toward the horses in the first moment of the alarm. He came back riding, leading two more horses, and at last the two who had been in front of the house stepped out of the shadows. The first, a short man with a round face and shoulders like a blacksmith, mounted up and gestured to the retreating guards to move faster. Only when all the men were behind him did the last outlaw mount up. He was dressed no differently than the others in loose-fitting Manganar breeches and belted tunic, bow slung over one shoulder, long knife at his belt, and sword sheathed on his saddle. Straight black hair hung halfway down his back. He appeared no more than average in height and slender, but every fiber of his body was rife with power.

"There's your man," I whispered.

The Yvor Lukash sat still in the saddle and cocked his head as if he were listening, then slowly scanned the trees and the ridge tops.

"Head down," I hissed, and even as I said it, in as soft a voice as I could muster, the outlaw's head jerked upward, and he looked straight at me.

I had never seen his face before. Lean. Hard. Bronze skin drawn tight over high cheekbones. Deep hollows in his cheeks, emphasizing a firm, jutting chin. Long arched nose. Dark eyes. Aleksander's suspicions were correct. He was Ezzarian. But even more astonishing . . . in that moment when he peered upward at the ridge where I lay . . . I knew him. An air of stillness surrounded him like the moon's corona on the night before a storm. No matter the face he wore. The sword of light . . . the white dagger. The man who wheeled his horse and spurred the beast after his comrades was the priest who had my son.

"After them," said Aleksander, springing to his feet and hurrying toward the path and the trees. "I won't lose them."

"Wait . . ." My mind was in tumult. I could not risk Aleksander harming the man, but neither did I want to lose him. I had no skill at infant-nurturing to offer my child, no home or healing to nourish his wakening soul, but I had a sword and a strong arm to keep him safe. I could not rest until I had made sure of those who cared for him.

The Prince was already into the thick stand of pines, while I stood staring at the mounted figures disappearing into the hills. If only I could shape my wings . . .

"What is it?" said Fiona. "Do you not obey your master?"

"Come on or the guards will drag you," I said, retreating from the cliff edge. Without wings I would have to rely on my feet and a horse, and meanwhile try to figure out how in Verdonne's name I was going to keep the priest out of Aleksander's hands long enough to find out who and what he was.

I took off running and caught up with Aleksander about halfway between the ridge top and the troops hidden near the valley mouth. The Prince was striding purposefully down the root-laced path through the trees. I wrestled with words and plans. How could I convince him to let me go after the outlaws alone? Whatever speech Aleksander had with a man leading a rebellion against him would leave no room to learn of my child or to discover what Ezzarian would risk the safety of our race and the demon war in such a rash undertaking. These were not matters to be discussed under bonds of uneasy truce or imperial forbearance. And even if I found the words to persuade Aleksander to hold back, how in the name of reason could I get the rebels to trust me? If the man guessed that I had been chasing after him with the Prince of the Derzhi, he would likely see me dead before I opened my mouth. He would have listened to me better when I was a slave, than now I was a free man.

I thought I would have at least a little time to sort out this dilemma. But we had gone no more than twenty steps together, when I felt the stirring of air some fifty paces in front of us, just around a curve where the path squeezed between a giant rock outcropping and a steep gully. Massive enchantment. Profound stillness.

Without time to weigh consequences or possibilities, I yanked on Aleksander's arm, stopping his mouth with an upraised hand at the same time I halted his steps. Fiona and the two Derzhi guards came up behind and almost ran into us. I flicked my eyes toward the boulders and prayed for Aleksander to understand what I was about to do. Then I snatched the startled Prince's sword and quickly and carefully whipped it across his cheek, leaving a shallow, bloody scratch from his left eye to his chin.

Aleksander slapped his hand to the wound and stared at the blood, then at his sword in my hand. "What the cursed—"

"I'll never go back," I screamed, aborting the Prince's erupting roar, even as one Derzhi guard shoved Fiona to the ground and another laid an arm the size of a tree trunk to my head. The second man stomped his boot on my hand, which had already let loose of the Prince's sword. Spitting blood and dirt from my mouth as the guards tried to twist my arms out of the sockets and pull my head off my shoulders, I cried out, "Put me back in your chains. But don't think you'll keep me forever. There's fire in your empire. I am not this Yvor Lukash, but your slaves will be free, whichever of us does it." I gave the warriors only enough of a fight to keep my tongue free and breath in my lungs. The messier I was, the better. "I will never serve you again, Lord Vanye."

For a heart-stopping moment I allowed one guard to plant his knee in my back and pin my arms behind me, and the other to bend my head back at an angle I would have declared impossible and hold a knife to my throat. Aleksander, pale and rigid with fury, blood dripping down his cheek, stared at me as if I were the Lord of Demons come to life again. Had he heard the name I'd called him—the dead man's name that was the root of our history together? Everything depended on his listening.

Trust me. Think. Even if you don't understand everything, remember what we have done together. You know I would never harm you.

Even as I willed him to understand, the Prince motioned to the guards. "String him up to the tree, give him fifty lashes, and leave him here to bleed. Let the wolves teach him a slave's true worth. I've better things to do than coddle a runaway. He's warned these bandits off, and now we'll have to report a failure to Prince Aleksander. He won't like it. I told him that talking to outlaws was useless."

When Aleksander pursued a deception, he threw himself into it with a vengeance, and somehow I always ended up bleeding for it. The well-disciplined guards—whatever their mystification, they did not dare question the Prince's strange reference to himself—bound my hands to a tree branch far above my head. Before they began with the lash, Aleksander walked around me as if to inspect that all was secure, stopping where his blood-streaked face looked into mine. Rings of gold banded the powerful arms folded tightly across his chest. I had walked his soul, shared such intimacy as brother and brother, father and son, or man and wife could not imagine, so I did not need to hear words to understand the question in his eyes. *Are you sure?*

"Tell your Prince that his empire will not survive as long as injustice rules," I said, "but if he heeds those who cry out to him, trusts those who have faith in him, his glory will never end."

"Fifty," he said, then turned on his heel and strode down the path. His hand lay on the hilt of his sword, but there was no disturbance as he disappeared into the trees.

No sorcery can blunt the pain of such a beating. What skill I could bring to bear faded quickly as torn flesh and battered muscle took their toll. Aleksander could not have given me less. Not for cutting him. Those I felt watching from the shadows would never have accepted it. *Stupid ploy.* There were a hundred less destructive moves that could have set up a confrontation, but I'd had no time to think of them. Aleksander had to believe that I was going to spy on his enemies, and the observers had to believe that I was going to die for my offense. How I was ever to untangle matters, once I had learned what I needed to learn, I had no idea.

At some time the two soldiers finished their work and followed the Prince out of the dim glade. To me, drifting in and out of hellish sense, the beating seemed to go on without end. The thought drifted through my murky perceptions that if the Yvor Lukash did not come to rescue me, then I would go down in history as the greatest fool ever to draw breath. I had no assurance that the presence I'd felt in the forest was that of the outlaw priest, though I believed it so. And I had no assurance that he would fall for my crude deception, though there had clearly been no artifice in the Derzhi warrior's hand. If ripped flesh and moaning misery bore sufficient testimony, then perhaps the outlaw leader would accept my story. For the immediate moment, I, too, believed I was going to die, hanging from a tree with my shredded body consumed in a fog of pain.

My head was too muddled to concern itself much with what story I might tell if anyone came. I scarcely had wit enough to pull together an enchantment to shear the binding ropes. Once that was done, I collapsed in an ignominious heap on the prickling carpet of pine needles. One more thing I had to do, quickly, before anyone came. Scarcely able to breathe for the agony of movement, I worked my hand underneath my chest and pulled the leather packet from my breeches, with the vague intent to bury the thing. But once it was in my hand, I had to stop and rest.

Deep in the gully to the side of the path a stream gurgled contentedly, unaware of the mortal doings alongside it. Astonishing how such a pleasant sound can so quickly become a torment. My mouth was ash. My throat parched. All memory of deception and larger purpose crumbled in the craving for water. Steeling myself for the unpleasant consequences of my excursion, I began to creep on my belly across the path toward the sloping gully. After no more than ten paces I stopped and buried my face in my arms, trembling, unable to move another finger's breadth. The fire in my back had me ready to scream, and I had no idea where I had dropped the packet . . . the paper with Aleksander's seal . . . my freedom. Another few mezzits progress and my head hung awkwardly over the edge of the gully, but I did not have the strength or the will to pull back. I was desperate for water.

Just then a tin cup filled with water appeared under my nose, and somewhere beyond the roaring in my ears I heard a quiet voice speaking in the soft accent of rural Manganar. "Might this be what you're after?"

CHAPTER 11

"You're not taking him with us?"

"What else do you suggest?"

"Kill him. He's but another Derzhi assassin come to clean us out. There was a whole troop of them. What else do you need?"

"More than that. He's got a number of questions to answer, and I would say he's had something of a falling out with his friends, if friends they were. Despite what you'd have me believe, thinking and listening are often as useful as bloodshed. Get a horse up here."

"You're a damned fool, Blaise."

"It would be a dull day indeed if you didn't tell me that at least once."

These pleasantries were going on across my back. The hands that had given me the sip of blessed water had also shifted me just far enough that my head was level, resting on a folded cloak. I felt like my body had been ground between two millstones. But at least I could hear.

A burst of enchantment from behind me came near splitting my head. Being facedown I could not see how the doubting man departed. The solid beat of hooves had me fooled into thinking there was a horse already in the glade. But the hoofbeats were too light . . . and it was some other kind of beast I smelled. Goat, perhaps. I was very confused and considered passing out for a while.

But indeed the cup appeared in front of my nose again to dissuade me. "So how did you manage to find me? Don't say you followed me from Vayapol. I know better."

Clearly, there was no use in pretense. I raised my head slightly and allowed him to tip the cool liquid into my mouth. "Thank you," I said. "How ever do you manage to conjure a mask for so long? I've never known an Ezzarian who could hold his face changed for more than a quarter of an hour."

He laughed, full throated, rich. A pleasant laugh. "So we are to play games, are we? Spar a bit. Question for question." I wanted to see his face, but could not muster the nerve to twist my head, fearing it might fall off. "I'll tell you this much. I am not an Ezzarian."

"But you look—"

"Oh, we share common ancestors, no question. But I'm not one of you. I've never lived in Ezzaria, neither before nor after the Derzhi had their way with it. I think we are very different."

He was rummaging around in a leather bag that sat on the ground just beyond my nose. I wasn't sure I liked my vulnerable position—facedown, back exposed to whatever an immensely powerful sorcerer wanted to do with it—but I had left myself little choice in the matter. He stood up and set off into the gully, light on his feet as he slipped and slid down the steep sloping land. In moments he was back, and I almost came off the ground when he laid an ice-cold wet cloth on my back. Then he had the audacity to start dabbing at the wounds. Clearly he was not experienced with a slave's lot in life. His effort was kind, but exceedingly clumsy.

"Sorry," he said, as I fought to muffle my moaning curses. "Such injuries heal better when they're clean. But then you look as if you've had enough of them to know that. Wounds of all kinds . . ." His finger traced the outline of the crossed circle on my shoulder. "This was certainly not your first lashing."

"No."

The forest was alive with sounds of afternoon. Two jays argued from a tree just over us. Tree limbs creaked in a warm, rising wind. Beetles and hoppers clicked and scraped about their business amid the pine needles and grass. My rescuer squeezed out the cloth, the red-tinted water dribbling into the grass, then he pressed it tightly against my right shoulder blade, where warm rivulets of blood were rolling down my side. Not Ezzarian ways at all . . . touching another man's blood without purification . . . leaving wounds open to the air . . . no jasnyr smoke to keep demons away. The man spoke to me again, but I had begun to shiver and my vision blur, and no matter how I tried, I could not keep my eyelids open. A mantle of numbness fell over me, muffling his voice and the forest sounds, muting the howling protests from my flesh and bone. For a brief moment it occurred to me that I had no idea what had become of Fiona. Good riddance. This was one place she didn't want to follow. From behind me came a soft whisper that I believed said, ". . . sleep . . . ," but I couldn't be sure, because I did just that.

The next hours were a jumble. Every once in a while I was jolted awake. It was dark, and I was sure that some demon-beast had at last had its way with me and was throwing me into the abyss. I dreamed I was burning in a dragon's fire, and another time that I had been slathered with acid venom from a monstrous snake. For a long time I was convinced that I was hung by my feet in the web of a giant spider, and I couldn't breathe because my stomach had fallen into my throat and my lungs were squeezed by the tight ropes of spider's silk.

"Easy, my friend." Strong hands held my wrists until I was lost again in realms of numb terror. Fading voices. "I would not live in this one's dreams for all the Emperor's gold."

"Holy stars, Blaise, keep him asleep. He almost took off my head when I put him on the horse. I think I've lost a tooth."

At last my eyes came open and stayed that way, though I had not yet regained any feeling beyond a general throbbing that pulsed in rhythm with my heart. It was enough to remind me that I didn't really want to come completely awake. So I drifted on the boundaries of sleep, noting in the disinterested way of sleepers that I was under a beamed roof, stretched out on a thin pallet that lay on a dirt floor. What I could see of the room by the light of a single candle was not impressive: a crude, soot-grimed fire pit beneath a hole in the roof, a jumble of animal skins, gnawed bones, muddy boots, battered pots, and unpromising bags of wheat and oats spilling their contents into the dirt where a mouse was boldly helping itself to the provender. The candle stub was perched on an upended ale cask. The flat taste of blood was in my mouth, and a spiderweb was stuck to my face, tickling my nose and threatening to make me sneeze. A disastrous prospect. I closed my eyes, trying to wish away the thought.

A threadbare blanket had been laid over me, and about the time I had convinced myself that I really could ignore all and go back to sleep in order to avoid waking up to the results of fifty lashes, someone tried to uncover me. The blanket stuck to my right shoulder blade and took a fair amount of skin and scab with it. I jumped. The sudden movement brought back reality with a rush, and it took several moments of rigorous discipline before I could hear someone speaking.

"Sorry, sorry, sorry. Don't mean to hurt. Just checking as the good Blaise told me. 'See the bleeding stopped and that no fever comes.' That's what he told me, and I've done it just right. No fever. No hurting. You won't tell him as I've hurt you. The cloth was sticky. That's all. Don't mean to hurt."

I twisted my head just a little to see a woman kneeling at my side, rocking back and forth and chewing on her knuckles as she looked at my back and mumbled her apologies. Her gray-streaked black hair hung lank and greasy over her face, and she wore a shapeless dress of brown sacking. She reached out a bony hand and passed it through the air above my back. I flinched, but my own movement was the only thing that caused me any discomfort. The woman's hand never touched me. Rather it—or something—left my back tingling as if on the verge of waking. But its sensations grew dull, for which I was very grateful.

"I know you didn't mean to hurt me," I said. "Thank you for helping."

She turned her face to me and brushed her hair aside. She was perhaps fifty years old, and at one time she had been a classic Ezzarian beauty. Her bones were fine, her eyes large and set wide apart, her full lips and arched nose balanced and well proportioned. But her skin was mottled and dirty, her cheeks hollow, her mouth slack, and her

eyes . . . Oh, gods in the starry heavens . . . her eyes were
dark and angled . . . Ezzarian eyes . . . but thoroughly mad
and, far worse, flecked with the ice-blue coloring of long,
deep-rooted demon-possession.

"I've done it right, then? I told Blaise I could still do it.
Others don't trust me. Only Blaise."

I tried to shrink away from her, but only then did I realize that my hands and feet were bound and that I could
move no better than if a millstone sat in the middle of my
back. *Don't panic. The woman is mad, but she's said she's
commanded not to hurt you.* The well-reasoned words did
little to soothe my terror. I was neither a Searcher who
could send a call for help back to Ezzaria, nor a Comforter
who could bridge the distance from victim to Aife with
enchantment. And I had no Aife to open the poor woman's
soul. All I could do was invoke every enchantment I carried
that might throw up some kind of protective barrier between us.

"A fine lad Blaise. Done right by us. Takes care of us.
We'll never want, he says. Others would have throwed us
away. Killed us like in the old days. Not him." She stroked
my head. Her touch was gentle and soothing. Maybe I'd
been wrong about what I'd seen, for the room was very
dim.

I was parched, and the dry tickle in my throat had me
nervous. "Have you . . . could I have water?" I rasped.

The woman was rocking again, and jerked her head
around as if she had forgotten I was there. "Water . . . aye.
I've got it."

"Please. If I could have some . . ."

"Give him a drink, Saetha, and loose his hands. He's
awake now and won't harm you. Will you?" The question
was directed at me. The questioner was the priest . . .
outlaw . . . sorcerer . . . whatever he was.

I shook my head. "I won't hurt anyone."

The woman nodded and bent her head over the knotted
rope that I had not managed to loosen despite my best
attempts. Somehow as she removed it, she also removed
my immobility, and though my feet were still bound, I was
able to wriggle up to my knees and creak to sitting. I did
not lean back on the log wall. The most immediate discom-

fort of the fifty lashes was still muted from the enchantment—the woman's enchantment, it seemed—but the stiffness and bruising caused by such a deep-rooted offense to the human body remained.

The woman brought me a cracked clay mug filled with clean water. As I took it, I looked at her with my Warden's sight. She was rank with demon. "Thank you," I whispered, averting my gaze. I gave my situation a moment's consideration, then closed my eyes and drank the water. As I had discovered when I was a slave, thirst is very powerful.

The young man folded his legs under him and sat gracefully on the dirt floor, tossing his long black hair over his shoulder. He took a similar cup from Saetha's hand, and smiled at her. "You've done well, Saetha. He mends nicely."

The woman smiled shyly. "You trusted me. I tried to do my best."

"As you always do. Now, go tell Farrol where I am in case he needs me. I want to visit with our guest for a while."

The woman left the dirty little cottage. I could get a better view sitting up. The cottage was no more than fifteen paces square and filled with all manner of unidentifiable litter. It smelled of rotted meat, cold, dirty hearth, and unwashed clothing. Every crevice was alive with insects; I needed a horse's tail to keep away the flies.

"You should stay away from that woman," I said quietly. "Do you have any idea what's wrong with her?"

"She won't harm you."

"But she's—"

"I won't discuss her with you. Now, if you will give me your bond not to run, I'll take off the rest of the ropes, and we'll go outside. Likely it would do you good to stretch a bit."

"You don't need my bond. You have my son." I dearly wanted to get away from the demon.

"So you still claim the babe is yours." With little more than a twist of his long fingers, Blaise made quick work of my leg ropes. His spare build gave no impression of strength or power, until you noted his large bones and broad hands. I was taller, but I guessed that he out-weighed me.

"Everything I told you was the truth, which is more than you can say."

He stepped back, offering no help as the blood rushed back to my extremities, and I stumbled to my feet. He tossed me a shirt of coarse brown wool, much like his own, and he watched with interest as I managed to get it on gingerly over my back—a necessary skill of slaves.

"We are not here to discuss my truth, only yours. I was brought up to mistrust Ezzarians, and I'll not be easy to convince. You were with the Derzhi willingly. You wear no slave rings, though I can see you've done so in the past. You walked Vayapol a free man. If you wish to live beyond sunset, I would recommend you tell me a good story."

"I'm surprised you would listen to my story. Your friend was ready to kill me."

"He is rarely wrong with such advice."

I followed him out of the squalid little shack and into the predawn stillness of a verdant valley, much like the one from which the outlaws had escaped. Four ramshackle houses set along the streamside; several more tucked back into the woods. A horse pen upwind. Rocks and trees. We walked along the bank of the stream that sparkled in the lingering light of a waning moon. No one was about. Only sleepers in the houses, watchmen at both ends of the valley, several men restless with injuries in a house deep in the woods. My own injuries stayed quiet as we walked. I had long wished for some such enchantment, but I had the un-easy sense that I would not like its making. I could not allow the demon woman to touch me again.

It was imperative that Blaise trust me, so I put aside my worry about the demon and told him my history as accurately as I could without revealing my relationship with Aleksander. I had been a slave of the Derzhi after the capture of Ezzaria, I said. I had served in a number of Derzhi houses, the last one being the Emperor's summer palace in Capharna. Two years previous, in the confusion of Prince Aleksander's arrest and near execution, I had escaped and returned to my people to take up my life. Then my son was born and sent away.

"And that drew you out of your forests, risking capture as a runaway in order to find him."

"I need to see him." To look into his soul and verify what Ysanne and three witnesses had claimed. "Our customs seem cruel, but there are good reasons that . . . some children . . . afflicted children . . . cannot remain in Ezzaria. As I told you before, I don't want him dead. I want him to grow up in safety with someone to care for him." Until I could enter his mind and remove the demon that had no business there. But this man was not going to understand that part. He had left me in the care of a demon-possessed madwoman.

"And how did you find me?" His stillness was profound. We had stopped on a wooden footbridge that crossed the dancing stream. I did not know what skills Blaise possessed, but he listened with all of himself, so I needed to stay as close to the truth as possible.

"There is a Derzhi named Vanye, the son of a powerful house. He was a bitter enemy of Prince Aleksander in the days when I was held in Capharna. He did this"—I pointed to the burn scar on my left cheekbone—"as an insult to the Prince. He thought that to mar the Prince's property would make him look stronger in other men's eyes. The Prince did not kill Lord Vanye, because the deed was not entirely unprovoked, and despite what many believe, there is a strong sense of justice in Prince Aleksander." Now, for the riskier telling. The lies. Aleksander claimed I was the world's worst liar. I hoped he was wrong. "As I was hunting you, I was picked up by the Derzhi. Vanye was hunting the Yvor Lukash—he thinks to regain favor with the Prince by doing so—and was sure that an escaped Ezzarian slave must know something of the rebels. He had learned of your hiding place and dragged me there, promising to let me go free again if I helped him capture and identify you. I agreed. I had no enmity for you; how could I, of all men, disagree with your goals? I just didn't think there was any way ordinary outlaws would survive the Derzhi attack. When I saw who and what you were—"

"You recognized me?"

"There are a great many things that define a person beyond his face. Why do you think I allowed you to keep my son?"

He looked at me quizzically. "Go on."

"I told the Derzhi to stop the attack, that you were fifty sorcerers and would bring down the rocks on his troops. When he realized how few you were, Vanye swore to put me through the Rites of Balthar again. If you have ever spoken to an Ezzarian slave, you know that death is preferable. If I had known you were coming up that way and could give me a hand, I might have thought of some less drastic way to get free of him. I thank you for your help. I've survived a great deal, but I don't think I would have made it through this one."

"You don't make it easy for me to trust you, admitting that you were ready to give us over to the Derzhi."

"My life is in your hands. I think that is a better place than in Lord Vanye's hands, though I believe there are a few things you ought to know about the world." If he could not recognize a demon and understand what it could do to him or his followers, then in no wise could he understand the risks of his activities.

We walked up a short steep path to an open meadow and sat ourselves on a flat slab of rock as the sun lightened the sky beyond the end of the valley. Blaise was silent. I waited for his judgment, reviewing my testimony even as he did, looking for flaws, slips, untruths that I would have to maintain or work around. Unfortunately, it was about that time that the demon woman's enchantment began to lose its effectiveness, and I began to feel cold and sick. The brown wool shirt touching my flayed back felt like acid-dipped claws. Blood seeped from the deep lacerations and dampened the coarse cloth, and a wave of weakness had my knees feeling like porridge. Even the glory of the red-streaked horizon was lost on me.

"I need . . . if I could go somewhere . . . lie down," I said. "I'm sorry . . ." All the questions I had ready for the man drifted away in a fog of misery, and what came next was quite unclear.

Blaise left off his pondering and took note of my condition. "I'm a dolt. I didn't think. Here . . . wait . . ." I curled into a ball and rolled to my side on the rock, trying not to be sick at the waves of fire consuming my back. My companion hesitated, then walked away into the tall meadow grass that surrounded our rock. I squeezed my eyes and mouth shut to keep from shaming myself before a stranger, and when I opened them again, Blaise was gone. Nothing remained in the expanse of meadow but waving grass, the distant line of trees emerging from the night shadows, and the birds of prey circling overhead looking for breakfast. I might have passed out then, but I would have sworn the sunrise still spread a rosy mantle on the grass when two people walked up behind me.

"I let him walk too far. Can you help?"

"I'll lay it careful on him. Longer than before. Deeper. But so careful as you've said to me always. Careful, Saetha. Careful. Careful. Careful. You're the only one who trusts me. He'll be well tomorrow. No fever. No hurt."

I heard the faint warning notes of demon music as the woman cut away my shirt and pressed her bony hands to my head. "No, please don't let her . . ." I said, panic overtaking my reason. "Demon . . ." But before I could stop her, my mouth sagged open and my eyes sagged shut, and I neither knew nor heard anything more that day.

On the next morning, when dawn poked its fingers under my eyelids, my wounds were healed.

CHAPTER 12

There had been times in my demon battles when I had been slathered with such foulness as was not found in human realms, the fluids and entrails of beasts so vile, imagination could not conjure them. In my years as a slave I had worked in stables and middens, and I had been required to clean up the vomits and defecation of drunken men or of women besotted with yaretha weed. Once I had been commanded to clean a castle where the entire garrison had died of plague, and once to strip hundreds of corpses that had rotted in the summer sun for three days. I had been revolted by such filth, but in every instance I had been able to cleanse myself in some fashion, to bathe or wash or wipe with sand or straw, or to purify myself with prayer or ritual or contemplation until I felt clean again. The filth was never a part of me. But on the morning I discovered that my wounds had been sealed with demon magic, I could devise no cleansing rite that could ever make me whole and could imagine no span of years that could ease my horror. If I could have ripped my back open again, I would have done it.

"What have you done?" I yelled at the ragged woman cowering in the corner of her hovel. "It is unholy . . . foul . . . unnatural." And so much worse because I had said nothing the previous day. I had allowed her to ease my pain. I had walked with Blaise and never gotten around to telling him that she was not to touch me again. I had lost all sense, all caution, because I was focused on my lies. But for her to close all the wounds . . . I felt as if worms were crawling beneath my skin.

"Does it pain you? I was so careful. The good Blaise

watched and said I did well. I'm so sorry, sorry, sorry."
Saetha twisted her fingers into a knot beside her mouth.

The good Blaise. The fool Blaise. I rubbed my head and
could not decide whether to weep or scream. All my superior rambling about demons who had no lust for evil was
forgotten in my revulsion. The demon would be laughing.
The woman reached out to touch me, and I jerked away,
stumbling to my feet and knocking over a barrel. "It's not
you. But I know what you are. I know what lives inside
you and what you've used to heal me. Vile, poisonous . . ."
Inside I was babbling enchantments of protection and purification. "Stay away from me."

"You know nothing about her." Blaise stood rigid in the
open doorway of the stinking hovel. He was dressed all in
black: breeches, shirt, tunic, and boots, and he wore black
beads woven in his hair that hung long and loose at his
back. His face was smudged dark with coal, and on each
side of it, from jawbone to brow, was painted a white dagger. His eyes were pools of seething midnight. "Saetha has
done you great service. How dare you speak to her so?"

The woman was crouched in the corner weeping, rocking
back and forth, her arms wrapped over her head.

"I don't blame her—the woman—but she is a danger
beyond your understanding. She is possessed by a rai-kirah.
Look into her eyes and you'll see it. Open your ears and
it will deafen you. Have you no lore to tell you of demons?
Do you have any idea of what they can do? There are
enchantments that can be bound with blood . . . terrible,
ruinous things." My years of training and experience demanded their say.

Her blue-flecked eyes told me that she was so far gone
in her madness that the demon would answer to her name.
Even had I an Aife to weave, I would have hesitated to
walk Saetha's soul. And she had touched me with her
magic . . . My gut twisted at the thought of it.

"Saetha has been a healer from the day she came of age.
She has saved more lives than the Derzhi have taken,
birthed children, healed wounds, nursed and blessed everyone she has ever touched. When I was a boy, I saw her
walk into a village where every man, woman, and child was
dying of bog fever. She could not save them, but she eased

their pain and soothed their madness, staying with them without sleep, not daring to touch food or drink until every one of them died in peace." Blaise knelt down in the dirt beside the distraught woman and brushed her hair back from her face. She bowed her head and laid it on his breast, and he wrapped his arms around her, stroking her filthy hair, soothing her shaking sobs. "There is no evil in her, whatever you think you've seen. Now that she has gone the way of the elders, no one comes to her anymore. But her skill has not died with her mind."

The sight was incomparably strange, the mad, grieving woman and the painted outlaw twined in a gentle embrace. My fear and anger receded as I watched. "I'm sorry," I said. "I know she was trying to help. You must understand . . . I've seen so much."

"But not everything." He pressed his hands to the woman's cheeks and smiled at her. "You've done well, Saetha. I'm proud of you. This Ezzarian did not intend to grieve you. He doesn't know us, but you've given him his first lesson, and I'm going to give him his second."

Saetha beamed at the young man and laid her finger on his painted cheek. "Lukash. Good hunting, Blaise, and go careful. Careful, careful."

He laughed and rose. "You can be sure of it."

Before I knew what was happening, Blaise pushed me out of Saetha's doorway and into the arms of a short, stocky man who was dressed and painted in the same fashion as himself. "Get him ready, Farrol. He says he's one of us, and he certainly has hard knowledge of the Derzhi. We'll see if he can fight."

"Wait . . ."

But they did not wait. Farrol and two women stripped off my boots and my bloodstained breeches and dressed me in black clothing slightly too small, and black boots, slightly too large, then smudged my face with coal and painted white daggers on my cheeks. They lamented my hair that hung only to my shoulders, but they loosed it from the tie that bound it and strung black beads in it. I asked what was their plan, but they laughed and said they wouldn't tell until we were there.

"Can't expect us to trust everything to you right off, now,

can you?" Farrol was very familiar. I was sure I'd seen him
at Blaise's side during their retreat from Aleksander, but
that had been only a glimpse. His voice told me he was the
one who had gone for horses when Blaise had found me
after the beating. But even that was not enough to explain
his familiarity. He was short and round, but in no way soft.
He, too, was Ezzarian, as was one of the women. The other
woman—a tall willowy woman named Jalleen—was Suzaini. She it was who buckled a sword belt about my waist.

Before I could get one decent answer, some twenty riders, all dressed the same, were mounted and ready. It was
difficult to determine their heritage save by their eyes. At
least four or five appeared to be Ezzarian. One man was
a Thrid, no coal needed to stain his dusky skin. Three of
the riders were women.

As the sun soared toward noonday, Blaise stood before
the group, facing north along the dirt track that led out of
the valley. He swept his arms in a wide circle and brought
his hands together in front of his face. In his gesture was
a splash of enchantment, but I could not discern its nature
nor could I hear any words. The riders waited quietly, their
heads bowed as if making an invocation to their gods. With
no other movements or gestures, Blaise mounted his black
horse, and we were off.

Some twenty others, men and women and even a few
children, stood along the track that led out of the valley,
waving and wishing the riders well. They were Manganar
and Suzaini, a Thrid woman, and even a few Kuvai, most
of them young, in their late teens or twenties. Only three
were Ezzarian, all of them in middle years, all wearing the
same slack-jawed look as Saetha. A prickling of foreboding
brushed my skin.

I rode between Blaise and Farrol. I had never been more
than an adequate horseman, and though Blaise and his fellows did not ride with the easy art of Aleksander, they
were far better than me. Feeling awkward and graceless, I
had to work to stay centered and keep from being jolted
from the saddle as we galloped down the road. It occurred
to me that we were leaving late in the day and going out
awfully fast for a long ride. I could not imagine what target
Blaise could have in mind that was anywhere near the

Kuvai hills. Yet it seemed no more than an hour until I looked up from my concentrated efforts to stay in the saddle and noted that the landscape had changed a great deal. We were in drier country, more like the fertile wheat fields of Manganar. Perhaps Blaise had moved his people farther than I had imagined while I was out of my head from the lashing.

Another short while and we were traversing a flat, wide land of parched grasslands and angular prominences. The terrain was very like the land near the Azhaki border, which opened onto the dune seas of Aleksander's homeland. But that was impossible. Unless I had fallen asleep in the saddle for more than a day, we had been riding for only two hours. We were coming from the south, and the sun was still high. The shadows of the thornbushes were just beginning to stretch to my right. No geography of my study matched what we had traveled.

Blaise led us into a dry riverbed, a long, narrow valley cut deep into the flatland. "I found a quick passage, but we must wait for nightfall," he said. "Eat and rest. The baron has left only fifty men to await this caravan."

I spent most of the afternoon walking up and down the narrow gorge, trying not to think of the demon fingers that had touched my blood, the grotesque words that had knitted my flesh, the cold blue eyes that had looked on my pain and fed on it. Saetha was a healer in her own right. Perhaps it really was her enchantment, not that of her demon companion. Yet the echoes of demon music scraped at my ears, and I could not summon the cleansing words to silence them. Was it distraction? Creeping corruption?

Blaise's riders lolled in the shade, sleeping or talking quietly, an odd sight in their paint and beads. The Thrid man laughed and took off his shirt, teasing a pale-fleshed Manganar to do the same and offering to paint his friend's skin to match his own dark coloring. Two slight Ezzarian youths, neither one older than eighteen, sat quietly playing draughts with chips of stone.

Blaise and Farrol sat apart from the others, talking intently and tracing their fingers in the dirt. Farrol was arguing his points vehemently. Hoping to discover what I'd gotten myself into, I perched on a rock where I could watch

the two, and I passed the back of my hand before my eyes
to trigger my deeper listening.

". . . good a chance to miss," said Farrol. "Take Nyabozzi
out of the game, and we'll halt the trade in this region for
three years. There's no single merchant strong enough to
take his place."

"I don't like it," said Blaise. "To burn him out . . . there's
no assurance we could get everyone away. A few more
raids and he'll take himself out of the game."

"You said it yourself. Time is just what we don't have.
You've shifted too much—"

"That's enough!" Blaise jumped up and faced away from
the short man. "I've done only what I had to do, and I'll
take whatever comes with it. But it's no excuse to be rash.
We need to be in and out quickly. We'll only have an
hour—two at most—before the baron brings the main
force. The plan is unchanged."

"What's happened to you? We agreed to be more
forceful."

Blaise turned back to his friend, but before he said anything, his eyes met mine across the heads of his resting
band. I was well out of range of normal hearing, but I
believed he changed what he was going to say. "We need
to remind the others that we have a stranger with us. I
think it's best we stay discreet until we know if we can
trust him." Though he had no reason to know I could hear
him, I felt he was speaking to me.

"Ezzarian shit. We should kill him." Farrol was not at
all discreet in his opinions.

I did not approach the outlaw leader or any of his companions during that afternoon. I recognized it as a testing
time, when silent observation was the correct behavior.
There was nothing to be learned until the testing was done.

As the sun settled into a thin smear of silver-gray clouds
in the west, the sleepers woke and the quiet conversations
and laughter died away. Blades were drawn from their
sheaths to be wiped and tested and caressed with soldiers'
invocations. Friends checked each other's paint, and nervous horses were soothed. The hot afternoon had depleted
the waterskins hung from each saddle, and I wondered if

those who stood draining them dry had some instinct that they would need no more for their return journey.

My own preparation was not without anxiety. I was not afraid of fighting—a battle with human opponents had little to concern me, and death would come when it would—but I was sorely afraid that I would be forced to betray Aleksander in order to protect my son. *Damnable stubborn people,* I thought. *Demons are altogether easier.* Ezzarians were not born to meddle in the sordid business of the world. I had to find some way to avoid involvement in the raid.

As if summoned by an alarm bell, the troop gathered about a tall rock. A man climbed atop the boulder, the hot breeze stirring his black tunic and pulling at his long dark hair. Though I could see nothing of his features in the growing gloom, save the painted daggers on his cheeks, I recognized the power of his presence.

"Once more we stand ready to test our resolve." He spoke softly, yet the force of his words drew me from my rock to the fringes of his band. I could not take my eyes from him. "Justice lives in our hands. No man is slave if our hands can free him. No child is hungry if our hands can feed her. No tyrant rules if our hands can bring him down. Our swords will bring light to this dark world."

"Lukash!" The whispered word swept through the twenty riders, spoken not as a cheer, but as a prayer. *Lukash*—light.

"You all know your duties. The gate will be open when you arrive. There should be no more than ten of the garrison on the walls, and no change of guard until after the caravan arrives. Be quick, my friends, and be strong."

Blaise stepped down, and I lost sight of him in the mass of black-clad bodies. It was Farrol who sought me out and told me to stay at his side. "Blaise wants you in on this," he said as we mounted and led the column of riders from the rift. "Though I've known him since we were cradled, it's beyond me as to why. But be warned. If you blink an eye at the wrong time, I'll have your heart out."

"Will you tell me where we're going?"

"You'll see soon enough. We're going to roust a devil."

With disciplined speed the band raced over the plains, past misshapen rock outcroppings outlined dark against the

stars. The air that lifted my bead-woven hair was cool and
dry, scented with sere grass and dust. That ride across the
plains, dressed in the color of midnight, evoked strange
sensations. I felt the boundaries of my physical self dissolving, as if I had melted into the darkness. Did my companions feel it, too? Was that what bound them so closely? All
I could see of them was the white paint on their faces. A
broad streak of white across the land. The sword of light.

Blaise was not with us. I was sure I would sense his
presence. And indeed it was Farrol who commanded the
party. He waved one hand, and two riders peeled off in the
direction where the last fading remnants of sunset had been
consumed by night. Within a quarter of an hour, the angular mountain in front of us took on an ominous shape. Atop
the rocky prominence was a massive fortification, a castle
of five towers and thick walls that could house a thousand
warriors. Two stone towers bearing gates of steel-banded
wood protected a steep causeway that wound up the moun-
tainside. I could not fathom twenty men and women being
able to disturb one stone of that rock pile.

Nyabbozi. The name was familiar, yet I did not trust my
memory of it. Nyabozzi was one of the Twenty Hegeds, the
oldest and most powerful Derzhi families. But my memory
told me that the stronghold of the ruthless Nyabozzi sat on
the western boundary of Azhakstan, where the Emperor's
Road crossed the caravan routes into the lands of the Veshtar and the Hammadi, only a ten days' journey from Zhagad itself, no less than four weeks journey from Kuvai.
Impossible. Yet it made the conversation of Blaise and Farrol settle into some sense. The Nyabozzi held the reins of
the trade in slaves. Verdonne's child . . . what had we
done . . . and what were we doing?

The riders slipped from their horses, and I grabbed the
sleeve of the short man as I dropped to the ground beside
him. "Farrol—"

He shoved his knife into my ribs, just enough to prick
my skin through my shirt. "You will stay by me and do
exactly as I say, or I'll give Saetha a bigger challenge than
she's ready for. I'll take your tongue before I'll let you
warn these Derzhi devils."

I was not ready to reveal my skills, or I would have

planted his paltry knife in his own neck. As it was, I pushed
his arm away. As soon as they began their foolish enterprise, I would find a way to stay out of it.

Two riders took the horses away, and the rest of us scuttered toward the gates that barred entry to the sloping
causeway. What could they possibly be thinking? Yet im-
possibility seemed no barrier that night. As we stepped
onto the hard-beaten roadway, a body, undeniably dead,
toppled from one gate tower to the rocks below it, and
soon afterward the steel-clad gates swung slowly open.
Quickly and silently we slipped through the towering opening. I followed Farrol into the shelter of the tower stair just
beside the causeway, while the rest of the group melted
into the jagged rocks alongside the path that led up the
mountain to the castle. The gates swung shut again behind
us. No sound. No alarm. I saw Blaise leap from the tower
stair and land lightly on his feet just ahead of us.

Mystified, wondering, I watched the outlaw run lightly
up the path, nodding, checking positions, waving one or the
other of his men or women a little farther up the path or
a little deeper into the shadows. A brief time of silence,
then I heard the call of the zhaideg—the scavenger wolf—
from a distance outside the walls, and Blaise himself disappeared into the darkness.

We held silent. Waiting. Soon, on a dry desert wind that
blustered about the towers and the rocks, there came a
mournful moan that was nothing of nature's making, and
tainting the scent of desert night was an odor of such foul
familiarity that my knees grew weak. The moan was everything of desolation—unbearable loss, unfathomable pain.
The scent was of unwashed filth and seeping blood and
rotting wounds, of sickness and horror and tainted food.
Slaves. Hundreds of them. The slow clank of chains grew
louder.

*Bodies . . . close around me, slimed with sweat or burning
with fever . . . no room to move save with the mass of others
like a crawling worm . . . no breath of air that was not laden
with the stench . . . feet torn and blistered from days of
travel . . . eyes bleared with sleepless agony . . . flesh shredded with the lash . . . wrists and ankles raw from the jerking
motion of the steel bands linked to hundreds of others.* How

many times . . . three . . . four . . . had I been moved in a slave caravan? The last time from Sikkorat to Capharna, thirty-seven days across the scorching desert. I took a heaving breath and commanded my stomach to be still. I drew my sword and crouched beside Farrol, who glared at me through his paint.

A challenge from the gate tower. A laugh and an answering call from beyond the gates.

I coiled my muscles. Ready. I needed no commanding.

The gate swung open, and two Veshtar in striped robes rode through.

Hold . . . hold . . . I could feel Blaise's will restraining his soldiers. Accompanied by the harsh cries of the overseers and the crack of the lash, the leading edge of the massive misery that was the slave caravan passed between the towers. As if we had planned it, Blaise and I cried out at the same time. "Now!"

The dark-clad outlaws fell upon the caravan, cutting down the overseers and scattering the guards. A few of the raiders carried axes with which they began to hack at chains and ropes, freeing the slaves before the garrison could come to the aid of the Veshtar. They told the stunned slaves to seek help in the temples of Khessida, a nearby city on the border of Basran, and to scatter quickly, as the baron would soon return with a large force and would be mightily unhappy to discover his valuable shipment dispersed.

I took down two snarling Veshtar guards, who were slashing at Blaise's riders with long, curved swords, then I got into a skirmish with a bewildered Derzhi, roused from his bed in the guardroom of the lower tower. He woke quickly and gave me a reasonable challenge before I bound him to a post with his gold-linked belt. Two of his fellows came out rubbing their eyes and staring at him in astonishment before noticing the melee about the gates. They were unarmed, and I stepped out of the shadows and urged them forcefully back into their rooms, piling barrels in front of the door so they couldn't get out again. I called up a wind and snuffed the torches that lined the causeway. Now that the slaves had scattered, there was less likelihood of killing the wrong person.

Farrol was engaged with another Derzhi. The warrior
had no weapon but his bleeding arms, and the outlaw was
forcing him to the ground with his sword, teasing and taunting the stunned, heavy-eyed Derzhi. I would have stopped
it—there was nothing to be gained by such slaughter—but
a Veshtar tried to slice off my arm just then, and I was
occupied for a while. When I looked again, the Derzhi was
dead, his throat gushing blood onto the dry stones. Killing
Veshtar slavers was one thing. Slaying unarmed Derzhi another. I backed away.

Some of the slaves scrambled back through the gates and
into the open, helping each other, snatching weapons and
horses and waterskins from the fallen Veshtar. Some wandered about in a daze, allowing themselves to be led to
safety. A few began to exact bloody revenge on the fallen
overseers. I looked away and reminded myself of despair.
A few were too weak to move and sat numb and weary on
the paving, waiting to be recaptured. To get all of them
away would be impossible.

For an uncounted time I was caught up in furious combat. A small troop of Thrid mercenaries arrived from a
guard post somewhere up the causeway. I could not see
others of the outlaws, and the thought crossed my mind
that Blaise and his men might think it humorous to abandon me in the midst of the carnage. But five Thrid gave
me little time to worry about anything.

A mounted Veshtar overseer, trying to control his maddened horse, flailed about with his whip, cutting a slave
woman across the face as she stumbled weakly away from
the fray. She fell to her knees in the middle of the roadway,
but the Veshtar spurred his mount forward, heading for the
safety of the castle garrison above us. He rode right
through her, his horse's hooves and spiked anklets slashing
her body to ribbons. In mindless fury I abandoned the sole
remaining Thrid, leaped over the unmoving woman and
gave chase, dragging the Veshtar from his saddle and sa-
voring the terror on his face as I kicked him onto the stones
and plunged my sword into his gut. I pulled out my weapon
and shoved it in again. Then again and again, expending
rage I had believed used up in bloody dreams.

I might have hacked at the Veshtar merchant forever,

but a steady hand fell on my bloody arm and I looked up into a coal-smeared face, painted with white daggers. Blaise. His stillness fell about me like a mantle. He pointed up the sloping roadway, and as the fire in my veins cooled, I heard running footsteps only a few sharp turns above us. Soldiers. At least twenty of them. Together we ran down the road, gathering up the others of our band, urging the lagging slaves to hurry into the protection of the night and the rocky hills. From the distant north, along the line of the Emperor's Road that came from Zhagad, a torchlit army of no less than five hundred men came into view. As we rode away, I glanced back over my shoulder and saw what would meet their eye as they approached the fortress—a man-high dagger of white, splashed on the ancient gates.

CHAPTER 13

No more than three hours passed before the tired outlaw band returned to the lush green valley where their fellows waited. By my reckoning we had traveled some three hundred leagues from the gates of the Nyabbozi baron's fortress. It was impossible. Just as it was impossible that Blaise alone had scaled the walls of the fortress, killed two guards while leaving the others asleep, and opened the gates to let us in. The plan had been foolhardy, but clever—so much more devastating to take the slave caravan within the very walls of the Nyabbozi stronghold than somewhere in the wilderness. How in the name of the gods had he done it? My body was mortally tired. My mind more so.

In the chill gray light, as birds fluttered from their perches calling mournfully to the coming dawn, I knelt by the stream and scooped water into my hands, scrubbing the blood from under my fingernails and the coal from my face, letting the dirty water drain into the grass. I longed for some answer for my confusion and some cleansing for my sickness of spirit; Saetha's demon healing and my frenzied vengeance on the Veshtar merchant weighed heavy.

Those left behind were celebrating our return with a bonfire and a slaughtered deer to roast on it, greeting the story of the well-timed assault and the scattered slaves with cheers and laughter. I wanted no part of celebration. I could not regret the death of Veshtar slave keepers, nor the freedom of those slaves resourceful enough to keep themselves hidden and safe. But the raid had been ill conceived in every point. The outlaws had no idea of the harsh truths of the world. I knew what would happen to the slaves who were recaptured and those too weak to run. I knew what would happen to the remaining gate guards when the baron found his fortress violated. And I knew what would happen to nearby settlements when the Derzhi found one of their own with his throat cut and no weapon in his hand. I could not bear the thought of Saetha's demon hearing the tale.

"A man of violence. I judged you rightly." Blaise was sitting on the opposite stream bank, leaning against a crooked pine.

"You know nothing about me." I judged myself well disciplined for not jumping out of my skin at his sudden appearance. Blaise's mysteries were becoming exceedingly annoying.

"You're weeping."

"Yet you name me a man of violence." Was I forever to be plagued with companions who could read my soul?

"I'd like to understand it." He leaned forward so that his dark eyes glittered in the last light of a fading crescent moon. "It's not just the slaves you mourn, is it? Farrol says you protected the Derzhi. And I suspect you weep even for the Veshtar pig you hacked into pulp. I was taught that Ezzarian sorcerers care nothing for the sorrows of the world."

"I would like to understand how we traveled six hundred leagues in a night's work and how you broached a Derzhi fortress that has not yielded to an enemy in five hundred years. Perhaps we could exchange a tale or two."

He shook his head, laughing. "Not yet. All I ask for now is that you warn me if you decide to kill me. I can think of a number of ways I would rather die than by your hand."

"And you will keep your friend from knifing me when I'm asleep? Unarmed?"

It was not a pleasantry I spoke, and Blaise did not laugh at it. "My friend is none of your concern. You are under my protection."

Somehow that did not make me feel any better.

The Yvor Lukash led his bandits on three more raids in the next two weeks. Each time I swore to myself I would not go. Yet each time Blaise made it clear that my participation in his war was the measure of my truth. I learned quickly that no one else in the band had the least idea where Blaise sent the Ezzarian children, and he had told no one that I claimed kinship to one of them. I could not leave without abandoning my son, therefore I could not refuse to go where he led.

One raid took us into the middle of Vayapol to steal hoarded tax revenues from a corrupt Manganar tax collector named Govam. Govam was known to inflate the tax assessments on prosperous merchants—keeping a good proportion for himself and paying his superiors enough to keep them quiet about his activities. If a man could not pay, Govam would take his home, his shop, his slaves, or his land. Poorer folk were required to tithe to the Derzhi, and many had to choose between feeding their children or paying their taxes. Govam pretended sympathy with their plight and allowed them to put off their payment, building up a backlog of debt. When the tax collector had squeezed all he could from the prosperous citizens of Vayapol, he would call these debts, claiming that his baron had discovered his generosity. Of course no one could pay, and even as he wept and apologized to his debtors, Govam would take their wives and children and sell them to the Veshtar as slaves. This practice was not uncommon throughout the Empire. Govam was just better at it than most.

Once I got over the churning discomfort at performing an act for which Aleksander would have us pulled apart with maddened oxen, it was somewhat amusing to see the stolen coins stuck to the inner walls of Dolgar's shrine with daubs of mud. The poor worshipers could come and exchange their snips of tin and iron for a coin that would feed their children for a year. I was pleased that at least there was no bloodshed involved. Blaise left the tax collector trussed up to a lantern post naked, his beard and hair shorn off. Proper justice. The tax collector had done the same to shame poor Manganar craftsmen who could not afford to pay bribes on top of their taxes. Farrol painted a white dagger on Govam's belly.

Though the raid itself went well, no one had bothered to make a reasonable plan to get us out of the city. The night was stifling, the city stink hanging thick in the narrow lanes. The Derzhi governor had lent the Manganar magistrates seasoned troops to give chase. With disciplined inevitability, they descended on us from every quarter, and I was sure we were done for. We raced down a narrow alleyway, kicking aside scrawny cats, crowding past slaughter pits and refuse heaps that were seeping in the heat, only to see torches and swords waiting at the other end. Back on our tracks, we pushed through gaping beggars who had come out to watch, up a worn stone staircase and into a dark courtyard filled with the choking stench of human waste and burning yaretha, the mind-destroying herb so prized by wealthy, bored women and the hopeless poor. We hurried across the foul nest, leaping over prone bodies—dead or alive, it was impossible to tell—intending to cut through a block of houses on the other side. But I held up my hand for a moment to stop the others. Horsemen held themselves quiet in the lane beyond the ramshackle buildings, and I whispered a warning to Blaise and Farrol.

"I'll find a way," Blaise said, and he ran back the way we'd come, disappearing into the shadows. He was back quickly, directing us through a maze of alleys and shops, only to disappear again. Four times he did the same, meeting us at each turning of the road to tell us which way to go next. He was never wrong.

The second raid took us to the crowded city of Dargonath in the extreme western reaches of the Empire. A season's supply of grain shipped from the south lay rotting in Hollenni warehouses, while a famine raged throughout the poor quarters of the city. The Derzhi factor had gone to Zhagad for horse races without authorizing any sale or distribution of the grain. Blaise happened to know that the man had been arrested for attempting to poison one of the Emperor's mistresses and would not be returning, but the factor's Hollenni assistants had refused to hear the pleas from the starving population and locked the precious grain away. Blaise found a way into the locked warehouses—finding a way into impossible places seemed to be a special talent of his—and the rest of us shared out the stores to the ravenous crowds. Farrol wanted to execute the traitorous Hollenni, but Blaise said he had no time to do it properly. He wanted to serve justice, not vengeance. Since the foray was even worse planned than the Vayapol raid, the city garrison was breathing down our necks, and Farrol had no time for his usual symbolic gestures. He had to be satisfied with abandoning the traitors undefended in the middle of the poor quarter.

The next venture took seven of us to a border outpost where a Basran guard captain was enriching his coffers with outlandish bribes extracted from travelers. As the little band set straw bales about the guard captain's house and the guardsmen's barracks and soaked them with lamp oil stolen from an unguarded storehouse, I tried to convince Blaise that reporting the matter to the Emperor might be more fruitful than burning people in their beds. Farrol accused me of Derzhi sympathies. "He must have found a master to his liking. Perhaps it was a mistress—a rich Derzhi cow to lick his backside and addle his mind."

"Even an addled mind can see the difference between legitimate grievance and pointless murder," I said.

"I need to make sure my lessons are noted," said Blaise. "I don't have time to beg or bribe the fifty different magistrates who sit between me and the Emperor, only to be scorned and refused every time with nothing gained. The Emperor cares nothing for justice, nor does any man who obeys him."

"There are innocent people in the house—children, slaves—and ignorant, stupid soldiers in the barracks. Most of them are illiterate conscripts from the borderlands. They have no power. What justice is served here? What lesson is taught?"

"Light the fire."

The other raiders threw their torches onto the straw, though they could have lit it as easily with their blazing fervor. But as we rode from the city, Blaise left us for a time, returning with blistered hands and half his shirt burned away. He would not answer Farrol's questions about what he had done.

I took part in all these raids, trying to understand how Blaise's magic was done, trying to keep my skin and my honor reasonably intact. My skin stayed whole. My honor less so. Deception ate away at me as acid eats paper. I learned nothing of the magic, which was very purposefully hidden from me, and little of Blaise himself, save that every man and woman of the outlaw band would die for him

without hesitation. The longer I watched and listened, the
more I came to understand it. Though I disagreed with
most of his awkward schemes, and thought his view of the
good and bad in the world far too simple, I could not fail
to recognize his worth. He was clever and generous, gentle
and devoted to his people—a population that seemed to
include everyone in the world who had need of what he
could give. His passion for justice was infectious. Whether
it was an illiterate peasant worked to death in Derzhi fields
or mines while his family wore rags and starved, or the
tenant farmer whose hut was burned because it offended
Derzhi eyes, or a child who was ripped from her family to
polish the insides of prized Derzhi oil jars from dawn to
midnight because her hands were small enough to do so,
no one was beneath Blaise's notice. I came to think that if
I could but bring about a truce between him and Aleksander, both prince and outlaw might find their lives a great
deal easier, and the world might be a great deal better off.

Farrol was a different matter altogether. He was Blaise's
right hand, doing much of the early planning for each raid,
while guarding his friend's back with ferocity and devotion.
I gathered that they were boyhood friends, bound by ties
so close that they could finish each other's sentences and
laugh at jokes that remained half unspoken. But I did not
believe the hard round man served Blaise well, and, in fact,
I wondered if Farrol's purpose was to lead his friend to
destruction. The stocky Ezzarian's plans were always
bloody, always ill considered, and they always jabbed at the
very tender spots that Aleksander would resent the most.
Blaise had slightly better judgment, but he had neither the
time nor the will to argue over everything. I was too much
an outsider to counterbalance the advising of such an inti-
mate. Farrol never trusted me, and never let Blaise forget
it.

As for myself, I was left very much alone. Blaise told me
nothing of what I wanted to know, but neither did he pry
into my own business. Only once did he bring up the matter, one morning some three weeks after my arrival, as I
took my turn cleaning fish our comrades had caught from
a nearby lake. He came and sat beside me in quiet companionship, as he did with everyone from time to time as they

worked around his camp. He handed me another fish from the flopping heap of them, and watched quietly as I made a quick incision around the head and stripped out the entrails cleanly in the Ezzarian way. Then I washed the remaining flesh, not in the stream as most people did, but with water scooped out and used only for the one fish. "You never ask about your son," he said after a while.

"I assumed you would tell me in your own time." I took another fish, my knife moving of itself through the familiar task, though my attention was most definitely elsewhere.

He nodded and stood up to go, rinsing his hand, not in the stream, but with water from the pail I had brought to hold it. "Exactly right." Then he strolled away and began helping an old man drag a heavy sled piled with logs. I wanted to throw my knife at him.

I was given a blanket and a straw pallet in a small barracks house with the other men. None of the raiders made any advance of friendship, but neither was I murdered in my sleep. After the Nyabozzi raid, Blaise began to ask my advice about Derzhi warriors' habits and my experience with Derzhi household routine, and though I was not trusted with any responsibility in succeeding raids, I was given some deference with respect to my fighting skills. After the third venture, Blaise asked if I would teach his fighters how to defend against Derzhi sword work, and we worked at it every morning for two hours. He stood beside his men and women, making every move with them, learning, asking questions, laughing at his own mistakes as I ran them through the simplest of drills. The warriors of the Yvor Lukash were farm youths and serving girls, a miller, and an apprentice blacksmith. None of them had the least smattering of warrior's training, yet all of them were prepared to die at Blaise's word. Their success was due to blind courage, foolhardy determination, and the skill and brilliance of a leader who could bind them into something more than they were.

One rainy evening as I sat by a fire, honing a knife which needed no keener edge, Blaise sat down beside me and asked if I would teach him "magic." I was surprised. "You seem to do quite well without any assistance from me," I said. "I've been thinking of asking *you* for teaching. You confound me: showing up out of nowhere, seeing things you had no way to see unless you were sitting on the moon, getting us from one side of the Empire to another before I can digest my dinner. What do you think you have yet to learn?"

He flushed and dropped his voice. "I keep finding mice in my house, and Kyor told me you'd done something to keep them out of the barracks."

I didn't laugh. I was too puzzled. Who could have taught him workings so massively powerful without taking him through the most rudimentary arts first? I was even more perplexed when, after half an hour of trying, he could not so much as cast a light from his fingers. The melydda was in him; he just had no more idea than an infant how to use it. I walked over to the shack he shared with Farrol and cast the vermin barrier myself.

"I had thought to teach my son these things," I said, once we were done and Blaise had thanked me for the lesson.

The young man cocked his head at me for a moment. "You're a good teacher." And that was that.

A few days after the foray to Basran, Farrol came to Blaise with a new scheme. "Jakkor the hostler says that every year at this time a train of horses is brought to Zhagad from the northern marches, bound for the Emperor's stables. He says he's heard that this year's lot is prime. Think what we could do with Derzhi mounts. Sell half of them to the Peskar warlords—they'd think it fit justice to take the Emperor's beasts—and we could use the rest. The sale price would feed the Kuvai for a year or pay off so many Thrid mercenaries, the Derzhi couldn't hire them. And it's easy takings. They'll have to pass through the Makai Narrows, and I've heard they'll be lightly guarded. The Derzhi bastards will never imagine anyone coming after them."

"For good reason," I said. "Do you understand that the Derzhi prize their horses above their houses, above their gold, above everything but their own children—and sometimes even that? And the Emperor's horses . . ." Gods of earth and sky, Aleksander's horses. He would go mad with it. There was nothing that would proclaim his weakness to his nobles in more glaring fashion than having his horses stolen from under his nose. "Their horses are the foundation of their wealth, the sum of their honor and status. Another tax collector . . . the royal treasury itself would be more sensible."

Blaise looked at me across the fire. "I've heard this about Derzhi, but I never believed it. Who could value a horse so much?"

"Believe it."

"He's just trying to keep us from disturbing his friends," said Farrol. "Why do you listen? He's always after us about bloodshed . . . well, there'll be no bloodshed this time. We'll be in and out in half a day. If it gets their attention, so much the better. It's exactly what we want to do."

There was no convincing them that a Derzhi would defend his lord's horses with his life. No persuading them that there was nothing more sure to invite the Emperor's wrath. They could not comprehend such value being placed on a beast, therefore they could not appreciate the consequences of their plan. The sinking dread that presaged every venture was tripled in intensity for this one.

On the night before the venture, I caught Blaise by himself, walking by the stream. "I can't go on this raid, and you mustn't, either. I don't want to see you dead." Again, I went through all the reasons. Again, the outlaw listened quietly, respectfully, and changed his mind not a whit.

"Why are you so disturbed about this venture, Seyonne? Don't you see that the reasons you give are the very reasons to do it? The Derzhi must learn to value their people more than their beasts. I can't spare you on this one. We need your skills." He slapped me on the shoulder. "We sealed our fates long ago. What are they going to do, kill us twice?" Though his lips smiled, his dark eyes challenged me to answer him—to tell him my secrets, to commit fully to his purpose or to explain why I could not. To prove my truth by fighting with him or to abandon pretense and leave. I could do none of those things, and he walked on alone while I stood cursing myself and fate and everyone whose name came to mind.

I needed to keep Blaise alive. He alone knew the whereabouts of my son. And truly, the young man was a mystery that was driving me to distraction; I could not let him die without telling me why he could take me across the Empire in a day, yet could cast no spell to ward his house from vermin. More importantly, he was a good and honorable man, a leader of such skill and worth that I could not see him dead from his folly. So when the day came, I, too, was dressed in black, my face stained dark and painted with white daggers. I just prayed that Aleksander would never find out what I had done.

The early morning was cool and damp. Thunder rumbled in the highlands of the Khyb Rash, the Mountains of the Teeth that would forever remind me of Parnifour, the city where I had stepped into Aleksander's soul to battle the Lord of Demons. The water and grass were sweet in the high valleys of the Khyb Rash, and the altitude helped horses build good wind for racing. So in their second summer they were taken from their desert stables into the mountains to train. Now it was autumn, coming winter in the heights, and it was time to take the prized beasts back to Zhagad and their proud owner. The train of horses and grooms and guards had to pass through the Makai Narrows, a quarter-league passage scarcely two horses wide. Not a good place for a fight—which was rarely a concern, since no bandit who valued his skin would attack the Emperor's horses. Clearly Blaise and Farrol and the others did not value their skin.

The Narrows was at the lower end of a high, sloping valley that had been scooped out from the mountains by an ancient watercourse. Most of the region was soft dirt and crumbling sandstone, cut out and smoothed by the ancient waterway. But partway down the valley, huge protrusions of harder rock had resisted the sculpting of the water, creating a narrow passage, like the neck of a bottle. Eventually the stream had given up and settled into a lake in the center of the upper basin, leaving the bottleneck dry and barely passable.

Blaise and I took a position atop a boulder at the upper end of the neck, where we could watch the train of horses cross the valley. As soon as we judged their numbers and

their timing, we would jog down the rift to join Farrol and
the others, where they held ready at the lower end of the
neck. The outlaws could snatch the grooms and guards one
by one as they emerged from the rift, and drive the horses
into a small side valley to the left of the opening. If the
assaults were quick enough, no one farther back in the train
would be able to see anything suspicious in the shadowed
gloom of early morning in the rift. Nor would they be likely
to hear anything over the clatter of hooves echoing from
the tall rock walls.

I didn't believe it. Nothing was that easy. The dark, narrow slot that was the mouth of the side valley had left my
neck prickling when Blaise and I passed by it on our way
to the upper watch post.

The thunder held its promise, and the first gray light of
dawn looked to be all the light we would get for the day.
Heavy clouds hung over the peaks like soggy wool, and a
cold drizzle trickled down our necks and left streaks of pale
flesh on our coal-smeared faces. "They might postpone the
journey," I said, wishing I could will such a thing to happen.
"It's too miserable to travel."

Blaise said nothing, his calm confidence a glaring reproach to my nervous babbling.

But it was only a little after first light when I caught the
sound of distant hoofbeats, slow and leisurely, rounding the
far end of the gray sheet of the lake.

"One . . . two warriors at the front," I said. I could
hear the measured tread of mature warhorses with riders,
different from the lighter, less disciplined hoofbeats behind.
"Four horses . . . then a walker, a groom most likely." A
groom would not be allowed to ride the Emperor's horses.
"Four more horses, then another walker . . ." The shapes
my senses had identified emerged from the curtain of drizzle, the wet gray world . . . mournful . . . Twenty horses,
five grooms, one for each four horses, the two warriors, and
two other riders, probably minor householders, following.
Nothing unexpected. The only trouble would be the warriors, and we were twenty.

"Let's go, then. You can take one of the warriors. Farrol and I can deal with the other." Blaise slipped down

from our perch and drew back into the upper end of the rift. But I kept watching as the procession moved slowly around the lake. Why did my back feel so exposed as I lay on the rock? I glanced over my shoulder at the walls of the rift behind me, their tops lost in the gloom. It made me think of Aleksander and how we had spied on the outlaws' hiding place from the cliff tops. I could sense no one there, but the clouds were heavy and the rain spattered in my eyes. I crept forward again and peered across the valley at the approaching men and horses. What bothered me so badly?

Blaise stood in the shadow of the rift mouth, waiting.

One warrior at the head of the train sat shorter than his fellow rider. He was slender but with powerful shoulders. He sat proudly . . . and so familiar . . . but I couldn't place him. His warrior's braid was blond. His braid . . . I glanced at the first groom. He wore a hooded cloak, and out of the right side of his hood hung a braid. A warrior? None but blooded Derzhi warriors wore a braid on the side of their head. What of the next walker? I couldn't see his hair, but he was tall and muscular. I glanced back at the warrior at the head of the train, now close enough that I could see his face. My blood went cold. Kiril. Aleksander's cousin, the Prince's dear and trusted friend. My friend. Lord Kiril, the Emperor's favorite nephew and foster son, would never be leading a common horse train. There would be a reason . . .

"Come on." Blaise's whisper was insistent. He wanted to get down the rift well before the horse party entered, lest they hear our footsteps.

"Wait." I needed to be sure. The second groom rounded the lake and looked up at the rainy sky. His hood fell back, and I could not mistake the braid. Another warrior. My mind flashed back to the gaping mouth of the side valley and to the cliff tops that had my skin creeping with more than cold. I dropped off of the rock and snatched Blaise back into the lingering night of the narrow passage, flattening us both to the wall beneath an outsloping rock. "It's a trap. Those are warriors, not grooms. And the leader . . . he is of the Prince's household. He would never be sent to escort horses." Only to trap outlaws.

"We'll take them. They still have to come through one at a time. Perhaps it's time we took a prisoner. Someone worth bargaining for. You say he's in favor?"

"No. No. Don't you see? They must know you've come . . . we've come. There'll be another party of them in the side valley. I'm sure of it. And another atop the cliffs. Someone has betrayed you. They're going to wipe you out."

Blaise's hard look made me feel unclothed. "You're sure of this?"

"He is the Prince's cousin. He will not be unprotected. We've got to warn your riders and get them away before the Derzhi close the trap. All of you are in terrible danger."

"And you?" His voice penetrated my fear like a cold knife.

I had no need to lie. "Worse." If Kiril saw me stealing Aleksander's horses, I was a dead man.

With no more discussion we set off running, but were brought up short by an arrow narrowly missing Blaise's back. I glimpsed another movement on the cliff top and threw myself atop the young man, slamming him to the stone underfoot. The shaft thwacked against the rock wall and fell on top of us. We rolled into the deepest shadows. "We need a bit of enchantment here," I said, getting back to my feet and calling up a wind to swirl the rain and cloud. "Anything you can provide might be helpful."

He pulled himself to sitting and gazed up at the cliff tops, sighing. "As you've seen, I have a somewhat limited set of skills."

"Well you'd best figure out how to warn your riders, or they're going to be dead. Weather spells are very difficult, and I can't deflect arrows from fifty places at once. There's nothing to burn, and I've never been good at large-scale illusions. My skills are somewhat specialized, too."

He laughed and stood up, patting me on the shoulder. "Then, I suppose I've no choice but to answer one of your questions. Get down the rift as fast as you can. I'll warn the others and take care of the archers." And with a massive pulse of enchantment that sucked the warmth from the damp morning, Blaise folded his arms in upon himself and was instantly transformed. A large bird of golden brown streaked with white flew up from the stone floor of the passage and into the wind and cloud. I flattened my back to the stone and sank to sitting, gaping so hugely with astonishment, it's a wonder I didn't drown in the rain.

CHAPTER 14

Shapeshifting. As far as any Ezzarian knew, I was the only one of us ever to experience such a marvel—the mystery of my wings beyond the portal—and I had thought myself blessed, skilled, powerful, supremely fortunate to have stumbled across an enchantment of such magnificence. Yet in the moment of Blaise's transformation, when I saw the exquisite harmony written on his face, I knew myself for a cripple. The revelation put my gift in true perspective for the first time, and the craving I had forced aside for so many years was now given such poignant substance that I believed I could never again suppress it.

My body felt like lead as I started down the gorge. I hugged the wall, moving steadily, but slowly, giving Blaise time to clear the way. No need to wonder anymore at how Blaise had opened a locked fortress or how he would dispose of the Derzhi archers atop the cliffs . . . landing so lightly behind the unsuspecting enemy, slamming a hand into the neck to lay him out. All I had to do was put another man's face in place of my own. Oh, gods, I wanted it to be me . . .

From ahead of me came shouts and the squealing of horses. *Focus, fool. You're caught in a trap between Aleksander and your child, and you'd best figure out how to get out of it. Since you can't fly, you'd better run.* I raced down the gorge, heedless of any threat from above. Blaise's brave farm boys and serving women would be no match for a planned assault of Derzhi warriors.

At the point where Farrol had set his ambush, the Makai Narrows opened into a wide, round grotto called the Makai Mouth. Very likely the place had once been a cave, for huge slabs of rock littered the ground, fallen from the erstwhile roof, and in the center of the grotto lay a wide and impossibly deep pool. Beyond the fallen stones and the pool, directly across the circular Mouth from the opening to the Narrows, was the way to the open world. Pillared stacks of stone made a gateway to the sloping treeless plain that stretched east along the foothills of the mountains toward the city of Parnifour, south and southwest over boundless leagues to Avenkhar and onward to the Azhaki desert and the Derzhi capital of Zhagad. To the left of the Narrows opening were the shadowed rock outcroppings where Blaise's people lay in wait for the horse train, and it was in the small, dark side valley on the right that the Derzhi lay in wait for the outlaws.

As I reached the lower end of the Narrows, the outlaws, warned by Blaise, were scrambling madly for their horses. The Derzhi, well armed and well disciplined, had begun moving out of their hiding place through its narrow slot-like opening. They were not attacking. If so they would have taken the shorter way left around the pool, past the Narrows toward the black-clad young men and women. Instead, they were moving to their right around the pool, picking their way through the fallen stones, and heading straight for the gateway to the plains. Childishly simple. Cut off the escape route, then drive the outlaws back into the Narrows, right into Kiril's arms.

But Blaise's warning had given his people their chance—along with the rain and the constraints of the awkward geography. Because of the tight entry to the side valley, the Derzhi could bring their horses into the Makai Mouth only one at a time. And because of the fallen slabs and the wide pool, they could not take a direct line anywhere or form up ranks. And because the rain had put out their torches, they could not yet see Blaise standing in the gloom beyond the pool, sword drawn, the tall Suzaini woman and the two quiet Ezzarian youths at his side, ready to block the Derzhi passage while his people bolted for the open skies. There wasn't much time. Kiril's party would already be in the Narrows behind me. And once they saw him, it would take only moments for the Derzhi to ride over Blaise and shut off the escape.

I could wield no enchantment to hold Kiril back. Though

my adversaries were not demons, my power was limited in
the human realm. Anything I might do in the Narrows—
pulling down rocks, crippling horses, flooding the gorge—
would risk Kiril's life and others. And there were too many
combatants to distract with smaller things like blistering
skin or the sensation of snakes in the boots. Even as I tore
at my brain to decide what to do, the lead Derzhi caught
sight of Blaise, yelled out a warning, and charged the young
outlaw. I heard the clash of steel and the grunts of the
men and the screaming fury of a wounded horse. No more
thinking. Only one thing could I do better than any of
them. I drew my sword and ran.

I smelled the sudden sweat and blood-roused horse even
before I joined the combatants. The woman Jalleen was
desperately trying to dodge a rearing warhorse while striking at its rider. She got in only one blow before her neck
was severed. Her lovely, lithe body fell lifeless to the stone,
soon trampled by the maddened horse.

"Get them out!" I screamed at Blaise, who was ducking
underneath a slashing blade and cutting upward at a warrior's leg. His sword sliced through empty air. "I'll hold
here." I grabbed at a passing leg and hauled the attached
body from its mount. Half a minute later, the Derzhi lay
writhing and cursing, clutching a slashed thigh muscle that
would no longer hold him upright.

The two Ezzarian boys were to my left, trying to protect
Blaise's back, but I was too busy chasing another Derzhi
to see how they fared. I let loose a burst of billowing fire,
an enchantment I had worked as I ran down the Narrows.
It was only an illusion and so wouldn't hold back the Derzhi for very long, but it distracted them enough that I could
take care of another warrior. He was very determined and
quite skilled. To get free, I had to kill him. *Stupid, stupid
fool. What are you doing?*

Blaise had pulled a Derzhi off of his horse and was holding his own, but he was too slow. The warrior would have
him in moments. "Go," I yelled again. "I'll be right behind
you." I ducked and spun around, leaving a bloody streak
on the warrior's back. A bubbling scream from my left was
one of the Ezzarian youths, watching his entrails spill from
his slashed belly. I grabbed onto a gauntleted arm as it

stretched a blade downward to finish the boy, and I dug in my boots to keep from being dragged, twisting the rider's hand until he bellowed and bone snapped. His terrified mount pulled him out of my grasp, but I gave chase and hauled myself up behind him, hanging on for my life as the beast reared.

Growling in pain and fury, the warrior did his best to stick a long, curved dagger between my ribs and throw me off his mount. He seemed to have seven hands besides the one I had broken, and he didn't seem to need any of them to control his horse. I would like to have ended it quickly, but somewhere in the sweaty, heart-pounding madness, it came to me that we were blocking the passage from the side valley. So I resisted the temptation to break the Derzhi's neck, and instead I clung to his back and managed to force his dagger point into his horse's flank, driving the poor beast into worse frenzy. I threw up another curtain of flame between us and the escaping outlaws, counting the time in my head—the brief eternity until I knew I'd better get off that horse or I was going to lose an eye or a hand or worse. Two more warriors had come in close and were waving swords at me. So I gave one last gouge to the rider's belly, enough to loosen his grip, then I dropped to the ground, rolled away from the flailing hooves, and scrambled to my feet. Breathless, battered, and limping from an annoying slash in one thigh, I took off running, right through my fading wall of flame toward the gateway.

From the corner of my eye I saw the dark shapes of Kiril and his riders streaming from the Narrows. If only I could shape wings . . . There was no possibility I could outrun them. The stacked pillars were too far.

A spear glanced off a rock by my right shoulder, and I ducked and dodged lest the thrower have a friend with better aim. While I was dancing in circles, a rider from the Narrows' party came up on my left. With a practiced move he slipped from the saddle, and while he landed lightly on his feet, his mount cut across my path and forced me into his arms. No one knew how to use horses in a fight like the Derzhi. I cast another fire burst to delay the rest of the party—it was difficult to be inventive in the midst of such a fight—and in a furious flurry of sword blows, I took the man down. He was a ferocious fighter, and only after I was standing over him, sword point at his throat, did a fading tendril of my enchanted fire drift over us to give me a good look at his face . . . and him a good look at mine. Kiril. I stepped back, withdrew my sword, and raised my arms in truce.

"Druya's horns! Seyonne?"

So much for painted faces. His soldiers burst through the wall of fire, and I took off running with no hope at all of escape. But at the same moment a dark shape shot from the direction of the escape route. A mounted rider, arm outstretched . . . Blaise. I reached and jumped, and somehow he managed to haul me up without slowing, then we reversed course, racing outward through the opening . . . and into a nauseating blur of gray nothing.

When my eyes were next able to focus on any single object beyond the black-clad back of my rescuer, it was a dead tree—actually quite a number of them, the blighted remnants of a burned forest that spanned a rocky hollow. A few charred logs and skeletal chimneys told me that a village had burned with the trees . . . a hot fire and not too many months past, as there were only a few spiky weeds poking out of the blackened earth and rocks as yet. The mountain-scape around us held no similarity to the valley above the Narrows, and, in fact, the sun was shining, though I was still wet from the morning's soaking.

Blaise threw his leg over the horse's head and slid to the ground, while I sat gaping tiredly at the bleak little valley. "We'll rest here for a little, then go home," he said. "Is the leg bad?"

My ripped breeches were soaked with more than rain, and as soon as the pulse of battle faded, my leg was going to hurt like the devil. "It will heal," I said, gulping the clean, dry air. "I just need to tie it up with something." He offered me a hand down, but I waved it off and got myself off the horse. I wasn't feeling particularly friendly. The plan had been stupid and ill conceived. Common thievery. Two of the outlaws—the laughing Jalleen and one of the shy Ezzarian boys—were dead. And I had killed at least one Derzhi . . . betrayed Aleksander's trust . . . made myself an outlaw, with Kiril, of all the bloody damned honorable people in the world to witness it. All of it for nothing.

"You saved our lives. My own twice." Blaise stood beside his horse. His companions were sitting silently on the charred earth, waiting. Several of the men and one of the women were clustered around the remaining Ezzarian boy, consoling him. The other youth, the one we'd left behind with his bowels spread all over the ground, had been this one's brother.

I sat on a rock and cut away my breeches. One of the women offered me a roll of dry cloth as I was attempting to tie the wet rags into something long enough to bind the wound. I nodded to her in thanks and kept my eyes on my business, though I could feel Blaise watching.

"We could have done a great deal of good with the price of the horses," he said.

"Enough to pay for the two you lost?" I knotted the bandage tightly around my thigh.

"They believed so."

"They believed in you. You might give a little more thought as to how you spend such wealth."

Only half of our exchange was expressed in words. I sensed how deeply he grieved for his lost companions. And he was trying his best to soothe my anger, though he could not have known the roots of it. I could not have explained the entirety of the tangled mess myself—only that I believed I had squandered something precious and irretrievable. But I didn't think he would have much sympathy with the price I had paid, unless I found myself a slave again, which was the most pleasant of all the likely outcomes.

Farrol hovered a few steps away, as if there were an invisible circle drawn about Blaise and me, one he was forbidden to cross. His round face was red, and he twitched and paced, starting forward toward Blaise, then stepping back, flicking sideways glances to the huddled mourners.

I stood up and tested my leg. "It will be fine in a couple of days," I said. "Can we find some water? I'd like to clean it."

Blaise nodded and waved to the others to mount up.

The barrier broken, Farrol descended on Blaise. "I don't know how they got wind of us. It couldn't have been Jakkor. He despises the Derzhi bastards." He shot dark glances my way. "Someone else betrayed us. They couldn't—"

"You damned, stupid fool!" I said. "I killed for you. You have no idea what you've done."

"We'll speak of it later," said Blaise. "For now we're going home."

I tried to settle my anger by peeling away the layers of enchantment as Blaise led us through his mysterious paths back to the green valleys of Kuvai. If I hadn't known he was working sorcery, I never could have detected it, and even knowing, I found it impossible to dissect his weaving. Never had I touched spells buried so deep in a man. It was something like trying to unravel the mysteries of a beating heart without cutting open the flesh. No skill at observation or listening was going to reveal the component parts of the event.

We arrived at nightfall. The bonfire remained unlit this time, a skeletal pile in the center of the valley clearing. The deer was butchered, but shared out among the men and women to cook over smaller fires. Songs were raised for the dead Jalleen. She had a sister in the valley, who donned red veils and sang the Suzaini dirges until the mournful music wound through the trees like a spider's web, binding us all in a net of beauteous sorrow.

As the music filled the night, I lit my own small fire back under the trees where I could be alone, heating barley soup to fill my stomach and boiling oak bark to clean the gash on my leg. About the time I untied the blood-stiffened bandage around my thigh, I sensed someone standing quietly in the dark trees behind me. "Come share the fire if you want," I said. "No need to stay in the shadows." It was the Ezzarian boy.

He was, perhaps, fifteen. In all my weeks with the outlaws, he had said no more than four words to me. He and his brother had trained with me, watching and listening, but had very pointedly refrained from any personal contact.

I gestured to the soup, but he shook his head and settled himself awkwardly to the ground on the opposite side of the fire. "I just wanted to ask . . . is there an Ezzarian death song?"

"Yes." I dipped a rag in the steaming oak water, gritted my teeth, and dabbed at the sticky sword cut. "It's much simpler than the Suzaini dirge." The Suzaini believed that death was only the first of a hundred trials before the spirit found its way to the land of the dead, which was not at all a nice place for all the work it took to get there. "But I like it better. A little less grim. Our gods—Verdonne and her son Valdis—are something more forgiving than Gossopar. Our chant is sung to honor the dead and to fix them in our memory." And to ease those left behind.

"I'd like . . . I don't have anything . . ."

"I'll teach you, if you want."

He nodded, the firelight reflecting in his dark eyes. And so we worked at it awhile, the more comfort coming in the action itself, I thought, rather than the words. I would say the verse in Ezzarian, which the boy did not seem to know, and then in Aseol—the common tongue of the Empire— and then I would sing the verse, showing the boy how to sit back on his heels and open his hands to set himself in the proper attitude of humility and respect. When I came to the phrase where one would include the name of the dead, the boy was ready to tell me his brother's name. But I held up my hand in warning. "Do you believe his soul yet lives?" I said.

"I want to think it." Hope. Sorrow. Uncertainty. Fear that he was wrong. The same as all of us.

"Then, don't speak his name to me, a stranger." Certainly not to one that was demon-touched. "Names are the entry to the soul. Never give them lightly."

"Is that why you don't ask our names? Da—my brother— thought you despised us. We'd always been told that no Ezzarian—"

"Your pardon, lad." Blaise stepped into the circle of firelight and extended his hand to the boy, who jumped to his feet, all his attention reverted to his commander. "I don't like to interrupt, but I need to speak with our new friend a moment. Here . . ." Blaise pulled the boy close to him and locked his gaze on the grief-ravaged young face. "I've not had a chance to mourn with you. At sunset tomorrow we'll raise him a cairn, and you can sing this chant you've learned." He gripped the youth's shoulders firmly. "His death will not be wasted. I promise. Now, go to Farrol. Tell him I'll be at Wellyt Vale until late, and he needs to see to the watch. Everyone's tired."

The boy bowed awkwardly before he left. "Thank you." He walked into the woods, but returned very quickly. "His name was Davet. I'm Kyor."

I nodded and pressed a clenched fist to my breast in the way of Ezzarians. *"Lys na Seyonne,"* I said, telling him my name as one does to a guest-friend. "Good night, Kyor."

As the boy ran lightly toward the other fires glimmering through the trees, Blaise kicked my boots to me. "We need to go for a walk. You said your leg was not too bad . . . ?"

"It's fine," I said, pulling on some dingy breeches that at least had both legs intact, and sticking my feet in the boots. "A walk would be good. Keep it from stiffening up." I was happy for any distraction from the day's disaster.

We strolled up a gently sloping path toward the southern end of the valley. As the faint track wound through the thickening pines and birches, the sounds and lights of the outlaw camp faded quickly, leaving only the last birdsong of evening and the gurgle of a stream from under the thick leaves of houndberries and foxgloves to break the silence. I waited for Blaise to begin. Clearly he had some purpose in mind. But he said nothing, and I had to be satisfied with the cool, clear night air, tinged with the first edgy promise of winter. We topped a rise, and Blaise led me through a thick birch grove before the path fell away into another valley that stretched eastward toward the rising moon. A trailer of wood smoke teased at my nose, as well as the smell of goats, and before long I heard the murmuring of another stream and caught a glimpse of lantern light ahead of us.

The sod-roofed cottage stood at the edge of the trees, overlooking a broad meadow, watered by a stream that sparkled in the growing moonlight like a jeweled band. A garden plot, full to bursting, ready for harvest, lay to one side of the house, and a large man was shutting the gate to a goat pen that lay on the other side. He held still when he caught sight of us walking out of the wood.

"I've brought a visitor," called Blaise. "I hope it's not too late."

"Just done milking," the man called back. "It's still early for us as work for a living." The big man's hearty rumble was welcoming. He didn't wait to greet us, but limped slowly for the cottage, a pail in one hand, a sturdy crutch in the other. I hadn't noticed when he was standing beside the fence, but the man had only one leg. "Linnie! Blaise has come with company!"

By the time the man reached the house, the door was open and yellow lantern light fell onto the path. The one-legged man, a Manganar whose brown curly hair and massive shoulders put me immediately in mind of a bear, paused in the light to greet us. A woman stood in the doorway with a blanketed bundle cradled on her shoulder. Her long dark hair was tied with a faded green ribbon, and her skin shone red-gold in the lantern light. Ezzarian.

"Welcome!" The man set down his pail and gripped Blaise's hand. "About time you came for a visit. It seems a year since we've had news."

"A busy time even for those who don't work for a living," said Blaise, smiling at him.

"Hush, the both of you," said the woman, the loving brilliance of her gaze belying her severity. "I've just got this mite to sleep, and whoever wakes him will have to deal with me." She allowed Blaise to kiss her on the cheek, and when their faces were so close together, it was not difficult to guess their kinship.

"My sister Elinor," said Blaise, smiling fondly at the woman who was almost his same height. "And her husband Gordain. This"—he nodded at me—"is a new man joined us a month ago. I'll let him introduce himself."

"Seyonne," I said.

The one-legged man motioned with his head that I follow his wife into the house. The place was clean and neat, though cramped for three grown men and the tall woman. A small table of smoothed pine was laid with two wooden bowls and two mugs that Elinor quickly made four. Three well-made stools sat along the wall beside a cupboard with shelves containing bags of flour and salt, packets of meal and herbs, a plate mounded with butter, and the other usual furnishings of a modest kitchen. The floor was wood, scattered with clean straw. The bed in the corner was neatly covered with woven blankets of blue-dyed wool, and a black iron pot hung over the fire, with a supper porridge bubbling in it.

"You'll sit down with us?" said Elinor, setting the table one-handed, while Gordain filled a copper pitcher with milk from his pail, then took the rest back outside. "You both look tired to death. My brother is a hard taskmaster, is he not?"

"I've never known anyone quite like," I said, taking the butter plate from her hand and putting it on the table.

Blaise drew up the stools and a barrel for the fourth, then took a knife from the shelf and cut bread, putting a chunk in each bowl. His sister took down a blue pottery cup that had perhaps two spoons of sugar in it and set it in the place of honor in the center of the table. "As soon as Gordain has put the milk to cool, we'll eat. I'll see if I can lay this one down for a bit. He does dearly love to be carried about." She pulled the soft woven blanket from the bundle on her shoulder, and turned to the side so I could see. "Seyonne, meet Evan-diargh."

It was a vision come to life—a vision I had created from madness and despair in the rocky desolation of Col'Dyath, now born in soft warm flesh of rosy gold, a dusting of black straight hair, and long, dark lashes that would shade eyes of Ezzarian black. With a hesitant finger I touched the rounded cheek, and the babe stirred, sighing and nestling his small straight nose closer to Elinor's long neck, though his eyes did not open. I knew him as I knew my own hand, as I recognized the sun that came up in the morning, as I knew the stars of Ezzaria. He was my son.

CHAPTER 15

I glanced quickly at Blaise, but he was concentrating on the bread. Surely he knew I would guess. Who was so blind as not to recognize his own flesh? So the young outlaw had brought me here for a purpose and was not afraid of what might come of it. What kind of fool was he?

Elinor laid the child in a basket near the hearth. Gently. Lovingly. I squatted on the floor beside her and watched as she tucked the blanket around his sturdy limbs and brushed her hand softly across his silken hair. "His name means 'son of fire,' " she said. "He is a beauty, is he not?"

I nodded, unable to answer. At the edge of my hearing whispered demon music. If his eyes were to open, I would see blue fire lacing the black centers.

"One of Blaise's foundlings, brought from Ezzaria itself. He's told you of them?"

"I've heard," I said, stammering like a student Warden at his first testing. "Tell me . . . what does he do? I've no experience with infants."

Elinor laughed softly and stood up, her hands on her hips. "Drinks milk and puts it out again. Sleeps and cries and laughs, and demands quite noisily to be held and carried every minute of every day. But he takes to the holding and carrying so sweetly, that I don't know he'll learn to creep or walk on his own until he's too heavy for us to heft. We don't grudge it."

"You've no others of your—"

"No others. I'm barren, as it happens." She smiled radiantly at the bearlike man who was just coming back in the door. "Gordain never complained, never spoke of putting me away, so this little one was a gift beyond compare. Once we learned how to get enough of Tethys' milk down him so we could get some sleep, we've never rued his coming."

Gordain had maneuvered himself onto a stool, setting his crutch aside, and begun questioning Blaise about the latest raids. Blaise told the somber story of the day's doings, and then went on to other news of the Empire and the outcome of recent raids. Elinor invited me to sit beside her husband while she ladled porridge in our bowls, then she sat down and joined in the lively discussion. From the sound of it, she had been a raider herself in the days before Evan had come to live with them. I ate what was put before me, wrestling with what I was to do. But as I watched and listened to the three of them in the golden firelight of that little house, talking, planning, alight with their ambition to remake the dreary world, the answer was very clear, as Blaise had known it would be.

What sort of Manganar would stay with a barren wife when his priests told him that the number of his sons would fix his place in the afterlife and the number of his daughters give him wealth and riches there? What kind of woman would take in a child discarded by an entire race for fear of it? With cold precision, I examined the hollow where my heart had once lived, and I excised the nubbin of life that had sprouted there. What more could I give my child than these two?

We stayed late, Blaise and Gordain drinking summer ale and talking of Derzhi nobles and Suzaini merchants, and what supplies the outlaw band might need for the coming winter. Gordain had evidently lost his leg on one of Blaise's early ventures, and though he did not complain or express any bitterness, he clearly chafed at being unable to join his fellows in their exploits. I helped Elinor clear away the supper, and I watched the babe, wondering if he would wake before time to go. He didn't.

Just as well, I thought, as I bowed to Elinor and Gordain, and watched from the path as Blaise kissed them both. To see him awake would have made things more difficult than they were already. As I waited, I cast a few enchantments around the cottage. A spell to keep the water clean. Another to ward off diseases borne by air. Another to give warning to Gordain and Elinor if anyone approached. And one to keep the goats and the fields fertile. It was all I could do.

"You are satisfied?" said Blaise after the cottage lights had disappeared behind us. The freshening wind of passing midnight stirred my hair as we walked.

"Thank you."

"You saved my life twice in one day, and the lives of many others. You eased a boy's pain that knew no solace. It seemed only right that I should do the same."

"You took a risk," I said, bitterness and grief competing for the remnants of my spirit. "I am, after all, a man of violence. And there is no small danger to your sister and her husband to leave him there. You must know it. He is possessed by a rai-kirah—a demon. He's only a child, but later . . ."

Oh, Verdonne's mercy, I did not want to think of later. I needed to tell Blaise how to find a Searcher to come for the child when he was old enough. So many things to tell the young outlaw before I left. No reason to stay any longer; I was sick of lies. The only remaining question was where to go. Not to Aleksander; the Prince would no longer believe I was his spy, not after today. Nor to Ezzaria; the glimpse of my child—beautiful, loved—had only made the breach with my people wider, our ignorance more inexcusable.

"So you haven't figured it out. Your eyes see so much that the rest of us cannot; I never expected it would take so long for you to understand."

"Figured out what?" I had been lost in my self-pity and believed I had missed something of the conversation.

Blaise stopped in the middle of a meadow, where the moonlight fell clearly on his tired, angular face. "Look at me," he said, pointing to his own eyes. "Pass your hand before your eyes and do whatever it is you do, then look at me. Tell me what you see."

With a feathered brush upon my spine, I did as he said and stared into his clear gaze as I had in the tavern the first time I met him, as I had done three times since then, trying to discover what made him what he was. Again, I saw the good and simple man. No arrogance. No slyness. A man at peace, awash in stillness. Again, I felt the faint dizziness and saw a scattering of images laid one upon the other. I had assumed it was my own state of mind that caused the ghosts of faces and landscapes to flicker through my head whenever I examined Blaise, as if somehow the hard, shining surface of his eyes was reflecting my own visions. But this time I realized that I was seeing Blaise's images, not my own. The Nyabozzi castle as he soared over its walls to open the gates. The streets of Vayapol as he scouted for Derzhi guardsmen. The Makai Narrows in the rain from a point higher than the cliff tops. Myself huddling to the walls in stupefaction at the enchantment I had witnessed. A thousand colors. A thousand shapes. Yet there was nothing to explain his insistence. He appeared to be the sum of his memories, as was every man.

"Now look again, Seyonne. Tell me what you see."

The lock of my gaze on his still held. Yet something had changed. Something was released. A thrumming at the outer reaches of my hearing set my blood cold. Denial came to my lips even as I pushed my seeing deeper. Even as I opened my ears. Even as I began to hear and see the truth that lay exposed before me . . . the dissonant music intruding on my soul, the blue flame that burned behind the dark eyes. *Demon*. I backed away, looked this way and that, trying to determine how I could get back to the cottage before Blaise could stop me.

His huge hand gripped my shoulder. "I am a man. Nothing more. Nothing less. I make my own choices. Live my own life."

Madness . . . fear . . . disbelief. The world was caving in on me again.

"Look at me, Seyonne. What has changed? Nothing of any importance. Nothing."

His passion held me still, forcing me to look, to think, to question yet again the most fundamental tenets of my life—to stand on my head, to walk on my hands, to listen and believe, not only paying service to intellect and reason this time, but to ignore all my deep-bred fears and allow the world to take on a wholly new aspect. I had to work at it a very long time before I could comprehend. Yet in one heartbeat, as spent storm clouds thin and vanish before the midday sun, all came clear. "You're one like my son."

Blaise nodded, but he did not smile, just motioned me to walk beside him. "We need to talk," he said. We had walked only an hour to get to Wellyt Vale, but it took us two to return.

"I was born in Ezzaria to a midwife, and one you call a Searcher," Blaise told me as we wandered through the towering pines outlined dark against the stars. "Though they saw what I was, they rebelled against your custom. My mother knew where children like me were laid out to die, and she and my father came for me as soon as the rites were done. My father had traveled widely in his work, of course, so he knew where to take us. For many years we lived on the outskirts of Vayapol, getting help from the priests of Dolgar when we were in need. As a skilled midwife, my mother was able to keep us fed, while my father searched the world for some help for me. Though they were sure that I would fall into demon madness eventually, a child could want no better loving than they gave me. They taught me nothing of Ezzaria, nothing of your ways, nothing of your magic—for fear, I think, that I would betray you all someday. But, as years passed and I grew up as any boy, I like to think their fear began to fade away."

"They must have been extraordinary people. To leave everything behind. To risk so much."

Love radiated from Blaise's quiet face. "Aye. They were indeed. And in his travels and searching, my father came upon other extraordinary people. A few, born like me, who had somehow survived. A few others, both Ezzarian and not, who had been 'possessed,' yet found their experience quite unlike the horror Ezzarians would expect. My father persuaded them to come together in Manganar, to learn from each other so that someday he could go back to Ezzaria and explain what he had found. It was his greatest hope . . . to go back someday. I've always marveled at this feeling you carry for your land and for each other." I thought this wistful comment odd. How can one miss what one has never known?

"So what happened?" We came to the top of a treeless ridge and walked along the crest, the wind lifting our cloaks as it spoke of the change of season.

"My mother kept in contact with one of her friends among the Ezzarian midwives. And in the years after our escape, she would take in others that were laid out to die."

"Farrol," I said.

Blaise nodded. "He is my brother in all but blood. I've not done right by him . . . I've let his rashness go too far . . . you see it so easily. But it's hard . . . There were seven of us altogether."

"Elinor?" I almost didn't ask it. I wasn't sure I wanted to know.

"She is my natural sister. But she's like you, rather than me and the others. Anyway, I had no idea of any of this. Everything was fine until I was ten."

"The Derzhi conquest." When the world had changed and every Ezzarian was required to be enslaved.

"Everyone went into hiding. Dolgar's priests took in as many of the children as they could, keeping us at the hermitage outside of Vayapol. I saw my father only once more after that. It was the middle of one night when I was thirteen and one of the old priests took Elinor and me out behind the goat pen to see him. He was sick. Starving. He could not get work anywhere, dared not be seen, dared not come to the hermitage lest he be followed and bring the law down on us. But on that night he had come to tell us that our mother was dead. A Derzhi woman whom she had once helped give birth had sent out servants looking for her, because she was ready to deliver again. My mother would not refuse, thinking that no harm would come from one of her friends. But as soon as the child was born, the woman's husband took my mother to the magistrate." Blaise studied my face intently, as if he could somehow squeeze out an explanation of such vileness. "She had no power of sorcery anymore. She had given up all practice of it because of me, and my father said that it had all faded away. But they put her through these rites they use for sorcerers . . . and my father watched it from hiding. He said she was dead when they took her out . . ."

It was a child's question, filled with knowing sadness, yet not quite bereft of hope. But I could give him the sorrowful answer. "It's not possible to survive the Rites of Balthar without using melydda," I said. "I had a great deal of power and used it all, and it was sixteen years before I knew I didn't die from the rites."

"Sixteen. I had wondered." The child was gone. Only the man remained.

"So you lived with the priests and decided to spend your life righting the ills of the world that killed your parents. And somehow you developed power such as no Ezzarian ever dreamed of."

"Not exactly. What power I have has been there all along. The shifting started when I was eight. I was lucky that my father's friends were close by. It was painful at first, of course, before they taught me how to manage it." He folded his arms in front of him and glanced my way. "When I shifted those first times, my parents were terrified. They were sure my rai-kirah was tormenting me, but I was just frightened. I was the first of the children to go through—"

"Wait just a bit." I said, my mind swirling in confusion. "The first? You mean the rest of them can do this . . . shifting?"

"Yes. Of course, all of us born this way—Farrol, Davet, Kyor, the others. Your son will do it, too. It's why you need to know—so you can help him. Farrol says I'm a madman already to tell you any of this. But we've lost all of the elders, those who knew anything of Ezzaria and the things you learn there."

I could feel his struggle to say these things, and even in my wonder at the revelation, all my burgeoning hope—that my son could grow to be a strong and honorable man like Blaise—was balanced on the point of a knife. "What is it you want of me?" I said.

"We need to know if you've been taught what happens to us. If you know how to prevent it."

The confusion was not improving. "I don't know . . . prevent the shapeshifting? Why would you want—?"

"Because we go mad from it . . . or worse." He broke a dead branch from a sickly fir tree and snapped it into ever smaller pieces as we walked, throwing the bits into the woods in disgust. "Gradually it gets more difficult to change back to human form, and there comes a day when you can't. You stay in the form you've chosen . . . a beast forever . . . locked in until you become one with it and forget what you were." He hurled the last stick into the sky as if it might catch the attention of some wayward god. "Or you can choose the alternative . . . equally happy. If you feel the change coming on and choose not to shift, you lose your mind. The more you shift, the sooner it happens."

"Saetha."

"She chose not to change. Her natural form, the easiest for her to shift to—you find it as you experiment with shifting—was a cat. She rarely shifted, so she was almost forty when the time came. She was a healer, and she couldn't bear the thought of losing her skill . . . to be so limited . . . to forget everything of importance to her. So she refused it and spent every one of her last days healing. In less than a season, she was as you see her now. I'm so afraid that somewhere inside her she remembers what she was."

I once knew a slave, a Fryth woman who fed me during a month I was chained to the wall in my third master's cellar. She told me that I should be at peace with my slave's lot, for her gods had told her that every happiness has its price, and that those who climb to the greatest heights are always those who have the greatest price to pay. I thought I had seen the living example of those words in Aleksander, but the Prince's tally had been nothing compared to this I heard from Blaise.

"And you change so often in this business of yours . . ."

"It is necessary. But it means I have very little time, and there's so much to be done. I know I'm not the only one who can do this work, but Farrol is rash, Kyor is young, and now Davet is dead." He shook his head and straightened his back. "Gods, what am I doing? I'd no intention of telling you so much. This is not about me. It's about all of us. It's about your child. I thought maybe you would be willing to tell us."

"But we don't know anything. I wish I could say differently. But I . . . none of us had any idea there was even such a possibility as this. I know of nothing that's been written or passed down to so much as hint at it."

"Ah, well then. Since no one ever mentioned it, I thought that must be the case, but then most of the ones I've asked were in no state to remember everything—"

I would not let him finish. "We learn new things all the time. I have skills. It's possible I might be able to help. I'll look again, and if there's anything to be found, I'll find it. I promise. And there is one matter I can certainly help you with . . . about the other . . . about these changes you're trying to bring about in the world. I need to tell you a few things about myself—"

"Blaise!" We had walked down the path from the woods and into the center of the camp. Before I could say anything more, Farrol came running, sword drawn, and with him four more of the outlaw band. Torches were blazing through the camp. "Thank goodness you're all right."

"Why should I not be?"

Farrol placed the tip of his sword in the region of my heart. "Because you've been consorting with a Derzhi spy. We've finally tripped him up. We've caught his accomplice, sneaking about the camp, ready to bring the villains down on our heads. And we've got the evidence writ in pen and ink. Sealed by the royal devil himself."

"I don't believe it," said Blaise, turning to me in puzzlement.

If I had been able to shapeshift, I might have picked that moment to become a worm and creep into the bosom of the earth. When Farrol placed a worn leather packet in Blaise's hand, I knew what the evidence was—damning, undeniable evidence. And I guessed who the "accomplice" was . . . and that my moment's opportunity to make peace was irretrievable.

"Where is she?" I said. "If you haven't killed her, I think I'll do it myself."

I found Fiona when I was thrown in a root cellar on top of her. We weren't going to be there for long. Blaise would take no chances on his people being set upon by the Derzhi. He was probably flying over the countryside, searching for royal troops at that very moment. But even when he failed to find them, he would move the settlement, leaving the two of us dead, no doubt.

I was almost too discouraged to be angry. "Did anyone ever tell you that you are the most damnably persistent, annoying, rock-headed imbecile of a woman that ever lived?" I said as I shoved her legs aside to give myself room enough to stretch out my wounded leg. "Did it ever cross your mind that you could just leave me be for one moment and perhaps the stars wouldn't come crashing to earth or the sun fail to rise?" A basket of onions took just that unfortunate moment to topple onto my head from the stacks that surrounded us in the dark earthen pit. I spat out the dirt that showered down in company with the smelly lumps, and I crushed the basket, trying to make a pillow out of it and my cloak. It had been a long day since the Yvor Lukash and his band had gone riding into the Khyb Rash.

"They would never have known I was here except the cursed horse got spooked. Some kind of a damnable goat came charging out of the brush. Demon beasts. Can't trust them."

I couldn't see her face in the dark, and I was in no mood to cast a light. I just wanted to sleep . . . perhaps for a hundred years or so. But with a twisting movement that caused yet another avalanche of earthy delicacies—potatoes and turnips, this time—Fiona launched herself upward, toward the wooden door that Farrol had slammed and barred so triumphantly. After a sprizzling burst of sorcery, I smelled burning rope.

"They'll be guarding the door," I said. "They're not stupid. You can untie yourself and burn out the wood—burn out the whole cursed camp if you want—but they'll be waiting with more rope and more wood and a few knives and swords. And they won't care what we do to them as long as they protect Blaise. They know what we can do and what we can't."

"So you've betrayed that, too."

I wasn't going to get into an argument with her. "I did what I had to do. Now, be still. I'd like to get some sleep."

Trying for the trapdoor one more time, she slipped backward, so the potatoes rolled out from under her backside, and she landed right on my wounded thigh.

I erupted. "Gods of earth and sky, what ever did I do to be cursed with a self-righteous twit of a watchdog who can't sneeze without drawing my blood? If you are so determined to see me dead, why don't you just stick your knife in me? It would be a damned sight easier on both of us."

"I'm sorry," she said when she got herself untangled and helped pull a hundredweight of potatoes out of my lap, throwing them back in their heap. "Are you hurt?"

I didn't risk saying anything more, but cast a light, lowered my breeches without regard to modesty, and worked at tying my bandage tighter so I wouldn't bleed to death in that wretched hole.

"You seem to get bloody enough without my help. Here, let me do it," said my cell mate. "I've got a clean kerchief in my pocket." She reached for the blood-soaked bandage.

"No! Don't touch it," I said, yanking it away. "You mustn't." I could not have her touch my blood, the blood that Saetha and her demon had tainted. After the revelations of the night, it seemed foolish to worry about it, but I didn't know what to believe anymore. Was Saetha the truer demon or was Fiona? Or Blaise . . . what was Blaise?

"Why not? I can help you take care of this. I'll keep it clean."

Realizing that no matter how tired I was, I was unlikely to sleep in that squirrel hole full of vegetables—not with the events of the day nagging at my head like shrieking jays—so I told Fiona about Saetha . . . and about Blaise and his followers, about Aleksander and the raids, and about my son. I hoped to shock her into silence while clearing my own head. "And so I've betrayed a man who shared his soul with me, who gave me back my life and my homeland," I said as my light died away again. "I've abandoned my oath, taken human lives like a blood-mad barbarian, and I have given up my child to strangers. My blood has been touched by a demon, and I am not sorry for it. Now, aren't you glad you've come? If you survive this mess, you can go back and tell Talar that I am truly corrupt. I name Blaise a better man than any Ezzarian I know, yet I've seen demon fire in his eyes. We don't know who and what we are, Fiona, and I have the terrible feeling that we are wrong about every single thing that we believe."

I seemed to have succeeded in my plan, at least where Fiona was concerned. She didn't say another word. I soon fell asleep. For the first time since I had come to Blaise, I dreamed of a frozen castle and a dark horror that devoured me from the inside out.

CHAPTER 16

Verdonne battled with the god all the years as their son grew to manhood. The cruel god stripped his wife of her clothes to shame her, melted her sword to taunt her weakness, and burned the fields and forests around her so that she would have no sustenance. "Yield," bellowed the forest god. "I will not sully my sword with mortal blood." But Verdonne would not yield.
—The story of Verdonne and Valdis as told to the First of the Ezzarians when they came to the lands of trees

Blaise did not allow me to explain myself when he held my rudimentary trial before the assembled outlaws. The men and women were already mounted, their wagons and horses loaded with their meager belongings. Fiona and I stood in front of Blaise, outlaw swords bristling around us like hair on an angry cat. I could have escaped if I chose— and Blaise surely knew it—but I put up with his little ceremony in hopes that he would let me explain.

Stumbling over the flowery language of the Derzhi scribe, his jutting chin daring anyone to make jest of his unskilled recitation, Farrol read the royal proclamation that declared that I was a free man and that anyone who harmed me was at peril of his life. The growls and murmuring of the outlaw tribe grew thicker than the lowering clouds of the damp morning. Several of the women spat at me, and more than one hand quivered on a sword hilt.

Blaise asked only one question. "You are the one named in this paper?"

"Yes, I—"

"Then, you can be nothing but a spy for the Derzhi Prince. It is usual to execute spies. But you fought at our sides and saved lives, my own included, and I won't have it said that I killed a man in payment of a life debt, no matter whether it served his own duplicity to save me. So you'll not die this day. As for the woman, I give you her life in payment for your service in our ventures. And so we are quit. Next time I see you, I'll know whose interests you serve, and I'll deal with you accordingly."

"Blaise, let me—"

"Tell your royal master that the Yvor Lukash will not rest until the day a Derzhi prince serves the lowest of his subjects with his own hand." With that Blaise motioned to his riders, who began to move down the path out of the valley. "I had hoped we might learn from each other," he said. "But I don't care to learn what you have to teach." Then he wheeled his horse and spurred it forward to take the lead of the slow-moving party.

Farrol and Kyor were left to guard us. As soon as the last stragglers had rounded the bend in the path, taking them out of sight, Farrol commanded the boy to get their horses. The short man glared at me and sheathed his dagger. With a grimace he tossed two items at my feet. One was my knife, taken from me when they threw me into the root cellar. The other was my leather packet. To my astonishment, the precious royal letter was crumpled and stuffed inside it. "Damned, cursed spy. I told him he should kill you, but he didn't even let me burn the paper. It's a sore temptation to disobey."

"Killing me might not be as easy as you think."

"Oh, I know you can fight. You might even take me down with your fine sword work and your magics. But then I've already won, haven't I? I found out the truth, and he won't be taken in by you again."

As I picked up the leather packet and slipped it into my shirt, I at last remembered where I had seen Farrol before—the beggar in the alley of Vayapol who had tried to steal the wallet from my pocket. He had been trying to protect Blaise even then, not caring for his own safety. He was no duplicitous enigma, but only a rash, foolish, loyal brother.

The sturdy round man checked his saddle girth. Quickly I took stock of my possessions. I needed something that was my own. My clothes, the black rider's costume, had been loaned me by Blaise, which left only the paper and the knife—a fine one that Kiril had given me as I left Zhagad on the night of Aleksander's anointing. I decided that I could replace the knife easier than the paper, so I worked a hurried enchantment, then ran after Farrol. He was just mounting his horse. At the sight of the knife in my hand, he backed away quickly and drew his sword, but I reversed my weapon, holding it out to him hilt first.

"When the day comes for Blaise, the day of this last change, tell him to find me. All he has to do is touch this knife and say my name, and he'll know where I am. I'll help him if I can."

"You've put a curse on it."

"I swear I've not. All I want is to help. But if you doubt me, then you carry it for him. If it happens that your friend and brother doesn't need it, that you don't need it, that Kyor here doesn't need it, then you can throw it in the fire for an hour to remove my enchantment, and you'll have a very good knife. But I'm going to find out what you need to know. I promise you."

Young Kyor watched all this solemnly. Worriedly. Such a burden of dread for a young man at the beginning of his life. The boy didn't say anything, just turned his mount to follow Farrol down the valley. But when Farrol deliberately threw my knife to the ground and kicked his horse to a gallop, Kyor slipped from his mount, snatched up the knife, then glanced at me furtively before leaping back into the saddle and riding away.

"Have you gone completely mad? You've just given a demon-infested outlaw a locator spell. He can find you whether you want it or not."

I jumped. I had almost forgotten Fiona. She had maintained a granite silence the entire morning. "It's likely he could find me anyway. You seem to have no trouble."

"Will he come?"

The last dust settled to the road. "I hope."

We didn't spend much time in the deserted camp. We had no horses, no food, no cloaks or blankets, and only Fiona's knife for a weapon. At least they'd left us our

boots. According to Fiona, we were ten days' walk from
the nearest town. A quick scout through the houses turned
up nothing more than a few shards of broken pottery, four
broken arrow shafts, five half-rotted potatoes, and two
handfuls of oats. We mended the pottery cup well enough
to hold water, and while I boiled the oats, Fiona cut lengths
of tough gray reppia vine and wove them into a sturdy bag.
We ate the thin oat gruel and a few tiny, sour raspberries
left on a late-flowering vine, then we packed the potatoes
and the cup into Fiona's bag and set off.

The walk was long and miserable. Autumn had decided
to arrive in Kuvai with a siege of cold rain and mist that
seemed to wash the green from the leaves even as we
passed. At night we wove sticks and leaves into crude shelters to keep off the worst of the rain, and we huddled into
piles of damp leaves and pine needles. Fortunately, Fiona
was quite accomplished at making something out of nothing. I could coax a sputtering fire from damp wood, but
she gleaned enough berries, wild carrots, and hedge-plums
that we did not starve, and even managed to trap a couple
of rabbits in the few hours we stopped to rest. I knew how
to set the bone in her hand, broken when she slipped on a
muddy bank and slammed it into a stone, but she knew
exactly where to look for the rare herb alcya to treat the
festering wound in my thigh. She it was who found the
spring after we'd gone two days with nothing but rainwater
to drink, and I had to trust entirely to her sense of direction, for the thick clouds prevented any analysis of sun
or stars.

Beyond the basic necessities of survival, we did not talk
for the first five days. I was morosely reviewing the events
of the past four months, trying to decide if there had been
any way to avoid making enemies of everyone in the world
I cared for and most of the people I didn't. Fiona trudged
alongside me league after league, her thin face fixed in
stony solemnity as if she were escorting me to my
execution.

In truth, I wasn't sure where we were going. Ezzaria, I
supposed. I needed to study. To read everything again. To
meditate on the mysteries I had uncovered and to talk to
Kenehyr and the other scholars and discover anything that

might help me know what to do for Blaise and Kyor and my son when they faced their too early doom. For Blaise it would be soon. I felt again the urgency of his followers, Farrol's rash, flailing grief. Months, I guessed. Maybe weeks. Not years.

Yet just as it had when I was leaving Vayapol, Ezzaria felt like the wrong destination. My home had faded into unreality—the people, the life they lived, their concerns and desires as alien to me as the life and thoughts of trees. And there was another worry. Since the night in the root cellar, the haunting dreams of the frozen castle had come back with such ferocious power that I woke exhausted and shaking, flinching at every sound, at every touch. I began doing almost anything to avoid sleep, only to have the dreams invade my waking. They would creep up on me as I walked. Rather than the cool rain on my soggy outlaw's garb, I would feel frigid wind cutting through whipping rags. My reluctant steps homeward were hurried by the compulsion to find my way into the ice castle. The quiet solitude of the Kuvai forest was invaded by creeping, frozen terror until I was checking over my shoulder every moment of the day. Never had I been so consumed by a dream. By the evening of the fifth day of our journey, as I huddled by our meager fire in the unceasing rain, I was half crazed with it.

My shirt was pulled up to my ears to prevent the cold dribble that was pouring through our twiggy shelter from running down my neck. Fiona was roasting some kind of thick white root on a stick. It smelled like burning flesh. As I stared at the fire, trying to stay awake and trying to ignore the hopeless growling of my empty stomach, the smoke shaped itself into spires and bridges, and in the flicker of blue and white flames, I saw the wraiths passing over the bridge. One of the wraiths turned to look at me just as the darkness swept over . . .

"What's wrong?" Fiona cut the charred root in half and offered me a portion. "You've been twitching like a nervous cat all day. You're not getting a fever again, are you?"

"No." Gingerly I slipped the soft, sagging mess from the stick, shifting it from one hand to the other until it cooled enough to hold. By that time it looked so unappetizing, I

could not think what to do with it. I glanced again at the
fire, and the wraith still shimmered in the flames. "Tell me
why you came after me," I said, closing my eyes, which did
me no good at all. The castle was waiting for me in the
darkness behind my eyelids. "You're weeks away from
home, in danger every minute. I don't understand it."

"It's duty you don't understand." She knew it was a feeble attempt, her voice thrusting out the words like a sword
made of feathers.

"Your duty was done with long ago, and your mistress
should be well satisfied, since I'm nowhere near Ezzaria.
Are you truly trying to get me murdered? What have I
done to you that you bear me such hatred?"

Fiona stared at the white pulp in her hand, then threw
it into the fire in disgust. "I don't hate you. I hate what
you do. How you make a mockery of the law. How you
came back and lived as if you were uncorrupted, pretending
that you cared about truth. I could see it so clearly. You
had violated everything, yet people honored you . . . for-
gave you . . . as if corruption could be dismissed like a
slip of the tongue. It was . . . is . . . my duty to prove
them wrong."

For that moment she pushed my visions aside. I didn't
think she was talking about me at all. This was something
deeper and more painful, something eating at her, like a
splinter in the heart. But I had no skill to get it out of her.
"And what have you proven?" I asked.

"Only that I am a more stubborn fool than you."

For the first time since I had known her, her perfect
honesty abused herself. I started to laugh at her. Yet her
face showed such wounding, as if she had pricked herself
with a needle only to find her entire hand lost from it, that
I softened my retort. "Well, on that we are agreed," I said,
raising the pottery cup of rainwater in mock salute. "At
last some common ground. I think we shall have an entirely
different relationship from now on."

Though she scowled at me furiously, my gibe seemed to
draw her out of whatever morass she had sunk into. She
reached for another wad of her white roots and stabbed
her stick through it. I had the uncomfortable feeling that
the roots wore my face.

"Since you've heeded my lessons in stubborn foolishness, perhaps I should mentor you next in madness," I said, leaning back against the cold, wet rock. "But I need to decide where the next lesson should be taught." I told her of my conviction that I needed to study demon lore and my hesitation at returning to Ezzaria. Just as in the root cellar, it suddenly seemed easier to talk than to be silent. Better to drown out the nagging terror than to retreat into maddening solitude. I did not mention my dreams.

To my surprise, she entered into the discussion quite seriously. "There is one source of demon lore outside of Ezzaria," she said. "Mistress Catrin told you of it."

"Catrin?" It took me a moment to recall the conversation at Col'Dyath and to remember that Fiona had been there when Catrin told me of Pendyrral and his strange demon encounter. "That was Balthar the Devil, she spoke of. I cannot, will not—"

"Then, you are a coward and a liar who has no intention of discovering the truth."

There are some fires that cold rain and long traveling cannot quench, and Fiona had found a way to light one. "You don't know what you're talking about," I snapped. "This is the same Balthar who discovered that burying a sorcerer alive and sending him visions that your worst nightmares cannot match will cause the wretch to expend every shred of his power. Leave the poor devil long enough, just to the edge of raving, and he'll believe his melydda is destroyed. Sometimes, of course, if you leave one buried too long, or if the Rites were not properly recorded and you put a person through a second time, or if the person happens to be one of our race who has no melydda . . . too bad, they suffocate or go mad, one or the other. And, oh, yes, tell the Derzhi Magicians Guild—a league of petty charlatans fearful of losing their stipends from the noble houses—so that they will be sure to use your enchantments on every Ezzarian man, woman, and child taken captive. What could such a man have to say that could convince me to exist in the same room with him? And don't bother to answer until you've lived what he has wrought."

Fiona's cheeks glowed with more than the heat of the

fire, but her resolve did not falter. "Did you know that Balthar had two children born demon-possessed?"

I stared at the woman. Though my skin still throbbed with disgust and fury, she had silenced my tongue quite effectively.

Pursuing her advantage, she continued. "The first was a daughter, laid out to die one hour after her birth. Balthar immersed himself in demon lore, even took himself outside of Ezzaria to learn more. He told his friends that he had learned things that would surprise them, things that explained some of our mysteries. But before he explained anything, his son was born. Another demon child. He barricaded himself in his house, refusing to allow the child to be taken, but eventually Queen Tarya sent in temple guards to remove the boy. Balthar swore he would take vengeance on all Ezzarians if the boy was harmed, and the Queen forbade him to leave his house until he could answer charges of corruption. But after that night he was never seen again in Ezzaria."

"And the child?"

"The gods destroyed him."

"How did you learn all this?"

"You asked me to find out."

"I?"

"You told me to think about what I had seen and heard in our last battle. To ask some questions. To investigate. So I did."

Clearly, there was to be no end to the amazements of life. I began to think I was either unendingly dull, everlastingly ignorant, or absolutely blind. Perhaps all of them. "It was you who discovered Pendyrral's story, not Catrin at all."

"It doesn't matter who discovered it. If you're going to learn anything, you're going to have to find Balthar. And no one in Ezzaria has any idea where he is."

I leaned my head on the heel of my hand, trying to press the visions from my eyes. "Oh, I know where to find out. It's the asking will be tricky business."

"How difficult can it be to ask?"

"I would recommend you stay well away." Only a very few people knew Balthar's whereabouts, and they were all housed in the Imperial Palace in Zhagad. I would have to be very careful. I didn't think Aleksander would be at all happy to see me.

It took us four weeks to make our way to Zhagad, the Pearl of Azhakstan, the desert city that was the heart of the Derzhi Empire. We were fortunate to take up with the caravan of a Suzaini wine merchant. I showed him my paper and told him that I had been freed for saving the life of a royal favorite—exactly true. Wine caravans were rich prey for bandits, so the merchant was delighted to take on another fighting arm—and one in royal favor—in exchange for food and company on the long route across Manganar and into the Azhaki desert.

Being a traditional Suzaini, he required that Fiona wear robes to cover herself completely and travel with the other women, which annoyed Fiona, but suited me very well. I was free of her scrutiny and of guilt about her danger. No one could see that she, too, was Ezzarian. She had no paper to ensure her freedom. I reminded her of that every time I had an opportunity to speak with her, offering explicit details of the fate that awaited her if she were taken captive, but I could not make her see sense and go home. She fumed and fretted and spoke hardly at all, but she wore the long white robes, traveled in the women's cart, and was not noticed.

My dreams continued, but got no worse. In the society of other people, it was easier to keep them at bay. I earned our passage fairly, helping the merchant fend off two raiding parties. Happily, neither party wore black clothing or had painted white daggers on their faces.

We entered Zhagad in late morning. The autumn cooling meant that it was possible to travel all but a few hours at midday in the desert, so we had made good time. I bid Dabarak, the wine merchant, a polite farewell and asked if Fiona could keep the robes, as I wished her to remain modest in such a wicked city as Zhagad. His eyes glinted green in the sunlight of the outer marketplace, a teeming center of commerce that had its only quiet hour at high noon. "Your woman walks proudly like a Suzaini woman, and reins her tongue as she should, but you should teach her to control her eyes. She does not drop them when you speak to her. I would chastise any of my women for such boldness."

"I've considered chastising her," I said. "But I've decided that it would be more trouble than it's worth. She doesn't take it well."

The man nodded sympathetically. Fiona's bold eyes stung my back so wickedly, I thought they might draw blood. We had scarcely spoken for four weeks, and I hoped such a public mocking might make her leave at last. I should have known better.

We took a room in a small inn tucked away in the merchant district, paying for it with coins taken from the defeated bandit party and shared out among the caravan guards. I had bought paper, pen, and ink in the marketplace, and after we argued over whether to share the one bed or waste money on two (Fiona prevailed—one bed; we would take turns sleeping), I laid my purchases out on the little table in our room. I sharpened the pen with Fiona's knife, then wrote a message.

My lady,
I hope beyond measure that this missive finds you prospering in health and fortune. At our last meeting, you offered to do anything within your power to aid me in time of need. I had hoped never to find occasion to redeem that pledge so graciously given in perilous times, but I find myself in grave circumstance too complicated to explain in a brief message. In short, I need a bit of information, and I have no way to obtain it, save through the influence of someone at the Derzhi court.

It is possible that you have heard ill tidings of me in these past weeks. I beg you withhold judgment until I am able to recount the full story behind these reports. I swear to you upon the work we did together two years ago that my faith, my honor, and my aims have not changed. My request bears not the slightest risk to the safety or honor of the one who brought us together, and, in fact, could be of benefit to the stability of his own work.

If you feel that giving me private hearing in any way compromises your own position, I do most gladly release you from your pledge. Short of that, however, I ask your indulgence and discretion.

With highest regards,
The lady's foreign friend

"Who is she?" said Fiona, reading over my shoulder. "Someone's mistress? Yours? With such a title . . . 'the lady's foreign friend' . . ."

"Not exactly," I said. "If the gods are wise, she will one day be the Empress of Azhakstan." It was always a pleasure to shock Fiona.

CHAPTER 17

The problem was that I knew none of the courtiers or administrators in the imperial palace in Zhagad, certainly no one likely to know Balthar the Devil's whereabouts. I had never served in Zhagad, only in the Emperor's summer palace in Capharna, so I was acquainted with only three people who could find out what I wanted in any reasonable length of time—Aleksander, his cousin Kiril, and his wife, the Princess Lydia. Aleksander was out of the question, and Kiril, whose warriors had died at my hand, would reflect his anger. The Princess was my only choice. Lydia was not what one would call serene, but she listened far better than her prince.

I returned alone to the marketplace and hired a public messenger to deliver my letter to Hazzire, Lydia's trusted intermediary in discreet matters. I hoped the man had moved to Zhagad with the lady upon her marriage to Aleksander. He would recognize the signature and know to pass the note quietly to his mistress.

For the rest of the day, I paced and fidgeted in the vicinity of the messenger's table in the outer market. I dared not stay still, lest I be noticed; yet I dared not miss the messenger, lest he take another commission and disappear before I received my answer. The withering heat of midday drove most people indoors or into the cool shadows of lattice-roofed gardens and walled courtyards. Only the most privileged residents had fountains that drew water from springs in the porous rocks under the city. But as the blue shadows of afternoon grew long, and the breeze blew in from the cooling dunes, everyone came out again. Men greeted friends and sat together at stone tables in the market squares playing ulyat or sharing cups of nazrheel—the hot, stinking tea the Derzhi loved. Women in floating, transparent veils came out to buy fruits and meat for dinner, and stopped to gossip with friends or relatives by the public wells. Merchants and vendors put out their best wares in the evening—jewelry, wines, exotic spices, and perfumes—for the wealthy residents of the city came out to buy in the pleasant evening. Only servants and slaves were out of bed early enough to shop in the cool of the morning.

I was just considering buying a wooden skewer of grilled sausage to take back to Fiona, when the blue-clad messenger came trotting down the dusty street from the inner ring of the city, where the golden domes of the Imperial Palace glinted in the sunset. "Do you have an answer?" I said, pouncing on the man before he could catch his breath.

"The gentleman says that he and your most devout friend will worship at the Temple of Druya in the outer ring tonight. They will discuss business after making offerings for the god's feast tomorrow. And it would needs be brief, as he has very important company at his residence this night and cannot be away from them long."

I flipped the man a coin and hurried back to the inn to await sixth watch, for Druya was a god of night and darkness, and it was always in the hours before midnight that a "most devout" Derzhi woman would come to the temple of Druya.

"I'm coming with you," said Fiona.

"No. She doesn't know you. I don't want to frighten her away."

"Surely a Derzhi princess is not one to be frightened easily. I'll wear these cursed robes, and she'll think you've brought your wife. It will put her at ease."

My wife . . . Filled with dreams and fears and journeying, I had spared little thought for Ysanne in the past months, yet she had always been at the back of my mind. I feared that this terrible thing that had come between us was but a symptom of a deeper problem that I had tried to ignore for far too long, sure that devotion would always lead us right. She was queen and had given her life to it. She had warned me repeatedly, but I had never listened. I was . . .

whatever I had become in our long years apart, and whatever we said of it, we had never been able to reconcile my discontent with her position. Her duty made it impossible that she trust me. And my history made it imperative she should. Now our ways had parted so decisively that I was afraid there was no going back. I wondered how she fared, and whether she allowed herself to think of our son . . . or of me. Lost in the empty ache of memory, I missed the rest of Fiona's arguments, but when I slipped through the bustling streets toward the bronze dome of Druya's temple, the white-robed figure trailed doggedly behind me.

The interior of the temple was dark, save for a bank of candles beneath the towering red and gold mosaic of the bull on the distant wall. The domed roof was supported by a forest of orange and red-striped columns, and you could never get an expansive view of the god's gigantic image, only glimpses of its majesty through the complexities of the space. The thick walls of the temple blocked out the noise of the street traffic, but strands of bells, large and small, silver, gold and brass, hung from iron hooks that protruded from the massive columns. The bells moved with the air of our passing, leaving a trail of chiming music behind us as we hurried through the dim light. A few worshipers moved about, leaving offerings atop the five altar stones that were already heaped with flowers ready for the next day's festival. I began to do the same, passing slowly from one granite block to the other, dropping a handful of the prickly villaine and musty-scented harrowmint I'd bought from the flower seller outside the temple gates.

"Have you said prayers enough?" said the small, neat-bearded Derzhi gentleman who lingered at my side after placing his own flowers on the third altar stone.

"Enough," I said.

"Then, let us be quick." He took my arm companionably, though with a quite firm grip that steered me toward a dark alcove between two of the altars. "And this woman who has been following you . . . ?"

"She's with me," I said, gritting my teeth. "Harmless. On my life."

"As you say. My dagger will watch and judge. You have a quarter hour, no more."

Before I could thank him, Hazzire fixed his attention on a mural that depicted Druya's mysterious cave deep in the fiery bowels of the earth. I stepped into the alcove, feeling Fiona slip quietly in behind me. A tall figure in pale blue silk hovered in the shadowed nook. Her shining hair was piled high, the red curls tamed into a queenly knot, exposing the long graceful curve of a neck no sculptor could duplicate. From the quivering tensions in the air, I knew the worst.

"Seyonne! You are mad to come here."

"Your Highness." I genuflected, but she did not offer me her hand, the slender hand so deceptively fine-boned and soft—I had watched the lady throw enough furniture in a half hour's distress to leave a man-high heap of broken sticks.

"Kiril was here a fortnight ago. I couldn't believe the things he told us." When I stood up again, her fiery green eyes, at a level with my own, were demanding to know why she should give hearing to one guilty of treachery to her beloved lord. "Aleksander has been beside himself for weeks, punishing himself for letting you go into such danger, for hurting you so badly, grieving that you suffered yet again for him. Then to find out you had betrayed him so wickedly . . . and how it was done . . . his horses . . . Have you the least idea what you've done?"

"My lady, I swear to you, there is an explanation. I am not blameless . . ." The demands of those green eyes would not allow me to pretend otherwise. ". . . but on my soul I have not conspired to harm the Prince. If his need required it, I would do again everything that is past, even to wearing his chains. If we had time, I would tell you all."

She shook her head. "Telling me accomplishes nothing. You know well enough how little words or wishes can change the ways of the world. Why have you come?" She flicked a suspicious glance to the white-shrouded Fiona, but I was not going to waste the precious time with introductions.

"I need to know the whereabouts of the man named Balthar."

The lady's rosy complexion faded, and her lip curled. "Balthar . . . of the slave rites?" Lydia was a longtime opponent of slavery.

"Yes."

"So this is about vengeance? I thought you above—"

"There is no human vengeance fit for this man; the gods must take care of such crimes. But I must discover what he knows of matters of grave concern to my people. Please, my lady, he may have knowledge of such importance . . ." How could I explain my fears, my questioning, the complexities of sorcery and worlds and history, of nobility of spirit doomed to madness? It would take five hours.

"It is for Seyonne's son, lady, a child born demon-afflicted." Fiona had slipped off her white veil and stared quite boldly at the tall Princess. "You understand that Ezzarians are hesitant to speak of such personal matters."

I wanted to choke Fiona. What idiocy had prompted her to make a revelation so fraught with risk?

"Your son!" Lydia's astonished glance shot from Fiona to me and back again. "Then, you are Seyonne's wife, the Queen who helped—"

"No." Fiona and I answered together.

"Hsst, Your Highness!" Hazzire swept into the alcove and took Lydia's arm. "There is a disturbance outside the temple."

"Forgive me, my lady," I said, grabbing Fiona and pulling away. I, too, heard the shouts and noise at the temple gates. "I would not have you compromised."

But for a moment Lydia stood her ground against her nervous steward, fixing her gaze on my face as if locking my image in her mind for later dissection. "The answer will be at the Gasserva Fountain at midnight."

"My lady, there is but one other way out of the temple." The dapper Hazzire was about to burst.

"I'll see she has time," I said. "Hold at the rear door until all goes dark." Before the words were out of my mouth, the Princess and her guardian were gone, and I shoved Fiona farther into the alcove, where a deep niche in the stonework made a hiding place just large enough for a child or a very small woman. "Stay here, out of the way, but be ready to run."

"Where are you, traitor?" Aleksander's anger bounced off the walls of the temple as if the majestic bull itself had set to roaring. "Coward! Deceiver!" The ordinary worshipers scurried away in shock and dismay. "And where is the one you came here to meet? What spell have you cast to turn her against me?"

I could not allow him to search for Lydia or to harm innocents in his rage. "I am here, my lord," I said, dodging behind one pillar and then another as I spoke, swiping at the bells to set up echoes and distractions. "I did indeed seek audience with an intermediary, hoping to plead my case with you. Hoping you would listen to one you cannot doubt, as you find yourself doubting me."

"Where is she? How dare you invade my household with your treachery?"

"She has refused me, my lord, and returned to tell you of it. She says I must submit myself to your judgment first." Lies came easier these days. And he couldn't see my face go yellow as he always claimed it did when I tried to deceive him. "And so I must beg your grace—"

"Do not beg anything from me!" His boots rang on the floor tiles as he strode through the columns, hunting me, searching, not with melydda, but with pure warrior's instinct. "All your talk of faith, of honor, of light and darkness . . . was it always a lie? Face me and say these things again, and let me applaud your art."

I shifted my senses, straining to hear. "No, keep them back," he said quietly to someone close by him. "I want everyone out of here. We have no idea what all he can do. And, Sovari"—I heard the unmistakable sound of a sword unsheathed—"if you find my wife . . ."

"I'll be discreet, my lord."

Soon the soft footsteps fell away, and there was only one Derzhi left anywhere close inside the temple—the one with the drawn sword. I closed my eyes and called up a wind to douse the candles. His steps halted when the darkness fell. I wished the Lady Lydia quick and silent feet.

"You can do whatever magics you wish, Seyonne, but one of us will take you. You will not live to betray me again." He was only a few steps away. Close enough that we could speak in normal voices, though I kept moving slowly between the columns, silencing the bells beside me or sending a wind to ring those farther away to keep him at a distance.

"My lord, will you not give me hearing?"

"I've listened too much. And do you know what I've heard? The story of how the Yvor Lukash and his rabble came near taking the Emperor's horses, and how a sorcerer toyed with my warriors and left two dead and one crippled. My nobles say that a man who cannot secure his own horses, cannot secure his own empire." His footsteps grew closer, and his voice grew harder. I heard the sound of flint and steel, and soon a torch blazed no more than ten paces from my position. "Some say this outlaw sorcerer is the same who invaded the castle of one of my barons and slew an unarmed warrior, and perhaps the same who stole my tax money in Vayapol not long after. Some say it is one who fights with more skill than the Lidunni Brotherhood, and I have seen only one man who can do such a thing. And I have heard that a man I trusted with my soul . . . one to whom I gave my friendship and such honor as I have given no other . . . has painted his face with daggers and made mockery of me. Is this the story you wish to tell? Or do you maintain the lie you told me at Dasiet Homol—that you are not one of them?"

"If you would but—"

"Druya, bear witness to my empty head . . . I believed you. Never again, Seyonne. Come out and tell me your story. But this time bring your sword with you."

I grieved to hear his rage and hurt. The ties that bound Aleksander and me were deeper than vows or kinship, more precious to me than my own life. But I could not assuage his wounding without explaining everything—if it was possible even then—and this was not the time to tell him of Blaise. Too much pride was involved. Too much suspicion. I had to find a way to keep the young outlaw alive and well. Only then could I consider how to make his peace—and mine—with Aleksander. "I'll not ask you to trust me, my lord. I know how hollow such words ring when the wound is so great. I understand—"

"Understand? Half of the Twenty Hegeds have called a meeting one month hence, and they have summoned me . . . *summoned me* . . . to attend them and explain what I am doing about the rebels. Do you *understand* what that means?"

I knew. Humiliation. And there was only one way for a Derzhi warrior to recoup such a loss of respect. War. Things were far worse than I had imagined, but I had no answer for him. "If it would help you set things right, I would yield to you, my lord. But my death—even if you make it a spectacle—will not solve your problems. Nor will making war on your own people, no matter how much your barons demand it. Stall them. Convince them. No one reads the hearts of men as you do. When your temper cools, you will remember why we cannot hide our truth from each other. You know me as no other man or woman in this world knows me. Give me time, and I'll show you how to end this rebellion. I swear to you."

"I have no time left. And neither have you." Aleksander then dismissed any lingering illusion that I could convince him of my good intentions. "I will not take back the gifts I have given, but you will never enjoy them, Ezzarian. I have issued a judgment of treason against the Yvor Lukash and his riders. I will take them, they will die, and their deaths will be on your head. And likewise any man, woman, or child who gives aid to the Yvor Lukash, who feeds, houses, heals or clothes any one of you, will be held traitor to the Empire and will die a traitor's death."

"My lord, please—"

"As for you, if you take one step to return to the land of your birth, your people will be held as your accomplices, and I will burn Ezzaria with such fires as no sorcerer can quench."

My blood turned to ice. I could scarcely answer. "No fear of that. They'll not have me back." But to have the choice removed . . . Even with my knowledge of Aleksander, I had underestimated his anger.

The Prince's voice fell to a quiet that was far more deadly than his fury. And his words were wrenching in a way no bluster could match. "I once thought that this 'shunning' your people practice was a coward's way of punishment. Now at last I understand it. Sometimes you cannot bear to see the ugly truth of something you believed was good. But I am a hardheaded Derzhi, and I must follow my own way. So you can surrender and stand trial with your friends, or you can fight me and die here. That is the only choice that remains to you. Surrender or die." His warrior's skills were not honed with melydda, but they were very good. He was no more than five steps away from me, and he knew very well where I was.

"I'm sorry, my lord. I can do neither one right now." I swept my hand in a circle, and an explosion of fire swept through the temple, setting every bell to jangling and tinkling until one might think an earthquake had set up housekeeping inside the place. I ran for the alcove, but Fiona was already ahead of me. We streaked for the back exit, hiding behind a pillar as Aleksander's soldiers ran to his rescue. While they were still blinded by the brilliance of the light and distracted by the cacophony of the bells, we ran right past them into the night, and we didn't stop until we were deep in the poorest quarter of the capital city.

"He thinks he still owns you," said Fiona as we slowed down at last, doing our best to disappear into the crowds of beggars, drunkards, slavers, thieves, and whores who plied the dusty streets.

I could not answer her. My head was reeling from strong enchantment and sick fury—at myself, at Aleksander and his hotheaded pride, at Blaise and his foolish idealism, at a world in which I had failed everyone I loved.

In the sickly light of sputtering torches, gaunt-faced women haggled with each other over diseased goats or bony chickens, while dirty-faced children clung to their skirts. A toothless Frythian beckoned to us to join in an alleyway game of ulyat—the prize a ragged, trembling girl of ten. "For work or pleasure," he said. "Not hardly touched as yet." I shoved the pawing man away, scarcely controlling the urge to stick a knife in him.

Fiona pulled me away. "You're not safe until you get out of this vile city."

"He won't hurt me." I clung to the thread of belief.

"He sounded quite serious about it."

"I know him better than he knows himself." But not well enough to expect he would turn against me so absolutely.

"You're an idiot."

"Indeed." A chill wind had risen up off the desert, and Fiona was shivering. She had already stripped off her white robes to make us harder to follow, and was wearing only her breeches and a thin shirt. I rummaged through a pile of old clothes laid out on the street beside a flint-eyed old woman, and found a ragged cloak that smelled vaguely of sheep and a short jacket of purple wool with an ominously dark-stained rip in the back of it. I gave Fiona the jacket while I donned the cloak. Though I could not believe Aleksander would harm me, I had no such illusion about his anger at the Yvor Lukash. "And now you should go home. Hide your face and get as far away from me as quickly as you can manage." Ezzarians were already at risk of enslavement, and if I had to show my paper to avoid capture, anyone with me would be judged as aiding the Yvor Lukash. And then she would be dead. Painfully and slowly.

"What of the lady's promise?"

The dilemma, of course. I needed to find Balthar. Now that I was forbidden to return to Ezzaria, I had no ready alternatives. But I could not risk involving the Princess any further. "I'll find some other way to get the information. Now, go and don't stop. If you stay and the Derzhi don't kill you, I promise you I will."

But my watchdog would not leave it. "She'll send a messenger. If I were to meet him, there would be no connection with you or the Yvor Lukash. I am not one of them. The Prince himself knows that."

"Too risky. I won't let you." I started across the miserable lane toward an alehouse, but Fiona shoved me backward until my back was against the wall of the alley.

"Won't let me? And since when have you become my protector?" Before I could answer, the city watch began to call the midnight hour. "Wait here. I'll be back before you can close your mouth."

"But you don't even know—"

"I know how to find the Gasserva Fountain. As it happens, I once killed someone there." With that, she disappeared into the crowd.

I shrank into the alleyway and wondered if I would ever see Fiona again. For the first time since I'd met her, I hoped I would.

CHAPTER 18

I left a trail of blood-streaked snow as I dragged myself toward the icebound castle. The sharp edges of the ice sliced through the deadness of my bare hands and feet. Still too far. The darkness would consume me long before I could get inside. As I forced another breath into frosted lungs, the majestic gates swung open and issued forth a host of the shimmering wraiths. In awe I watched them ride, tall and straight and proud, across the luminescent bridge, flickering in and out of the realm of my seeing as they moved through the pelting sleet. Beautiful. Dangerous. A rider at the front of the column led a white horse, decked out in black and silver trappings—a riderless horse, huge, powerful, and spirited. The wraith army wound through the gloom, farther and farther from me, until, at the very limits of my sight, they came upon a figure dressed in black and silver, a man standing alone in the swirling storm. He was the sovereign of that storm, the master of any land he walked. He wore power, strength, and danger with the same magnificence as his garments of silver and black. As the man mounted the riderless horse, I cried out a warning, for I knew the rider was born of the same darkness that was creeping into my frozen soul, and that the cold fire gnawing at my entrails was his work. But no matter how I screamed in pain and desperation, the wraiths could not hear me over the wild wind. And no matter how I tried, I could not see the dark rider's face.

"When are you going to tell me what's happening?" The strained voice from behind me dragged me back yet again. "Bad enough you scream in your sleep, now you sit here with your eyes rolled back in your head, looking like you're going to keel over dead right here in this filthy boat. If you think to leave me drown, why don't you just push me over the side?"

"Sorry." I caught my breath and dragged at the oars. The flimsy craft of leather stretched over thin spars had started a slow spin and was almost broadside to the current, the dark green water lapping eagerly over the low sides.

"So what is it?"

"Maybe I'll explain it when you tell me who you killed at the Gasserva Fountain."

"I don't have to tell you anything."

So I didn't tell her of the dream that was again creeping into my waking hours. Worse than before. More urgent. More frightening. The black and silver lord who stood waiting in the storm . . . his power and his danger froze my blood.

"I never heard of this place," she said. "Why ever would anyone live on an island? Makes it nasty difficult for visitors."

I bent my back to the oars, pushing against the strong current, and wondered yet again if Fiona had been born solely as an instrument for the gods to punish my multitudinous sins. There was not a horse but was a bucking demon to her, not a turn in the road that was anything but crooked, not a day that was not too hot or too cold or too windy or too wet, and certainly not an action that I could take that was not too hasty, too slow, cowardly, or ill considered. Since the night she had returned with the information that Balthar lived alone on an island in the Sajer River, she had not been silent for the span of ten heartbeats in any hour I was awake. For all I knew, her complaining might continue while I slept. Perhaps she talked so much in hopes I would forget what she had said about killing someone by the Gasserva Fountain in her days as a gleaner.

Gleaners were the thieves Talar had sent into the cities during the years of Derzhi rule, to steal the things the Ezzarians hidden in the forest needed for survival, but could neither grow nor make nor find. Gleaning was fraught with danger, the gleaners at constant risk of enslavement. Those who survived became very good at spying and subterfuge. No wonder Fiona was so capable. The strangest part was that Fiona had ever found herself in Zhagad. What would have taken Ezzarian gleaners into the heart of the Empire?

I gave her plenty of opportunities to tell me about the incident at Gasserva, thinking she must have mentioned it for a purpose. But in all the leagues we traveled from Zhagad and all the words that passed through her lips as we rode, I learned nothing more of her past. Now we were about to beard the despicable Balthar in his den, and my watchdog would still not leave off either her watching or her talking. "Do the clouds ever lift from this miserable river? Three days since we turned north at Passile, and we've not seen the sun even once."

"Just row, Fiona. I want to get this over with." The closer we got to Balthar, the less sense the visit made. Why would such a detestable wretch tell anything of importance? He had shown himself willing to destroy Ezzarians for his revenge, and even if he had found the answer to the demon births in all his searching, he'd not been willing to share it with the rest of us. He'd not come running back to save anyone else's children.

Fiona and I had traveled west and north from Zhagad, keeping to ourselves, using the last of the wine merchant's reward to buy supplies and a chastou for the desert crossing. Once into the hilly sheep country north of Basran, we sold the chastou at the market town of Passile, and made inquiries until we learned of a bargeman who had a boat to rent. Unfortunately, we were left with a long day's row across a lake and a short stretch upstream to Balthar's island. We could have waited for one of the regular merchant barges that carried cargo across the lake into the western Empire. For a price they would drop us and our little boat near the mouth of the Sajer, but barges were often used by slavers, and eyes were already taking note of Fiona's Ezzarian features. I dared not let myself be seen in Passile after Fiona heard soldiers talking about the Prince's new edicts concerning the Yvor Lukash. We wanted to be out of the place before anyone decided that there might be some reward bound up in our skins.

The dream had plagued me during all our traveling, worse every day. As we rowed toward Fallatiel, I could scarcely hold two thoughts together.

Though it was sometime in mid-afternoon, the light was almost gone. Thick gray mist swirled about us, leaving a damp film on skin and clothing, packs and oars. The afternoon was cool, but my limp hair was pasted to my face, and I could not tell whether the droplets that rolled down my neck were rain or sweat. I was steering by sound more than sight, listening for the break in the current where the river curved west and split, skirting the island of Fallatiel.

On the western side of the island, so the bargeman had told us, we would find an inlet and a strip of sand and shingle suitable for landing. Once a year a supply of salt, flour, oil, candles, and other such items was left there, though to his knowledge no one had ever seen the resident of the island. Someone in Zhagad sent payment, but he didn't know who.

"Ease off a bit," I said. The plopping and gurgling of water warned us of the rocks, and soon two giant shapes loomed out of the mist. "There are the boulders we were told of. We should be able to steer a little to the right and let the current carry us onto the shore."

A short time later I was able to wade through the shallows and haul the boat onto the small crescent of sand. A kingfisher sat brooding on an overhanging limb, waiting to plunge into the river to catch his supper. A flock of swallows gibbered at us and fluttered about in the mist, disturbed from their evening's roosting in the rocks surrounding the landing spot.

"Hello!" I called. The fog muffled my cry, so I wasn't surprised when no one answered. "Let's walk up. I'm not going to stand here and wait for him to come down and invite us in." I brushed the damp sand from my feet and pulled on my boots that I had removed to haul in the boat, while Fiona dragged our vessel well away from the water's edge and tied it to a clump of willows.

A narrow track led up from the beach between the giant boulders and into a thick forest of hemlock, spruce, and pine. Birds shrieked at us as we passed, and small creatures skittered under the blackberry vines that grew thickly under the trees. "Hello," I called again.

We wandered for a quarter of an hour, finding no sign of habitation, only more trees, more rocks, and more birds.

I began to wonder if we'd been misdirected. But then I sensed movement behind us and touched Fiona's arm in warning. "It's only reasonable that he would be shy of strangers from Ezzaria," I said loud enough to be heard at a distance. "He has no way of knowing we've only come for information."

"I've heard he is our only true scholar in these matters," said Fiona, catching my intent. "It would be a shame to miss . . . oh!" She stopped short at the top of a climb that I thought must surely take us to the high point of the island. But before us on the crest of the next rise stood a ruin—five pairs of tall, graceful columns standing like ghostly couples in the foggy evening, ready to take up a dance suspended for only a moment. The wooden roof had long rotted away, but the elegant curves of the carved stone lintels were still visible, some in place atop the columns, some through the heavy growth of berry thicket and flowering vines where they had fallen.

I had seen a number of the ancient builders' ruins—all of them lovely and well designed, hinting at a culture of refinement and intellect. Everything my mother had tried to teach me of artistry, of proportion and balance, symmetry, and grace was exemplified in their stonework. But never had I seen one of their structures so complete or of this precise shape. This could be the archetype for every Ezzarian temple, though after seeing both, one would never mistake the small, crude imitations for the glorious original. Someone of my ancestors had seen this place and found in its simple harmonies a model for the work we did—seeking wholeness for human minds—and they had built its replicas all through our own lands. How ironic to discover it just when I had come to believe that we ourselves were broken.

In the tree-flanked hollow between our position and the ruined temple was a rectangular pool, its stonework borders still intact, tendrils of mist rising from the dark, unmoving surface of the water. In eerie unison, Fiona and I walked down the almost invisible path to the pool, bent over, and peered into the water. What we expected, I could not have said, but it was certainly not what we saw in the reflection. For peeking out from between our shoulders was a merry face . . . round cheeks, small mouth, two bright black eyes,

slightly angled, and a short fringe of white hair on a bald
skull.

"Do you see anything in there? I've looked quite a number of times over the years, but I've never seen anything
interesting. Water. Stars. Wind. Myself. I'm sure there must
be something to see, else why would it beckon us
to stop and take a look." He looked from one to the other
of us. "Do I know you?"

I popped up and spun on my heels, relieved to find a
very solid figure standing behind us, not some specter observing us from the pool. "We've come here to see. . . ."
I looked at the cheerful, clear-eyed old man, scarcely taller
than Fiona, and I could not make myself believe he was
the monster.

"Don't say the name if it bothers you. Or say it as you
please. I don't worry about it anymore. And, of course,
there's no one about, so I don't hear it so often as I once
did. Sometimes I come near forgetting it, and that indeed
might be a fine thing. Names carry so much baggage."

A man who can prattle so ingenuously while carrying
such a burden of horror, death, and madness . . . the worst
kind of monster. Awash in purest loathing, I passed the
back of my hand across my eyes. With a full focusing of
melydda, I examined him for demon infestation, but I saw
only a ragged little man with stringy white hair whose wide
brow was crumpling into a frown. He flinched as if he could
feel the assault of my seeing.

"Not a friendly guest. Not at all. And you"—he cocked
his head at Fiona—"not quite so terrible as your companion. You dislike this business altogether, but you are curious at least. His hand can scarcely keep from his knife. My
first visitors in ever so long, and I'm like to end up dead
from it." He sighed. "Can't say as I mind."

He clasped his hands behind his back—he was wearing
some kind of shapeless gray gown—and strolled around the
pool, peering into it as if checking again that there was
nothing to be seen there. After a moment, he looked back.
"You can come, of course. I'll show you where everything's
kept, then you can kill me or not as you please."

He took a few more steps. Neither Fiona nor I had
moved. "I've been waiting all these years, you see. And no

one's come. I couldn't leave, for no one would believe me without seeing, so there wasn't much point in it. But someday, I thought, someday they will send someone. I knew what you would look like. A Warden, I have no doubt. I can smell your melydda, it is so strong in you. Taste it. Myself, I never had so much that anyone could sense it without probing. Quite mediocre always. What glory you must have known, and yet . . . well, that will come, if you are patient before the killing. Come. There's a fire and spiced wine—I always have them send me wine. Two casks to last me the year. They'll send anything I ask, but I don't ask anymore. Just let them send what they've always sent. Easier, you know."

He shook his head and stepped between one pair of the pillars. "Well, come on. Anyone would think you were a pair of these." He slapped his hand on the pillar, chuckled softly, and disappeared into the temple.

Once the spell of his odd rambling was broken, the two of us moved to follow him. We did not speak. What could be said of such absolute reversal of expectation? Ours and his. He thought we were there to kill him . . . which I had always feared that I would do if I were ever to confront the villain . . . and in truth we were there to hear his story . . . which it seemed was exactly what he wanted.

The steps of the temple were broken, thick green vines poking up through the cracks, but the floor within the ring of pillars was smooth and undamaged from what I could see. A tidy fire crackled in the fire pit, hot—no smoke at all—and a copper pot hung over it. The air was redolent with hot wine and cloves. I stood by the fire and let it heat my damp clothes, but when the old man offered me a cup of his wine, I refused it. "I did not come here to drink with you."

"No. No, I can see not." He was staring at the burn scar on my face, where Aleksander's enemy had branded me with the slave mark of the Derzhi royal house. "You must be an extraordinary man. You have been through the Rites, yet retain your melydda. Would I could persuade you to tell me how you did it." With a deep sigh, Balthar turned and offered the cup to Fiona. She glanced at me, then took the cup and held it close, letting the fragrant steam wreathe her face. She was so thin that the chill affected her quickly. I had no skill to test the drink for poisons. I hoped she had.

Balthar poked another stick on his fire and twitched his fingers. Instantly the stick burst into hot clean flame, burning away the gloom that was encroaching on the temple. A splash of color caught my eye, bright red and blue from the floor beyond the fire pit. Mosaic. Just as in our own temples. I had never seen evidence of floor mosaics in the other ruins I had visited. Perhaps they had been destroyed with so much else, or perhaps it was only in this kind of structure they would make them. What had they used this place for? Likely not for walking souls.

"Go ahead and look at it," said Balthar. "It's taken me a very long time to put it back together."

"We've not come to look at ruins," I said. "Nor to kill you. Only to seek knowledge of rai-kirah."

The old man continued poking at the fire and rearranging his copper pot. "What would you learn of demons? Surely you've not found the scrolls inadequate after so long." He chuckled as he poured himself a mug of wine. I would have been offended at his sarcasm if I had not borne my own growing disdain for Ezzarian scholarship.

"Two matters," I said, approaching what I believed the easier one first. "You once studied a demon encounter where the Warden—a man named Pendyrral—claimed the demon was of a different nature than the usual."

Balthar did not turn, but his hands fell still. "Yes."

"Someone else . . . I . . . experienced a similar encounter. I need to understand it."

He turned his moonlike face upward. "And it made you so desperate as to bring you to Balthar the Devil. What did you think after it happened? Did you think yourself corrupt?"

"I don't believe in corruption." I was surprised at myself. I had never voiced the sentiment quite so bluntly, even in thought.

Balthar slapped his knee and laughed uproariously. "Of all the things I never expected. You have confounded me right here at the beginning. Have Ezzarian mentors forgotten their discipline? Are our Wardens now permitted to agree or disagree as they choose?"

"I believe in evil—I've seen too much to disregard it—just not in corruption that floats in the water or creeps up through cracks in the floor."

"You believe that I am evil."

"Yes. I've seen . . . I have lived . . . your legacy."

"How can you keep your sword sheathed, then? If I am evil, then you would do the world a service by removing me." He spread his arms out wide. "Or is it that I serve some purpose . . . some balance like that which holds us from destroying the rai-kirah?" These words were not spoken casually, but wrought with care and gilded with profound mystery.

The whispers of my dreams tickled my ears, and a frosty breath sighed down my neck. The scene before me wavered for a moment like sheets hung to dry in the wind. "I need to get away from here," I said, throwing up my hands and retreating to the temple steps where I tried to get a lungful of the heavy air. Suddenly I seemed incapable of sensible conversation. I wasn't sure what I was doing there. I couldn't remember the questions we had come to ask.

Fiona took up the challenge and explained the case. "The demon this Warden encountered claimed it was welcomed by its host, an artist who had given up family, friends, and a lucrative contract to decorate a local castle. He preferred to paint pictures of flowers. When questioned, the Searcher verified that the claims of madness were made by the victim's wife and other acquaintances who saw no value in the man's pursuits. The wife was a wealthy woman who had borne the man nine children. She had used her father's influence to get her husband the castle contract. The victim displayed all the signs of demon-possession, save that of deliberate taste for evil—unless one counts abandoning his wife as deliberate evil. The wife certainly did."

"And what was the nature of the encounter?" Balthar reflected Fiona's matter-of-fact tone.

She told him of my experience, almost word for word as I had told it to the Mentors Council, though she had not even been in the room. And the other information . . . where had she found it? I stared at her narrow face and wondered if I knew the young woman at all.

"A Nevai . . ." Balthar said to me in wonder. "You've drawn out a Nevai. What are you?"

"He said nothing of—"

"He spoke of the Gastai, the 'brutes' he called them—yes, yes—and the Rudai—they are called the 'shapers,' though of what I don't know—and he referred to the 'rest of us,' which names him a Nevai, one of the inner circle, the most powerful of their kind."

"How do you know of these things?" said Fiona. "I've read no such lore."

But Balthar's full attention was on me. "You dream now, do you? Ah, yes, I see it in your face. You dream, but you believe it is not dream. Pendyrral had dreams. He died without learning what they meant." Balthar's finger tapped his chin rapidly. "What was the second matter you wished to learn of?"

"The children," said Fiona harshly, before I could answer. "The children born like yours were born. Demon children."

The old man nodded until his whole body was rocking slowly. I would not have been surprised if he had started chewing his knuckles and moaning like Saetha. But he was quite composed when he answered. "I suspected as much. Only logical. 'The man has sired two of them,' you say, 'and if he has learned anything, he must have learned what caused him to commit crimes of such horror that his name will ever be the very name of sin.' Is that not the reasoning?"

So simple, so quiet was the echo of profound sorrow in his words that I almost missed it.

"For two years I searched for the answer, after my daughter was born and murdered. I read and studied every writing. I read the journals of the Wardens, the journals of the Searchers. Did you know there were at least three more such encounters? And those just in the past hundred years. Before that . . . who knows how many went unreported or were excised from the records? It would have been seen as evidence of corruption. Only in the recent past have we felt it reasonable to keep the written record as complete as possible."

He was talking faster and faster, then shook his head as

if to cool his rising eagerness. "I went back to Pendyrral and begged him to tell me again about his encounter, for I wondered if by some chance my child could have been held by such a demon. Yes, I see you have wondered the same about the children." He peered at me again, curiously, then went on. "But Pendyrral had already told me everything he could. At last I decided to try to find the woman herself—the victim who carried this kind of demon. But I couldn't locate her. It had been too long. Instead I found myself at the place where the Searcher and Comforter had taken the woman to link her to Pendyrral and his Aife."

He looked up and waved his hand at the ghostly columns around us. "One of these ruins. Built by a people so ancient no mention is made of them in any written history. It had been a square building of some kind and was overgrown with weeds and trees. The walls and floors were rubble, the tiles of the roof scattered and crushed so that even the poorest of the local people could not glean anything useful from the place. Scarcely anything left at all save the melydda. So much power, always around these ruins. Why did we never investigate them more thoroughly?"

"They are none of our concern," said Fiona. "Our business is the war."

"Ah, yes. The demon war. Protecting the world from the horror of demons. Our noble sacrifice. Our entire purpose for being. Did you never wonder why?" Balthar's eyes glittered like black gems in the firelight.

"So tell us what you learned," I said, refusing to be drawn in by his excitement. "What enlightenment was given you?"

Balthar came to where I stood by the steps of the temple looking out upon the fog. "No enlightenment. What I found that day was only a fragment. A beginning. I dropped my knife, you see. I was trying to cut an apple, but my hands were shaking because I was weeping. I had found no answers. I dropped my knife into a pile of rubble, and I had to scrabble through the pile—crumbled bits from an inner wall—to find it. But this is what I found." From his shirt he pulled a piece of cord that was tied about his neck, and from the cord hung a bit of gray stone about half the size of my palm. On the ancient bit of stone was etched the figure of a man with wings . . . the very same figure that was sketched on the Ezzarian Scroll of Prophecy . . . the very same figure that could be the image of myself as I transformed beyond the portal. I stared at it uncomprehending, teetering on the edge of revelation. An image from Ezzarian lore scribed on the walls of the builders . . .

Balthar did not give me time to sort it out, but dragged me along as relentlessly as the Sajer current. "For two years I searched every ruin from Parnifour to Karesh, and the first thing I discovered was that there was nothing to be found. No drawings of the ones who built the places, no paintings, no writings that anyone could translate. Everything had been destroyed. Everything. Why? Was there a war against these builders? A grudge of such long-standing that every relic of their life had to be obliterated at once?"

The night air had me shivering, though there was no trace of frost in the river valley. Balthar took me by the arm and drew me toward the splashes of blue and red that gleamed in the firelight.

"It was years later that I found this place. After my second child was born a demon and destroyed, I was in the throes of madness and lust for vengeance, and for a long time all I did with what I found was create the horror that you know—my legacy to the world. But as the years passed, I pieced together the true tale. I came to see that what I was and what I had done was small beside the sin of our race, and that the gods had sent us these demon-devoured children as just punishment. Look down," he said. "Read the history of our people as I have learned it, then tell me which one of us is better than the other."

The mosaic was not complete. Hand-sized holes and gaps were littered with crumbled bits of stone and mortar. And it was not a true mosaic, where the images are created solely from the bits of colored stone. Instead the patterns were etched and painted on larger tiles, which had been broken into tiny fragments and pieced back together again. But spread before us was a story that covered half the floor and that drew me to my knees to examine it.

Set into a background of red and blue were thousands of fragments, none bigger than my thumb, bits of line and color that created a pageant of shapes: men with wings, women with the bodies of horses, children transforming into birds and deer and foxes, life in a forest of towering trees and graceful-columned structures like that in which I knelt. A life of sorcery and mystery. Around the borders were tiles that formed words and symbols, but they could not draw my eye from the pictures. All of the figures had black hair, bronze skin, and slightly angled eyes. Ezzarians. I was drowned in wonder.

Fully half of the images seemed to be a depiction of everyday life. Large and small drawings of every kind of activity were crammed together as if the artist kept remembering more that he wanted to show and squeezed it into a painting that was already complete: eating, sleeping, washing, spinning, growing and harvesting, braiding hair, building houses and temples, playing music. Starting somewhere in the middle just beyond a large gap, the story became more precise. From the left to the right in square after square of carefully constructed evidence, I saw a group of men and women—five of them who were the same from picture to picture—performing some elaborate ritual, with fire and smoke and music, with knives and mirrors. A larger group of men, women, and children stood nearby. All of them were horrifically afraid, their hands gripping each other, their eyes hidden or closed or scarcely daring to watch what was coming to pass. In each succeeding panel of the story, a shape appeared slightly larger than the one before, an ominous smudge that might have been the symbol of storm or plague or any number of terrors. It took form only in the final picture. In that one, the group of five stood before the others, their heads bowed, tears drawn on their cheeks, their hands lifted in a clear display of horror, shame, and fear. And just beyond the two groups the formless mass had become a third group . . . monstrous shapes that had lived in my memory since I was seventeen and first encountered one of them . . . demons, held at bay only by the same knives and mirrors used in the rituals. I could not comprehend all that was before me, but Balthar voiced the conclusion that had formed in my head as I gazed on the creation.

"You see, Warden. We are responsible. With our magics and our wonders, we ourselves created the demons."

CHAPTER 19

"How could you possibly think such a thing?" Fiona was standing just behind me, yelling at Balthar. "Even if this mess meant anything, it's not complete. You've got holes all over it."

"Twenty-seven years it's taken me to get this far, and I don't know that I can do more. My eyes are not so good as they once were, and the tiles that remain are broken so badly, it's difficult to see any pattern on them. They were in the water for a while, you see, thrown in the river by those who destroyed the temple. I think the river must have changed course soon after, for few were lost or ruined. But that's a small part overall. No, it's all there. Easy to see. Very clear."

"But you can't be sure what it means. How could you know?"

"Don't you see, girl? They came and destroyed the evidence of their own crimes. When they saw what they had unleashed on the world, they could not allow others—ordinary folk—to know. They . . . we . . . had to remedy our mistake. We declared war on our own creation, and we have lived with our guilt every day for a thousand years. And if we think to forget, the gods send us the children to remind us—our own children possessed by the evil we have done. I found the answer."

"You can't know all this."

Fiona's denial rang hollow. Of course, Balthar was right. The knife in the picture was the image of the knife I used to slay demons. The mirror was oval, the size of a hand. Was the one holding it Luthen himself? And the one singing, was she Ioreth? The origin of the demons was Ezzarian sorcery. There was no denying it.

And the rest of it . . . I brushed my hand across the winged figures and felt the burning in my shoulders, the craving in my belly, the aching emptiness in my chest. What had happened to us? "You're wrong in at least one thing," I said, my voice tight with hunger. "The children could not be our punishment. What we suffer is not half of what they must endure, and we don't even see it, for we kill them or send them away." I could remember the expression on Blaise's face as he folded his arms and became the thing that was a part of him. It was not pain or discord, captivity or possession, but purest joy. I could recognize it only because amid the rubble of my life of violence, I had been fortunate enough to experience a few moments of it. Blaise's stillness was a perfection of peace, of completion that I could not imagine. Only the end he faced was terrible.

"What do you know of it? Nothing." Balthar shouted so loud that a flock of chittering sparrows rose from the nearby trees in a gray cloud. "The children would have destroyed us. We were right to destroy them first. I hate it, but that was the way it had to be. Our punishment was the necessity to kill them for what we'd done."

Of course Balthar resented my inference that his theories were incomplete. But he couldn't know. He had never met Blaise.

While I tried to piece together the mosaic of my experiences, Fiona tried to outshout the old man. She argued all the points of Ezzarian tradition—that the demons were only a force of nature, not evil in themselves, that it was only our gift for sorcery that obligated us to oppose them. Nothing in our writings laid blame upon us. But the very incompleteness of Ezzarian evidence left her hanging; she could not tell another story, for we didn't have one. So she fell back on telling Balthar about Blaise and Saetha and demanding to know how his theories explained them. Balthar called her a liar and me worse. I couldn't blame him. If he believed that demon-possessed children could grow up whole and undamaged, then his carefully built accommodation with his own children's death was shattered. But I had no pity to spare for Balthar.

"You are both fools," said Fiona furiously, almost stomping her feet on the colored tiles. "You, old man—murderer,

slaver—you've invented this perversion from your own evil.
You're trying to redeem your sins by pretending there's
something worse. And you"—her glare was hot on my
head—"you are rank with corruption. Your sight is clouded
by your own impurity. I won't believe either of you."

"I do not deny my crimes," said Balthar, spluttering and
stumbling over his words. "But you . . . willfully . . . stupidly
blind. It's just as I expected. Because you didn't see it first.
Because the despised Balthar found it. The mosaic could
reveal that the sky is blue, and Ezzarians would deny it.
How could I ever have thought to teach any of you anything? If there were harder truths . . . more terrible things
to know . . . what would you do then, eh? You would slay
me before I had a chance to tell."

They continued yelling at each other until I wanted to
scream at them to take their arguments elsewhere. The answers were floating around in my head, waiting to be captured if I could but find the right hook. If I could just get
peace enough to think.

On the upper left of the picture was a small frame depicting a young girl changing into a deer. With only a few
strokes of his brush, the artist had etched pain on her
face . . . pain that had endured a thousand years to tell me
something of truth. About her neck she wore an amulet in
the shape of three linked circles that allowed me to identify
her in more of the pictures. A woman laid a hand on the
girl. Comfort, enchantment . . . whatever it was, it had
eased the child's hurt. As I studied the complex images, I
came upon the girl again. Older. Still wearing her amulet.
Carrying on the same activities as the others: cooking, reading, writing, weaving. I looked further to see if she appeared again, and I found her repeatedly, sometimes shown
as a young woman, sometimes as a deer, sometimes as
other creatures, sometimes as a combination of woman and
beast—always marked with the three linked circles so I
knew it was the same woman. I saw her wed to a young
man who took the form of a bird. I saw her give birth to
a child.

Excited, I began to ignore the other images drawn and
etched on the tiles, hunting the single figure that might tell
me more. There, a tiny image out of proportion to those

surrounding it. The young woman, half changed into another form, pain and distress etched into her face and body,
was giving her child to her husband, and then—it was so
difficult to see, for the tile was cracked just beside—the
deer was shown inside a rectangular outline. A doorway?
I peered closer. The edges of the rectangle were rippled,
not straight, and within it were the faint outlines of
strangely shaped trees, unknown flowers, all blurred at the
edges. It was a portal. The familiar shape emerged from
the flat tiles as if an Aife had woven it. Frantically I
searched further. I needed to know what happened next. I
was almost up to the part about the magic and the demons,
and I was afraid that I would find nothing more of ordinary
life . . . but there . . . in a series of tiles just before the gap
and the square where we met the five sorcerers, there was
a small rectangle with the deer inside it. And again. And
again, tucked into the corners and backgrounds of every
square. *No, no, no. There must be another answer.* When I
was just at the point of frustration, I found her again.
Greeting her husband and child . . . a visibly older child.
She had come back from wherever she had gone beyond
the portal. A few more images . . . some in the deer form,
some in the human. No other anymore. But she was not
mad. Not trapped.

I sighed and sat back on my heels. The image offered no
immediate solution. And certainly it could signify a thousand possibilities. But hope. Surely it was hope.

Time had meandered on its way. I had not even noticed
that the arguing had stopped. A silent Balthar was messing
about with fire and food, while Fiona sat on the floor across
the mosaic, her chin on her knees, watching me. "And what
do you think you've learned from this ridiculous fakery?"
she said, in a far more even tone than I would have expected considering her earlier tirade. She seemed tired.

"Nothing but more questions," I said. "That we created
the demons is clear enough, but why do they affect Blaise
and his kind so differently than the rest of us? Is it the
demon drives them into madness or makes them stay a beast?
Or is it that they need . . . something . . . somewhere"—I
touched my finger to the image of the woman/deer entering
the portal—"that we don't know how or when or where to

give? All I've learned is that the shifting is a natural part of them, which one day's observation could tell anyone. We're the ones who are broken."

"You're as mad as he is." This time it was a quiet accusation. Almost friendly.

Balthar and Fiona had reached some accommodation, perhaps agreeing that they were both so stubbornly entrenched in their positions that it made no sense to discuss the matter any longer. My own limbs felt like lead, and when the old man brought us hard, dry bread and barley soup, I could not summon the will or the indignation to refuse him. The two of them talked only of mundane things while we ate: of river currents and game and the once-a-year delivery of supplies—the blood price provided by the Derzhi Magicians Guild. They had stepped back from the risky precipice we had trodden that evening, but I could not. My eyes and my thoughts never left the mosaic, tracing the outlines of the figures, trying to probe and penetrate their mystery and the thoughts of those who had created the images. When I had silenced the growling of my belly, I bent over the pictures once more until my eyes blurred and my musings circled upon themselves for the twentieth time. Then I wrapped my cloak about my shoulders and fell asleep, my hand resting on the puzzle.

The dream came again, of course. Even as I lived it repeatedly through the ensuing hours, I held enough conscious thought to wonder if it assaulted me with such intensity because I slept in a place exploding with melydda. I lived and died a hundred times that night, my limbs frozen, my longing unsatisfied, my eyes blinded, my breath choked with horror and darkness as I watched the one in black and silver take command of his legion. But when I woke to the dripping fog of morning, I knew the answer.

"Tell me, old man, what did Pendyrral dream of?" I shook Balthar awake from his mattress of dried leaves. It was difficult to keep from bruising the dazed old man in my anxiety. "And the others who had these encounters— what of them?"

"A castle," he mumbled. "Pendyrral dreamed of a castle in the snow and how he needed to get inside. Cathor, too—

he was one of the others. He wrote it down. Something the same. Odd that it was like. Fellyd disappeared after his encounter. Some said he went north."

"And there were beings who lived there . . . wraiths . . . beautiful, glorious beings who could not see him?"

"Yes. Yes. Pendyrral described them so." The old man sat up and scratched his head. "Why?"

Dreams . . . dreams of belonging. The craving to go inside that castle in the frozen wasteland. These rai-kirah had been trying to tell us something, to draw us closer. As my people had always feared, a demon had found a way to penetrate our minds . . . but not to fill it with fear and madness, but with wonder and hunger and the certainty that there were mysteries that we needed to unravel. But why? I could not believe it was only to lure us to destruction.

"Did Pendyrral feel the darkness devour him or did he see the wraiths leaving the castle, riding out to meet someone in the storm? Someone he believed—he knew—was everything of evil, immensely powerful, one whose very touch was destruction?"

Balthar screwed up his face. "No. I don't recall anything like that. Neither one of them. They feared the dreams, feared their desire to live them out. Not the beings in the dream, though. Not afraid of them at all. Pendyrral said they were beautiful."

Only the outsider was fearful in my dream, the darkness that consumed me when I could not go where I needed to go.

"Gods, it fits." I leaped to my feet and paced back and forth, my hands pulling at my hair as I reassembled the pieces I had put together in my dreaming. I had seen it so clearly. Pendyrral and Cathor had not understood, because they didn't know Blaise.

Fiona walked up the steps out of the foggy morning. "What fits?"

"The answers to some of the puzzles. Who the children are. Why we can't bring ourselves to kill the demons. Why the demons come seeking warmth and life. The meaning of corruption and impurity, and why we've been told to be so careful lest the demons find their way into our souls." My skin was blazing hot—the fever of truth scalding my veins. "We did not create the demons, Fiona. The demons are a part of us."

"You're mad!"

"They're a piece of our own souls, a piece that was torn away by this magic." I fell to my knees beside the mosaic, the words crowding their way out of me, the ideas structuring and restructuring themselves in my head, the world reshaping itself before my eyes, just as Blaise had reshaped himself. "Look at it. Shapeshifting. They lived it. As much a part of them as cooking and birthing. And portals . . ." Now that I recognized them, the faint rectangle shapes appeared everywhere in the early frames. ". . . they passed through them easily between these two places, one very much like our own home, and this other place where everything is different . . . perhaps like Blaise does his journeying. And then this"—I pointed to the gap just before the story of the dreadful magic. "We need to know what happened here, and perhaps the whole thing might make more sense. But whatever it was, the people were afraid, and the magic was done. Look at them afterward. It's the first image where not one among them is shifted. There are no portals. The other place is no longer visible. And these monsters that we call demons are separate. It all happened at once."

"Never," said Fiona. She backed away from me and shook her head, her thin face losing its rich bronze color. "You will never make me believe I am a demon."

"You're not a demon. No. Of course not. But neither are you whole. Nor am I. Nor is Ysanne nor Talar nor any of us. Only the children." My son. In the midst of upheaval, the foundations of the world quaking beneath my feet, I clung to that one thought—that he was as he was supposed to be. "We have always said that rai-kirah were not evil of themselves, but only hungered for warmth and life. The Scroll of the Rai-kirah claims it is only the possession of a soul that is the evil, and that's why we send them back instead of killing them all. Don't you see? They are a part of us as truly as our hands and hearts and desires, and in the dreams, where we can see them, we understand it. In this time a thousand years ago, we were ripped apart"—I tapped the picture of the sorcerers who had worked the enchantment—"and these five were determined we would never go back. Think of the rules we have lived by. Think of our uttermost fears hammered into us from childhood. They didn't trust us with the reasons, and they destroyed everything so we would never discover what we had been." Unvoiced was my growing conviction that my dream . . . the warning . . . the Precursor . . . all of it was connected with the gap in the story, the cause of everything.

Balthar had said no word since I'd begun, only listened and stared, rocking himself very slowly. His full lips hung slack, his round cheeks suddenly sagged and wrinkled. His arms were wrapped tightly about his legs, and his chin rested on his knees. One might have thought him shocked into immobility, but the fingers of his left hand hammered on one knee like a woodpecker's beak on a dead tree. But as I paused to run my eyes over the mosaic yet again, trying to extract more of its secrets, he spoke very softly. "Pendyrral thought that the demon had taken him and was only biding his time until entering his soul. Then the dreams kept coming, and he was mad to go find the place. He said he belonged there with the wraiths, that they were calling him. He killed himself, you know . . . so he wouldn't go there. He had a wife and five children. Couldn't bear the thought of going mad or becoming a demon." The old man shook his head aimlessly, all life, all animation gone out of him. His bright eyes had gone dull, and from his lips there came a soft keening. I did not think there were easy answers for any of us.

"What else do you know, Balthar?" I said. "There are things . . ." Pendyrral had not dreamed about the darkness or the rider. Something had changed since his day. I had defeated the Lord of Demons . . . the Naghidda . . . the Precursor. My dread would not stay buried. What had written such fear on the faces of the people as the ancient magic was done? What could cause a people to cripple themselves, to destroy their history, to bind their children's children in a war that would never end? "How do the prophecies fit with this story?" I said.

"Nothing! There is no more of it. No more. It's all broken. Take your guesses and go away. None of this does

any good. What does it matter?" His fingertips were now
hammering on his bald head, as if he was trying to make
himself remember something . . . or perhaps to forget.

"First I need to know everything you've learned of
demons. Unless you've lied about your knowledge."

My sharp questioning drew Balthar out of his preoccupation. "I know little of prophecy, but I know more than any
person alive about demons, which, if you are correct, leaves
a great deal still to be learned. I can teach longer than you
can listen, I'll be bound." He picked up a stick and threw
it onto his hot fire so hard that red coals bounced out of
the fire pit.

"Then teach me."

"Why should I?"

"Because I lived for sixteen years with the horror you
created. You owe me something."

Balthar made no answer, but for the rest of the morning
instructed me in demon lore. He had been a demon scholar
long before his children were born possessed. He spent the
first half of his life studying every word written, every
rumor, every experience of every Warden that he could
gather, and then he had gone out into the world, and gathered the legends of other peoples. The stories of the Derzhi
and their battlefield spirits. The tales from Manganar campfires of the warrior spirits that would devour the unwary
soul. The legends from Basranni storytellers and Kuvai
minstrels. "I wrote it all down," said the old man, "but I
didn't let anyone read it. I wanted it to be complete, so no
one would accuse me of corruption. When I left Ezzaria I
burned it. But if I had paper and ink enough, I could write
it all again."

He had come to believe that there were three groups of
demons; circles he called them. The demons that the Wardens encountered were almost exclusively from one group.
My demon had called them the Gastai, and Balthar had
run across the term before. "They are the hunters, the ones
who come searching for sustenance. Their violence is in
proportion to their hunger."

I had learned of such behavior in my training, but never
of the names.

"Some of these Gastai we encountered many times over.

You know the stories. If you fight very often, then likely
you've met some of them—demons who follow the exact
patterns of earlier encounters. Worse every time they
come back."

I nodded. We never gave them names lest it give them
power or permanence. But our mentors made sure we were
prepared for certain demons who had been encountered
multiple times throughout our history.

"Then there are the Rudai. The shapers. A few demons
have claimed Rudai connections in their boasting. Some
Kuvai legends tell of spirits who shape worlds of stone and
wind, and I thought the tales matched with the experiences
of several Wardens. Ayolad and Teskor both encountered
demons who reshaped the Aife's weaving to confuse them.
They both claimed to have encountered the same demon
several times, but their accounts were always brief, and I
always wanted to ask them why. But all mention of the
shapers was far in the past—Ayolad six hundred years ago,
Teskor two hundred. A few others in between. I don't think
we have encountered any Rudai in my lifetime, unless
you . . . ?"

I shook my head.

"And the Nevai . . . only a whisper. The proud. The
hidden. The innermost circle, the most powerful of them
all, farthest from any contact with us. I've wondered . . .
Tales say the Derzhi god Athos was once an earthly king,
big and handsome and golden fair, who could transform
himself into any kind of beast. His reign was so magnificent
and his subjects loved him so dearly that the lords of the
sky—the stars—became jealous. They persuaded him to
transform into one of themselves, then worked magic so
that he could never return to earth. They thought he would
be lost among them, and the people of earth would turn
their eyes back to the stars. But his glory grew and captured
half of the sky, and the stars were afraid they would lose
even the part they still held. So Tyros, the Lord of Night,
adopted Athos as his son and anointed him as the ruler to
follow him, and so day follows night. The sun participates
in the lives of men, but the stars . . . I believe the stars are
the Nevai. They watch us, and are jealous of any who intrude upon their power, but they do not touch us. They

feed upon the sustenance brought by the Gastai, but crave power more than life."

He touched a few of the words scribed around the edges of the mosaic. "These words are unknown to me. Neither our own language nor anything like the demon words we know. But look. Here is the word for Nevai, and here Rudai and Gastai. So these ancient ones knew their names. Perhaps these words could tell us more about them"—the old man's voice shook—"if we wanted to know. Some things . . . some things it's best not to know."

"Power-born, skill-born, service-born," I said. "Valyddar, eiliddar, tenyddar. We have our own circles."

"Daughters of night . . ." As Balthar lectured me on his years of learning, my eyes did not stray from the images on the broken tiles: the woman/deer, the man with wings, the alien trees that appeared beyond the gateways. By the time the fogbound sun slipped away to leave the world in darkness again, I could re-create those trees in my head and others that were not portrayed on the mosaic. I could touch the baskets given reality by a few brush strokes, and I could imagine what was in them, fruits that grew on no vine in my experience, bread that tasted of grains unknown in the Derzhi Empire, gems that glittered with colors my eyes had never seen. As her child and husband watched from one side of the portal, the woman/deer ran along a road through a flower-filled meadow, and I believed I could describe what lay beyond the next curve. How was it possible? As truly as I knew my own name, I believed that the road she had traveled still existed somewhere, but I was dreadfully afraid of what I was going to have to do to find it.

"I need you to weave for me, Fiona."

Fiona had sat on the temple steps all day, listening to Balthar's tales without speaking. After we had shared a meal of cheese and dates, she and Balthar had gone to check the safety of our boat and empty the old man's nets and traps—I think Fiona wanted to make sure the old man took his catch cleanly—while I spent a long evening of thinking. Now she was back, sitting cross-legged by the fire splitting branches for kindling. Balthar had fallen asleep. I sat leaning against one of the columns.

"Weave? A portal? The old man may be a madman and a villain, but he is not demon-possessed. And I don't believe a Warden can walk into his own soul, even if he had all his wits—which you most certainly do not." She ripped the shaggy bark from a hemlock branch. "And, besides, you're forbidden to step beyond a portal."

"I am forbidden to engage in demon combat. I have no intention of that." Even as I listened to myself explain what I wanted, I agreed with Fiona's judgment. I was mad. What man sets out to follow the road of his worst nightmares?

Soon Fiona was standing over me, shouting. "It's murder. Worse than murder. I can't do it." She stormed across the temple, as if to put the maximum distance between herself and my plan. But she was back in seconds, and dropped to her knees so as to be on a level with me. "What will you prove by it? All you have is this madman's whimsy to go on. And a dream and a vision of a demon that you met when you were out of your mind with exhaustion and grief."

"Tell me what else I am to do, Fiona. I am convinced . . . convinced . . . that there is a danger to this world that is worse than the Lord of Demons. The only way we can withstand it is to be united under strong, capable, honorable leaders . . . and that means Aleksander and Blaise must find an accommodation. But before that can happen, I've got to find the answer to Blaise's fate, and I've got to find out the nature of the threat, so we'll know what they're up against. And the only way I can do those things is to fill in this." I pointed to the gap in the center of the mosaic. "Where else can I go to find that answer?"

"You can't believe all this."

"Tell me another story. If you can think of one, please tell me. This is not what I would choose."

"What of our own people? The Queen, Talar . . . many others. This is why you are so dangerous. Because you're not willing to do things properly, listen to those—"

"Ezzarians have done what was needed all these years. I believe that. Our strength and faithfulness have kept the world safe. But it was never meant to be this way. These

five did not do this thing from greed or pride or grasping
for power beyond what they had been given. Look at the
picture. They acted from profound terror. We can't fault
them. But the demons were an unexpected consequence.
See their faces. They're appalled at what they've done . . .
and so they bound us—their children—to remedy their mis-
calculation. The problem is that they didn't trust us with
the reasons, and now something has happened along the
way. Something has changed. My dream is different from
the others. Nothing that they left us predicted the Lord of
Demons or the kind of threat he posed to this world. He
was called the Precursor. I can't help but conclude that
whatever our ancestors feared is coming to pass anyway,
and we don't know what to do to prevent it. Gods of night,
Fiona. We kill our own children because we're ignorant
and afraid. The time has come to look elsewhere for answers. Tell me where."

"Find someone else to weave."

"There is no one else. I can't go back to Ezzaria—Aleksander will do what he says if I try it—and there's no time
for you to go and send someone here in your place. Ysanne
said she would have no one else weave for me, and I cannot
fault her judgment in that matter."

"You'll be dead."

"And if so, who is to care? Except perhaps you, for your
duty will be done, and you'll have to deal with your own
demons. And I trust you to be a good witness. If I die, the
responsibility to tell the others all this will rest with you."

"You can't force me to do it." She was weakening, which
I was in two minds about. In so many ways I hoped she
would keep refusing me.

"I can ask. I can say you got me into this mess . . . which,
to be honest, is only partially true. I can say you owe me
your life; my illusion with the rabbit kept you from being
Derzhi sword practice. But I must assume that the reason
you're still with me is your duty. You are compelled to
uncover those things that threaten Ezzaria and our war—
not just evidence of my corruption. There is enough evidence here . . . enough mystery . . . that to refuse to investigate it, even with such a flawed instrument as myself, would
be irresponsible on your part. If you're searching honestly

for answers, then you will come to the same conclusion—it's worth a try."

She stared at me expressionless. Unflinching. "We'll need clean water. I won't let you skip steps."

"I wouldn't think of it."

I didn't sleep much that night. I wasn't afraid. There would be time enough for that. I just didn't want to dream. Someone had been intruding on my dreams, and I wanted some time for my own. The stars had found their way through the fog and shimmered in icy remoteness above the dark trees.

Fiona pretended to sleep. She rolled in her blanket and lay still. But at dawn when I returned from Balthar's spring with a filled waterskin, she was already laying out her white Suzaini robes and the spare shirt I had bought in Zhagad, smoothing out the wrinkles with her small hands. We did not speak. She began whispering the verses of cleansing as she swept the dust and leaves and ash from a wide circle around the fire pit. I poured half of the water into one of Balthar's pottery jars and left it beside her robe. Then I took the waterskin and the clean shirt down to the pool. While I washed myself, I wondered what Fiona was telling Balthar or whether she would just prepare him tea and drop in some herb that would make the old man sleep while we borrowed his soul. But then it was time to close off such thoughts.

I spent an hour at the kyanar, using the slow, studied motions to focus my thoughts and prepare my body. Then I drank the water, put on the clean shirt, seated myself by the pool, and began Ioreth's Chant. As the sun burned off the last of the fog, I laid aside my connections to the world—a task that was pitifully easy—and soon I was in the state of readiness, halfway between the world in which I existed and the one I would walk.

At some time—moments later or hours or days, I could not have said which—a figure in a white robe came for me and led me into the temple. I knelt on the floor beside a quietly sleeping man, and the white-robed figure sat on the other side. "It is time, Warden," said the one who knelt opposite me. "Come with me if you choose again this path

of danger, of healing, of hope." She reached out her hands
and I touched them, and the world disappeared.

You'll find a spot that is familiar. The cool voice spoke
clearly in my head. *It will be your lifeline, your anchor, and
will not fade until I permit it. Even in chaos you will be
able to find it. Once every day I will weave a portal and
wait there for an hour. Until you return.*

I peered through the gray rectangle that hung in the air
before me and glimpsed a ruined tower on a bald, rocky
knob. Col'Dyath. *I'll not forget this*, I said, smiling. I felt
no smile returned.

The path was steady beneath my feet. Unyielding. I
stepped through the portal onto the familiar rock, then
took a deep breath. *Now.* With startling speed the sky
began to spin, the ground to crumble beneath my feet, and
the light to fade. Fiona closed the portal behind me, as I
had asked, and I stood alone on the brink of the abyss.

CHAPTER 20

The elemental spirits, who ordinarily care nothing for the affairs of gods or mortals, watched as the mortal woman challenged the mighty god. They marveled at her courage and took pity on Verdonne. They gave her sunlight as her cloak when the god took her clothes, and thunder and lightning for her weapons when he melted her sword. They gave her rain to wash her wounds, wind to bear her up, and fire to sustain her.

"Yield," bellowed the forest god. "You are mortal, and when you die I will have my way. You have no hope." But Verdonne would not yield.
—The story of Verdonne and Valdis as told to the First of the Ezzarians when they came to the lands of trees

I believed I was familiar with fear. I had been only seventeen when I first stepped into a madwoman's soul to face a demon. While enslaved in Capharna I had come face-to-face with the most powerful demon of my experience, believing I had not the melydda to ward off a flea. For three days entombed in Balthar's coffin, and again during my summer on Col'Dyath, I had felt my mind slipping into madness. But my long-held conviction was sorely mistaken. I had never known true fear—abject, soul-consuming terror. Not until that day, when the last solid foothold gave way beneath my feet and the last shreds of light were swallowed by absolute night.

"Aife!" I screamed. Only the panicked vibration of my chest told me I had succeeded in my cry, for my voice was lost in a vast nothingness. I was deaf, for there was naught to capture sound. I was blind, for there was no substance to the darkness, no contrasting shadow to work against another. And there was nothing to touch, nothing to feel: no cold, no heat, no air to soothe my skin with the assurance of my existence. I was numb to everything but terror as I began to fall. My stomach heaved. My arms and legs flailed. I tucked in my knees and wrapped my arms around them lest my limbs fly off and lose themselves as irretrievably as my senses.

Oh, gods of earth and sky, what have I done? Too late to grow my wings. The needed words were already lost in the chaos of my dissolving reason. I had known I was going to fall—I had been close to the abyss several times in my demon combat—but I had deliberately not triggered the enchantment when the portal vanished. In those last moments of rational thought, already so far removed from me as the vision of earth must be from the stars, I had told myself it would be a waste of melydda. I could not fly forever, and if I was to find some other existence beyond the realms of the soul, then I might as well get on with it. Or if I was to die when the portal dissolved, no reason to put it off.

Imbecile! Prideful, wretched idiot.

I begged the gods for help . . . though I could not remember their names. I fought to control my bowels that spasmed like those of the dying. I longed for the impact of solid earth, though it might crack my spine and crush my head. But I continued to fall, and I felt the wail of madness rising in my throat . . .

The brush of frost on my cheek saved me. Only a moment's variation in the emptiness as I plummeted into that well of endless night. But it cooled my fevered panic just long enough for my training to take hold. *No. No. No. You will not enter this realm like a squalling infant, whether it be the realm of death or demons. You are a Warden of Ezzaria. Your whole life has prepared you for this. If those who wait in this darkness are your kin, then you'd best scrape together a bit of dignity.*

Dignity. Too grand a word for a quivering lump of terrified flesh, but at least I was not screaming when invisible fingers began to pick at my clothes and my hair. And by that time, though my churning stomach and entrails had not yet realized it, I was no longer falling.

"I am the—" I had to clamp my teeth to cut off the familiar challenge. I smelled demons. My skin crawled with the nearness of them—the strength of them. But I was not in this place for battle. "I've come in peace," I said, my voice almost unhearable in the void. I tried to remember the words I had so carefully crafted for whomever came to greet me in the abyss. *"Dargoth viagh*—let us bargain."

No answer. Only a hundred cold fingers feeling my limbs, tracing my bones, probing my mouth and my ears and every other part of me, inside and out. When they reached inside my head, and into my chest and stomach, exploring the bones and muscles and organs they found there, I twisted and tried to push them away. As I resisted, the probing touches grew sharper, scoring my flesh with thin, stinging cuts inside and out until my skin was on fire. I lashed out, but no solid mass anchored the invisible fingers. *Hold patient. You're here to learn, not fight.* Was this what it felt like to be possessed? Exposed. Nauseated. Violated.

"I seek answers to what happened to us—my people and yours—back at the beginning. The reason for our war. Why it is that we fight, though it wounds us so terribly to kill each other. Please let me speak. I won't harm anyone."

"Sykkor. Asethya dv svyadd."

"Mezzavalit."

The whispers crept up my spine, a cold, oily salve on the fire of my skin. I tried to be still and decipher the words, but I couldn't concentrate, couldn't remember. Though I didn't recognize the words, what I heard was indeed the language of demons. Ezzarians knew only a few words of the demon tongue. But if I had possessed any remaining capacity for fear, these words would have filled me to over-flowing. They were the very vocabulary of hate.

"Yddrass!" That word I recognized. Warden.

"I've not come to fight. I'm unarmed." I would have laughed, had I remembered how to. I wasn't even sure there was substance under my feet, much less whether these beings cared about my intentions or noticed that I carried no weapon. All I knew was that I heard . . . felt . . . three different voices, and that as soon as they realized I was a Warden, they started arguing among themselves. I didn't have to know the words to figure that out. Nor to discover how they felt about Wardens. The cold fist that had held my stomach captive for at least an hour reached for my entrails and came near pulling them out of my body. And that was only the beginning.

Warden's training warned of the consequences of demon captivity. It was all speculation, of course, based on the virulence and methods of a thousand years of demon opponents. The warnings were meant as encouragement to judge your skill and your opponent wisely, for there was certainly no additional teaching as to how one might cope with those consequences. Just as well. Our estimate of cruelty and torment and pain was so under-calculated as to be but a dust speck beside the mountain of the truth.

One of the cold fingers wrapped itself about my neck and dragged me, choking and gagging, through the darkness. The ground beneath me felt like great slabs of ice, though when the dragging stopped, I could no longer feel my surroundings at all. I could force my hand through the floor—the darkness that was underneath me—or the ceiling—the darkness that was above me—or to any side with equal ease. The air was bitterly cold and very still. I could not tell whether I was out of doors or inside a structure of some kind, but I believed, for a moment, that I was alone. Carefully I sat up and with trembling fingers tried to cast a light. No luck.

"Garaz do tsiet, Yddrass." The hissing breath was just in front of my face, enveloping me in the stench of an open grave.

Even as I recoiled, gagging at the smell, a powerful blow to my stomach took my wind away. Another to my back cracked a rib. I reached out to grapple with my attackers, but my hands came up empty. "Wait! I've come just to learn—"

"Garaz do tsiet, Yddrass." A blow hammered my head. The red lights I saw were only within, for there was no light in that place of horror. I rolled into a knot to protect myself, but the cold fingers grabbed my wrists and ankles and forced me to spread out. Then someone dropped an anvil on my chest.

"Stop! There's some danger to us all. One of your own warned—"

"Garaz do tsiet, Yddrass." And it began raining anvils.

Eventually I learned that those words meant, "fight me now, Warden." They might well have meant "you're going to be sorry you're alive." In those first hours, they beat me until every bone in my body was broken. I fell insensible a number of times, but they always woke me up again to demonstrate how this arm or that finger or that foot or this rib was in multiple pieces. Only when I was shattered wreckage did they leave off.

Not at all what I had hoped.

Empty silence. Frigid darkness. A floor beneath me that was not a floor, that left me with a constant nauseating terror that I was going to fall through it. I could not breathe, could not move, could not imagine living a moment more in such pain. Each limb, each muscle, each bone cried out its ruin, finding a distinct pathway to send its message until my body lost its solid substance. I became a fibrous jumble, each thread a fiery torment. Perhaps I was already dead. I had just never expected it to hurt so wickedly.

I lay in this state of misery, drifting in and out of gruesome consciousness, for some hours. The fifth or sixth time I came awake, I smelled something new. Food. Not pleasant-smelling food, but then nothing would have smelled appetizing at that moment. I wondered if there was drink beside it, and the thought became obsession. From the smell, the food could be no more than an arm's length from my head. Might as well be on the moon; I wasn't sure I could move any of my broken limbs. But the throbbing in my left arm had eased a bit, so I cautiously shifted it out from under me. I didn't die. In fact, as I dared move a little more, I realized that despite what I had experienced as painful truth, only a few of my ribs were broken, together with both of my ankles and several fingers on my left hand. Everything else was only battered to the edge of ruin.

I ignored the metal dish of food—meat, none too fresh—but pulled the cup close and managed to raise my head to drink. I spat out the first mouthful. Never had I tasted drink so foul. But it had no ill effect, so I kept it close and, as

soon as I could steel myself, tried again. My thirst muted,
I slipped into a painful stupor, only to be kicked awake
before I could gain any benefit from it.

"Garaz do tsiet, Yddrass." And they began it all again.

In an eternity of darkness, I was subjected to every horror of nightmare. I was drowned fifty times, consumed by
dark fire fifty more. Between beatings that left me pulp and
lashings that left me in shreds, I lay in a huddled knot and
wished for death. They knew each nerve ending to scald
with burning oil and each tender bit of flesh to pierce with
iron spikes. From my deep-buried fears they drew images
of snakes and entombed me with a thousand of them. And
they discovered my horror of mutilation and made sure I
knew every form it could take. Once I lay for what seemed
an entire day believing that both my arms had been severed
at the shoulder. Sometimes I believed that they actually did
the things I felt, but healed me or reversed the damage
after, so they could have the pleasure of doing it all again.
Sometimes I was convinced it was all illusion, grotesque
visions punctuated by enough reality to linger until the next
time. I never knew the truth of the matter. The only surety
was that every fiber of my body was in agony every moment of those endless days.

They tried to invade my soul as well. At the beginning
of each session I would feel one or the other of them pawing at the door, hunting for the way inside. *"Seggae llydna."*
Speak your name. It was the only fight I won, yet I knew
it was only a matter of time until they had their way with
me in that, too. But for the time they had to be content to
remain close by as the day's work was done, licking at the
scraps of my pain and despair like cats in a milking stall. I
did not scream or beg for mercy. Though they hungered
for it, and things might have gone easier if I had given
them their fill, my long years of practice would not allow
me to feed a demon's lust. But when I was left alone, I
buried my mouth on my filthy, bloody arms and sobbed in
muffled agony. I craved one moment's peace. One glimpse
of light.

I was fed regularly—raw, rancid meat. Perhaps it was not
real, or perhaps my senses were merely deceived into think-

ing it the worst filth I could imagine. But at least I had been accustomed to eating whatever came when I was a slave. Though I longed to die, stubborn instinct would not allow me to hurry it along, so I ate enough to keep myself alive. ·

Never was there light. Never was there warmth. Never was there a word that was not hatred or vengeance. Day or night had no meaning, nor did hours, or weeks, or months. After a time I could not even remember what to wish for . . . only for an end to what was. Of course I tried to use my melydda to make a light, to weave some protection. But I could not summon power, and any attempt drew the demons down on me in frenzy.

Early on, in the brief hours of respite when my tormentors were otherwise occupied, I tried to crawl away, for the place where I was kept was not a cell with walls. Each time I worked for hours, scarcely able to drag myself along, hoping that I would find something to touch, to feel, to hear, or that at least I would not die in their hands. But I arrived nowhere except where I had always been, and my jailers had no difficulty finding me. Their first cold touch, just behind my eyes, was the worst of all.

Desperate to find some reason to keep breathing, I tried to fill my mind with images of those I loved. But I could not conjure their faces, and the fading echoes of their voices were more painful than the bodily torment I endured. *Prophecies will not shield you from the law if you come back tainted this time . . . Sometimes you cannot bear to see the ugly truth of something you believed was good . . . I thought we might learn from each other, but I don't care to learn what you have to teach . . . I see no reason to contradict the saying of the Council. Your Warden's commission is revoked. Your oath is void.* No comfort in those voices.

The one thing that prevented my complete disintegration was the remembrance of Fiona, somewhere back in the world of light, her small, stubborn face set in the mysterious trance of an Aife, doggedly weaving her lifeline in a sleeping Balthar's soul. For one hour of every day, there was the possibility of escape. I had no idea how to reach for it, or whether I would ever have the strength or ability to use

it, but the possibility was enough. No one in the world—
not Aleksander, not Ysanne, not Catrin—no one would I
trust the way I trusted stubborn, relentless Fiona. She
would be there, and one day I would find a way to use her
gift. Until then, I would just have to survive.

"Yddrass, gzit!"
I was dizzy and sick from another wicked beating, curled
up in a ball, trying to steel myself to eat the disgusting
mess they had left for me, when I felt the creeping touch
of demon fingers. "Leave me alone. You've had your fun
for a while." It certainly wouldn't stop them—I didn't think
they understood anything I said—but it gave me heart to
know I could still put words together. Two of them pulled
me to my feet and backed me to a cold iron post, which
seemed to manifest itself whenever they had need of it.
The third demon bound my hands to it.

Though I never saw my three jailers, I had learned to
tell them apart by their voices, their touch, and their pleasures. One was the most vicious, always inventing new torments and always the most disappointed when I did not
give him what he wanted in return. I thought of him as
Jack-Willow—a nasty character who appeared in many Ezzarian children's stories. One of the three I named Gyyfud,
because he reminded me of a boy I had known in my youth
who had burned down his parents' home by playing with
fire. The demon Gyyfud had the same dangerous habit,
only it was my hands and feet he liked burning. The third
demon I thought of as Boresh, for he reminded me of a
household official in the palace in Capharna. His delights,
too, were always degrading and obscene.

"You'll get nothing from me. Nothing." But of course
they would. Eventually they would.

"Yddrass . . ." It was a new voice. Higher. Tinny sounding. The visitor was astonished at my presence, and I had
to endure his nasty investigation of my substance.

Though I relished any novelty as evidence that time had
not abandoned me, I was not at all excited to have someone
new come to visit. Only once had any but my three jailers
entered my prison. On the second or third day of my captivity, a soft-voiced visitor had come and stripped away my

clothes, then taught Boresh in mortifying detail how to inflict the most private indignities upon a human man. Visitors were dangerous.

Jack-Willow babbled at this new visitor without stopping,
and it came to me that he was boasting—showing me off.
I had no way to estimate demon intelligence, but I didn't
think his proud display accomplished what he intended.
The visitor stole me.

Perhaps for an hour after the two had left, I lay in the
throbbing stupor that passed for sleep. A cold appendage
twined itself about my neck, and before I could protest, a
fist-sized lump of nothing was lodged in my throat. Amid
furtive whisperings, I was dragged away, a very long way,
and deposited somewhere else. That is, I assumed it was
another place, though it was truly no different at all. Absolute darkness. Bitter cold. It smelled like a charnel pit. Or
perhaps that was just my own stink.

"Yddrass," said the one with the tinny voice. *"Seggae
llydna!"*

"No." I shook my aching head. I would not yield my
name. Not yet.

"Dol fysgarra, Yddrass?" I had no idea what that one
meant. *"Garaz do tsiet."* They yelled these things many
times, pounding me to the floor after each repetition as if
the blows might make me understand, then prodding me
to stand up again. Eventually it was impossible for me to
rise, and they had to stop.

"So you've won your point, whatever it was," I said as
soon as I got breath enough to speak. My face was pressed
against the quite solid floor. "But I only came here to ask
a few questions. I want to find one of the Nevai."

"Nevai!" They found great hilarity in that. Stomped on
my hands and kicked me in the face while they laughed. I
thought perhaps they were the Nevai.

These fellows were not so inventive as Jack-Willow, but
they seemed to quite enjoy every minute of their activities.
Their particular pleasure was to hold mock combats, to
flatten me while I was holding a weapon—no matter that it
was impossible for me to do anything with it. *"Dol fysgarra,
Yddrass?"* And so the misery continued as before.

*   *   *

After I had been with the second group as long as with the first—weeks, months, a year?—I began to lose my memory. My head was never clear, and my thoughts drifted away before I could catch them. To concentrate on the mental exercises I had used to keep some semblance of sanity became impossible. I never truly slept anymore; everything hurt too much. But I was never really awake, either. I could no longer remember what evidence had convinced me to come to this place. Something about a dream. A picture, a blur of colors. Something I needed to know, but I couldn't think what it was. I lay in the dark and laughed at that, as I throbbed and ached and bled. Who would step into the mouth of a shengar because of a picture? Who would surrender his soul because of a dream? Only a madman. I had a vague remembrance that in some time long past, friends had judged me mad. They must have been right. But it worried me more that it took me a very long while to name the colors in the picture.

"Yddrass, gzit."

I stood up as quickly as possible. Getting up was painful, but you paid a price if you weren't quick about it. Ham-fist hated it when you didn't get up right away. He was the leader of my third set of captors. I wasn't sure when his group had taken me. I knew only that I once woke up hanging by my wrists with different voices whispering in the dark.

Ham-fist was very strict. He commanded his henchman with as much zeal as he battered his prisoner. But on this particular occasion, he sounded nervous. Perhaps I was about to be claimed by someone new. Someone unfamiliar stood close by in the dark—someone who didn't smell bad, which was very unusual.

"Hyssad!" This new one spoke softly, but with altogether more substance to his voice, as if perhaps there were a physical body behind it. If so, I pitied him. Physical bodies were dreadful things . . . useless things . . . always so much pain . . . hungry, thirsty, stinking . . . forever . . .

"Dego zha nevit!" The words were unknown to me. Though I had come to understand a few brutally simple

commands, I still knew very little of the demon language. Within the soul of a possessed victim, demons spoke in the tongue of the victim. Only when he had killed the demon's physical manifestation was a Warden forced to bargain in the demon tongue. But I could hear that Ham-fist was very angry. He didn't like being told to leave. Demons hated the word "hyssad." But the newcomer stood his ground, and soon my jailer was gone. Silently as always. I had never gotten used to the absence of footsteps. It kept me jumpy all the time, for I could never hear them coming. I never knew when or from which direction the next blow would come.

I wasn't sure I was going to enjoy meeting someone who could order Ham-fist around. Chances were he wouldn't like Wardens, either. I shrank into as small a space as I could, and wrapped my arms over my head. Best to be prepared. I wished they would leave my head alone. I didn't like being so muddled.

"I won't hurt you."

At first I couldn't figure out what made the comment seem so strange. A moment passed before I realized not only were the sentiments unusual, they were expressed in words that made sense—Ezzarian words. When a warm hand took a firm grip on my arm, I almost came out of my skin. A normal human hand. I thought it might burn a mark into my flesh.

After a moment's hesitation, I reached out and felt the solid muscular arm connected to the hand. "Who?" My voice shook, for suddenly I was trembling with the cold, with weakness, with fear and despair and a deluge of emotions let loose by four words and one touch. I had lived for so long in the dark.

"A survivor. How long since you took up with this lot, lad?"

"Don't know. Forever." My teeth were chattering.

"I don't doubt it seems so. Here"—he helped me sit down—"careful of your eyes."

I was too slow. A searing pain split my head as a sun bloomed in front of my face. I buried my face in my arms and suppressed a moan.

"Oh, hang it all, I'm sorry." The flame beyond my eyelids dimmed. "Now, try again. Slow. For certain true, they keep it pitch down here."

I could see little but brilliant whiteness. My eyes were watering so badly, it was no use keeping them open. For a few moments I had to enjoy the change in brightness through my eyelids.

"Don't you worry. There's naught so much to see. I'm the homeliest fellow was ever born 'neath a tree, and you . . . by my boots, you are a rascally sight. I just caught the rumor that the mad ones had snatched them a captive. Gastai can't keep a secret worth the devil—and devils aren't worth a sow's tail, as you fairly know, since you've been living with a pack of them. How in all that's holy did you end up with these particular villains? They're so rotting mad, they're not even sent out to hunt anymore."

I tried another peek and caught a blurry image of a stocky, flat-faced man with long, straight hair, just turning gray. He was human. Solid. Ezzarian.

"Please"—I rolled forward as a wave of pain from my belly met the lancing fire from a torn shoulder—"can you help me?" My immediate misery precluded any consideration of how one of my own people had come to be walking about freely in the realm of demons.

"It's possible. In the ordinary chance of things, no one interferes with these brutes, but Kaarat won't allow them to destroy a Warden before he's had a crack at him. You *are* a Warden, am I right? The ways of the world haven't changed so that some other kind of fool is sent here?"

"I am. Was."

"The only one was fighting for quite a long while? The one who changes himself? Shifts? Wings, I heard—what a wonder—and who did for the Naghidda? That's you?"

Warning bells rang in my tattered mind. I craved human speech. I longed to pour out everything I had left . . . then perhaps I could find the things that had gone missing. But I could not silence caution. Tears rolled down my face, tears not caused by the brightness of his light. "Please, I cannot—"

His hand lay gently on my shoulder, and his voice dropped to a whisper. "Sorry, lad. Not fair to press. It's just been so damnably long. I'm so hungered for news, for some sign that we're still strong in our duty. I do their bidding here in this place, but I command my own soul. I vow it."

"I've come to learn. To find truth about demons."

"Truth?" He chuckled softly. "From the look of you, I'd say you've already learned that you've come to the wrong place." But then his voice dropped even lower. "See here, now. You've no reason to trust me, and you're right to be cautious, but I've a bit of influence. I promise you've no other ally here. The brutes claim you had no weapons. But perchance you did—being a Warden doesn't go far beyond a portal without—and you found the clever skill to hide them. If you was to tell me how to fetch them, I might have better luck getting you out of here. Once you're out, you can take me or leave me at your will."

"It's so hard . . ." So hard to remember. "No. I didn't have any. I came . . . a demon warned me . . . something terrible to come . . . a Nevai came to me . . ." He would never believe me. "I had to come here to learn more of it."

My visitor was quiet for so long a moment that I thought he was gone. I cracked my eyes open again, and he was staring at me in puzzlement. "A Nevai warned you? Who the devil . . . ? What did he tell you?"

Ham-fist started yelling murderously from a short distance away. I cringed, drawing up my knees and stuffing my hands between my thighs.

"Confound these cursed devils!" said the Ezzarian. "I've got to get out of here before they decide to keep me. I'll do you no good torn to pieces. Keep yourself together, lad, and here . . ." His wide, warm hand rested on my pounding head for just a moment, leaving behind a tingling sensation. ". . . a little gift. Maybe it will give you some amusement. I'll see what I can do for you."

The light vanished. Darkness settled around me like the dirt thrown on a coffin. "Don't go," I cried. "Oh, gods have mercy, please don't leave me." I waved my arms wildly, trying to find him. I had used up all my pride, and the thought of being abandoned in the dark again came near destroying me. I was ready to tell him anything. But he was already gone.

Ham-fist and his fellows let me know what they thought of interfering visitors. By the time they were done, I wasn't sure anyone had come. Perhaps it had only been another blow to my head.

CHAPTER 21

I did not see the Ezzarian again for a very long while, but I did come to believe he was real. From the moment he touched his hand to my head, I could speak and understand the language of demons. Unfortunately, I had already learned most of what my captors had to say. Things like *dol fysgarra*—where are your weapons?—and *garaz do tsiet*—fight me now. Constant demands that I tell them my name and how I had managed to kill the Naghidda—the Precursor, a powerful demon they admired. Though I could not remember when or how, I supposed I had indeed done such a thing—killed a powerful demon called the Precursor. I was a Warden. My duty was to fight demons. The demons spoke most eloquently with their invisible whips and clubs and knives, and I was sure that if it went on very much longer, I would not remember anything at all. But somehow hearing their speech and understanding it, crude as it was, gave me a point of reference. I was no longer so alone in the painful darkness. Creatures with words were creatures I could hate, and that kept my mind alive. Barely.

On one day—until that point no different from the endless days preceding it—I was crouched over my lump of raw meat, gnawing at it hungrily, trying not to think about what it was, only that if I could get enough, it might keep me living. I had developed an unceasing tremor in my hands, and as I worked at the tough, gristly mess, I concentrated on making my hands be still. They refused.

"You will give him over now."

I fumbled at my feast, despising the way I flinched at every sudden sound or movement. Quickly I downed the last dregs from my cup. The liquid was thin and sour, but

I would need whatever sustenance I could get if they were coming for me again so soon. I wiped my mouth on the back of my trembling hand and tried to clear my mind, inviting emptiness.

I had taught myself to embrace emptiness, to immerse myself in it. The effort neither blunted the pain nor strengthened my mind, but at least I could protect the few fading memories I had saved from their ravaging: a smattering of words and phrases—words that would make a difference in the world, words that would tell someone why I had come—and a few precious images—a babe's soft fair cheek, a soaring bird of brown and white, a braid of bright red hair, a stone tower. I could not put names to these images anymore, nor remember why they were important, but when I was alone, I would take them out like a miser's jewels and savor them. My secrets proved to me that I was yet my own master.

Ham-fist was very angry. My bones quailed at the memory of his rages. "He stays here. Don't care who wants him. We've not done with him. We make him pay, that's what. He's the one as done us all these times just gone. The one as done for half our cadre, and the Naghidda, who promised we would hunt again and have all the *yladdimari* we wanted." *Yladdimari*—human lives.

"Kaarat will have him tried. If he's judged guilty, you'll likely have your wish. No one will want anything to do with the slayer of the Naghidda, if this is indeed he. Many yet honor the fallen Tasgeddyr."

I dug at my ears with my fists, trying to decide if the newcomer was human. I was always hearing things that weren't there. The voice didn't sound like the Ezzarian. I knew better than to hope. It had been months . . . forever . . . since he had come.

From one corner of my eye, I glimpsed a streak of red and purple. Sometimes I imagined I saw lights or colors in the everlasting blackness, but usually that was when the brutes had battered my head again, or stuck something into my eyes.

"*Yddrass, gzit.*" Ham-fist kicked me. I wasn't very fast at getting to my feet anymore.

"You claim this creature killed the Naghidda? Impossible."

"He is the one, and we'll have him back."

"You'll have whatever you're given, beast. Servants of the Nameless, what a mess . . ."

I felt a shove at my back and staggered forward . . . into a churning, whirling, formless pool of gray cloud. A few moments of it, and I heaved up all the foulness I had just eaten. And so I was dizzy, confused, and slimed with bloody vomit when I stumbled into a stormy twilight.

"Is this him?"

"So say the mad ones. Doesn't seem possible. I thought you might want to get a look at him before I take him out for testimony. Give you something interesting to top Yasnit when he starts his battle stories again."

I had fallen to my knees on hard-packed snow, unable to open my eyes more than a slit. A bitterly cold wind ran razor fingers over my naked back and down my throat, setting me to coughing, and someone was poking at me with the toe of a boot, as if I were a dead cat found in an alley.

"Doesn't seem very fierce. Not like the stories. How'd you get wind of him?"

"Kaarat heard they'd captured one of the creatures and plans to put him on trial. But the vessel has emptied a thousand times while the mad ones had him, so there's probably not much use to it. Ylad don't keep much of a mind if they've been in the pits too long. And they always end up dead once they're out."

What was the burden of dread that weighed so heavy whenever I thought about how long I'd been imprisoned? Something beyond the horror that they would send me back. It was so hard to remember.

"I've heard that Denas has taken an interest, because of the connection with the Naghidda."

The two voices drifted lazily over my back. "Denas! I didn't think he cared for anything but his ambition . . . and Vallyne, of course."

"Hush, Vilgor. You mustn't bandy her name about so freely—and certainly not in the same breath with Denas's.

She doesn't take well to it. Even when Denas does exactly as she wishes, he finds a way to displease her."

"So when will you be done with her garden?"

"Never. She's demanded more roses and fifty new kinds of flowers . . ." The two of them rambled for some time. Though I could translate their words, the meaning was lost on me. It was so miserably cold. Who could make sense of gardens and roses while battered by this sleet-laced wind? I must have mistaken the words.

And then they started gossiping: who was allied with whom, and how someone had revealed a plot and been poisoned for it, but some other person had put them up to it and that one had vanished. Dead, it was said. Who knew where it would end? Their voices dropped low when they began to talk about a disagreement over who would lead "the great venture," and how Rhadit was still looking for the one to open the way. "There'll be more disappearances. You can be sure of it," said the gardener. "Someone's hired the assassin. He's strutting about as if the Naghidda lived again."

"Never trust him, Vilgor. I've heard what's said about good Zelaz. He was the last who knew—"

"Hold your tongue, friend."

None of it made sense, and my thick head could not seem to grasp any information that might serve my needs. Still huddled to the snowy ground, I pressed my tremulous hands to my eyes and tried to get a glimpse of where I was and who were these people who spoke of intrigues that seemed more fitting for an imperial palace than the demon realm. I could see no one. The gray light was dim, and my eyes kept blurring and watering, stung by flying ice crystals. Streaks of red and purple danced at the edges of my sight, and I was afraid that my eyes had been permanently damaged, until at last I managed to focus them on something closer.

I blinked a hundred times to make sure I was not imagining it—a perfect frozen image of a butterfly. Not living, of course. Perfect only in shape and size and the detail of its patterned wings, for it was carved of the very stuff of winter, a fragile creature of frost. The coloration was quite faint, only a pale suggestion of the radiant reds and yellows and hard-edged black I knew were the reality. But there was such vivid truth in the shaping of it that I held my breath lest it startle, fly into the raging storm, and be shattered.

I wrapped my arms about my shivering self and struggled to my knees, squinting and blinking away my freezing tears so that I could see more. Indeed the butterfly was only the beginning, Perched upon a leafy bush, also carved of ice. Upon the bush were roses in every stage of their blooming from tight-closed promise to the poignant perfection of full bloom, doomed to fade upon the next hour's passing. The merest hint of pinks and reds, deeply buried in the ice, gave memory to their missing colors, and I sniffed the faintest tinge of sweetness on the air. Was it only my starved imagination that made me smell them.

Beyond the one sculpted bush were thousands more flowering plants of varieties wholly unknown to me, stretching in every direction as far as I could see in the gloomy grayness. And in the midst of them, trees, tall and marvelous, every detail of leaf and branch recorded in exactitude, unmoving despite the raging wind. Winding paths through the frozen garden led to fountains that showered frost-carved droplets in unchanging patterns over images of birds and maidens and children dipping pails into the ever-still water. Delicate bridges arched over frozen ponds.

Perhaps they intend to leave me here, I thought. I could well have been the bony, battered gargoyle left to frighten evil spirits from their glorious garden. Indeed I was so cold and broken, I could scarcely move, yet in truth the piercing beauty of the frozen images, the unyielding purity of their perfection, took such hold of my withered soul that I did not want to leave. *To die here in beauty. Not so bad a thing.* I had forgotten beauty.

In my childhood, people had told me stories of the demons' frozen land, but never had I pictured castles and roadways and bridges formed from the ice, much less gardens and butterflies. The bitter cold was the only thing we had right . . . and the monsters in the pits.

The two voices were still whispering of conspiracy and intrigue, but I could see no one about. The lack of substance to my tormentors drove me to despair. All my fighting skills had been useless, and now I was such wreckage, I could likely not lift sword or fist.

But then I blinked and saw the red streak of light bend toward the butterfly. The delicate creation was moved from its branch to rest upon a half-open rose that took form even as I watched. In sudden enlightenment, I smiled to myself. I watched the red light shimmering in the gloom and waited until the butterfly was firmly settled. "Did you make it?" I said, my voice sounding harsh and strange as it formed the demon words.

And as I expected, the red shimmer flickered into the form of a man when he turned to look at me—a gnarled, little brown man in red shirt and breeches—and beside him another man—younger, quite thin, and very annoyed—dressed in a flowing purple cape. Forms of light, not flesh, but with expressive faces and limbs perfectly shaped, though they had no more substance than lightning.

"Did he speak?" said the one in purple. Vilgor, the gardener had called him.

"He did," said the one in red. "And the answer is yes, I made it. Why do you care?"

"M-m-arvelous," I said through chattering teeth. "Exquisite." The two looked so shocked that I almost burst out laughing at them. "Only a little m-m-ind left and that half frozen, b-but enough to recognize an artist w-w-worthy of p-p-praise."

"Insolent vermin."

I wasn't at all prepared for the powerful burst of enchantment that instantly snatched me away from the garden and back into the swirling murk.

". . . No doubt of it, good Kaarat. We displayed him to the hunters before bringing him before you, and more than two hundred identified him. He is an yddrass, the very villain Warden who has tried to starve us these times just gone. The cruel hand of the Aife scourge. And because there has been no other but this one for so long, he is certainly the one who gave Barrakeval no choice in his outcome, but killed him savagely, violating the codes of his own kind. This Warden must be punished. Destroyed." The one in purple was speaking. Vilgor. I recognized his voice, though I could not see him.

I strained to see anything through the gloom. Hours had passed since I had been able to make sense of my surroundings. I had been dragged, bullied, shoved, and prodded into storm-wracked settlements, into buried dens peopled by shadows, and murky rooms flickering with light, all of them packed with hatred so palpable I could have molded it with my hand. Finally we had arrived at this somber gray room, long and narrow, with gracefully arched walls that shot up steeply to a high peak lost somewhere in the ever-present shadows.

Though it was still wickedly cold, we were no longer in the wind. I was grateful for that, as I was bound to a slender column of some sort, my hands over my head, my battered flesh abjectly exposed. At least a hundred demons were present. I could see only a few of them who were turned just at the angle they became visible to me, but I could feel their hot blue eyes on my wretched self—naked, bruised, caked with blood, vomit, and worse. My knees were quivering so badly, they kept threatening to cave in and leave me hanging from my sore wrists. My hair hung lank over my face, some of it stuck to my cheeks and lips with frozen foulness.

"How came this yddrass here? We've no record of engagement in the time given." The stern, calm questioning came from somewhere in front of me.

"The mad ones claim he surrendered himself to them in honor of their past ferocity," said Vilgor, "if one can believe them. For myself, I think he must have battled with a rogue and got himself captured. Perhaps he killed the rogue, but too late to escape, and then he fell into the pit with the mad ones. But that is no matter. The only question, good Kaarat, is what punishment do we devise, and who has the privilege and pleasure of meting it out."

"Hmm. A difficult question." The speaker turned where I could see him as a spare, gray-haired man of advanced age. "Where is Merryt? He's the one who brought this to my attention, and he asked to speak at the trial. What does he have to say of it?"

Vilgor, the purple-clad demon, was incensed. "The *ylad*! Surely you won't listen to the vile—"

"I will listen to whomever has light to shed on the matter. Has anyone seen Merryt?"

The judge had raised a commotion. Apparently many others shared Vilgor's displeasure at mention of this Merryt. An *ylad*—a human. My sluggish blood began to move.

"I am here, noble Kaarat, and greatly value the honor you do me by permitting me to address the Rudai Meet. May the Rudai Circle ever be complete." The owner of the substantial voice stepped out from behind me, a stocky, gray-haired man who bowed to Kaarat and did not shimmer and disappear. "I bring word from Denas." Silence fell, as if the storm beyond the gray walls had stopped its raging. "He has commissioned me to tell you that he has no interest in this case. A captive Warden is proper fodder for his Gastai, as has always been the custom."

Kaarat sighed. "But surely this Warden should be interrogated. I've been told he can still speak, and we've had so many questions about this particular one. He's different. Powerful enough to destroy the Naghidda. And he changes form. We've much to learn. Matters are moving more swiftly than we're accustomed to. And if Rhadit's legion is to embark on the quest—"

"My noble Kaarat, I have no advice upon this business. I only bring you the word of Denas, as he commanded me. As an Adviser of the Rudai Meet, you must determine your own course where it may deviate from Denas's recommendation."

Kaarat was flustered. "All right, all right. What insights could I have that would change what passes anyway?" He stood up, flickering in his pale blue brilliance. "I concede that this prisoner is indeed a Warden responsible for multiple deaths. Because he took Barrakeval's life savagely—without warning or negotiation, thus violating our terms of battle with the *pandye gash*—he properly belongs to those of Barrakeval's cadre, those who took him captive. Send him back—"

"No!" I croaked, trying not to panic. "Please let me speak, honored sir." The room erupted with so many flickering lights and forms, all of them shouting and babbling, that I had to close my eyes to concentrate. "I've come to meet with those like you. We didn't know what you were . . . all these years . . . so much misunderstanding . . . Please—"

A powerful fist in my gut aborted my plea. I opened my watering eyes to see the gray-haired Ezzarian glaring ferociously into my face. "You will be silent, prisoner. The noble Kaarat has spoken his judgment."

"But I've come unarmed," I wheezed, trying to force the sound beyond the broad, flat face to the troubled judge. The words I had held safe for so long in the dark were desperate to get out. "There's a danger . . . warning . . . please hear me. A Nevai—"

Another blow and I could no longer protest. Vilgor came for me then, elbowing Merryt aside. The purple-caped demon mumbled under his breath as he unhooked my hands from the column and shoved me toward a wavering door. "Cursed Nevai meddling. Who asked Denas to send his mongrel to direct our business?"

I stumbled and fell, retching from the blows, though there was nothing left inside me to lose. Dizzy, doubled over in pain and sickness, I fought to control my terror. I could not let them send me back to Ham-fist and Jack-Willow and the darkness. The Gastai were going to make me forget everything. They were going to crawl inside my soul and stay there forever, feeding on the horrors they inflicted upon me. What if they never let me die? With some mote of foolish resistance, I lashed out at the purple-clad demon. "Hyssad! Begone! I am the Warden—"

I never got out the rest of it, for something exploded in my head, and when I woke again, there was no light.

I could not bear to open my eyes. My head felt like a cracked melon. My gut like fire. My hands trembled unceasingly. When would they come? When would they begin again? I rolled over onto my knees and rested my throbbing head on the formless darkness of the floor, fighting to muster some shred of strength. I would not tell them my name. I would not yield my soul. I would not scream. I would not. I refused to feed a demon's hunger until there was nothing left of me to care.

"Here, come on." Hands reached under my shoulders and dragged me up. "And quietly about it."

I pulled away, wobbling, flailing with impotent fists. "I won't. I won't," I said, mumbling through lips numb with cold and swelling. "You can starve."

The hands gripped my wrists. "Come, now, hold on. I'm sorry I knocked you about, but I had to silence you. Here . . . lean on me . . ." The whispering man draped my arm across his broad back. "You need to learn how things work in Kir'Vagonoth. Never go about anything directly, and never, ever, let anyone know who your friends are. Now, hush you, lad. We'd rather not allow these devils to know I've come for you."

Through the fog of my fear the voice took hold. "Merryt?"

"Would you please keep your voice down? Since when are Ezzarians so dastard free with names?"

He dragged me stumbling through the cold darkness, through another sickening whirlwind, and into a long dim passage. The only light came from the walls themselves, built of pale gray stone or ice. After threading our way through a maze of such grim passages, we came to a small room, piled from floor to ceiling with clothing, dishes, boxes of candles, balls of yarn and rolls of leather, bars of metal and sticks of wood, and all manner of other things. A half-open wooden chest held hammers and chisels of various sizes, and the walls were hung with loops of rope, lengths of chain, and bundles of leather thongs. "This is a useful hideaway. Can't keep anything safe in my quarters in the castle. They haven't found this place yet, and I don't intend they should. The devils imitate everything that's been seen in our world, but don't know the proper use of half the things they shape." A small desk was littered with pens and ink and papers half written or crumpled. "Some of them shape themselves bodies, too, as if wearing flesh will make them human."

As I stood hunched and shivering beside the door, Merryt threw open a flat-sided brass trunk, yanked out a small leather pouch, and stuffed it in the folds of his cloak. "I need to teach someone how to speak respectfully," he said, once the trunk was closed and locked again. He stood up and raked me with his dark eyes. "Damn, you are a wretched mess."

The Ezzarian disappeared into one corner. He came back with a silver pitcher and filled a crystal goblet, which he gave to me. I stared at it dully, as the contents sloshed over my trembling hands. Cold and clear. Water.

"Go ahead and drink it. There's no time for anything else. I know you crave a cleaning and a bed and something fit for a human to eat, but it's best you stay as you are for a bit. You don't want to appear threatening."

Threatening. I squinted at what I could see of my bent, scarred, filthy self, and I started to laugh, sagging against the cold gray wall. I couldn't stop, and Merryt had to catch the shaking goblet before I dropped it. He was missing two fingers on his left hand and one on the right.

"Come on," he said. "We need to go. Denas is waiting. He's the most powerful of the Nevai circle, and the only one who could get you away from the pits. I told him you might be useful. Make him think so, and things will be better soon. There are interesting occupations for Wardens who keep their wits about them. I could mentor you." He refilled the goblet and held it to my lips. Never had I tasted anything so marvelous. Three times he filled it, then he set it down and took my arm. "We must go. I'd advise you keep your counsel. Your secrets are your only coin in this realm."

"I thought . . ." To think was difficult. "I thought this Denas had no interest in me."

Merryt leaned his head out of the door, as if checking to see if anyone was coming, then he dragged me into the passage. "It seemed that way at first. For all this time, he's refused to pull you out. But things change. As I mentioned earlier, don't ever believe what anyone says. If someone says up, it's likely to mean down or very possibly sideways."

"But then everyone knows—"

"Not exactly. That's why we had to take the risk to send you back to the mad ones, and why we'll not let anyone know you've been dragged out again. Your story is ended as far as most everyone knows. Denas wants an advantage in his enterprises. Perhaps he thinks you can serve."

"Thank you." I said no more than that. I did not want

to weep in front of him. He had already witnessed the depths of my degradation.

Merryt clapped me on the shoulder, then led me through the passageway and out into the storm. My head was bent into the wind, and I was following just behind the man, doing well to stay upright and move fast enough that my bare feet and hands did not freeze. Merryt had a bit of a limp, and it was the only reason I could keep up at all. But after a long time slogging through the bitter storm, something in the sighing note of the wind set my jumbled thoughts quiet and uneasy. Wary, I looked up. In the distance stretched an arched bridge, long, graceful, an impossible span over a jagged ice gorge, a rainbow of pale colors leading into the soaring, ice-carved fortress of my long-forgotten dreaming.

I stumbled to my knees in gaping wonder, the frigid wind scraping my lungs and making me cough until a fine spray of blood reddened the snow. *Wake up . . . wake up . . . before it comes.* Merryt was already disappearing into the gloom. "Please . . . help . . ." The wind snatched my voice away, and the man did not slow. *Get up. Move. This is not the dream.* My feet were unfeeling blocks of ice, but I got them under me and staggered forward. "Wait . . ."

Merryt turned just as I fell again, and he came and hauled me up, my arm across his shoulders. "Mustn't leave you out here to freeze. Not until we see what you're about, at least. Just a little farther."

More than a little, but I didn't care. I was not collapsed in the snow being devoured by the darkness.

We did not cross the bridge or enter the castle by its magnificent gates, guarded by towering forms of winged jackals, hacked from the ice. Rather Merryt took me a long way around, climbing up a jagged ice mountain to a back gate tucked inconspicuously between the castle wall and the frozen cliffs behind it. While he unlocked the gate, I stood shivering and gazing down onto the storm-wracked plain where I had lain so often in my dreams. From this vantage I could see the outline of a city in the distance, spires and roofs and towers sprawled across a small segment of the horizon. The city was dark, as if it were deserted, consumed by plague, perhaps, and waiting for the storm to bury it in winter. Just to the right of the city, stretching in a long arc to the base of the castle mount, was a sea of flickering lights. They put me in mind of a warrior encampment on the eve of battle. We'd just come from there, I believed.

"Come along. No one outside the castle is supposed to see us. That's why we came the long way around." Merryt held open the gate and waved his three-fingered hand for me to pass.

I took one last look at the bleak wilderness. He was out there waiting, the one in black and silver, the horror I had felt in my dreams, ready to devour what light remained in this dark place and in the world I had near forgotten. Merryt gave me a push, and I stumbled into the castle.

CHAPTER 22

Merryt stuck me in a holding room of some kind—a plain, tall-ceilinged, forbidding place that appeared unnervingly like a prison cell. He warned me not to move or speak unless I was told. As in the other place—the warren where Merryt had shown me the room he called his hideaway—the walls gave off a faint light of their own, enough to find one's way from place to place, but scarcely enough to read by if one had possessed the luxury of books. I stood shivering, hunched over, wondering dully if it was possible that I was in the midst of some grotesque nightmare. After pinching and prodding both flesh and mind in an attempt to rouse myself, I came to the sad conclusion that I was already awake.

"How have you come here?" A deep voice, as strong and cold and hard as if it, too, had been shaped from the ice, rang out clearly, making me jump halfway out of my nasty skin.

Wits. I needed to get some wits about me. This Denas was someone powerful enough to alter the course of Rudai judgment with a simple word of "disinterest," someone who could send me back to Ham-fist with a twitch of his finger. It had been so long since I'd needed wits. From my thick head I dragged the words I had saved. "I was invited," I said at last, my whole being clenched in prayer that I guessed rightly about a place where plotting and intrigue seemed the business of existence.

"Invited by whom?"

Your secrets are your only coin in this realm. "He did not give me his name."

There was a long pause. No matter how I squinted and stared I could see no one in the room with me—neither a being of flesh nor one of glimmering light—yet I could feel his formidable presence. "You carried no weapons when you were taken. Where are they?" And he was sounding neither friendly nor interested.

"I brought none." Words crowded to my tongue, begging to be heard—babbling entreaties, promises to tell whatever I could remember. What if I said too much or too little and was cast into the pits again? I clamped my trembling hands under my arms.

"You would have me believe that a Warden, the slayer of the Naghidda, has come into this realm undefended? Do our enemies yield when they yet hold mastery of our prison?" I had no idea what he meant.

I closed my eyes and searched for words in the battered pulp that was my head, trying to recapture the reasoning that now eluded me. My hoarded words sounded absurd as I stood naked before a demon lord. And I had to be careful. My own surrender was one thing, yet somewhere Wardens were still fighting, Wardens who had not forgotten what they were about. I could not jeopardize them. *You don't want to appear threatening.* Merryt's advice was probably worth heeding. But I had sworn to myself through months of horror that I would not lie to those who might question me, or grovel before them in shame. I'd had enough of lies. *So, dolt of a Warden, remember what it was you wanted to say.*

"I no longer speak for the Aife and her Wardens," I said at last, spending what little coin I possessed. "I have been cast out of my own land because I believe our long-held enmity is wrong. I have come here not in surrender, but to seek refuge and truth." With what dignity I could muster, I sank to one knee, straightening my back and keeping my head unbowed. "I ask for sanctuary."

"Sanctuary!" He was indeed surprised. "And if I refuse?"

I scraped together the last of my words. "An honorable enemy would send me back to my home unscathed to face the reckoning of my own people." I longed to go home. If I just knew where it was and why I had been thrown out of it.

A mistake. The darkness gathered in that room like a

summer thunderstorm fills the sky. "You dare think to instruct me—"

But a silvery thread of a woman's laughter cut off the questioner's mounting anger. A magical, beckoning sound, like the clearest bells in Druya's temple. My eyes flicked upward and to the sides, but I saw no one. Never had I heard such bright music in laughter. The shadows shrank into the corners of the room at the sound of it.

I waited several moments for more questions or a verdict. But empty silence soon gave me to understand that the observers were no longer present . . . if they had ever been. Wearily I sat back onto the cold uneven floor, propping my arms on my knees and resting my head on them. My hands shook—quite on their own, as if they belonged to some other body.

I sat there for perhaps an hour, too tired to sleep, too spent to think or plan or be afraid anymore. I sought emptiness. Not as shelter from pain this time, but for its own sake. I drew it over me like a woolen mantle, warmth and softness against the bitterness of existence. Then somewhere in the depths of emptiness there came a whisper, pricking my mind like a bee sting on tender flesh. *Do you yet live, Warden?*

Every cell of my body came awake. What marvel was this?

I clutched those whispered words like a starving man hoards newfound crumbs of bread, wanting to caress them, to savor them, wanting to laugh aloud, yet terrified at drawing any attention that might take them from me. And if I consumed them with too much haste or too little care, they would be gone, and I would not be able to bear it.

Hesitantly I probed my innermost depths, the place where melydda lived, the place that had been cold and dead for all the months I had languished in the pits of the Gastai. I found something there . . . and like the thready pulse of a dying man, the power wavered and fought for life beneath my hand. I coaxed and prodded tenderly, carefully, until I felt it strengthen just enough to push back the shadows of my mind and give me voice. *I live. Whoever calls . . . I live. Help me.* From a distance so far I could not fathom it, I felt a hand reach out in eager astonishment . . .

"Come on, then. You've not sat here and died on me?" The broad face of weathered bronze was no more than a handspan from my own. The Ezzarian was shaking my shoulder so hard my teeth clattered in rhythm with my hands. "I'm to take you to meet Denas and his guests."

"Denas . . ." The weight of waking disappointment came near crushing me. I tried the slightest touch of melydda, but found nothing. It wasn't real. I must have fallen asleep.

"You've done well, it seems. Got them interested at least. You're an experienced player, then?" Before I could summon words from beyond despair, Merryt put a thick finger over my mouth and escorted me from the waiting room. "Never mind. Time enough for talking when your position is settled."

Exhausted, hungry, confused with injury, cold, and searing disappointment, I scarcely noted where he took me. A brief journey through a windy courtyard, innumerable turnings through long, gloomy passages, and we arrived at a modest room that was draped in heavy curtains. The bed was a long mat or cushion piled with billowing coverings, and red cushions were scattered on a rug of white fur that softened the stone floor. In one corner was a small gray block with nine candles sitting beside it, their glow a bright smudge in the darkness—an Ezzarian mourning stone. A tall doorway opened onto some larger space, but it was too dim to see anything beyond it. If I could only be permitted to fall onto that glorious rug and sleep, I thought, I could want nothing better. That was only until my escort spoke to someone at his door and came back with a huge bowl of steaming water, setting it on the bare floor beside the rug.

"Go on," he said, nodding toward the water, clearly annoyed. "Be quick about it. We've no time to dawdle. Everything's changed, and not one of the cursed demons has bothered to tell me what's going on."

I knelt beside the bowl and dipped my trembling hands into it, surprised to find the water cold, despite the steam. But it was clean and fresh, and I scooped the precious liquid and splashed it on my face. A fresh gash on my forehead stung with it, but I groaned in animal pleasure and did it again.

"You'll have to learn to make it hot or cold for yourself.

They can make the appearance, but there's never any certainty as to the feel of it."

I could not speak. Just as well, because I didn't understand him in the least. Perhaps there would be time for understanding. For the moment I reveled in the water and the bit of cloth he gave me to scrub with.

"You've got a quarter of an hour. No more. Doesn't do to keep a Nevai waiting. They have more ways to twist a mind than an Ezzarian has prayers." Merryt grunted like a wild pig as the water turned black. "A pox on the mad creatures! I've never seen a body so cursed filthy. Nor such a variety of villainy." With no attempt at politeness, he inspected my lifetime's harvest of scars. "You are quite a rugged fellow, it appears. To have survived so long in the pits, and so many injuries of longer history. And this"—he touched the left side of my face with his three-fingered left hand—"it may be you have as little use for the humankind as I. I do so wish we had time to talk. There's a tale here somewhere, and I don't like being left out of it." He disappeared into the next room. "I'll be right back."

By the time I made one swipe at everything and used his knife to hack off my mat of filthy hair, I felt one small step back to human. Meanwhile Merryt returned with brown breeches and a long white shirt of nubby linen, black hose, and boots. Best of all was a thick cloak of black wool.

"Can't have you come naked before Denas this time. He has guests. An interesting story you gave him—sanctuary. I'm fain to see how it plays . . ." He paused very briefly, as if to see if I would explain a little more. But I was fumbling with buttons and laces—no easy matter with hands that would not stop shaking and eyes that could scarcely focus in the gray light—and I wasn't even sure I could remember what I'd been thinking when I spoke of sanctuary. Once I had released the hoarded words, my mind had fallen into a jumble. Everything was so confusing. Merryt shrugged and went on. ". . . but Ezzarians are never at their best unclothed. Sorry I've got no extra human togs to put you in. I won't wear the demons' pretty rags myself. Only human-wrought. Just in case I find a portal to take me home—wouldn't want the demon rags to vanish and leave me naked, now would I? But you'll have to do with these. It's best to make a good appearance no matter what deviltry they're up to. Now, I've got you this far alive, might as well keep you that way long enough to see how it suits you here."

I had only time enough to wrestle the boots onto my scabbed feet, when Merryt hurried me out of the room and back into the gray maze of Denas's castle. Our route was little more than a blur. Merryt moved quickly despite his limp, and it was difficult to keep up. Something inside my lower back was torn, making movement impossibly painful, and I was so hungry I could have eaten the boots. Occasionally I saw flickering lights and felt the passing of demons; I even glimpsed a few humanlike bodies in rooms that we passed. Eventually we descended a broad circular stair into a lavishly vaulted atrium. The gray-and-white patterned floor tiles left me dizzy, as they were almost translucent, and I could scarcely see the tops of the twisting columns that supported the vault. Tucked into every nook of the circular space were ice sculptures, huge, translucent carvings of birds and beasts; fountains, I realized as we passed them, their sheets and whorls of water frozen in place. In only one, a very small one placed in the exact center of the atrium, did the water actually flow. Its faint trickle sounded something mournful amidst the echoing clatter of our boots.

"Here we are, then." The Ezzarian paused for a moment before tall doors, carved with a jumble of flowers and vines. He reached for the gleaming handle that was cast in the form of a snake, but before he could open the door, I plucked at his sleeve.

"Thank you," I said. "Will you tell me who you are?"

"A survivor, as I told you. If you get through the next few hours, perhaps we'll have occasion to get acquainted. More likely not. Denas dislikes humans something dreadful. It may be you're too porridge-headed to bother with."

This room was much larger than the last, with soaring walls of blue-white ice that reflected the flames of a thousand candles. But for all the fire in the room, there was no warmth and precious little light, so that I could only make out the furnishings closest to the double doors. That was plenty to consider. It looked as though they had stuffed enough rugs, cushions, chairs, tables, statuary, and brass in that room to furnish two Derzhi palaces. You could scarcely walk three paces without having to dodge a marble-topped table, a rearing bronze horse, or a needle-work-covered footstool. Elaborate candelabra hung from the high ceilings, and somewhere deeper in the room, silver lamps were set upon tall poles, casting weak pools of light upon vats of ice-carved roses. As everywhere I had been, the colors were pale and dull—as if the artist who painted the world had spilled a vat of gray paint upon his palette, spoiling all the colors so that none were true.

"Ah, Merryt. I want you to play draughts with me to-night." A small, puffy-faced man walked out of the gloom. At least he appeared as a man, with a body one could view from any direction, until I caught the demon shimmer riffling around the edges of his human form. He was short and balding, dressed in an odd suit of gold brocade—tight breeches and a sleeveless coat that fell to his ankles. He seemed to have forgotten his shirt, and he wore only one boot. Certainly not Denas. The voice was not at all right. "And this is the impertinent newcomer." He put his hands on his hips and stared rudely.

I kept my mouth shut.

Merryt gave a slight bow. "I would enjoy a game, Seffyd, but first I must deliver this one to Denas."

"It's *her* as wants him, you know. Denas has no time for schooling prisoners. He'd as soon see you all dead."

"I'm well aware of Denas's disregard for yladdi . . . but I thought he wished to question this one himself." Merryt seemed discomfited.

"Nope. It's her."

"What use does Vallyne have for him?"

"It's just more of this confounded bargain that's set them quarreling. Can't have a decent game without their arguing getting in the way of it. Everyone is over there"—Seffyd waved a limp hand into the gloom—"somewhere. Who knows? Have you seen Vilgor these past hours? He's sup-posed to bring me a new game, but no one's seen him. He's usually prompt—"

"Perhaps Vilgor has let his loose tongue wag once too

often." Merryt tugged at my arm. "I'm sorry, Seffyd, but Denas wants the prisoner right away, so I'd best move on."

"Ah, no matter. You're no challenge at a game anyway. A Gastai has more wit." The gold-clad man sniffed and went on his way, crowding past us in the aisle and knocking over a small wooden table, which shattered into a thousand pieces.

Merryt, muttering to himself, gave me a rough shove. I stumbled and came near falling into a frozen pool before he caught me. "Sorry, lad. These cursed demons . . . always keeping a man out of balance. Always lying. You never know what they'll do." The man nudged me forward more gently, whispering in my ear as we wound through the forest of furnishings. "For example, never beat Seffyd at draughts—or any other game for that matter. He's a fearsome loser. I've seen him send opponents to the pits for winning too often, and he'd likely do worse if they were human."

I was trying to sort it out. "They send their own—other rai-kirah—to the Gastai?"

"Well, they like to have something other than just annoying each other or clapping each other in dungeons. Gives them a nasty bit of fun. They can force each other to take solid form and do all the things they did to you and worse. But it takes a wickedly powerful demon to kill another one. Most of them can't do it, especially one that's in their own circle." Merryt slowed for a moment and jerked his head toward the silver lamps ahead of us. "Watch yourself, my friend. These you will meet are very old. Cunning. Dangerous. The Nevai dress themselves up like something fine, but the faces you will see are no more real than the seven-headed dragons you met in your days as a Warden. They can make your life livable, or they can make it worse than what you faced before."

I nodded and wished yet again that I'd had some time to sleep before needing wits again. How many hours had it been since the purple-robed Vilgor had dragged me away from my dark prison? I followed Merryt toward the sound of talk and laughter under the silver lamps. Music was playing . . . all too familiar . . . the dissonant harmonies of demon enchantment, not just a nerve-scraping reflection in the mind, but in full grotesque voice of harps and flutes and viols. The aura of demon—the soul-wrenching certainty of their presence gleaned from smell, taste, hearing, and the very touch of the air, and recognizable from hundreds of mortal encounters—grew so strong that my feet slowed and my hand cried out for a blade.

"You'll get used to it." Merryt dragged me on until we stepped beyond a folding screen of intricate silver work into the blazing light of the silver lamps. At least fifty demons occupied that room. Perhaps more. Some wore physical bodies as Seffyd did, with solid flesh and hair, clothes and features that looked like those of any humans, save for a lingering corona of colored light that hovered at their edges. Others appeared in their gleaming, light-drawn forms, their faces and shapes sometimes visible, sometimes not as they turned in and out of my view. Those who wore physical bodies were arrayed in extravagant costumes of silver and gold satin, trimmed with ruffled collars and feathered caps, rich embroidery and an emperor's treasury of jewels. The others—those who were light-formed—appeared in simpler attire, softly draped tunics and breeches or skirts of vivid, jewellike colors that were a startling contrast to the washed-out hues visible everywhere else in the demon realm.

Whether formed of flesh or light, the guests were engaged in lively activity. Some were dancing to the dreadful music on the floor of black-and-white-patterned tiles, some were sitting on red velvet couches or fat cushions of blue satin, engaged in animated conversation. Some were drinking pale wine from crystal goblets, and some were playing at games with ornate game pieces of ivory, jade, and ebony.

But as Merryt led me into the light, all conversation, laughter, and music stopped. The silent, staring crowd parted, moving smoothly to the sides as if a slave were drawing them apart like his master's bed curtains. We walked between them until we faced only a group of three rai-kirah: one a light-drawn figure of golden radiance, two with forms of flesh. The golden demon, tall and powerfully built, stood looking on in annoyance as the other two faced each other across a small table, apparently playing a game. I needed no introduction. The handsome, fair-haired Nevai appeared something near my own age, and the haughty brilliance of his presence left me no doubt that he was the owner of the castle. Though he did not wear a physical body, there was more solidity and substance to his shimmering form than in most humans I had known. When his cold stare shifted to me, it came near halting my steps. Yet my eyes did not linger on the demon lord. The two other players took my breath.

They alone among the crowd kept on with their activity, the intensity of their friendly combat causing the rest of the world to fade into insubstantiality. On the left was a woman arrayed in a silver gown, studded with diamonds that sparkled in the light as she leaned forward to move the carved game pieces. Her hair was a cloud of gold, caught up on one side with a diamond butterfly. Her laugh was the sound of chiming bells I had heard earlier, and her porcelain cheek flushed with triumphant delight as she knocked her opponent's game piece away with a slender hand, ringed with sapphires. I wanted to close my eyes before I looked into hers. Cold blue demon fire had no place in a vision so strikingly beautiful.

Her opponent was less remarkable in appearance than either of the others, a slender, fair-haired man of middle age and middling height, with a short, neatly trimmed beard. His aura was a brilliance of blue and purple and swirling gray-green, and indeed he wore a tight-fitting shirt and trousers of deep-hued blue and purple, shining black boots, and a gray-green cloak that shimmered like water in dappled sunlight. Yet it was on his face that my eyes settled and with his laughter of resigned good-humor that my blood took fire. He stood and bowed to the lady, yielding the field of battle to the beautiful victor, and when he at last turned his face to me, I saw a cocky smile and eyes that burned blue with demon fire and unending good humor. He was the one, the rai-kirah of my last battle, the cheerful being who had destroyed my life, who had driven me mad with dreams, the demon who had lured me away from the world I knew and into the heart of all my fears.

CHAPTER 23

"So what shall we call him, Vallyne? You know it will be three hundred years until he yields his name. He's shown himself a stubborn fellow. Can't just call him Yddrass. There'd be unending confusion, since we now have two Wardens, even though we do not abuse Merryt's name—much to his sorrow." The slight, blond-bearded demon wrinkled his nose in distaste at my escort, then chuckled and walked around me as if I were a piece of statuary. "I suppose we'll have to make something up, like 'Visitor,' or 'Horse thief'—not to offend you, ylad, as I've no reason to believe you have ever stolen a horse—or 'Bonechewer.' I think the Gastai once called him that. Or maybe we could call him 'Scarface.'" With his hands clasped behind his back, he stood on his toes and peered at my left cheek. Nothing in his· frivolous chattering gave any sign that he had ever encountered me before.

"I see no need to call him anything," said Denas. The storm that had gathered during our first interview had only receded. The brooding anger was an extension of his luminous form, spreading across the room as if the lack of solid boundaries to his body allowed his raw emotions to spill out. "He is ylad filth." With nothing more than a slight tip of his head, the grim demon lord dismissed the rest of the murmuring onlookers. The gaudy crowd retreated slowly—reluctantly it seemed—into the cluttered shadows of the vast room.

The lady did not move from her seat at the game table, but rested her chin on her hand as she watched the rest of us, amusement playing over her features. I kept trying to look away, to judge and learn of this place and its inhabitants, but I found it very difficult. She was extraordinarily lovely. Her lips were wider than the accepted form of beauty in my world, but they balanced her wide-set eyes perfectly, as if nature had saved such a combination only for its most sublime subject. Those eyes—their radiance promising mystery and magic like the stars of the night sky—were huge and green. Of course no artifice of color could mask the truth of her nature. Yet never had a demon been housed in such a pleasing form, and never had I felt such danger as I did in the moment of her attention. "I think we shall call him *Fyadd*." Her voice was low and warm, disturbing senses I believed long dead beneath the ruin of my flesh. Exile, she named me.

I bowed to her, not trusting my voice to answer, hiding my shaking hands behind my back. Their condition was not likely to improve if I was to see much of the lady.

She fastened her green eyes upon my own and smiled, a radiant beam of sunlight piercing that gloomy world. "And don't think to carry him off to your den of torment, dear Vyx. He is my very own. Denas offered me any gift of my choosing to prove his affection, and this is what I've chosen. I think my lord is much annoyed with me and not affectionate at all. I think perhaps he rues his bargain." Her wicked humor had the demon lord bristling, and I wrenched my eyes away from the two of them, lest my noting of it set loose the hurricane he held in check by such thin tethers.

The slender, bearded demon she called Vyx spun about in an eye-blurring twirl, ending up reclined on a cushion at the lady's feet. His physical body had disappeared, and only his light-drawn image remained—the same mischievous face, the same slender shape, but the purple and blue and swirling gray-green were now his essence and not just the color of his clothing. "Ah, but lady, to find you trifling with grim Denas and a mind-dead ylad . . . it is just too wretched. I thought you were to be mine alone."

"What you thought is of no consequence, mad sprite. I've heard tales of this Warden, and I *will* have him as my companion. Denas is full of himself and his plans for glory. You are full of mischief and your wanderings. You've left me without amusement for far too long. No, this one is mine until I tire of him, and you'll have to devise some quite spectacular entertainment to get him away from me. Now go. Summon a servant to put him with my other pets."

"As you say, dear lady." Vyx bowed elaborately and vanished.

Denas growled and folded his well-muscled arms. "You've no idea what you're playing at, Vallyne. Merryt says he is half a simpleton, but he is still an yddrass, and he killed the Naghidda. We should interrogate him and be done with it. There are important questions to be answered before Rhadit leads us . . ." Denas glanced at me with bitter hatred. ". . . to our destiny."

"We had a bargain, good sir" said the lady. "I claim my prize, and you can do nothing about it. What do I care for your quest for glory?" The lady, her silver gown and her diamonds glittering in the light, smiled wickedly and held out her empty wineglass to Denas, who snatched a carafe from the table and refilled it. She took a sip, then raised the glass to the guests who yet lingered in the shadows. "No matter where fate and plotting take the rest of you, my life will ever be here in Kir'Vagonoth."

Only when her eyes passed over my companion did Vallyne's radiance dim. "If you remember, dear Denas, I told you to keep your vile messenger out of my presence." She drained her glass of wine and beckoned another demon to her game table.

Denas jerked his head at Merryt. Merryt nodded politely, but his fingers dug deep into my already bruised arms until I thought the bone might snap. "What the devil does she want with you?" he mumbled. As a shimmering green figure appeared in front of me, extending a cold demon hand to wrap itself about my neck, the Ezzarian bowed to the lady's back, whispering from the side of his mouth, "If there is a rotted soul among these villains, friend, it is she who claims you. Watch your tongue and your back. I'll find you again when I can."

Merryt's advice was lost on me. The lady was laughing as I was led away, and despite every warning, including the screaming signals of doom inside my own head, I let the music of it fill my emptiness. Chiming bells, singing strings of harp and lute, the first birdsong after silent winter—never had I heard melodies so lovely, played on an instrument so sweet. Even the parting glare from Denas gave me no pause. All I wanted was to sleep forever with that music playing inside my head. I was so very tired.

Fortunately my desires were modest. I sensed that I would derive little enlightenment from the next phase of my life in Kir'Vagonoth—the name the demons gave to their land of snow and wind and frost butterflies. With his invisible leash the green-clad demon dragged me through room after room of opulent furnishings and magnificently set tables—all of them dim and deserted—into a barren courtyard paved with gray brick and sheltered from the worst of snow and wind by high walls and a latticed roof. There he gave me a green loincloth in exchange for Merryt's lovely warm cloak, boots, and clothing, and promptly deposited me in a corner with fifteen snarling dogs.

"You will speak to no one without the mistress's command. The gate to this yard is locked and will warn us if you attempt to escape. The penalties for disobedience will be severe." He tightened his invisible grip on my lungs, shutting off my breathing quite effectively until my eyes went dark. When the demon let go and I had breath again, I nodded and shrank back into the corner, sinking to the floor with my back to the cold brick wall. I understood severe.

The demon—whose physical appearance was exceedingly hairy and less than intelligent—flickered into invisibility and departed, and I was left alone with the uneasy beasts, all of them large and all of them with a great many teeth. Seven of them took the point, standing around me growling, legs stiff, tails dropped, showing their teeth, and—from the amount of drooling—contemplating the succulent tenderness of my throat and liver. I willed my heart quiet and my breathing smooth, and held still in the corner, allowing the beasts to posture and sniff and nose about me as they would. Fortunately they were more unsettled at my intrusion than truly vicious. A quarter of an hour seemed to convince them I was no threat, and they settled into large hairy lumps to sleep. A few of the less intimidating beasts I encouraged to come closer, and I curled up among them.

For the first time since I had stepped into the abyss, I slept warm and had no dreams at all.

Life with Vallyne's dogs was not so bad. Though it puzzled me that I was left unquestioned and alone for so many days; there were no beatings, no torture, and I could sleep as much as I pleased. The tiled courtyard was barren, but clean and slightly warmer than the pits. Though the light never changed from the stormy gray of everlasting winter, at least it was not darkness.

I enjoyed having company—though I quickly came to realize that the dogs were no more real than the frost butterfly. Less so, actually, for the butterfly had physical substance and could be shattered at a careless touch, whereas the dogs were but illusion. A sword through its belly could not kill one of them, but a sorcerer's word could dissolve it into nothing. The truth of the matter struck me when I patted a hairy, knee-high beast with drooping eyes and realized it had no heartbeat. I investigated further and discovered that although some of the dogs were warm, others were quite cold. Some had tails and some did not. A few had no teeth. They appeared very much like the cast-offs in a potter's studio, each with a flaw that kept it from being quite finished. I wondered why anyone bothered to feed them. But they were very good illusions, and I came to think of them as real. When they piled around me to sleep and I rubbed their bellies and furry necks, I blessed them for their uncomplicated companionship. I couldn't betray them. They couldn't despise me. Somehow that seemed a comfort.

The food was far better than that in the pits of the mad Gastai. I closed my eyes and let my imagination tell me what I ate, since the taste was often unrelated to the food's appearance. Occasionally I got bread, cooked meat, or cheese that looked like scraps left from someone's table. None of it had much taste, and what taste it had was something off. Not spoilt, just wrong. Vaguely sweet when it should be tart. Musty where it should be fresh. The texture hard or smooth where it should be juicy or crumbling. The variety was pleasant, though I learned to avoid anything that resembled cheese if there was enough else. I would have said someone had taken out all the cream and left only the mold. But I wasn't about to complain. Though their edible creations had never seen pig, fowl, vine, or tree, the rai-kirah were able to create something near enough that it could nourish a human body. I did not starve.

My injuries began to heal, and after a number of days spent huddled untidily in the corner, not daring to look about or think, starting at every sound, I decided I had better start moving or I would never remember how. On the first day I stood up and walked about a little. No one objected. On the next, I walked a bit more and began to stretch out my stiff and twisted muscles. Again, no one seemed to notice. On the third day, I began to train. In the beginning I spent long hours doing the slowest, easiest exercises of the kyanar, trying to build some semblance of strength and balance. Then I went on to more difficult movements, and I started running with the dogs in their aimless chasing around the perimeters of the courtyard. After a week of collapsing quickly with lungs and legs on fire, I began to make good progress.

The movement, sleep, and freedom from constant pain allowed me to regain some clarity of mind. I began to mark the days—counting the periods I slept as night—and scratching my tally on the tile work in a corner. Though my hands still trembled constantly, I could think again, and, if I worked at it, recall brief snippets of my life: my earliest school days, bits of Warden's training, Ezzarian ritual, isolated events from my years in slavery, unending demon battles.

Unfortunately I found that, no matter how hard I worked at it, I could not remember the most important things: my personal history—family, friends, how I had come to be a slave or been set free of it—how I had come to Kir'Vagonoth, what it was I had risked my life and reason to discover, the nature of the fears my dreaming had aroused. My memory was like a manuscript carefully written, then blotted with pools of ink—certain text in absolute clarity, the word right next to it totally obscured.

I wasn't sure I wanted to discover what was hidden. Every door I tried to open seemed to have something terri-

ble and painful behind it. For the moment I preferred to
work at physical exercise until I could not lift a toe, and
then to practice chants and recitations that took my mind
away from past, present, and future, until I collapsed with
the dogs and slept. There would be time enough later to
remember. Or if I was going to die or be eternally captive,
then what did it matter?

I had no thought of escape. I allowed myself to believe
it was because the walls were high and smooth, with only
one gate of thick black bars, and that the lock was sealed
with an enchantment I had no power to break. The roof
was a latticework of the same black bars, and even if I'd
had some confidence that I could bend them, they were
more than twice a man's height above my head. And my
melydda was dead—damaged, injured, fled, I didn't know
what—my words of enchantment as useless as a deaf man's
ears or a blind man's eyes. The moment's stirring power I
had felt at my interrogation had clearly been nothing but
a dream. But no reasoning could mask the truth. If I tried
to escape, the demons would send me back to the pits. The
terror of that bound me as no chains could ever do.

Never in all that time did I lay eyes on Vallyne or Merryt
or Denas, nor on the one named Vyx, the strange demon
who had drawn me to Kir'Vagonoth with terrifying dreams.
Only the green-clad servant came to the courtyard, to bring
food and sweep up our leavings—happily the illusory
hounds were not exceptionally foul—and make sure that
the rivulet of water that trickled through a stone trough
had not been blocked or clogged. Ofttimes he just sat on
a bench in one corner of the yard and watched us. He
never spoke to me or gave me any indication that I was
not just another of the burdensome beasts. But on occasion
he wore a solid body instead of his flickering demon form,
and when he did so, he strutted proudly. I didn't think it
was for the dogs he preened. It set me laughing to see him
adjusting his drooping breeches or running his thick fingers
through his shaggy brown hair or over his full, drooping
lips as if to make sure they were put on straight.

I made no attempt to speak to the servant. I had no wish
to invite consequences, severe or otherwise. But on one day
when the dogs kept getting in his way as he was sweeping, I

whistled to them and started them running with me while he did his work. When he was done, he nodded to me very slightly, and I smiled and bowed in return.

Soon after this he watched me dipping water from the trough to wash myself, then running and shivering until I was dry. On his next visit he left a clean drying cloth beside my mound of food. I made no attempt to bridge the distance between us, even when he seemed on the verge of speaking to me, but whenever he wore his body, I bowed to him—not in mockery or excess, only enough to show respect.

A few days after he brought the drying cloth, he came in wearing his body, walking stiff and slow, half bent over as if he couldn't straighten up. He tried to lay down the heavy trays of food for the dogs, but he grunted painfully and held still for a moment. Being familiar with every variety of injury, I surmised that he had strained some muscle in his back and did not know enough anatomy to reshape himself and relieve his discomfort. But when I stepped close and held out my hands to help him with his load, I saw bloody streaks on his thin tunic of green silk. I took the trays and set them aside, then led him to the trough. With gestures I told him to remove his shirt. Indeed he had been beaten, with a cane, I guessed, and I remembered what Merryt had said about the demons locking each other inside a solid body and treating it cruelly. I took his shirt and wet it, then dabbed the cold water on the fresh stripes. I knew how to clean a wound without making it worse, and how to press on one place hard enough that he would not feel what I did to the others. When I had done all I could, I gave him his shirt and motioned him on his way. Either my efforts were exceptional or demon-created bodies did not feel injury so harshly as our human ones, for the servant bowed to me and proceeded with his work as if nothing were wrong.

I should have known better. On the next day I had a different guard—an ugly demon woman, very harsh. She carried a stick and beat the whimpering dogs if they came near her. She glowered at me and waggled her stick in my direction, her stormy blue-gray light pulsing with her movements. Not tempted to test her ancient form or her

flimsy-looking weapon, I curtailed my activities. I did not
cower or grovel, only stayed quiet in the corner, watching.
When she left, I went back to work.

After several weeks of training, I began to regain my
strength. The long hours running improved my wind, and
dodging the carousing dogs honed my agility. I drew on
every technique I could dredge from memory to harden
muscle, sharpen senses, and eradicate my lingering terrors.
But my hands still shook, and though on several occasions,
at the end of a good day, I experienced the first faint stir-
rings of melydda, every waking found my soul cold and
dead.

After one particularly vigorous day's work, while I was
cleaning myself at the trough, wishing I had the old woman's stick to use for sword practice, someone rattled the
gate locks and burst into the courtyard. It was a short,
plump young woman—quite solid and human looking—the
bodice of her yellow gown half torn away. Her round face
was flushed, her long brown curls disheveled, and her
breath ragged. When she noticed me, her small eyes widened in surprise. "Oh!"

Shouts rang from the halls beyond the courtyard, and
heavy footsteps pounded on tile floors.

"Oh, please, sir, can you help me? This cruel lord says
he will have me or throw me to the mad demons. A hundred years I've been imprisoned in this castle."

It was very curious. Her words were empty. Despite their
meaning, there was nothing of true fear in her voice. Fear
and I were old acquaintances by then, and it set me
wondering . . . and wary. Careful to utter no word, I motioned to the barren walls and shrugged my shoulders. With
gestures I suggested that she might wriggle under the heap
of dogs. If she had been the most desperate of fugitives, I
would have had nothing different to offer.

"But he would find me there." She stepped closer, laying
her folded hands upon my breast. Very cold hands. Her
quivering closeness did not leave me unaffected, however.
And little of sympathy or protectiveness could have been
found in the sudden onslaught of unfamiliar sensation. I
had to force myself to hear her pleading instead of only
the rush of blood in my ears. "I've heard there was a sor-

cerer—a human man with a soul—kept in this yard. Oh, kind sir, will you not aid me with your magics?" Her pleading was very pitiful, but whoever she was, she had not learned to match her eyes with her voice.

I stepped back to a safer distance, shook my head, and held out empty hands.

The shouts grew louder. "Where are you, vixen? You'll suffer for this. My knife, my whip, and my hand will teach you who is master."

They almost had me, for the man's voice was a very good imitation of Denas's roar. But not quite good enough. When the angry shouts drove her into my arms again, I spread my arms wide and gave her no harbor.

"Wicked villain!" She struck me on the face, which caused the dogs to run closer, growling. But no sooner did they sniff about the woman than they began to whine and wag their tails.

I took their cue and changed my widespread stance into a very deep bow, quickly smothering the disbelieving smile that insisted on displaying itself on my face. It was well I did so. When I raised my head, the short, plump refugee had become a woman of my own height, majestic in her bearing, the torn yellow dress revealing a full, perfect breast and sculpted shoulder of such vibrant loveliness as set my skin on fire. Vallyne stood before me, tapping her foot in irritation. "All right, so tell me, when did you guess?"

Wits. Where were my wits? I motioned to my mouth and raised my eyebrows, even as I devoured her with my eyes.

"Yes, yes, you may speak. You *will* speak. Are you so cruel a man who will not rescue a distressed woman?"

I thought it best not to inform her that her playacting skills were no better than her cheese. The dogs were a much better illusion. "I'm in no position to rescue anyone at present," I said.

"And you're not like to be if you don't do something interesting soon. Days and days you've been here and not one attempt to escape, not one flicker of sorcery, not one secret word to the kindly guard, not one soulful moaning moment to touch my heart. Only sleeping and mumbling and this unending running and dancing about with these pestiferous beasts. And yet you are clearly not dead in the mind as is usual for those who come from the pits. Are you made of stone?"

A number of things became clear just then, one of which was that I was most certainly not made of stone, nor was I dead, which had been my frequent supposition. And she had evidently been watching me enough to know my habits . . . or had it been a spy? "Though I am not at my best, my lady, I did make friends with the guardsman as you likely know. A fine, gentle fellow who upheld your interests quite clearly. I thought things were progressing quite well until he was removed. And your dogs, though somewhat limited as to their capacities, have been my boon companions. If I'd had any idea that more was wanted, I would have given it consideration."

"You've an insolent tongue, Exile."

"I believe I've been told that before. It is company brings out the best . . . or worst . . . in me."

Her wide mouth could display every subtlety of humor—this time wicked teasing. "Are you saying that you have no wish to remain with my pets?"

"I've come here to learn, and I think I've learned all your pets can teach. I was hoping you could do better."

She cocked her head at me. "So what will you give me in exchange for my teaching? Perhaps you will tell me your name." Curling tendrils of golden hair brushed her bare breast, and I became uncomfortably aware of my skimpy loincloth.

I cast my eyes to the safe, dull paving and shook my head, hoping to discover my duty somewhere in my uncontrolled imaginings. "Ah, lady, that is a difficult thing. The custom of my people is to give names only to guest-friends and kin. You and I have scarcely met. Perhaps there's some service I could offer you instead."

A cold wind gusted through the dark lattice of the roof, and a blurring before my eyes left the lady swathed in a white fur cloak with a hood draped gracefully over her lustrous hair. She smelled of flowers and wine and scented candle smoke. "Do you play music?"

"Alas, no. Instruments go out of tune at my touch," I said.

"Sing, then?" Laughter and teasing flitted across her face like summer lightning in a clear sky.

"Only when sacred duty demands it. I've been told I sing like a wild boar." Someone had told me that when I was sixteen. For one brief moment I could see a different face . . . beautiful, too . . . but then Vallyne traced an ivory finger across my chest, and the violet eyes of my memory brightened to blue-touched green, red-gold skin paled to alabaster, and dark hair caught golden fire. I could not remember the other one's name.

"Games, then. Perhaps you could give me a challenge that my usual opponents cannot provide." The lady took my arm, and we strolled toward the black-barred gate. The dogs whined and whimpered about my bare feet.

"I'm likely to be better at games than music, but I'll confess I have less experience at them."

"What kind of useless man are you? Clearly an uncivilized brute warrior, and I have a surfeit of those in this castle. I'll wager you're illiterate as well." The gate swung open without word or touch.

"On the contrary, madam. I cannot claim wide scholarship, but I can both read and write. There was a time when I was employed to do those things." My heart twisted as I said it, and I thought that a curious reaction. Who finds poignancy in memories of servitude?

The gate swung closed behind us, and my friends the dogs howled in sorrow as the lady led me into the castle passageways. "I have no use for writing. Who would read it? But reading . . . I delight in books. I shall have to try you at that."

"As you wish, my lady."

I wondered if I was to be a slave again. Though Vallyne's hand lay softly on my arm, I could not shake the sensation of manacles being locked about my wrists. But as we walked through the castle to her chambers, I forgot to care about it. She filled the passageway with the music of her laughter, and I drank it in as the desert sand drinks rain.

CHAPTER 24

"This will be your resting room," said the flickering demon, whose voice sounded like tolling bells and who smelled as if he were late for his own funeral rites. I pressed my hand discreetly to my nose to block out the stench. His physical form shifted between human-shaped and piggish, and the more agitated he was, the more of the foul odor poured out of him. His name was Raddoman, and he was some minor functionary in the lady's household. "The mistress wants you kept close, so you can attend her as she pleases. She has commanded clothes to be shaped for you and human food to be made and brought as you need it." He clearly did not approve of such condescension.

He waved me into a small room, crowded—as were all the rooms in the castle—with furniture, artwork, and objects of every kind. Painted dishes were piled on wooden chairs that were lined up against the walls. Vases of frost flowers stood on tables stacked with brass boxes and wooden cups, baskets and bottles and statues of horses and dogs. Two black-lacquered footstools were stuffed under tables, because there was no room beside any chair where you might have wanted to use them. A rolled-up rug blocked the opening of a hearth, and stacks of wood and hods of coal stood in a corner behind a tall bookshelf, quite unreachable. Somewhere behind a cabinet with glass shelves, loaded with all manner of trinkets like mirrors and brushes and enameled cups and magnifying lenses, was a tall, narrow window. Snow blew in through the open shutters, frosting everything in the room with a fine dusting of white. Nowhere could I see a bed or anything similarly useful.

"Thank you, Raddoman. You're very kind to show me the way."

"I do as the mistress commands." He snorted and shifted into his piggish form, disconcerting since he was taller than I. "I don't like ylad."

"I understand. Perhaps we can get to know each other better."

He shuddered, and I worked not to gag at the cloud of stink. "I don't like you."

"I'm sorry."

"But mistress said to ask if there was anything you wished brought here, as ylad have different needs."

"She is most kind." I surveyed the mess again. "If there was water to be had . . . a pitcher of it, and a bowl I could use for washing . . . I would be very grateful. I think I can find enough else here."

The demon grunted and disappeared.

In the next hour I sorted through the jumble, clearing a space in one corner and piling several rugs, some flat cushions, and some layers of cloth, unrolled and folded, into a fine bed. Though tempted to slip in between the layers and get warm, I kept up my exploration of the room. A lidded, knee-high jar such as merchants use for cooking oil would serve for relieving myself. I pushed and shoved at the furniture until I could squeeze in behind the shelves and close the shutters. Since the shutters did not quite come together properly, the effort succeeded in cutting down the wind and snow only by half. For good measure I unrolled another rug and stuffed it in the window opening. Better. Not warm—my blood felt like slush—but at least the storm was outside and not inside. Though I managed to unblock the hearth and get wood and kindling enough to lay a fire, I could find nothing to light it. A brief interval of blinding frustration reminded me that my hopes of returning melydda were but illusion, so I left it to go on to more profitable activities.

From the glass shelves I retrieved a comb, a spoon and cup, and a small, round red box holding scented cream I could use for soap. I felt as if I had unearthed treasure when I found two sharpened quill pens and a few sheets of coarse paper in a poorly woven basket, and I rummaged

through boxes and trunks until I came up with a stoppered
bottle of brown liquid that smelled like oranges, but behaved very much like watery ink. Somehow it seemed imperative to do something with my finds, as if touching pen
to paper might give substance to my wayward memory.

I cleared off a small table by dumping a pile of coins,
gaudy jewelry, nutshells, nails, and bits of string into another tall jar, then pulled up a flat cushion and settled myself beside the table. With the paper spread out before me,
the pen dipped in the orange-smelling liquid, I considered
my experiences and prospects, and wrote slowly and carefully, *Day 1.* Almost unreadable. My constant trembling
spoiled my scribe's hand; the fine brown line wavered and
wandered this way and that like a drunkard's path. For a
while I could not think what else to write. At last I added,
*I was taken from the dogs by Vallyne. Demons cannot play-
act.* Nothing else presented itself, so I stoppered the ink
and wiped the pen on a scrap of fabric torn from a larger
piece. After another brief search, I folded the paper, put it
in the small silver box I'd found, and set the box beside
my makeshift bed, feeling a vague sense of satisfaction that
seemed entirely out of proportion to the event.

When that was done, I sat on the bed, put my head in
my hands, hoping to retrieve something of my mind. But
before I could dig out my little hoard of treasured images
from the depths where I had hidden it, Raddoman returned. This time he wore his figure of a bulky, sagging
man with greasy brown hair and a wiry beard that stuck
out in front of his protruding chin. An odd thing about the
demons, even though they could appear a hundred different
ways . . . or only as a streak of light when angled out of
vision . . . it seemed quite easy to tell them apart. I would
never mistake Raddoman for Kaarat or Vallyne or Denas
or Vilgor, the purple-clad demon who had taken me from
the pits. Even when they took on solid form, appearance
was a very small part of their presence.

"Here's clothes and this water foolishness. Be quick. The
mistress will have you to her book-room." He set down a
fat pottery jar of indeterminate color, and threw a wad of
black and red silk at me.

"And where is the book-room?"

"Cursed ylad!" the servant growled. "Can't find your own backside if someone lays your hands on it. You'll find the book-room beside the mistress's resting room."

Before I risked his further displeasure by asking where the mistress's resting room could be found, Raddoman twisted into a streak of mud-brown light, venting his stink and some long pent anger. "You oughtn't be here, ylad. Bad enough you took what was ours, now you come here like you own this, too. I heard how you come . . . no weapons . . . saying you was here to see us and learn of us. Like you belonged. Like you thought to rule this land. Where will you send us when you steal this place away as you did the last?"

"Took what? Please, I don't understand. I didn't come to—"

But he didn't let me finish; just tossed a pair of boots at me and left.

The clothes were very fine. Gray breeches, embroidered with black thread down each side. A wine-red silk shirt, open at the neck, with long full sleeves and buttons made of black pearls. Knee-high black boots of leather as soft as a woman's cheek. I washed myself as well as I could with the icy water and the cream from the jar, and used the comb to make some order of my ragged hair. I told myself that it was only right to make a good appearance before the lady. She held my future in her hand. But truly it was her hand that I was thinking of, more than my future.

When I had the boots buckled, I peered out of my door and saw only a gray passageway. No one was about, so I stepped out . . . and was not in a passageway at all. Rather I found myself in a small room crammed with chairs of every type: tall backed, round backed, with arms and without, simple, ornate, with cushions, and plain. The room looked like a salon where low-degree petitioners might wait for a royal audience, though no one was there. I looked back through the doorway and saw my own room again, but across a small, empty foyer and up two steps. No use to worry about it. I threaded my way between the chairs toward the only other door. Another corridor. I stepped through, prepared for another unsettling transition, but this time the passageway stayed put. Movement through De-

nas's castle was like going down a stairway in the dark,
where you prepared for one more step but jarred your foot
on flat ground instead. The passageway had innumerable
doors leading off it, but I quickly found what I was after.
The first opening was a tall, narrow doorway that led into
an immense room completely lined with books.

Never had I seen so many books in one place. I had
vague remembrance of living in a house where the owner
valued books—a house where I had been a slave, I believed—but that collection could have been nothing compared to Vallyne's library. The book-room walls were at
least five times the height of a man, their true dimension
lost in the gloom. Railed galleries on every side allowed
access to the upper shelves, and there were three sets of
stairs to reach them. Of all the things I might have expected
to find in the demon realm, I had not conceived of books.

In the center of the room were three thick pillars
wreathed with ice-sculpted vines, and from the pillars hung
crystal lamps, creating a bounded pool of brightness in the
universe of shadows. In this lighted triangle five elaborately
dressed demons, three women and two men, reclined on
pale red-cushioned divans, murmuring to each other even
as they stared at me.

Vallyne was standing in front of them in her demon
form—a silver brilliance in the light. When she turned to
greet me, I had to force myself to keep breathing. She wore
a gown of sapphire silk, draped enticingly about her pleasing shape and caught at one shoulder with a single diamond. Her green eyes widened with pleasure at my
appearance. My flesh caught fire at hers.

"Exile! I thought you would never come. My guests despair of entertainment."

"I'm sorry . . . I didn't know . . . was not fit." My tongue,
which had babbled so glibly in the courtyard, kept trying
to escape my control. "I didn't know the way."

"Well, now you are here, you must not make a fool of
me. I promised you would find a good tale. So"—she waved
her hand at me—"go find one." I stood stupidly until she
fluttered her hands again. "A book, Exile. Find a book to
read to us."

I wrenched my eyes from her and walked to one wall.

My fingers brushed over the bindings—every color of leather, cloth, and paper, some old and shabby, some pristine—and with dismay I noted that the language of the titles was unknown to me. I moved down the row, examining each one, squinting vainly in the dim light, hoping my eyes were fooled and that the words would make sense if I but looked hard enough. Faster and faster I hunted. I rounded the corner, and was relieved when the characters of the engravings took on familiar shape, at least, if not familiar words. So different languages were represented. That gave me some hope. A little farther and I came to one of the stairs. I climbed up and recognized a few titles as the language of the Fryth. A problem—I didn't know Frythian. Up to the third level.

"Do you think to find your way out of Kir'Vagonoth by the stairs, Exile? Or is it you are collecting books enough to fill a new book-room? Only one volume will do, I think."

"One moment, madam. I'd like to find something enjoyable." I hoped she would not take it ill that I might think some of her books were less than enjoyable, but unless I found something soon, rudeness would be the least of my offenses.

There, Kuvai script. I knew a smattering of Kuvai, though not enough to make sense of anything but the simplest book. But surely if she had Kuvai works, there would be something in one of the languages I knew well. I rounded another corner, and fell on my knees, elated to find a shelf which displayed titles in Aseol. Now to find something that looked entertaining.

Birds and Beasts of Basran. Basran. I smiled to myself in delight at seeing a name that was familiar. I was so far from home, I had begun to doubt what little memory I possessed. But though the illustrations were fine, it didn't seem like what the lady wanted, so I kept looking. *Astronomical Theories*, *Tribal Languages*, and *Trade Routes of the Khyb Rash* looked too dry. *The Feine and Ankient History of the Lutte* was far too long, and written in archaic speech. But I found a small book bound in wine-red leather called *Ships of Fortune: Ten Stories* that looked to be tales of a Basran adventurer. I pulled out a second book entitled

Myths and Fancies, just in case the first turned dull, and I hurried back to the waiting demons.

"I hope this will suit, madam," I said.

Vallyne had reclined on a gray divan and waved me to a low wooden stool. "Hurry up, then."

I propped the book between my knees as my wayward hands could not hold it still enough otherwise, and I began to read. " 'List, oh reader, to a story of wonders. I am a man who hath traveled far, and I have seen things which mine own father would name impossible . . .' "

No wonder the book had taken my fancy. Perhaps I could write such a story with my pen and brown ink.

Sarakhan was a young Basran sheepherder who had tired of his dull life at the edge of the desert and set off to find the great ocean, a myth among his people. At first, as I read, I methodically queried my memory. Had I ever seen the ocean? Had I sailed in a ship or climbed in its rigging? Had I met pirates or eaten the fruit of purple-leafed trees with strange names? Had I ever fallen in love . . . had a woman . . . a wife? Oh, gods, why could I not remember something so important? But after a while I glanced up to see how my audience received the story, and my eyes met two large green ones, flecked with demon-blue and rapt with shining wonder. In that moment all else fled from my consideration. ". . . Set sail . . . again . . ." My words faltered, and blood rushed to my face. I forced my gaze back to the pages. *Careful, Warden. There is such danger here as you have never imagined.* Ten more pages I read until Sarakhan touched the shore ending his first voyage.

"Go on." Vallyne looked puzzled that I had stopped. My throat was dry—with more than reading. "There is more to the book, is there not? This can't be all of it."

"Yes, madam. And I'll be happy to go on, but at some time, I'll need water or wine to ease my throat." Somehow it seemed crude to mention it.

"Yes, yes. Just tell us when it's needed. For now, go on." The other listeners were nodding their heads in agreement, but my attention was all for my mistress.

I read two more of Sarakhan's stories without stopping. The green eyes dragged me on until I started coughing. Even then I tried to squeeze in the words to please her, to keep that light of wonder blazing in her eyes. Just at the point where I was going to be forced to stop, Raddoman appeared at my elbow with a cup of wine. I downed the bittersweet stuff in haste without looking up from the page, and then continued, only to find, somewhere after the hundredth page, that the following page was blank. In panic I thumbed through the rest of the leaves. All blank. *Idiot. Why didn't you look?* Even as I said it, I knew the accusation was foolish. Who would expect such a thing?

"Why do you stop? We gave you wine." Vallyne sat up on her couch, and the storm on her pale brow twisted my gut.

"My lady, the book"—I took the book to her, showing her the blank pages—"it seems to be defective. I didn't know."

The lady snatched the book and riffled the pages, then threw it hard so that it skittered along the gray floor tiles. "Next time make sure of what you choose."

"Of course, my lady. I just didn't—"

"Do you know the rest of the story? You read it so easily; perhaps you've heard it before."

"Know it? No. I'm sorry. It was new to me. I could read something else . . ."

The other guests were rising from their couches and bundling their cloaks about themselves as if they had been asleep, and Vallyne turned her back to me in order to attend them. The heavy cold of the room came over me like a mantle, and I began to shiver, the emptiness of my mind and heart and stomach unable to stave it off. Had it been only her attention that kept me warm as I read?

I sat waiting, scarcely able to contain my impatience, until she had bade farewell to the last of her guests. When she returned to the pool of light, I jumped up from my stool. "I have another book. Perhaps I could begin it for you."

She cocked her head to look at me, and then she smiled, which sent lightning down my spine and eased my shivering. "No more books just now. But you read very well. We will do it again. Go back to your room and rest if you wish."

"Perhaps we could talk for a while. I came here to learn."

I didn't like the sound of desperation in my voice. What was wrong with me?

"Alas, no. I'm expecting a visitor, and you should not be here when he comes. Later perhaps."

I could think of no more arguments, save falling to my knees and begging. I was not so far gone as to do that, though I certainly gave it consideration. Instead, I bowed and retreated, vowing to douse my head in cold water and quench the mad fire she caused in me. I felt like I was fifteen again—awkward, obvious, and unable to control the simplest urges. And she was a demon. What was I thinking?

I found my way back to my room—no simple task since the way seemed to have changed even from my backward look upon my arrival at the book-room. But I seemed to know which way to turn, and though I peered into many doorways to see what manner of rooms I passed, I knew they were not my destination. Little interested me, and later, when I pulled my paper and pen from the silver box, I wrote, *Demons collect junk. Much of it is broken or imperfect.*

Like me, I thought, as I put the writing things away. Then I stripped off the fine clothes and climbed into my makeshift bed. I could not remember anything so marvelous as the warmth and softness of my motley layers of rugs and fabric and cushions. I told myself that I if I died there in my sleep, I would be happy. But instead I dreamed of Jack-Willow and woke many hours later to a dry mouth and trembling hands.

I sat up and rested my head on my knees, folding my arms over my head and forcing my breathing to slow and my pounding heart to settle as I realized where I was.

"So have you tried to make love to her?"

I jerked backward, slamming my back against the wall, which caused something metal to topple off a stack of bowls and baskets and clatter noisily to the floor.

"You can't, you know. Not without telling her your name."

"Merryt!"

CHAPTER 25

"So how do you fare?" asked the Ezzarian, as he dragged my writing table to my bedside. "I've brought food—breakfast, I suppose, from the look of you." On the table was a carafe of wine and a basket containing plums, grapes, apples, hard sausage, and bread. He cut off a chunk of the sausage and tossed it to me, then cut one for himself.

To see him work so deftly despite his missing fingers was fascinating. The little finger and the one next to it were missing on his left hand, and the third finger on his right. I tried not to stare, though my own fingers were counting each other under my blanket.

"I've tried to get word of you these past weeks, but Vallyne does not share her pretty schemes with just anyone. Especially when they're designed to prick Denas into fury. He went to all that trouble to get hold of you discreetly, and now she's showing you off to everyone, making him look the fool."

"I'm well enough," I said. "Far better than I was. Thank you. I've no words to say it properly."

Merryt was a big man, now I saw him with eyes that could focus. Leather breeches and vest, brown leggings and rust-colored shirt strained at the seams with his bulk. His long gray hair was pulled back tightly, making his broad, square face appear all the larger. But he was in no way fat. I guessed that he had kept up his Warden's training. He swallowed a huge bite of his sausage and poured wine into two silver cups. "I've no doubt you'd do the same. It's fine to see a human face—one of my own brothers." He took a great draught of his wine and set the other cup where I could reach it. "There's not been another of us down here for ever so long. None others still living. I wish I could

promise you an easy road, but there's no predicting with
the Nevai and their unending plots. You may not thank me
when all is done."

"For getting me out of the pits, I will bless your name
to my children's children," I said, and raised my cup to
him. The Ezzarian's eyes settled on my shaking hand. No
time for pride. The man had saved my life and the dregs
of my reason.

He raised his cup and drank generously. He seemed to
do nothing small. "So, are you ready to tell me how you
come to be here with no weapons? And this story of a
Nevai and a warning . . ."

An Ezzarian among the demons. My instinct for danger
was not completely buried in my mind's wreckage. Even if
I could have remembered half of what I needed to know,
I wasn't sure I would or should reveal it. "I'm sorry. Everything's a muddle since—"

Merryt raised one hand. "No matter, lad. I won't press.
I understand a Warden's reluctance to bare his soul to one
who's made a passing peace with rai-kirah." He leaned
back against a heavy wardrobe and popped a grape in his
mouth. "But someday . . . I've been hearing tales of you.
The wings. The Naghidda. So many battles. I'm damned
curious, and I'd like to think you'll come to trust me
enough to tell."

"Thank you for the breakfast. This Raddoman doesn't
quite approve of feeding me." The taste of the sausage and
wine made me realize how hungry I was. It wasn't as good
as it looked, but it had been enough hours since my last
meal that I wolfed it down. And once I had satisfied the
immediate ravening of my stomach, it was easier to pay
attention to other things. Mostly at how guilty I felt about
keeping secrets from the friendly Ezzarian. "I want to trust
you. Of course I do. But right now I don't trust myself far
enough to spit, and I can scarcely remember my own
mother. I just need a little time. Maybe if you were to tell
me a little about yourself . . . this place." The questions
Merryt raised were beyond counting. And he seemed to
know as much about me as I knew myself. Perhaps more.

"I'll give you whatever you want to know. I've naught
to lose, and a friend and ally to gain. I just can't tarry here

too long. Doesn't do to cross your mistress. I've seen her change form when she's angry—and you've seen naught in your demon combats to compare. It's why she dislikes me so wicked . . . because I know what she really is." He propped his boots on a cushion. "No, you're wise not to trust any of us here. Don't trust anyone ever. That's a lesson it took me a few lifetimes to learn."

He wore the animal confidence and easy grace that marked a man who believed in his own power. "I was forty-three when I was taken captive," he said. "In my prime. I had fought for seventeen years and never lost a battle. My Aife—my wife—had been ill, but was well recovered, so we thought. But it seemed an easy combat—a newly possessed young girl, innocent until she was taken—and we felt guilty that others had been answering our calls. I would not partner with any other Aife . . . more the fool. So, well, there's not much to tell. It was a hard battle, lasted a fair time, but my wife could not hold the land steady. Kept changing around me. I was on the verge of snaring the demon, but before I had a chance, the whole place starts falling to bits, and I see the portal closing down. Whatever the reason, my wife was too weak to hold. I think perhaps she died from it."

"I'm sorry."

He shook his head and twisted his mouth into rueful resignation. "No need. It was a very long time ago." He turned the silver wine cup around and around in his hand until it flashed in the soft light of the gray stones. "It was my good fortune—if ought of such a happening could be called good—to be taken by a Rudai. Only rarely do those of the Rudai Circle hunt. They are what we would call quite civilized, whereas . . . well, you've met the worst of the brutes, but the others aren't much better. Wardens taken by Gastai are given no choice in their fates. They are judged in the Rudai Meet, questioned, examined, and given back to be done with as the captors wish. It's how the Gastai are paid for their hunting."

"So the others . . ." All the missing Wardens—those who never came back. Lost . . . captured. We had never known what became of them. So many mourned. Prayed for. Wardens always watched for signs of our own kind when we stepped through a portal, but had never found evidence of them.

"All dead. A few survived for a while imprisoned, a few walked free for a time, only to run afoul of some devil or other. But it's been a number of years since the last passed on. I was lucky. My captor told me the secret to staying healthy."

A hundred questions came crowding to my tongue at once. "Will you tell me?" First things first. If I was to accomplish whatever I'd come for, then I needed to survive.

"The she-devil held me captive for a while, letting the Gastai take what they could get of me. Unpleasant enough, as you know better than I. But eventually she asked me if I would prefer to live or die. I said I would not live a demon, and she revealed to me a most surprising thing." He leaned forward and raised his thick eyebrows at me, opening his black eyes wide and pointing at them. "We are prizes beyond compare, and the rai-kirah will do most anything to get one of us for their own. But they'll not force themselves into us. A Warden isn't like other humans out in the real world. We have all these skills and protections to hold them off. If a demon forces us to take him and we keep resisting, then they can't hold onto us tight enough. So then another devil can come along and fight him, trying to push the first one out and take us for himself. That kind of assault is very damaging to them, and worse for the poor bastard they're fighting over. After a few changes of owner, we're not worth much, and they get raked over by the other demons for wasting a human. I've seen it happen to a few of us over the years." He shook his head grimly and rummaged in his basket for more sausage.

"They invade . . . fight each other inside a human soul . . . like we do?"

"Mmm. Something like. Nasty business. So if they can't beat us or scare us into serving them, what they try to do is get us to take them willing. Make us think we've no choice. Make us think we'll be happier, more powerful, or maybe that we could get back home somehow. Like I say, I was lucky Magyalla told me all this, and now you can reap the benefit of it as well. For if you take a demon willing in this place . . . well, that's something different altogether. After the first few hours, it becomes very difficult—impossible, so I've been told—to separate the two ever again. Worse than any case of possession we've seen in the human world. But they do want us to join with them . . . ever so much." His three thick fingers kneaded the plump purple surface of a plum. "They've promised me such power as you can't imagine."

"But you've not done it. Not even this Magyalla?" I said it in the way of a child claiming there were no monsters lurking in the nighttime shadows. The demons knew his name, and why would his captor have told him all this if he were not willing? That part made no sense. But then a large proportion of the world made no sense at that moment, so I let it pass and kept listening.

"Won't say I haven't considered it. Stay here a few lifetimes and see what you think. I've seen a few of us try to strike a bargain for joining—and all the other rai-kirah got wicked jealous, and the poor bastards ended up dead anyway. But for myself, I've never had the brass to do it. Who would rule, human or demon?" In one motion he devoured the juicy pulp of the plum, spit the seed onto the floor, and wiped his mouth on the back of his three-fingered hand. Then he gave a mock shudder. "Even after so long I get queasy at the thought. No one controls my destiny but me! But, whatever the reasons, they won't force us. You just need to be very careful. All the cursed demons are treacherous. Denas and Vallyne are the most powerful and dangerous of the Nevai. And they're quarreling, which makes them even worse."

"What of the other one that was with them—the bearded one? Is he the same?"

"Vyx? Nah, he's a fool. He flits about their courts pretending to be important, doing mischief—I've heard he's the one who set Denas and Vallyne at odds. But he can't get through a game of ulyat without forgetting what he's doing. No. Vyx is nothing. It's Denas rules this place, and you don't want to cross him. I hear he's out to control the whole lot of them and will do whatever it takes to get what he wants, but at least you can predict what he'll do. The witch Vallyne is more dangerous. She's like a spider, always weaving plots to snare herself a fly."

He pointed at his eyes. "Here, take a look and see what you will see. It's no rudeness. We're a long way from Ezzaria, and you may want a friend someday."

I examined him with what senses I could bring to bear, as he invited me to do, and indeed I could see no trace of demon. Somehow it did not settle my unease. "I don't understand why they want us," I said. "We're no threat to them here. Not without our own weapons. And we're not in any position to do much wickedness to feed them. Why not just kill us and be done?"

Merryt raised his wine cup. "Aye, that's the puzzle it took me a while to find out. It's all because of this, you see. We taste this pale, crude fakery of wine, and we know it's a pale, crude fakery. They can't tell. The bodies they create for themselves claim that the taste of this sausage is perfect, but they know it's not. It drives them wild that we can taste and feel and know the truth of such things, while they cannot. It's why they send the Gastai to hunt—to find true life and sensation and bring it back to feed them."

True life and sensation. I'd never thought of it that way. "So it's not just evil they seek."

"No, not just evil. We had that part wrong. They hunt everything that physical senses can give them—human life itself."

"How?" I said. "How could such a thing be done?" I felt I was on the verge of some discovery, if I could but recognize it when I found it. I had come to learn, or so I kept repeating to myself. But learn what? What question was I trying to answer? I wanted to shake Merryt. To make him say the word that would make me remember. *Everything that physical senses could give them . . .*

Merryt sighed and drained his cup. "Someday I'll show you how it's done. But there's no need to get everything poured into you at once. You'll learn all about it and a hundred other things. If you choose to live—though I wouldn't get my hopes up terrifically, because you never know whether you'll actually get the choice—there's nothing else to do but find your place here. I've not let them scare me into something foolish, and I've made use of my skills, so I've survived. I'm hired to the Rudai Meet—their idea of a court—though their judgments have no more to do with the merits of a case than does that of the Derzhi Emperor. And the Nevai find me useful when it suits. In special situations you might say. Opportunities, I would call them, that take advantage of my skills. It's not a bad life. Interesting. Always something going on. But I will say it's fine to have a human ear to babble into." He grinned and filled our cups again. "It won't make you drunk—they haven't got that part right, either. But we can have a jolly time pretending."

He took another giant swallow, but before I joined him, I asked the question that had been nagging at me since he had begun his story. "How long have you been here, Merryt?"

The stocky man leaned his head against the wall and closed his eyes. "By my best estimate—which is none too accurate—something on the order of three hundred and seventy years."

Our bodies were the problem, of course. The awkward, pain-ridden, breakable shells we carried about with us. They did not seem to age while confined to the demon realm and they encountered no disease, but they also made it impossible to escape. We had walked in through an Aife's portal, the physical connection she had made between this plane of existence and the one we knew. Merryt said that the only way to get out again was to walk back through an Aife's portal . . . if one could find one, which in three hundred seventy and some odd years he never had. I did not mention my aborted dream. I remembered enough of my years in slavery to know how crippling it was to hope for escape. And truly . . . a man who had lived with the demons for so long . . . no matter what he had done for me, how could I trust him even with a dream? Even my thick head knew better.

"The rai-kirah, now," Merryt had said, "they can travel where they will for the most part. It takes a mighty enchantment to keep them out of a place. They travel out into the wasteland and find a passage, a seam, a crack that will lead them into an ordinary soul, and they can pass between as easy as a Peskar warlord slips between his mistresses' beds."

And that had led him back to the subject of lovemaking. He had me squirming, and he took great good humor from it. Few Ezzarians were comfortable discussing such private matters, and the fact that my childish infatuation was so obvious made me feel even more foolish. "You may hold out for a while, but when you finally come to believe that there's no going back, and that there will never be a human woman to hold onto when you lie here alone in the dark . . . it's not so bad a thing. But these bodies they make can't feel it right. They have to get inside *you* to feel it. That's why they need your name and will do anything to get it."

I didn't ask him if that was why he had yielded his name. It was not important why, only that he had done so. I had only his word that the demons would not use it to force themselves into his soul. And about the lovemaking . . . I didn't let myself think of that at all.

Merryt promised to return when he could, saying he would be happy to show me about as soon as Vallyne left off watching me so closely. His was a cheerful face in that grim place. I looked forward to meeting him again. Once he had gone, I pulled out my writing paper—my journal as I thought of it, a safeguard in case I lost the rest of my wits. *Day 2. How long is forever?* After that happy thought, I put the paper away.

Not long after Merryt had gone, Raddoman appeared in my doorway. The odiferous attendant brought me water and a small bowl of pasty white mush that smelled like onions. He snorted and took on his piggish shape when he saw the remnants of Merryt's feast. "Seems like you can take care of yourself, then," he said. "Don't need me."

"Not at all," I said, bowing respectfully as I took the gold-enameled urn and the small chipped bowl and set them on my table. "This visitor will likely not come again, and he brought me no water. I appreciate the chance to clean myself. I'm most grateful for your assistance."

"I didn't do it for liking." Nor for any instruction in how to clean himself for certain. I did my best not to inhale while he was close.

"All the more reason for me to thank you. It's not easy to help those you dislike so sorely."

"Don't know why the mistress puts up with you. I know what you are. You're a *pandye gash*—one of the hidden yladdi. The ones who stole Kir'Navarrin. And you're a butchering yddrass. You've killed us, despised us, sent our hunters back here to ruin. Why did you come here?"

I had no answer for him. "I don't understand it all myself," I said, which was a mild way of putting it. "I've come here to learn."

Raddoman clearly had no interest in my learning. He was already out of the door and halfway down the passage. I leaned into the passage and called after him. "Can you tell me what I am allowed to do? Must I stay here in this room? No one has explained what is expected of a . . . guest. I don't wish to violate the lady's hospitality."

"If it was me, I'd send you back to the pits," he said, pausing long enough to glare at me, his blue eyes flaring like twin candle flames in the dark corridor. "Or hang you up by your nasty body and leave you freeze."

I nodded politely, hoping that he would progress to something more enlightening.

"But the mistress says you may have the use of the room and the things in it, and you are allowed to move about her wing of the castle. Not to trespass on her own resting room nor stray into Lord Denas's rooms. You'll feel the hurt of that if you disobey."

"So where—?"

But Raddoman wasn't telling me anything else. He vanished, leaving only his stench behind.

I sat on my makeshift bed in the gray gloom and pulled up the covers to hold off the chill. Munching on the grapes Merryt had left me, I tried again to remember why I had come to Kir'Vagonoth. To learn, I had said. To find truth. To find refuge, because I no longer spoke for Wardens and the Aife. Because the strange demon they named Vyx had come to me in dreams and warned me of . . . something . . . or perhaps he had lured me to the demon realm only to destroy the last experienced Warden. These were words I had saved through my ordeal with the Gastai, but I could make no sense of them anymore. Everyone wanted to know my secrets, but my secret was that I didn't know.

Unnerved by my own ignorance, I swore that before another hour waned, I would open at least one door to the past. I had been enslaved to fear, and it was time to break free of it. I closed my eyes and delved deep. *Aife. Who is my Aife? I should be able to remember her of all things. My partner. The one who weaves for me, who sends me into combat with care and well-wishing and skilled enchantment. Did she send me on this mission? Is she the one who waits for me beyond the boundaries of my dreams?* I tried to envision the person on the other end of my dream, but came up only with confusion. Multiple faces. Sorrow . . . estrangement . . . mistrust . . . dislike. The combination made no sense. Every thought of my Aife was a dagger in my breast, and the echo of my own words haunted me: *I no longer speak for the Aife. I have come seeking sanctuary.* I was terribly afraid that I belonged in Kir'Vagonoth because I had nowhere else to go.

My head came near cracking with the effort. I pressed the heels of my hands into my eyes as if I could squeeze some sense from the faulty workings behind them. Lost in paths of darkness, I did not hear a visitor enter the room. Not until she laid cool hands on my burning head.

"What battle is this you fight, my Exile?" With soft fingers she pulled my hands away and stroked my eyes open. Her face was only a handspan away . . . translucent ivory, flushed with faintest rose. Her human visage was not quite so perfect as her light-drawn demon face, yet the coloring of her cheek was enough to make me lose the feeble progress I had made.

"I don't know," I said, lifting one shaking finger to her lips as I had longed to do since my first glimpse of her. She allowed me to do it, and to run my other hand along her neck. Indeed if I had possessed any mind, it would have escaped me at that moment. I was astonished at myself . . . offering such intimacies to a woman I hardly knew . . . a demon woman. "I can't remember."

"So don't try," she said. "Think only of what happens now. And now I want you to walk with me in my garden."

"As you wish, lady." My voice fell harsh upon the ear compared to her sweet music.

She took my arm and drew me up, giving me the black wool cloak the servant had taken when I was left with her

dogs. With a blur of enchantment she was clad in white
fur, and we were standing at the edge of the frozen garden.
"Is it not wonderful?" she said as she led me onto a white
graveled path between a pair of spreading oak trees in full
frosty leaf.

"Marvelous," I said. "I never imagined anything like
this." Though the sky surged with clouds of black, gray,
and bruised blue, and the wind threatened to shred our
cloaks, the beauties of the garden glowed with their own
light and remained untouched by storm.

"I've had the shapers working for quite a long time," she
said. "There's no use in waiting forever to go back. We
must make what we can of what we have. Look, here's a
gamarand." She pulled me toward a tree with two yellow
trunks, wound about each other in a never-ending embrace.
Its arching branches were laden with round pink blooms
nestled in cups of pale green leaves. I envisioned the glory
of that tree, translating its pale hues into the truth of life
and color that still lingered in my head. Though I was sure
that nothing like it grew in the lands of my birth, its shape
and color were so familiar, I hung back staring at it as
Vallyne tugged at my hand.

"Come along! There's so much more. I told them I
wanted everything as it was in Kir'Navarrin, and if they
forget, I make an illusion to remind them. I did that with
the dogs, and then I couldn't bear to give them up, though
truly these are so much more like."

"What is Kir'Navarrin?" Raddoman had mentioned the
same word.

"How can you not know of it? You are of Kir'Zarra—a
pandye gash." Her brow was wrinkled in puzzled astonishment. "What thief forgets the thing he's stolen?"

"I've forgotten a great deal, but this . . . I don't think I
ever knew of it."

"Kir'Navarrin is the land we walked before the *pandye
gash* cast us out of it."

Pandye gash—hidden warriors—the demon name for
Ezzarians. So Kir'Navarrin must be their name for the
lands the Aife wove, I thought, the souls of humans that
we would not allow them to keep. "Please tell me about
it, my lady. I want to understand."

"Not now. Let me show you this first. Here, see?" She took me to a sculpted pile of dogs, playing in a glade of frost flowers. I recognized them as the portrait of my companions, and it was as she had said. These ice-carved beasts were masterfully shaped, perfect in every detail, where the lively illusions of the courtyard were not. Yet neither illusion nor artwork lived.

She pulled me along the path again, through vine-woven arbors, laden with frosted grapes, across lawns of palest green, bordered with terraces of faint-hued blooms. We stood on a delicate bridge, gazing down at a silent pool where swans in full spreading wing were forever at the verge of settling on the still water. Groves of white-barked birches, their autumn yellow pale beside other wan reds and golds, branches bent with unfelt breezes. An infinite variety of trees, mosses, and rocky ponds. All of them made of ice. All of them unmoving and silent beneath the doleful canopy of the clouds. As Vallyne leaned over a bronze-work balcony to point out a magnificent oak, so broad a Frythian family could have hollowed out its trunk for a home, I pulled my cloak tighter and shivered.

"What troubles you, Exile? I thought you were enjoying my garden."

"It does not change, lady, and it is so very cold. Those are its only faults."

"Such is the way of our existence." She laid her chilly hand gently upon my scarred cheek, gathering in my soul with her green gaze. "Neither do I change."

"But in you . . . that is not a fault," I said, and I bent down and kissed her. Her lips were cold, and she did not move, only gazed at me expressionless when I pulled away. Then she took my hand and led me down another path.

We walked the entire garden. Vallyne did not speak of what I had done, but, of course, it never left my mind. As I admired her trees and flowers, fountains and figures, my flesh pulsed with fire, threatening to melt the frost-sculpted creations with my shame, fear, anger, and sorrow. The shame and fear and anger were easy to explain. She was a demon. How could I have abandoned caution so completely? How crippled was I, how pitifully fallen, to be swept away by a beautiful face and a kind word from one

I should assume meant only harm? And she had known exactly what I would do and exactly how she would respond; I didn't like being toyed with. But the sorrow was the most complex and the most worrisome. I could not help but grieve for Vallyne—to see such brilliant light bereft of warmth. My body ached to give her something of myself that could elicit the same wonder in her face as stories. It was madness. She was my enemy.

I was bewitched. I knew it as I knew my own name, and with every breath I told myself to beware. Yet when the lady commanded me to come and read to her in her book-room after we had finished with our tour, I trailed after her like a besotted boy. I picked out a book of Derzhi legends, and while she reclined on cushions beneath a crystal lantern, I sat cross-legged on the bare floor, held the book in my shaking hands, and buried myself in words. The Derzhi were a warrior race, but they had a long history of wild and romantic stories. I dared not look at Vallyne while I read. Once was enough, to see her lips parted, her eyes shining in the soft light. All my questions and fears slipped away; my missing memories were no longer of concern. I could see only that if I stayed near her, she would drive me farther on the road to madness than the Gastai had ever done.

CHAPTER 26

And so I settled into life in Kir'Vagonoth. I spent several hours every day reading to Vallyne and varying groups of her friends. For the most part the other demons were as mesmerized by my reading as Vallyne. I thought of what Merryt had told me about the wine and lovemaking, and I came to think it was the same with books. The demons had the skill to decipher each word on a page, but I believed it took a human voice to build the words into stories.

When we were not engaged in her reading sessions, I was assigned to be her companion. I played games with her—variations of ulyat, draughts, and warriors and castles—or I walked with her in her garden, or sat and listened to her play music on a lap harp—terrible, screeching stuff, altogether unlike the sweetness of her voice and laughter. She had me sing a bit, but agreed with the forgotten critic who had judged me unsuited for the art. "Your voice is rich and full of melody," she said. "Serviceable enough. It's only the notes don't come out right." She had me laughing, and I counted any hour successful if I could do the same for her. We talked of the books I read, and she had me tell her of animals and trees and the lands and races of my world. She never asked me of my life or friends or family. Just as well, as those were the very things I was incapable of telling her. I took up running through the castle corridors, and she donned breeches and leggings and ran beside me, never tired, never breathing hard, always trying to learn what it was I enjoyed and craved about the activity.

My investigation—the formless curiosity as to the life and truth of demons, which was all I could grasp of my purposes—went nowhere. I was never introduced to anyone, was never allowed to mingle with Vallyne's friends, and none of them came over to my stool to speak to me. Vallyne forbade it. But I took pleasure in learning which streak of colored light would turn and reveal, which of Dena's gyossi—castle guests.

The gold-brown one, ragged at the edges, was Seffyd, the demon who lived for gaming, and thus never paid quite enough attention to his shaping. He would leave off hair or ears or half his clothes. The slowly shifting blue-white was Kaffera, a robust, ageless female with fine, delicate features that spoke only good humor, who indulged Seffyd in his games while kindly nudging him to shape his breeches. Tovall, whose light was a deep, rich purple, wore skin darker than a Thrid. Her drooping earlobes were thick with hair, though her gleaming ebony head held none. Her booming laugh made the candles quaver, and it was so compelling that the cold stars themselves—if there were such above the turgid clouds of Kir'Vagonoth—must have laughed with her.

Gennod appeared as a man of middle years—pale brows and lashes above cold eyes, a long straight nose, and a squared-off jaw that would have made him strikingly fine-looking were he ever to smile. His dark red light pulsed with power that made me wince, and he was constantly engaged in furtive conversation with other serious rai-kirah. He listened to the reading, but the acquisitive eagerness in his expression spoke more of gathering information than pleasure. When the activities turned to dancing or gaming, Gennod would politely take his leave.

Denkkar's shimmer was sparkling yellow, appropriate for one who brought such light to these gatherings. He worked closely with the Rudai shapers and took unending delight in showing off their latest creations. As for his own shape, it was something different every time he turned around, sometimes male, sometimes female, sometimes bird or beast . . . until it came time for dancing. Then he would take on the aspect of a tall, lean gentleman of sixty or so, and begin to whirl and step and bow with dignity and grace, his whole being pulsing with yellow delight.

Twenty others I came to know by sight, many that I would be glad to count as friends, some that awed me with the power and anger that seethed beneath their stunning beauty. All of them were wondrously beautiful to me, no matter how unusual the form they chose—beings sculpted of living light, raw passion, and emotion unmuted by flesh.

Though I never heard a word between Denas and Vallyne that was not irritation, teasing, or scathing insult, the demon lord attended many of the lady's gatherings. We lived in his castle after all, though no one ever explained to me why Vallyne held sway in a goodly part of it, while the two of them were feuding. Perhaps it was just too much trouble for her to move elsewhere—or perhaps there was nowhere else for her to go. I could not imagine her residing in the long low building where Merryt had shown me his hideaway. And the city on the horizon was dark. Vallyne did not belong in the dark. I assumed there must be more residences like the one we occupied, but the talk of comings and goings was not clear enough to know for sure.

As for Denas himself, the handsome demon was forever angry, his brooding fury lurking in the shadows even when he was laughing at someone's humor or conversing seriously. Whenever Vallyne commanded me to read, Denas would throw down what he was doing and stride out of the room, taking two or three followers with him.

Vyx was the cipher that I was still waiting to untangle. Not a gathering occurred without his purple and blue and swirling gray-green presence. He prattled endlessly, upset game tables, told humorous stories that were incomprehensible to me, drank endless vats of wine, and dodged not a few angry blows from irritated demons. He never spoke to me, nor did he seem to listen to my reading, though, unlike Denas, he stayed in the room. Whenever I looked up from my book, I would find that he alone of all the crowd was watching more than listening. But I was unable to guess his thoughts from his expression. His eyes were too distracting. He did not hide the blue fire as did many of the demons when in human form, but rather left it burning like a torchlight at the gates of himself.

As for Merryt, I saw him very little. He did not attend Vallyne's reading sessions, nor any other entertainment that I observed. I learned that he carried messages for Gennod, and once I saw him leaving Gennod's apartment when I was sent to return a book that Vallyne had borrowed from the red demon. On occasion I would catch sight of the man limping through the castle corridors. He would nod or wave, then hurry on his way.

"Does Merryt ever read to your friends as I do?" I asked Vallyne once, after glimpsing the big Ezzarian skulking in a corner as we walked past.

"There was a time when I employed him in that way," she said. "But he was not suited to it. I'll not have him in my chambers." She paused in her steps and gazed at me thoughtfully, as if it had never occurred to her that I might be interested in the only other human in the demon realm. "He has chosen other paths, Exile. He is your kind . . . but he is not like you. Never think it. Stay away from him." She changed the subject and, as had become my habit, I allowed her to lead me where she would.

One morning I was told that Vallyne was occupied and would not need me until three hours had passed. The clever Rudai shapers had solved the problem of sunless days and starless nights. In the center of the grand entrance to Denas's castle was a hive-shaped vessel filled with water. The vessel had markings on its interior, and a small opening at the bottom where the water ran out into a fountain. Vallyne had told me that as the water passed each marking, so passed another hour, though they did not know which one, or whether it was a part of night or day.

After washing and dressing and checking the time—and chastising myself for the hollow disappointment of her temporary abandonment—I decided to set out for the book-room to find a supply of tales to read for her. I disliked making a hurried and risky choice each time she took the whim to listen.

The book-room lamps were not lit, which meant that the gray radiance of the ceilings, columns, and few mezzits of bare wall were all the light available. I berated myself for not asking Merryt how to make fire in this place. If he wanted my trust, perhaps he could give me some truly useful information. I climbed up to the third gallery, where I had found the books written in Aseol, and I spent several hours sitting on the floor and taking out one after the other, examining the pages, looking for stories. More than three-quarters of them had blank pages—even books that looked well-worn—and many illustrations looked entirely wrong. Some had letters so small I could not read them in the weak light. But the most interesting revelations of the day were not from books.

". . . in here. There's no one about, and we'll know if anyone comes." Denas was talking to someone as he walked into the room through the door at the bottom of the opposite stair. His golden light illuminated the dim book-room as no candle, lamp, or hearth fire could ever do. Denas never took on physical form. Perhaps he knew that it could only mute the power of his presence.

"I want nothing to do with your scheme. It's too late to change leaders. Rhadit is weak, but he knows what needs to be done, and we can afford no delays." The second voice was unfamiliar, as was the sickly green light that flickered on the ceiling alongside Denas's gold.

"There will be no delays," said Denas. "We are committed, and Kir'Navarrin awaits us. The Rudai say they'll soon have the ylad hosts in place, awaiting our passage. The venture will occur, whether under my banner or Rhadit's. Better it be mine."

The tenor of the conversation told me from the beginning that I was in trouble. Conspiracy has its own particular voice, and eavesdropping does not harmonize with it. Unfortunately, there was no retreat, so I shrank into the shadows.

"Better it be one who has the key to open the way. Turn the yddrass over to Rhadit as he demands, and Rhadit will force the vermin to join with one of us. With you to prevent our greedy kin from disrupting the joining, we can use this ylad as we will."

"Then, how will you get him out?" Denas said. "Has anyone, in their mindless determination to use this cursed ylad, come up with a way to get a human out of Kir'Vagonoth? We should make our own passage to the human world and find someone there to use."

"The Gastai claim the yddrass himself knows a way. If he truly came here of his own will, it would make sense. And once we have him under control, we'll know it, too. It's foolish to gamble that we might find a suitable partner in the human world. We must use this one, Denas. He is the most powerful of their kind. Gennod is sure he can open Kir'Navarrin. Then we will be the masters of our own fates once again."

"My aims are the same as yours. But the rest of the *pandye gash* are still in the way. Rhadit underestimates the villains."

"They have few warriors left—and those weak and inexperienced I've heard. Since this one fell into our hands—"

Golden lightning streaked the shadowed ceiling. "If Rhadit believes that was an accident—or that an yddrass has come in truce or for sanctuary as he claims—then he is as mad as those in the pits. This ylad has powers we've never seen in any other. He's likely telling his fellows everything he learns of us. The *pandye gash* want to send us back to the dark times. I won't do that again."

"All the more reason to use this one. I'll force him myself if that's what it takes." Denas's conspirator sounded like no one I wanted to meet. "Nesfarro has said he is willing to sacrifice himself for the joining. Kryddon would be better. He has more intelligence, if not the strength of Nesfarro. I've heard whispers that Gennod will do it. Imagine it, Denas, one of our own circle! Success will be assured with a Nevai and an ylad of such power. Rhadit favors him—some say Gennod is the fire behind Rhadit—so perhaps he would not be so willing under your banner."

I tried to become one of the shadows. From my cowering vantage I could not see who was the other demon, and there was not motive enough in the universe to make me move. Only Denas was visible beyond the vine-festooned columns, the dark hurricane still pent up behind his glimmering gold light.

"It doesn't matter which ylad we use; many of the cursed *pandye gash* have power enough. And it doesn't matter which of us joins. Once the way to Kir'Navarrin is open, I'll kill the perverted creature, no matter whether it is Gennod or you or anyone. What matters is who leads. We have only one chance, and I'll not see it wasted with weakness or incompetence."

"The dark times will be nothing to what will become of us if we don't do something soon, Denas. We've just had to force another cadre into the pits. They were destroying their hosts before taking anything from them. We need to move quickly . . . so either give Rhadit this prisoner to use or kill the vermin. He destroyed the Naghidda. We don't want any ylad with that kind of power lurking behind us."

"I would gladly throw him back into the pits," said the golden lord, "but Vallyne will not give him up. She would go hunt with the brutes before she obliged me with a step out of her way."

"Of all times for you and the lady to quarrel."

"Either way, it is my game, not Rhadit's. Rhadit is dead already, as is anyone else who thinks to go in my rightful place. My assassin will see to it when the time is right."

"By the Nameless, Denas! You're more determined than I thought."

"I will lead. No one but I."

"Come, let's go talk to the others. . . ."

Hurrying footsteps faded, and the green and gold light vanished, leaving the book-room dim and gray once more. I lay prostrate on the floor for the best part of an hour, and when I got up the nerve to creep down the stairs, a kayeet could not have scurried back to its desert den any faster than I raced back to my room. They were speaking of Wardens. Of Ezzarians. They were afraid of us, and that was good. Afraid of me, which was not so good, especially as I knew there was so little reason for it. What was this thing the demons wanted of me? I pulled out my writing paper, and under Day 12, wrote, *Beware of Denas. What is Kir'Navarrin?*

Denas remained an angry mystery. Why he had pulled me from the pits or allowed Merryt to do so, I was not told. As I had heard him claim he wished to kill me or send me back to the mad Gastai, it seemed odd. Nevertheless I held a spot of gratitude ready for him should he ever decide to accept it from a human.

Only Denas of all the demons could put Vallyne out of sorts. One day when she was particularly irritated with him—ostensibly for using her servants for his own tasks—Vallyne had me accompany her to a vast, empty courtyard in the heart of the castle, a torchlit practice arena where

Denas and others of the Nevai worked at fighting skills.
We watched from tiered viewing stands as the demons battled each other in various beast forms and with such bloody
mayhem that I was sickened by it—the more so when I
found myself critiquing their form and thinking of more
efficient alternatives to their attacks. They did not die from
their combat. The victors simply reshaped their bodies and
walked away. Vallyne said that those most damaged would
be unable to shape themselves a body until they had
recovered.

Denas defeated every opponent decisively, demonstra-
ting exceptional strength and endurance, and awesome skill
in shaping himself into a beast of war. Seldom had I witnessed such ferocious, single-minded devotion to destruction. I could not but measure his prowess against my own—
an unsettling exercise. I hoped I would never have to test
myself against him. I wondered if that was perhaps the true
purpose of my presence, for Vallyne certainly did not enjoy
the activity. As we left the venue, I asked her why we
had come.

"It torments Denas when I watch," she said. "And to
have you with me makes it all the sweeter. He so dislikes
taking a solid shape of any kind, and to do so in front of
an yddrass . . . He would rather spend his entire existence
with the Gastai."

"Then, why does he do it?" I said. "And what enjoyment
is there in doing something you dislike so much only to
goad one who already spoils your pleasures?" For myself
I found Denas's rage unnerving.

"Our existence depends on our ability to fight," she said.
"And those who fight for us are going mad. Soon, if noth-
ing is done, we may all be going out hunting. I will credit
Denas that he does not ask anything of others that he will
not do himself." She glanced over her shoulder to see
Denas in a bear shape rake a giant cat with steel claws.
"As for my own pleasure . . . Denas has chosen to go his
way without concern for it. And so I take enjoyment where
I may."

I tried to ask more questions, but she refused to answer,
and I soon forgot them.

*   *   *

Nothing was simple in Kir'Vagonoth. Nothing was as it seemed, and the relationship of my mistress and the demon lord was no exception. A few days after our venture to the practice arena, Vallyne gathered a small group in a sumptuously furnished sitting room very near my own apartment. A circle of tall candles filled the room with the smoky scent of autumn grass fires—and the guests and I were seated on silken cushions inside the ring. I was just beginning the second tale in my book, when someone burst through a distant door and called out from the shadows, "Feasting this hour, Vallyne!"

"Denas!" Vallyne jumped to her feet, strangely unsettled by the sudden interruption. "I told you I was having guests." The four demons who reclined on Vallyne's pillows murmured to each other, raised their eyebrows, and vanished quickly. I stood up, curious at the abrupt intrusion and ready, as always, to do the lady's bidding.

"Forget this madness and come with me, Vallyne." The golden demon came into view just beyond the circle of candlelight.

"I have company enough, my lord." Vallyne wrapped her arms around one of mine.

Perhaps it was because of my own experience with the lady that I recognized the yearning in Denas's invitation. And so I also understood something of the fury that clouded his broad face when he saw me there. He clearly did not expect it.

"Send him away," he said. No winter's frost could have been more sudden or more bitter than his change from warm invitation to cold command.

"He's coming with me."

"He has no place in this."

Vallyne did not move, and in the moment's pause, I felt such a struggle of wills that I thought the candle flames might bend with it. "He has cast his lot with us of his own choice, Denas. And he is your gyos. Where else should your guest be but with us?"

"With his own kind. In Kir'Zarra with sun and rain and trees that move in the wind. Not here. Not tonight. I'll kill him if I see him near the feast."

"He is mine—"

"I'll kill him, Vallyne. Don't bring him." Denas whirled about and vanished, the wind of his passing snuffing the candle flames.

"My lord is a bit testy tonight," said Vallyne, sighing and relinquishing my arm. "Though I care nothing for his pleasures and think it time you shared more of our life, I would not have you dead from it. Perhaps you had best go to your room. And, Exile . . ."

"Yes, my lady?"

"Stay there until Raddoman comes for you. I command it. Things will go harshly if you disobey."

"I would not distress you in any way, lady."

She lay her cold hand on my cheek and explored my face with a trace of sorrow quite at odds with her usual cheer. "You are not at all what I expected, Exile." Her physical body dissolved, leaving only her silvered shimmer.

"Nor you, madam." I swept a wide bow that drew my cloak through her gleaming shape and left my empty hand poised beneath the image of hers. I bent my head toward her hand, then gave a sigh of my own, slightly exaggerated. "What man is comfortable kissing his own hand or laying his heart at the feet of the lightning?"

She laughed gaily, and I returned to my room planning to relive the sound of it until I fell asleep.

Just before I dozed off, someone slipped quietly through the door. I held still and wary in my nook, watching for the telltale demon light that would reveal the identity of my visitor. But instead of light, it was a bulky, dense form draped in shadow that crept around the stacked furniture—Merryt.

"Are you awake, brother?"

"Aye," I said. "At least half. And glad for company." I was happy to see someone who did not flicker out of view when I was nearby.

"I'm not here for society," he said, squatting on his haunches by my bed and casting nervous glances over his shoulder. "I thought I might take you on a short journey. See where your loyalties lie. See if you want to know the truth of demons."

"Truth . . . yes, I came for truth, but . . ."

"They're at their feeding in the black heart of this pile

of ice. No artifice. No pretending they are kin to humankind. If you seek truth, it's there to find. We'll need to be quick and quiet."

Amid the echoes of Vallyne's sweet laughter was her very serious command, *Stay there until Raddoman comes for you.* . . . I looked away from Merryt's probing eyes and down at my hands that still trembled like those of a thief sprawled at the Derzhi Emperor's feet. "I cannot."

"You cannot?" The big man paused only for a moment. "Ah. I see." He stood up and started for the door. "I've heard she keeps you close reined, flaunting you in front of Denas until he is half mad with it. But I never expected you'd be a willing slave. Clearly the Gastai tales of you are exaggerated."

"I was commanded," I said. But he was already gone.

Commanded. My own word stung deeper than Merryt's assumption of cowardice. I had been commanded to inaction by a demon woman who held me captive with beauty and laughter. No matter what lay beyond the barriers of my damaged memory, I could not have come to the realm of demons to find a lover. I was a Warden of Ezzaria. Ignoring the nervous sickness that accompanied my newfound resolution, I jumped up and ran after Merryt.

"You're right," I blurted out as I caught up to him in a gloomy passage.

He whirled around, fists raised, and broke out laughing at my nervous flinch. "So you're willing to risk a lovers' quarrel to see her true face, eh? I'll warn you. It may be you risk more than that. I was caught watching the demons' feasting once . . ." He held up his mutilated hands. "Are you willing, Exile?"

"I came to learn. So teach me." My words were very confidant and brave. Also quite misleading. I was terrified.

Merryt motioned me to follow in silence and caution. We crept through the cold gray warren like castle mice, pausing at every turn, skittering past doorways, hiding at every noise. No one was about. Only once did we have a close call. We were just about to step into a small courtyard, when Merryt abruptly shoved me into a dark niche and squeezed himself in beside me. He was a great deal more nervous than he showed. His heart was racing, and his shirt was damp and stinking with sweat. Three guards hurried across the snowy yard and took up positions beside a pair of double doors. Slowly we retreated back the way we'd come, and found a longer route that bypassed the courtyard.

Once out of earshot, Merryt breathed slightly easier, though our moment's proximity had revealed such quivering under his skin as could not be easily quieted. "Vallyne's sentinels," he said. "The lady and I don't get along, as I've said." He led me down a winding stair and into a narrow, bitterly cold tunnel.

At the far southern boundaries of Ezzaria were bottomlands, where the meandering streams that kept our land green and fertile came together and grew sluggish and slow as they approached the wide Samonka River that watered the jungles of Thrid. As a youth I had hunted in the Samonka swamps, training, of course, learning to endure the hot, humid climate, where the air was so clouded with insects, you had to wear cloth over mouth and nose as the Derzhi did in desert sandstorms. In some places the Samonka mud was chest high, so thick it sucked at your limbs as you fought to move. Every step through the downward tunnel under Denas's castle was a similar struggle. My limbs were lead. My muscles failed me. Vallyne's proscription blazed in my head like a fire in the forest, choking every other sense, threatening to destroy the flimsy structures of life I had rebuilt in my head. I was not just violating her command, but her trust . . . the bridge our strange relationship had built between her kind and my own. I could not bear the thought of it, and my reluctance seemed to take on physical shape in my incapable body. "Merryt . . . I can't do this."

"We're almost there." Merryt shot a quick glance over his shoulder as we passed by the dark opening to a side passage and arrived at a low-arched opening barred by a gate of rusty iron. The Ezzarian pushed on the gate, and it swung slowly away from him, creaking loudly. Beyond the arched gap lay a vast darkness . . . revealed by the smell of sour mud and old stone and beast venom as the demons' practice arena. "You've come for truth, remember? We've just got to cross the field and sneak through the gate on

the other side, and we'll come to the feasting rooms. We'll
have ourselves a fine place to watch."

I stopped and bent over, leaning my hands on my knees
and gasping for breath, unable to take another step forward
as my mind forced my body's revolt. What was wrong with
me? Never had I faced such complete physical incapacity
from my mind's forbidding. "Thank you for trying to help,
but I can't. She trusts me. I've got to go back."

"Afraid, are you? Can't bear to remember these are rai-
kirah that you're sworn to oppose? You'll know it when
you see what they're about. Let me tell you a bit . . ." He
stuck his broad face close to mine, telling his grotesque tale
with an unseemly eagerness.

Early in his captivity, Merryt had sneaked into the
demons' feasting trying to learn of it. What he had come
upon was a scene of horror—living visions of depravity.
"All the worst things we've seen possessed souls do in our
world . . . the demons gorge themselves with the taste and
feel and sound and smell of them," he said, near spitting
in disgust to tell the tale. "They live the deeds over and
over again, and the experience of it puts them in a frenzy
of fighting and mating and gorging themselves with food
and drink, until they fall upon the floor to sleep." He
sneered at me. "I suppose you're afraid to see it."

My reason told me I should go with him, but neither his
challenge nor my own could mute my body's overwhelming
surety that it would be a dreadful mistake. I shook my head
and turned back . . . and believed the action saved my life.

Three demons stood behind me, arms raised. Yelling at
Merryt to duck, I slammed away a heavy cudgel just as it
began to fall toward my head, then I dropped to the
ground, kicking a demon's hand as he let fly a dagger. The
weapon clattered to the stone, wide of any harmful mark.
The passage was too narrow. We were outnumbered and
could scarcely see, and I had no idea what kind of battle
we might face. So I rolled backward toward the gate and
bounced to my feet in the darkness just beyond it, flattening
my back against a wall just inside the archway. Merryt was
right beside me, cursing with a dedicated fervor I'd not
heard since living with the Derzhi.

"There's at least three of them," I whispered. "And perhaps one more."

My surmise was correct. A wooden club whacked into the wooden beam above my head. The wall behind our backs was the support for the viewing stands, so the attacker was just above and behind our heads. I dodged a second blow, then reached up and grabbed the arm that had thrown it, pulling the attached body over my head and slamming it to the ground so hard I heard the bones break. A wad of leather strapping fell from the viewing stand on top of the sturdy red-bearded body, so he looked like a fat fly caught in a spider web.

"You take the first one that comes out of the passage," I said, "and I'll take the next."

Merryt hesitated for so long that I thought I was going to have to go after all of the attackers myself. Burly shoulders emerged cautiously from the archway, as did a booming voice. "Have you secured him? Our master says to—" With a bellowing curse, Merryt launched himself at the searching demon.

The two others ran out on the big one's heels, and I snatched up the fallen demon's club and spun, letting all my strength flow through the arm-length weapon. The first demon was stopped instantly when the club smashed into his chest—stopping his wind if not his heart. A quarterstaff dropped from his hand. Having put everything into the blow, I had to duck and roll to give myself a chance to recover and see where the other fellow had gone. As I passed by the toppling figure, I grabbed his staff. A good thing, for just as I rolled to my back, a bludgeon came whistling through the murk, aimed at my head. With the fallen rai-kirah's staff, I held off the blow long enough to get to my feet, and in a blurring motion his bludgeon transformed into a quarterstaff of his own.

The demon was a fine fighter and untiring, easier to manage when you were half again as tall as a man, had scale like armor on your torso, and had three right arms. He kept shouting to his comrades to come after me, but two were flat on the ground and Merryt was occupying the fourth somewhere off in the dark. I was rusty—practicing moves in one's head until the body learned them was a

skill Wardens were taught, but was no substitute for true
weapons training. I had not lifted a sword or staff in
months. As I circled and attacked, straining to see in the
dim light, hoping strategy and experience would wear down
my opponent before he assessed my limits, I felt a sudden
sickening lurch in the depths of my being, an explosive
wrench of power, soon followed by a second and a third.
Reeling from the waves of darkness that flooded my soul,
I stepped back, only to see my opponent scream in fury.
"What do you think you're—"

But he never finished it. He fell to the ground with an ax
buried in his thick neck. Before I could gather my thoughts,
Merryt was on top of him, holding aloft a palm-sized oval
of glass that gleamed softly in the darkness. The pulsing
shape of light trying feebly to crawl away from the dead
body was stopped instantly. Paralyzed. And before I could
cry out in protest, Merryt plunged a silver knife into the
demon form.

"What are you doing?" I said, horror-struck. Nauseated.
"You've destroyed them!" Not just the bodies that could
always be remade, but the rai-kirah themselves.

"I've no patience for Ezzarian rules anymore." Merryt
stood up and wiped the Warden's knife on his victim's
clothes. "I've seen too much. Lived too long." He dropped
the knife and the mirror into a small leather bag, and he
gripped my arm. "I couldn't let them kill the only other
human in this place. Now we'd best be away from here.
Whoever it is hired them will be hunting."

I looked over my shoulder as he dragged me back
through the passage, watching the corpses slowly fade and
vanish, one by one. The physical bodies were nothing but
enchantments. The demons were already dead. No one
would ever know exactly what had happened. Only the one
who had sent the attackers would even suspect that we'd
had a hand in it.

We returned to my room, and Merryt took a hasty leave.
"My apologies, Exile. I'd no meaning to lead you into such
danger. I thought that way was safe." He paused in the
doorway. "Did you recognize the brutes?"

I shook my head. I was numb. Shaken. "Thank you for
saving my life. Now I owe you twice over." How could I

tell him how I detested what he'd done? Or how foolish it had been to kill our attackers without discovering who they were?

But evidently Merryt recognized them. "A dirty business in a dirty place. I'd best be off. Watch your back—those were Denas's Gastai." He slapped my shoulder and disappeared into the gloom.

The horror of the demon deaths took a long while to dismiss. The lingering images of the fading bodies made it worse. Like the one in the viewing stand, each of the attackers had carried a coil of leather strapping—exactly the kind used to bind me when I was in the pits. Merryt had believed he was saving my life . . . but I didn't think so. The attackers weren't trying to kill me. Denas planned to send me back to captivity—worse than killing, one might claim . . . unless you were a demon, whose death was so starkly empty. No body to burn or bury. No family to mourn or remember. To fade away so that no one could even see where you fell or how you met your end. And what came after death for a being of light?

I pulled the blankets over my head and dived into guilty sleep. I dreamed of Ham-fist and woke up screaming.

CHAPTER 27

After my deadly excursion with Merryt—an incident that might never have occurred, for all I heard of it—I could scarcely force myself to leave my room. What if someone had seen us in the tunnels or at the courtyard or in the practice arena? What if there had been a fifth attacker who had witnessed the fight? What if Denas saw my guilt-scribed face and made the connection with his missing Gastai? What if he tried it again? Yet when Vallyne summoned me, I could find no excuse to stay in. If I pleaded illness, she might detect my lie.

Two days after the ill-omened adventure, the lady invited me to walk with her in a long gallery where the walls were painted with stripes and swirls of every color. At first I thought the place only a failed venture into art, useful for nothing but making one dizzy. But Vallyne taught me to relax my eyes and let myself fall into it, allowing the colors to surround and enfold me like a painted ocean. The experience was gloriously pleasing, as if the colors—so weak in the rest of Rudai shaping—had taken on a life and energy of their own, very different from their role in the world I knew. As we stopped to enjoy a section of deep blues and purples, someone came hurrying out of the shadows and almost knocked the lady over. Merryt. He stopped just in time.

"*Gryallak!*" hissed Vallyne. The word was a demon curse of great ugliness that had no corresponding word in any language I knew. It meant something like "your vile person makes me want to chew up your essence and spit it out, and if someone else doesn't do it soon, I will." She made a small twisting gesture with her hand. "You trespass where you are forbidden, ylad. You will pay the price of it."

Merryt blanched and backed away. Before he could run, three Rudai guards appeared behind him. He wrenched his arms away and twisted his body fiercely, but to no avail, and he ended up facedown upon the floor, cursing. One of the demons stepped deliberately on the Ezzarian's outflung hands. "We should take the rest of these," said the Rudai, grinding his boots on Merryt's remaining fingers. "Make sure he's up to no more of his evil ways."

"Wait! Don't . . ." With this paltry protest I moved forward, hoping to stop it, but Vallyne touched my arm, halting my steps. One of the Rudai ripped a leather pouch from Merryt's belt, peered inside, and gave it to the lady. While guards dragged the protesting Ezzarian away, Vallyne pulled two objects from the bag: a silver Warden's knife and a Luthen mirror.

My face was scalding. While holding me motionless with her cool gaze, Vallyne handed them back to the Rudai and gave him his orders. "Show these to the ylad Merryt's friends and then destroy the wicked things. And see him punished appropriately."

Vallyne began to stroll along the gallery again, in a direction opposite to the way they had taken Merryt. I remained where I was, looking stupidly one way and then the other. Vallyne returned, took my arm, and pulled me with her. "He has been warned, Exile. He knows what it is he risks when he comes this way, carrying such foul implements." Vallyne's passionate hatred for the big Ezzarian was unlike anything I had felt from her.

The next time I glimpsed Merryt—limping through a crowded passageway—his broad face was one large bruise. Vallyne would say nothing more of him, but only reminded me of her command. In guilty confusion, I stayed away from him.

Indeed, I never again ventured outside the bounds Vallyne set for me. I took no risks, asked few questions, sought no information. Cowardice was not the only reason I abandoned my purpose. Though I pompously pronounced to myself that I was observing demon life so as to learn of it, in truth my every waking thought was of Vallyne.

For a while I told myself that I was bewitched and tried

to hold onto some semblance of reason when I was with her. But as the water clock was refilled again and again, I lost my remaining sense. I buried my fears in her laughter, allowed her beauty and wit to answer my every question, abandoned the search for my own mind in the delights of hers. My desire for her grew like mushrooms in the dark, and no amount of frenzied training exercises could distract me from it. Whether asleep or awake I dreamed of loving her. I told myself that her body was incapable of human sensations. Demons never touched one another, even when they danced. Their senses were broken and confused. She could not judge the taste of wine; she balked at food that I thought fine and relished other that made me ill. And so, though I longed to teach her enchanted body the truth of human passion, my touch could as likely give her pain as pleasure, and the thought left me half crazed. In the dismal light of my cluttered room, I would huddle in my empty bed, sick with desire and loneliness. Never did Vallyne mention my kiss or my quite obvious obsession with her. Nor did she change her own nature, which was to tease and taunt and torment even as she tried to soothe my mental miseries with distraction and kindness. Never did she ask me to yield my name, though the secret hung between us like a dark blot upon the sun.

I scratched more nonsense in my journal. My hands continued to shake. My past still lay hidden behind walls built of pain and mortared with blood, and I made no further attempt to recover it. I lived with beauty and could think of nothing else.

On the occasion when I completed reading a set of ten books of romantic epics, Vallyne expressed her desire to give me a gift. She did not ask me what I wanted—she well knew the truth of that—but instead presented me with a horse. The beast was an illusion, of course, for there was no life in the land of Kir'Vagonoth save the rai-kirah and the two captive humans. The lady wanted to take me riding into the storm-wracked countryside. I thoroughly disliked the idea.

I had come to the conclusion that, other than the demons themselves, the weather was the only reality in Kir'Vagonoth. The sole variety in it was the occasion's particular intensity of virulent cold and the shape of the penetrating wind. The demons suffered terribly from the cold, and no thickness of walls or layers of fur could shelter them. The bitter wind sucked the very brilliance from their light when they stepped out into the weather. All except Vallyne, who seemed to thrive at any challenge.

Of course, even beyond the frigid desolation, the grim wastes of snow and ice gave me the shudders. I had not completely forgotten my life-destroying dreams. And there were dangers in the wasteland that were neither frost nor dream. The Gastai lurked everywhere, and they were going mad.

On our third or fourth riding excursion, Nevai guards at the jackal gates tried to prevent our leaving the castle. A rugged, shovel-faced fellow named Heddon argued with Vallyne. "A party of rogue Gastai has raided a Rudai workshop, my lady. Ruined the tools and shapings, destroyed twelve Rudai of Kaarat's jurisdiction after using them cruelly. Denas has forbidden any to go out until he has controlled the raiders."

"He did not intend his orders to apply to me."

Heddon's light flickered nervously. "My lady, he expressly commanded us to stop you from leaving. The mad ones are everywhere."

"And if I refuse to obey?"

"I will be punished for permitting you to pass."

"But of course you cannot prevent me, Heddon." And then she spoke a word somewhere between a snake's hiss and the sigh of a lover. Until that moment I had never felt the fullness of Vallyne's power. For one brief instant, the clouds ceased their churning movements, and the relentless wind circled back upon itself, as if it might suck the earth and sky and all of us who inhabited them into its source. The soot-stained light of Kir'Vagonoth was dimmed as Vallyne's demon form gleamed alongside her physical form, the two images shifting one upon the other along with vague outlines of a hundred larger shapes. It was only a moment. Yet for the duration of it, I could scarcely move.

The guard bowed his head. "Of course not, my lady. I can only ask."

"You may tell Denas that I threatened worse punishments than he. I'm feeling too confined and need to be out for a while."

"Indeed, my lady. But please be cautious. The mad ones leave you nothing. It's like the dark times again, so I've heard."

"Thank you for your warning, Heddon." And so we rode on.

Ordinarily Vallyne would chatter unceasingly as we rode, the activity brightening her spirits even as the oppressive terrors of the wilderness sent mine plummeting. She would spur her mount up and over the rises and whoop in wild delight as it galloped down again, kicking up plumes of powdery snow. But on that day she said very little, riding aimlessly it seemed, circling slowly this way and that, winding between the icy hillocks instead of challenging them. A fine mist settled on our cloaks and in our hair, freezing them stiff. I had to trust that the lady could find her way through the heavy blue-gray clouds that had sagged all the way to the ground.

"How is it the Gastai can kill others of your kind?" I said, trying to shake loose my nagging fears with conversation. "I thought it impossible."

Vallyne kept her face straight ahead, her fine, squared jaw raised proudly as she rode. "It is a sickness in these Gastai—to hold one of us in solid form and kill the body, not allowing the true being to leave the shaping. Only after the body's death do they take the victims far into the wilderness and release them. The ones so treated cannot remember what we have learned in all these years, what we have made for ourselves. They can't find their way back here, and so it is like the dark times all over again for them."

I shifted uneasily, thinking of the Luthen mirror holding the demons paralyzed as Merryt killed them . . . as I had done so often in the past. A sickness. Yes. Perhaps it was.

After three-quarters of an hour, I caught the stench of demon on the blustering wind—thick, foul, raising my defenses as had not happened since my first hours in Denas's castle. "Vallyne—"

She held up her hand to silence me, then pointed down

a modest slope from our position toward a thickening in the clouds: a huge, dense black clot that seemed to grow as we watched. Howls of beast rage spewed from the blackness, soon drowning out the thundering wind and accompanied by a fury of yips and growls, the snarling lust of wild dogs that have scented fresh blood.

My body knew what it was I saw and heard—so familiar, yet magnified a hundred times from my past experience. My muscles tightened, every sense instantly alert, searching in vain for the melydda to feed it. A demon battle raged in the midst of the storm—not practice as they did in their arena, but a death battle. Monstrous shapes took form in the roiling clouds—a pack of huge jackals with bloody muzzles, apelike creatures with six arms, a giant cat with a snake for a tail, and, in the midst of it all, scarcely visible in the murk, a leather-winged dragon.

"Hyssad hwyd zhar! Faz dyarra y vekkasto." Golden fire split the churning mass of diseased enchantment as the command rang out. "Begone from this place! Back to your pits or become nothingness." Denas . . . the dragon . . . powerful, magnificent. He had not used that form in the practice arena.

The howls grew louder and fiercer. The jackals tore at the leather wings. The cat screeched, and everywhere was the sound of pain and mad fury as the dark cloud thickened, obscuring the vicious combat. My bones ached at the sound, and the reins slipped from my shaking hands. I bent forward to reach and take them up again, but stayed low, as if I might hide behind my horse's ruddy mane. Then a towering geyser of darkness shot into the clouds and collapsed instantly to the snow-covered wastes, and in the next moment I felt the explosion of sickness, the world-splitting, soul-darkening release of power that was the truth of demon death, magnified a hundred times.

Vallyne sat rigid in the saddle. Watching. Waiting.

Slowly the blackness thinned and broke apart, releasing pent-up deadness like the opening of a grave. Yet even as I shuddered at the foul vapors and spat to take the taste of it from my mouth, there rose from the drifting remnants of that enchanted storm a haunting song of mourning, a warrior's chant expressing loss so profound that it summed

up everything I knew of sorrow. As it reached its climax
and faded, a single frigid gust swept the remaining darkness
away, then even the wind fell silent for a moment, as if to
respect such grief. Five rai-kirah, their lights dull, their
faces tired and wounded, were riding up the rise toward
us, Denas in the lead. When he came even with our position, the demon lord reined in his mount and motioned his
warriors past us. He did not so much as glance at Vallyne,
but cast me a look of bitter hatred. He seemed on the verge
of speech, but as soon as the others were past, he jerked
the reins of his unliving mount and followed his fellows
toward the distant castle.

"Did they lose a comrade?" Instantly I regretted my query.
My curiosity seemed crass, desecrating the lingering echoes
of Denas's grieving.

"No," said Vallyne. A sudden gust of wind swirled snow
about her face, and she tugged sharply on the reins to turn
back and follow Denas toward the castle. "He sang for
the Gastai."

On the forty-first day of my life with Vallyne—approxi-
mately forty-one, as the days and nights were indistinguishable, and I may have missed a few or added extra—she
took me riding to the city on the horizon. I was surprised
at this. I had learned that there were indeed other castles
in Kir'Vagonoth. Rhadit, for one—the much maligned
leader of the "great venture"—had his own fortress. But I
had never been taken to any of them or to the workshops
of the Rudai that were the long low buildings half buried
in the snow. That was fine with me, as the black and silver
terror of my dreams still lurked somewhere in the freezing
tempest along with the mad Gastai.

I tried to avoid the outing. "I found another book about
mountains," I said. "I swear that it's complete and makes
sense from start to finish." We had found that many of the
writings took off in odd directions, as if the end of one
book had been pasted onto the beginning of another. "And
we've never finished the poem you were composing. If
you're going to make it rhyme as you wish, you need to
work at it a bit more."

"But you've never seen the city, and the Rudai worked

so hard on it. It is their greatest proof that we have come out of the dark times."

I could not refuse her, of course, and so I bundled myself in cloak and gloves, and we rode over the arched bridge into the wilderness. "Tell me of the dark times," I said, seeking anything to distract me from the terrors lurking in the howling wind and my unhealthy desire to love a demon. The "dark times" were oft mentioned, but never discussed among the Nevai.

"It was the time after Kir'Navarrin was stolen away. When we first found ourselves in Kir'Vagonoth," she said, matching her horse's pace to mine. "We could not remember our names or our shapes, could not find what we needed . . . could not feel . . . could not see. And there was nothing but this." She waved her hand to the bleak landscape. "A savage time. A very long time. Though we must remember it, it is very difficult to talk about."

Her face took on a new character as she spoke, as fine wood takes on a new luster with careful use. For just a moment her demon form flickered silver, overlaying her fair young woman's visage with a beauty that was older, sadder, prouder. Merryt could not have it right. Her true face was not monstrous . . . for I believed I had caught a glimpse of it. I promptly forgot what she had said, as well as my other questions.

In the way of demon travel, we were not long upon the journey, and soon we were riding on brick-paved streets between houses and shops, towered temples, sprawling courtyards and palaces, parks, fountains, bathhouses, and grand colonnades . . . all of them deserted. It was a city of grace and art and largeness of mind, expressing the power and intellect of a civilized people, worthy to be matched with Zhagad itself. But snow had drifted into doorways and windows, clogging streets and alleys, piled atop hanging signboards that swung aimlessly in the wind. Darkness hung thick in the wide streets and majestic buildings. Everywhere was silence.

"It is a marvel," I said. "Why does no one live here?"

"Some tried," she said, running her hand along the basin of a flower-shaped fountain. The water, frozen hard, should have been rippling about her fingers. "But we could never get it right. We didn't know what to do with it."

We explored the farthest corners of that city, wandering up and down the deserted streets, into vast sculpture gardens that would be the envy of the Kuvai. We left our horses for a while and gawked at the vast spaces of the temples, the sky-brushing vaults that should have been filled with sunlight from their patterned windows. I climbed two hundred steps to a bell tower, interested to see that the steps were cupped in the center as if worn by a thousand years of boots, though Vallyne said it was unlikely anyone had ever ascended them since their making. At the top I pulled the hanging ropes, but when the bell sounded, its tone was off, and the eerie echoes reminded me of my first impression—a plague city. I laid my hand upon the bell so it would not toll again.

"Come down, Exile, and tell me if I've found my proper place!" Vallyne called up to me, and as ever when she beckoned, I hurried my pace down the steps. I found her standing atop a carved lion in the square before the tower. "Is this not what you read to me about this beast?" And she roared into the storm, raising her arms in defiance of the everlasting wind. When she jumped down from her perch, I caught her in my arms and laughed with her and let the wind whip her golden hair about my face so that I was lost in a jungle of light. Lost. I wanted to be lost.

"I could teach you," I said, my voice breaking as I pressed her to my breast, knowing full well that she understood my desire. "Let me try."

"You forget. You came here to learn, not teach," she said. "And I need to be back to the castle. Don't linger too very long." Her physical form vanished, and for one moment I embraced only her demon radiance. *Fire . . . glory . . .* I was engulfed with such passion and power as could consume a city . . . but only for one instant, one heartbeat . . . and then she was gone.

"Vallyne!" I cried out in despair, for I did not think I could take another breath without more of what I had just tasted.

But as with all fools who believe their mortal existence bound up in another's touch, my heart beat again. And my lungs filled again. And the cold wind whipped my cloak about my empty arms. I walked slowly back to the desolate marketplace and found the horse—the illusion that would bear me back to the castle. Hers was gone, though no hoof-prints marred the newly drifted snow. Even the terrors of the wasteland were no matter beside my desire. I mounted the false beast, but sat drained and purposeless upon its back, my hands shaking in their unending coward's rhythm. When the horse ambled into the maze of streets, I paid no attention to what direction it was going.

All I had to do was tell her my name. Of course it would not make her love me—if she were even capable of love. And I knew better than to claim I loved her. I had not mind enough for love as yet. But to know her better . . . to give her what I could of life . . . to let her music fill the void within me . . . how could I ever know what was possible if I kept such a part of myself hidden? I could not believe the lady wished me ill. If I told her my name . . . what harm would come of it? And the possibilities . . . they made thought and reason and caution impossible.

But then I wrenched myself back from the brink of such appalling weakness. *Sentimental fool. Broken, mindless wreck. You are enchanted.* Surely that was it. This was all some game of witchery to make me surrender what I had suffered so dreadfully to protect. For if I fell . . . I pulled at my hair with my quivering fingers, as if I could wake the dead mind within my head. I had once wielded a great deal of power. What if this were just another combat? Merryt had warned me. I didn't know Vallyne's true face. She was not human.

An hour of this fruitless arguing, and the horse had carried me beyond the deserted city. When I realized that I could not see Denas's castle, a knot of fear strangled my moonstruck babbling. My mind began conjuring Gastai lurking in the darkness. *No matter*, I told myself. *All you have to do is ride the perimeter of the city, and you'll come on the point where you can get a view of the castle. Then a straight ride across the plain will get you behind walls.* I took control again, spurred the horse to a slightly faster walk, and bore to the left around the city. Every few hundred paces, I stopped to scan the horizon.

At my third stop I saw the tower. Not Denas's castle that had ten separate towers linked by roofs and battlements, but a lonely finger of stone atop a ridge of low hills. A ruin, the crumbling walls exposed to the weather, only bits of its smooth white facing-stone intact, only visible among the ice pinnacles because of a momentary lull in the storm. Hardly worth noting . . . except that it had no place in Kir'Vagonoth. It belonged in Ezzaria . . . on a bald, wind-swept knob of rock . . . my refuge . . . one of the images I had protected for so long.

Heedless of time and terror, I took out through the swirling snow, urging the unliving beast beneath me ever faster. In a frenzy to discover its meaning, I dared not even blink lest the ruin vanish in the blue-gray clouds. My mount was knee-deep in powdery snow as we pushed up the rise. My cheeks and nose were numb, my eyebrows stiff with frost when I dropped to my feet from the horse's back in front of the tower. For a moment I held still, closing my eyes, centering my thoughts, summoning the calm focus I used to detect sorcery. It was almost unneeded. No trace of demon working marred the immense enchantment.

Two steps took me through the jagged opening, where a thick wooden door had long rotted away, and into a circular room strewn with rubble. A blackened fire pit in the center of the broken floor. A dented copper pot and a pile of kindling beside it. A bed of dried pine branches—from trees that had never grown in Kir'Vagonoth. I passed my hand before my face, shifting my senses to intensify my perception of the world, and in the time it took for the air to shift about my hand, I knew where I was.

"Aife," I whispered on the frail breath of hope, opening my deepest heart and exposing it to the bitter winter. "Are you here?" Such silence wrapped the crumbling stone that my words jangled in disharmony. A gust of wind flapped my cloak like a giant trying to get my attention, but my attention was fixed on my hearing, on the hope for a voice from beyond the storm.

Warden? Is this a dream?

I leaned my head back and laughed as I had not laughed in ages of the world. "A dream, yes, for certain. No waking of my knowledge could match it, and if I should see a portal, I would think it the fairest dream ever graced a night's sleeping."

I heard her laughing, too. Tired, life-giving, exultant laughter. Laughter of pride and purpose. In the shadows of that tower, the air glistening with frost shards, took shape a gray doorway taller than a man. And beyond the doorway, wavering like heat shimmer in the desert, was a gold-green brilliance so glorious my eyes could scarcely bear to look upon it. Unthinking excitement and hunger propelled me forward, and I was just on the verge of stepping through the portal, when I heard a faint call—worried, searching—from the wilderness outside the tower. "Exile!"

I thought my being might rip in two. To walk away from Vallyne, to break the tethers that bound me to that strange and terrible place . . . The consideration left me desolate. Yet that was not the whole of it. For even as I stood in the Aife's shelter, enveloped in her enchantment, the walls of memory crumbled and my life came flooding back, giving name to my hoarded treasures—Aleksander, Blaise, Evandiargh, blessed, faithful Fiona—and purpose to my empty words. What was the missing piece of the mosaic? What had caused my ancestors to destroy themselves and condemn these bright spirits to this hellish wasteland? Was there remedy for the flawed wholeness of my child and Blaise? The fog suffocating my senses dispersed, and the edges of the world became clean and hard. The bits and pieces I had learned despite my crippled mind now took on new shape and urgency. And with memory came pain, of course. Without answers, what awaited me in my own land? Nothing. No one. The cold wind twined about my ankles.

Hurry, Warden . . . My time is almost done. I've promised the old man. Only the hour we agreed.

"Ah, my good Aife . . . I cannot . . ." Never had there been words so difficult to say. Never had I been forced to turn my back on a vision so enticing. . . . not yet. I'll come back when I'm able and tell you more."

Not yet! But you said . . . Are you mad?

"No longer, Aife. You've healed me. But my work here is not done. Tell the old man that Kir'Vagonoth is beyond his imagining. Ice and snow and cold and darkness, yes, but they have made beauty here in this horror. And the circles are just as he named them: the Gastai brutes, the Rudai, shapers of such skill they could remake his temple in an instant, and the Nevai . . . I cannot describe their glory or the strength of their passion. Tell him . . ." Another bit fell into place—the truth that had presented itself so clearly through the fog of my days in Kir'Vagonoth if I had not been too preoccupied to pursue it. ". . . tell him that they are not complete in themselves, any more than we are."

I'll tell him.

"I will survive, Aife. There is another human here. A Warden lost in a battle hundreds of years ago. Is it not a wonder? He—"

"Exile! Where are you?" Closer. I had to get away from the tower.

"I must go."

Are you sure, Warden?

"I'm sure of nothing. But there are answers here, if I can just discover them. And more in another place called Kir'Navarrin. Can you hold the way a while longer?"

Never doubt it. Never. I will hold until you walk upon the green earth once again.

The most stubborn and faithful of Aifes. "I will come bringing answers."

Bring yourself, and my duty will be done.

She left the portal hanging there for a few moments more, perhaps in case I changed my mind. But the choice was made. I closed my eyes to the green-gold world and walked back into the howling wind.

CHAPTER 28

Then came the day when Valdis reached his manhood and laid his strong hand upon his mother's shoulder. Verdonne smiled and stepped aside, and Valdis wrenched his father's sword away and stripped his father of his power. But instead of keeping these things for his own, he laid them at his mother's feet. "You have shown your people the selfless strength and faithfulness of a true sovereign ruler. These are rightly yours."
—The story of Verdonne and Valdis as told to the First of the Ezzarians when they came to the lands of trees

Vallyne did not see me come from the tower. I made sure of it by riding down the back side of the hill and threading my way through the snowy hillocks until I was as far from it as I dared go. It was risky to stray from the path I knew, but the tower was my refuge, my escape route. No one could know of it. The concentration required to keep my course straight and the direction of the city firm in my mind precluded any consideration of my newly reclaimed purposes or what light my experiences in Kir'Vagonoth could shed upon them. With profound relief I turned toward the city walls, and when I saw Vallyne racing toward me through the driving sleet, her silver shimmer like a beacon in the night, I came near forgetting everything I had just remembered.

"Where have you been, Exile?" Concern was written on her pale brow, and she reached out and took my hands. Like a slave's tether chokes off his breath, so her touch began to strangle my newfound reason. "I thought you were lost or run away. You are my gyos, and a guest should not stray so far from his patroness's protection."

But I held tight to my freedom, determined it would not be lost again to beauty and desire and whatever enchantment she had woven with them. I had a wife, a son, and responsibilities that could allow no more distraction. "I was only riding," I said. "Thinking. It's been so hard to have a clear thought since I was with the Gastai."

"The Gastai are everywhere out . . ." She paused and glanced down at my hands that lay in hers, then back to my face. A whisper of puzzled curiosity creased her brow, but she went on without mentioning its cause. "They hate your kind and will try everything they know to steal you back to their pits. They don't forget."

"No, I'm the one who forgot everything."

"But that's not such a bad thing, is it? You said you came to us for refuge. Your life must have been terrible to make you seek sanctuary with those you've sought to destroy. Why would you want to remember?" Vallyne released her grip, motioned toward the distant castle, and we nudged our horses to a walk. "There are many things I would give much to forget. But it is not a skill we possess."

"You've never asked me about what happened to me or why I believe I can find truth here. Nor has Denas."

"Why would I want to know? You've left that other place behind. This is your life now, and I take pleasure in your company. As for Denas, he is a fool and a brute, and has no right to question you. You needn't worry about him." Her acting had not improved. But I couldn't tell whether her performance was for me or for herself, or which part of her reassurance was the lie.

Time to be about my business. "Will you tell me of Kir'-Navarrin, Vallyne?"

She glanced at me sharply. "No," she said, kicking her horse to a faster pace. "Not yet." She said nothing more upon that cold journey, and we rode across the arched bridge in silence. It wasn't until I undressed, ready to fall into my bed, that I knew what had puzzled Vallyne when she held my hands. They were no longer shaking.

* * *

So where to begin? The more I considered my life in Kir'Vagonoth, the more convinced I became that I had been wearing blinders not of my own making. Yes, the Gastai's torment had wounded me, but not so much that I would forget my wife and my son and all the others I had left behind. Not so much that I would forget Aleksander and the changes we had wrought in each other. Not so much that I would forget my conviction that my people shared a common history with the demons. Why would the demons care what I remembered? And why would they not question my need for sanctuary or my claims of warning and goodwill? The foolishness with the dogs . . . Vallyne had been watching me. Testing me. And then she had bewitched me.

Sitting on my bed after several hours of restless sleep, I pulled out my journal. The childish scribbling was scarcely readable, and most of the entries made no sense at all. Sweet Verdonne . . . in one day's entry I had written the first four letters of my name! Without thinking, I called up fire to destroy the treacherous paper, and before I could curse myself for forgetting my helplessness, I had to drop the blazing sheet. I jumped up and doused the flames with water from the enamel bowl before they could set the cluttered room alight. Then I licked my singed fingers and came near crowing with delight at the quiet thrum of melydda in my veins. So my power had also been hidden beneath the suffocating bonds of demon enchantment. Merryt had warned me. I was allowing the lady to steal away my soul without a fight.

I made sure the mess was cleaned up, then poked and fidgeted about my room, waiting for Raddoman to come in for his daily visit, scarcely able to contain the fever of long-delayed curiosity. Perhaps I could learn something from the growling fellow. Of all the demons, he seemed to speak his mind forthrightly. I was anxious to meet each of my demon acquaintances with my newly opened eyes.

He appeared with his usual bluster, shifting from his demon form into his disheveled human-shaped bulk. "Here is water. Food. The mistress is occupied and will not see you until the reading time." He dropped a flowered plate of bread and cheese on the table and slammed a brass pitcher down beside it.

"Thank you, Raddoman. Wait! Before you go . . ."

He poked his chin out belligerently. "What do you want now?"

It was time to test my theories. "Why do you claim we stole your homeland?"

In the space of a heartbeat he shifted three times between his human form, his demon form, and his pig form. Settling on his human form, he grumbled. "Treating me like I am the captive, are you? Questioning me?" The stink of him wafted through the cold room.

"No. I've come here to learn, as I said. It's important that I understand how we came to be at war. My people have no tale of it. No memory of it. No writing or picture to tell us. So what do your stories tell?"

"It is no story, ylad. We remember. We lived in Kir'Navarrin in the light. We had our own bodies, and we knew who we were. And when came the terror and the dark times, we found ourselves here in Kir'Vagonoth. Would I could make every one of you *pandye gash* live the dark times as we did." He turned to go, his stink wafting through the room.

I was right. Kir'Navarrin was much more than the realm of the soul—the landscape of demon combat. "Teach me, Raddoman. I want to learn. I want to understand."

Raddoman shifted slowly to his demon image, his bearded face and hot blue eyes now facing me again, though he had not turned around. With a sigh—of satisfaction, it seemed—he bowed. "As you wish, ylad." He extended his hand toward my face, forcing me backward until I sat on my bed, jammed against the wall . . . until his wide palm covered my eyes and nose and mouth, the light-sculpted flesh closing off smell and speech and the gray light of the castle . . . I could not move, and the darkness deepened, suffocating . . . paralyzing . . .

. . . *burning . . . no, it's cold . . . bitter, bone-cracking cold. What is this darkness? Hold, think . . . someone is there, weeping . . . Who's there? Where are you? I cannot see . . . anything. Have I gone blind? The sun shone like*

polished gold this morn . . . but now it's gone . . . and I can
feel nothing. Nothing but this dreadful cold. Am I dead?
No, surely not. I have but few years compared to . . . so
many. Where was I when this came to pass? In the
garden . . . planting . . . new trees for the spring to come . . .
saplings we brought from the Mountains of Lorrai. But then
I smelled the jasnyr . . . and I lost my way . . . forgot what
I was doing . . . Holy stars, it is so cold. If I could feel my
cloak, I would wrap it about my arms . . . but I cannot even
feel my arms. These winds cut through me as if I had no
flesh. I must be numb already. The wind . . . right through
my head . . . no wonder I cannot think . . . this bitter wind
chills my brain. Think back to the sunlight. Think of what
happened . . . As I dug and planted, the elder, Lu— What
was his name? Can't think of the name, though I've known
him all my life . . . my father's brother . . . he called us
together and said the time had come. All would be well. We
would not remember . . . before the change . . . and the
danger locked away in Tyrrad Nor—this dreadful danger
from the beginning of the world, the danger that wears no
name—would not come to pass, because we had chosen
safety. We would still have our power, more of it because it
would not be wasted on useless shaping, and we would live
in beauty as always. Then everything smelled of jasnyr, and
I fell asleep. But of course I remember. I worked in my
garden this very morn . . . I who was born . . . come, it will
say itself . . . the name I was born with . . . that my wife
speaks with love . . . my wife . . . No! What's happened to
me? No one forgets his wife's name. Where is she? She was
with me in the sunlight, milking, far gone with child . . .
another daughter to grace our garden. Love, where are you?
I would call your name, but I can't remember. How can I
find her in this darkness without her name? She will be cold.
She hates the cold so sorely. I need to hold her. Warm her.
And our little ones . . . three . . . are they the ones I hear
weeping? Oh, holy gods of day, what are their names? And
my father who touched my hands with earth and called me
"son of the land, born to nurture trees . . ." Where is my
father? Where are my children? Where are my hands?

*   *   *

Hopeless, lonely grief was devouring my spirit as the light came back—the cold gray light of Kir'Vagonoth that was the very essence of despair. My fall into the pits had only approximated the moment of desolation I had just lived. Such loss. Such hunger. Physical life vanished in an instant. The only sound the wind, and the faint wailing of other lost souls. For a thousand years to have all the demands of bodily existence—hunger, thirst, desire—but nothing to soothe them. The demons had shaped their present existence from distorted memory and the stolen lives brought them by the Gastai. Holy Verdonne, what had we done to ourselves . . . and to the world, which had borne the burden of our deeds?

I slumped against the chilly wall, drained, sober. The demon form shimmered in the doorway, turned where I could see nothing but his light. "I'm sorry," I said softly. "I didn't know. None of us know."

"Gather the circle," said the demon softly. "It was all we could think. But it was a very long time before we found the others of our circles. We could not recognize our kin. Even now . . . Denas himself could be my brother or my father or my son, but I would not know it. Only the bond of the circle did we know. When we gathered at last, the hunters went out to find something to feed us as they had ever done, though what they found was not what we expected. Not meat or drink, but images of life—sounds and sensations and memories from bodies that were not our own, but could be given us to share. What they bring satisfies our hungers . . . some hungers that we never knew before and never wanted to know, for those depraved sensations are so powerful and the easiest to harvest. And so we have survived, except that your kind—the ylad *pandye gash*—fight them and kill them or force them to return to this realm broken, as if they were in those dark times again and again. Do you understand, Exile? It is your own evils and your own war that have corrupted the Gastai until they are gone to ruin. It is clear that you—the *pandye gash*—are the same who sent us here, and why else would you do it, but to take Kir'Navarrin for your own?"

"But we don't live in Kir'Navarrin. We don't even know where it is."

He shrugged his shoulders. "Perhaps you're afraid of what you would find in Tyrrad Nor. Perhaps your people know what is the danger and wait for us to go back and fight it for you. Or perhaps there never was any such thing, and it is a tale you told us to get us out."

"Tyrrad Nor—the Last Fortress. What is it?"

"As I told you, we don't know. You took that from us, too. But we lived alongside it once, and we will do so again. We will chance any danger to get our homeland back again, if not the lives you stole from us. We wish to survive. We have no choice. Now I need to be off. The lady calls."

"I'm sorry," I said again. What more useless words could a man utter? "We don't know any of this. Whoever made you forget did the same to us. All these years we've been fighting, when we are the victims of the same deeds."

"Just think of it," he said as he stepped into the passage. "When we leave Kir'Vagonoth behind, it's you who'll be left here alone. You and the other ylad. And there'll be no one to feed you, and no one to tell you your name."

"Will you ask the lady if I can see her?"

"She won't. I told you. Not until the reading time."

"Ask her, if you would, please. I'm anxious to speak with her about these things."

"I'll ask." Raddoman's brown-gray light vanished.

So much to consider. And even in this memory I had lived was the hint of the threat. What was the Last Fortress? What was the danger that had no name—the "danger from the beginning of the world?"

I waited for nearly an hour, but the servant did not return. Other than Vallyne, Raddoman, and the unapproachable Denas, I had exchanged no word with any demon. I didn't even know how to find most of the ones I'd seen, much less which of them might be receptive to my questioning. So, impatient to get on with my long delayed quest, I set off in search of someone I knew how to question. Merryt.

I had no idea how to find Merryt's rooms. I had been too confused and ill when he had brought me from the pits. But he still carried messages for Gennod, and I knew where Gennod lived. It was only a matter of waiting until the

Ezzarian showed up. I crept through the castle with caution, a tactic wholly unlike my oblivious wanderings of the past weeks. How could I have been so completely mesmerized by the demon woman, so careless? To forget all those I cared for. To forget my training. Swearing to harden my heart and my resolve, I waited in the dark behind a spiral column outside Gennod's chambers until I saw the Ezzarian come out.

"You'll see the message delivered, ylad." Red light flickered in the gloomy doorway. "Rhadit is waiting. I'll tolerate no delays."

"Of course, good Gennod," said the big man. He bowed respectfully and limped down the corridor, muttering under his breath. I stepped out of the shadows to intercept him. "Exile!" He was genuinely surprised.

"I'd like to talk," I said.

"I'm surprised to see you off your leash." He pointed down a spiral stair. "Let's go somewhere private, eh? When a fellow starts lurking in niches, one gets the idea he's got something on his mind."

"I don't want to get you in trouble with your master. This is the only place I knew where I might find you."

Merryt glanced up and down the passage, then grabbed me by the shirt and pulled me close, whispering in my ear. "Gennod is *not* my master. He keeps up the appearance of it to put off his rivals. We have some interests in common at present, that's all. A Warden must look to his oath now and then, even if it doesn't seem to matter much, eh? Or have you forgotten your oath while you dally with the beauteous Vallyne? I saved your life, Exile, and what have I got for it?"

"I'm sorry I didn't help you in the gallery," I said as we entered the rooms where he had gotten me washed and dressed for my first meeting with Denas and Vallyne. "I've had a lot on my mind that wasn't of my own choosing. It's only in the past hours I've come to myself again."

He thrust a number of oddly colored pillows out of the way, and we settled ourselves by his hearth. "Mind-stealing, is it? I warned you." He tossed in two handfuls of wood scraps from a tarnished brass bin, and sparked a fire. "So what do you want with me? I'd come to think you felt no need of corrupted brothers."

"I'd like to talk to you about the reasons I came here."

"Ah. So I'm to hear the great secret at last?"

"I can tell you some of it." Actually, I told Merryt a great deal: about my meeting with Vyx beyond the portal and the dreams he had sent me, of how I had been forbidden to fight, about the mosaic and my beliefs about the demons, and a general description of my experiences with Denas and Vallyne. Not everything. Nothing of Fiona. Nothing of Blaise or my son or how close I had come to surrendering my soul. Nothing I wanted to keep private from anyone, demon or human. I just hoped that perhaps the Ezzarian could give me a few answers I could understand. In my telling I came full circle to the essential question. "So what . . . where . . . is Kir'Navarrin?" I said. "Raddoman says that the demons once lived there, and we threw them out of it and into this horror of an existence. Vallyne says that her garden is the image of it." Only as I described it for Merryt had I realized that everything in Vallyne's garden could be found portrayed in the mosaic— the trees, the flowers, even the layout of the roads—but not in the foreground. Only beyond the faint rectangular images of the portals. I could not sit still as I thought of it, but jumped to my feet and paced the length of Merryt's room as I told my story. "Denas and his fellow conspirator believe I can open the way to it. Can I?"

The Ezzarian listened carefully to everything, poking idly at the edge of the fire with his boot, rubbing the stumps of his missing fingers with his wide thumbs, his rugged square face settled in sober concentration. "Not right now," he said. "But you could. You wouldn't like the learning how, I would guess. But any Ezzarian with melydda enough could serve their need. No . . . the worrisome thing is what Vallyne and her friends are planning. There's more to it than the opening . . ." He looked up at me, narrowing his dark, angled eyes, as if he'd not quite ever noticed my face before. "They believe they can force you to it. They see something in you . . . a man who claims he's come willing to the demon realm . . . Who, of any of us in Kir'Vagonoth, could know what to make of such a one?" He paused for a while, staring at me, then shifted his posture, settling back on his cushions as if he had come to some internal resolution. "Let me tell you a little tale. I thought we had some time to learn how things are like to fall out among the devils, but it appears that matters are getting out of hand. I think it's time we take charge of events ourselves."

The neglected fire snapped and settled into pulsing coals as he continued. "The demons dearly want to get back to Kir'Navarrin. They say it's where they came from—maybe we did, too, or maybe not; I don't take to that part of your tale. I am not one-half of a cursed demon. But they're set on going back. They think that once they're home, they'll be warm and taste their food and recognize their kin. But there's something blocking their way."

"Which is?"

"Us. Ezzarians." He dropped his voice almost out of hearing, drawing me close until I was sitting on the cushions beside him, peering right into his broad face. "What would the Queen of Ezzaria and her Wardens and Weavers do if there came a demon legion riding into the world? All of them invading human souls at once?"

"A demon legion . . . thousands . . ." Enough to drive a whole city or a whole race into madness at once. Impossible. Inconceivable. My mind balked and gaped—aghast at such a vision. No words could possibly address it.

"Yes, I see you understand. She would do everything in her power to stop it. Unfortunately, the gateway to Kir'Navarrin lies in our world, in a wild place—or at least it was wild when I last knew of it—in southwestern Manganar, just over our border. A ruin—gods' teeth it does fit with what you've said—the Place of the Pillars it's called. But no matter where. Because the demons are the only ones that know of Kir'Navarrin and its magics, a demon must open the way. And because the gateway exists in the physical world, the demon needs a human hand to open it—one with a great deal of melydda behind it, a powerful sorcerer joined with one of their own. They tried for a hundred years to persuade me to do it, but I wouldn't. And so they've planned to find some other Ezzarian sorcerer and take him by force as they make their way to the portal."

"But why . . . if they could force you, why didn't they?"

"Because they said"—for just a moment Merryt raised his maimed fist in front of his face—"because the lady would not allow it. She convinced the others I was not worthy . . . because I saw her true face when they were at their feeding. She could not forgive me for that, so she had me—" He took a deep breath and smiled tightly, rubbing his stumps again. "Well, my melydda serves me for little but magician's tricks anymore, and it would do nothing for them. But you . . . you've a great deal of melydda, so I've heard. Exceptional. It sounds as if someone thinks to use you and has drawn you here for that purpose. But first, before they attempt the gateway, they plan to destroy the Ezzarians."

Merryt's story was jumbled, clearly skewed with his own anger and resentment. He did not like to be found wanting, even by a demon who wished to possess his soul. But everything he said fit with what I had heard from Denas—Denas, who was planning to lead "the great venture."

"Why now?" I said. "Why haven't they done this before? There have been other Wardens, powerful enough surely. . . ." But perhaps not so easily manipulated as one who had been a slave, whose pride had set himself up as the judge of law and tradition, who had teetered on the verge of corruption.

"For a long time the Rudai held back. They're happy enough here and had no inclination to risk losing it all again. But the Gastai keep them all fed, and the Gastai are going mad, thanks to our war. The day is coming soon when the Gastai will be uncontrollable. Then who will feed them? The Rudai are next in line to go hunting. They don't like that idea and have come willing to the venture at last. The only thing that's hindering them is the Nevai's everlasting bickering over who's to command the legion. For you killed the Naghidda, and, of course, this was all his idea to begin with. All the most powerful Nevai have been killing each other off until you'd think there'd be none of them to fight."

"We've got to stop it, Merryt." I knew it as I knew my own name. I could see it so clearly . . .

. . . *mounted demons riding across the luminescent bridge into the storm that raged outside the castle walls. The terror*

*waiting for them . . . the one in black and silver . . . ready
to lead them to destroy Ezzaria. And at the edge of the trees
stood Ysanne and Catrin and young Drych and Tegyr, and
behind them in the moon-cast shadows the remnants of my
people . . .*

. . . but not me. I would not be there to defend them,
and none of them would know the truth. "It will destroy
all of us," I said, "Ezzarians and demons together—and all
hope of righting this great wrong that was done. We've got
to warn Ezzaria, and to find a way to convince them all—
both sides—that it doesn't have to be this way. There must
be another answer."

"A novel idea to be sure. I think the Gastai addled your
head." The Ezzarian sighed and poured wine from a crystal
carafe into two silver cups and shoved one of them into
my hand. "As to warning the Ezzarians, it's not going to
happen unless one of us can get out of this place. Maybe
you'll be more fortunate in finding a way out than I've
been. As to convincing . . . you've heard Denas and his
like speaking of ylad. Not exactly begging to get back into
the family. And I can imagine what my Ezzarian elders
would have said if I had tried to tell them that our war
against the demons was self-murder. I would have vanished
from their sight before I had the words out."

So was this invasion the key to my dream? Had Vyx
been trying to warn me of the demon plot? It would explain
why he had made no public acknowledgment of our meeting, no advance of friendship. If he was trying to undermine
the demons' venture, he could not dare reveal what he had
done. And yet that explanation seemed too simple. The
terror of the dream was all-encompassing, devouring
darkness . . . led by a being magnificent in power. "Merryt,
what do you know of the place called Tyrrad Nor?"

"The Last Fortress? There's naught to know. Rumors
from the dark times. Nothing more," said Merryt, leaning
back on his cushions and propping his feet on a flat box.
The wine cup held in his right hand was quivering ever so
slightly. "There's not any of the devils can say what gives
them the frights. Just ask them about it. You'll see. If it's
something so wicked, you'd think one of them would
remember . . . if the place even exists. Think on it, lad. If

there were some danger locked up in Kir'Navarrin, then why would they be so anxious to go back?"

If Raddoman was to be believed, the rai-kirah had no choice in the matter. It was go back or become like those in the pits. Risk the unknown danger to prevent the known. But what was the true risk? "It was fear that caused us to split ourselves apart a thousand years ago. We need to know—"

Merryt slammed his cup on the table. "I'll vow it matters not a whit what happened a thousand years ago. All that matters is what happens next . . . in the real world, where there are Wardens and Aifes and Searchers and Comforters who won't let these bastard demons possess anyone who takes their fancy—much less a host of thousands. That's where the battle will be won or lost. You need to get your head out of the past, lad. The devils plan to destroy us, and if we fall, havoc will rule. No phantom in any fortress can do worse than that."

He was right. The invasion was the immediate danger, worse than he knew. Neither Merryt nor the demons understood how few of us there were since the Derzhi conquest. However the confrontation came about, the Ezzarians would be destroyed, leaving the world at the mercy of the rai-kirah. So. One thing at a time.

Merryt leaned forward, motioning me to sit close. His voice dropped low. "You are set down in the middle of a very nasty fight, my friend. Unless you have some deep-held wish to be a demon, you'd best look to your soul." As if yielding this morsel of wisdom had eased his mind, he settled back again and drained his wine cup. "The biggest surprise is Vyx . . . the fool in the thick of the plotting. Clearly he has deceived us in many things. Maybe he was warning you, but I think it more likely he was just trying to get you here to use for the joining. But I can't credit that it was for his own play to command the legion. And if not for himself, then whose interest is he taking? Rhadit never had wit enough to come up with such a plan . . . and certainly it's not Denas. Denas has despised Vyx for fifty years. Had him beaten not too long ago for some petty insult—in front of twenty witnesses. There are only a few other contenders. Nesfarro might work with Vallyne and Vyx—but this is

plotting beyond the ordinary. Kryddon is too weak. The
legion would never follow him. As for Vallyne herself . . .
she's strong enough, but she cares only for her own pleasure. So who, then? Someone who's persuaded her to make
you into the instrument they wish." Though the fire had
died, Merryt blotted his square forehead with a blue kerchief. "It explains why you were left with the Gastai so
long after Denas told her about you."

"She knew?" All my confused speculations about threats
and dangers and dreams were erased in the instant. A
demon fist in my belly could not have felt so cold.

He raised his wiry eyebrows. "Of course, she knew.
Denas was the only one who could get you out. I couldn't
fathom why he wouldn't latch on when I dangled the prospect of a new human ally in front of him. When I went to
him a second time to plead your case, he told me of this
lackwit bargain that gave you to Vallyne. She's the one
who kept you in the pits, Exile, and Vyx along with her,
for whatever Vallyne knows, Vyx knows. These are no
common enemies, my friend."

No. No common enemies. So it all fell into place, now I
had wits. Indeed I had started losing my memory before
Merryt's first visit to the pits. Everything since was hazy;
every moment of my time with Vallyne was obsession. She
had left me in torment until I forgot everything, until I was
so empty she and her friends could fill me with whatever
lies and distractions they wished. All of it—the rescue, the
trial, the teasing, and affection—all of it had been
scripted . . . a mummery . . . a dance . . . to make me do
what they wanted. To yield my name. To let them take
possession of my soul so they could use me, at the same
time as they were destroying my wife and my friends and
my home.

In disgust and fury, I blurted out the secret I had no
intention of sharing just yet. "We have a way to send a
warning to Ezzaria. And when the time is right, when we've
learned enough, we can go ourselves."

Merryt's eyes were huge. "Then, what you've said is
true . . . how you came here willing . . . I never
believed . . ." I thought his bellowing laughter might melt
the frozen stone of Denas's castle. "By the Nameless God,

brother, this changes everything! A way out! After this eternity . . . to see sunlight . . . and to turn this devil's dance upon itself. I need to think on it." His dark eyes took fire with excitement. "We can cause havoc if we but put our minds to it." He jumped up, in clear indication that it was time for me to go. "Stay careful, friend. Don't let them know you've got on to their plan. If they think you'll refuse them, they'll have no more use for you, and they'll do to you what they did to me. We'll stop them—all of them who've done us ill. By all that's holy, we will. After all these years"—he raised his mutilated fists before his face and grinned ferociously—"it will feel damned fine to get back in a fight."

CHAPTER 29

Plotting. Conspiracy. Manipulation. Those were not the answers I had come looking for in the demon realm. I certainly did not trust Merryt implicitly—I was already uneasy at my hasty revelation of Fiona's tower. His story was self-serving, a jumble of hearsay and guesses, and his glib dismissal of the mystery of Tyrrad Nor rang false. Yet Raddoman had dismissed it, too, willing to risk its uncertain dangers in order to reclaim his home. It was my own deepseated dread that kept twisting my gut. But everything Merryt had revealed of the demon plan fit with what I had already learned. No wonder Vallyne had never questioned me. Vyx and Vallyne knew very well what had drawn me to Kir'Vagonoth, and they didn't care in the least what other reasons I might have had. They had their own plan.

I strode around the corner of the castle and was almost knocked off my feet by the wind. After leaving Merryt, I had gone outside to walk off my churning anger. Anger at allowing myself to be so duped. Anger at the demons for their shimmering beauty, for the pity and admiration they raised in me. What warrior had room for pity? And such disappointment—all my hopes for understanding, for peace . . . What kind of fool had I been to think that one man's insight could stem the tide of violence that engulfed our history?

Yet even now that I knew of Vallyne's duplicity, what real difference would it make? That was the most distressing part. So many had suffered for so long. So many were destined to face the truth of suffering. If opening the way to Kir'Navarrin could set right the horror my ancestors had worked. . . . My stomach gnawed upon itself, rebelling against the terrifying idea that was growing in me as I re-built the mosaic in my mind for the hundredth time.

If I had been a Rudai shaper, I could have reproduced the images of shattered stone in the slightest detail: the trees, the figures, the portals that opened onto a place that was the image of Vallyne's garden—the garden that was itself the image of Kir'Navarrin. In that chain of images lay one of the answers I had come so far to find. Now I knew where Blaise and Kyor and Farrol and my child would find their healing. The woman-deer, in pain and torment, had left her family in the human world and stepped through the portal into Kir'Navarrin, then had come back eased to take up life again. Something in that place had made her whole. I pulled my cloak tight and ducked my head into the wind that thrashed about the desolate courtyard like a caged beast.

"Exile!" Raddoman called to me sharply from the balcony. "The mistress is waiting for you. She is most irritated at your absence. Where have you been?"

"Walking," I said. "Trying to wake up." I needed to be careful. "No luck at it, unfortunately."

"Her guests are in the book-room. I'd recommend you make your way there straightaway."

I looked up at the light-sculpted figure on the balcony and wondered if Raddoman, too, was part of the game. Likely so. They would have left nothing to chance. Only by Fiona's grace was I awake to know it, and as I walked into the dwelling carved of ice, I wished that I had never seen her tower. Then I wouldn't know what fate was demanding of me.

"I've been waiting a very long time, Exile," said Vallyne when I walked into the shadowy book-room.

I pulled out a slim brown volume from a shelf where I had put books that looked to be complete and sensible. "I'm sorry, my lady. I have no sense of time here. I'm not used to . . ." To telling time without sunlight and moon and stars, I was going to say. Yet even in my anger, it seemed cruel to mention it. "I was outside walking and lost track of the hour," I said.

I went to my stool, pressing the book between my knees

as I always did, trying to ignore the green eyes that were staring at me so unashamedly. No doubt she was watching to see if my hands were trembling or if my face gave any sign that I had caught on to her game. Conspirators had no rest, as well I knew.

There were three other demons—Kaffera, Tovall, and Denkkar—reclining on the soft couches of the reading room, talking and laughing with each other, turned so that I could see only their light. Vallyne did not recline, but sat in a chair watching me, and I felt the fingers of her enchantment reaching out to tangle my thoughts again. She was dressed in a flowing gown of green, deeper in color than her eyes, and her hair was all wild curls of gold, pulled back on one side by an emerald clip. My blood pulsed with the memory of the moment I had embraced her demon fire, making me stumble over the opening words of the poem.

Ill-chosen reading, fool. It was a Hollenni ode, the story of two young lovers, pledged in marriage on the day of their birth as were all Hollenni, but not to each other. Hopeless love, unending grief, as the two sought a few moments together, pursued by relentless fortune. The language was overdone, the characters foolish and simple, the verse mundane. But an explicit description of tender lovemaking was not at all what I needed to hear when I was trying to maintain a wall of anger between myself and those green eyes. Recognizing the disease did not cool its fever. One slip and I would be lost again.

I broke off halfway through the long tale. "The book is flawed," I said, jumping down from my stool. "I'll find another."

Voices of drowsy disappointment murmured behind me, as I stuffed the guilty book on a shelf and searched blindly through my other selections for something less risky.

"No matter, Exile. Put them back." The melodious voice spoke softly in my ear. Much too close. "My guests have gone."

I stayed where I was, crouched in front of the lowest shelves, not daring to turn around and look at her. Her presence enveloped me like a cloak of heavy-scented flowers, stifling every other sensation. "I'm sorry. I'll find—"

"Come to my resting room later, when the time vessel is

at its lowest ebb. Bring the book and read me the rest of this story."

"It's incomplete."

"Then, you will complete it for me."

Before I could come up with an excuse, she was gone. *Damnable, cursed, demon woman.*

I deliberately left the volume of poetry in the shelf and took a different book, one claiming to tell stories of the gods. Gods were not at all romantic. On my way back to my room, I took a small detour past the time vessel, the trickling passing of the moments echoing in the vast, empty entry hall of the castle. I peered inside the gray, carved vat. The slowly descending surface of the water was just above the seventh mark. Seven hours. Forever.

Once back in my cluttered little haven, I occupied a few moments with the bread Raddoman had brought me earlier. I'd not taken time to eat any of it before setting off in search of Merryt. The thought of the long-captive Ezzarian led me into other channels where I had no wish to go, so I cast a light from my hand and opened the book. For an hour I read the god-stories of Kuvai and Manganar, of Basran and Thrid and Fryth, and twenty other peoples I had never heard of. So many were similar. Gods seemed subject to all of the same foibles as their human worshipers: love and jealousy, grief and celebration. Some of them were human heroes, tested and tempted and elevated to godhood. Some were immortal teachers who grieved at their students' straying. What use to be a god if there was no relief from the pain of ordinary life?

My reading left me contemplating the teachings of my youth . . . the story of the mortal maiden Verdonne and her romance with the god of the forest, and of their half-human, half-divine son Valdis. The god had grown jealous of his son, so the story went, for the boy was handsome, intelligent, and generous, and was loved dearly by mortals. When the god threatened to destroy the unfaithful humans, the courageous Verdonne had sent her child to safety and taken up a sword, setting herself between the heavens and the earth to protect the human world from her husband. She had stood alone—reviled, taunted, wounded by the god—until Valdis grew to manhood. Then the young god

had challenged his father and defeated him, not taking the
throne for his own, but giving it to his mother and making
her immortal, saying that she had shown the world how a
god should behave . . . protecting her people at whatever
cost to herself. He was content to rule at her side, her
strong right arm.

How profound was the impact of myth. My people
claimed that this story was why Ezzarians had a queen, but
no king. And why we felt safe living in the forest, and why
we found our source of melydda, the "Gift of Valdis,"
among the trees. Or was it that the story had been shaped
from the substance of our lives, the truth that existed
among us, given form and glory by a minstrel's tongue?

As I sat there musing, tracing the warp and weft of my
dingy bedcovering with one finger, the tale began to nag at
me, but I could not touch on the reason why. My mind
drifted idly to the end of it. Valdis had not killed his father,
but imprisoned him and taken away his name so that mortals could no longer worship him and give him power over
them. *Taken away his name* . . . The book slipped from my
hand, as I sat up slowly on the bed. What was this creeping
unease? The tale was naught but myth. I had just read
ten similar stories. Yet an image came to me—a scene of
devastation, blood and bones and a destroyed city—and a
voice—Vyx, when I had met him beyond the portal—telling
me, "This is where such sentiments take you. Into the
realm of one . . . Unnamed." And only a few hours before,
Raddoman had shared with me a piercing memory of a
"danger without a name" in a fortress called Tyrrad Nor.
Was there more truth here—hidden in myth? The source . . .
the Nameless God . . .

"Hsst!" The hissing sound came from beyond my small
circle of light. Distracted from my ill-formed theories, I
brightened my light and discovered Merryt pressed to the
wall just inside my doorway. He waved a hand toward the
dark passage and shook his head vigorously. Someone was
outside my door. Puzzled, I motioned Merryt around the
cabinet with glass shelves, and he quickly slipped between
the cabinet and the rug-stuffed window, while I snuffed
my light.

"Are you alone, Exile?" Raddoman popped into view,

his brown shimmer ragged at the edges like hastily trimmed hair.

"Does the lady wish me to come?" I damned myself for the ease with which that thought obscured every other consideration.

The demon shaped his human form and poked his wiry beard this way and that as he peered about the room. "No. The ylad—the other yddrass—was seen intruding upon the mistress's wing. He is not welcome here. You should have nothing to do with him."

"Am I a prisoner, Raddoman?"

The demon's glance latched onto me. "No, ylad, you are not a prisoner. The mistress has petitioned Denas that you not be constrained, and the good lord has granted her request. You know how the mistress dislikes—"

"Then, leave my room and knock before you come in again. Such is ylad custom."

"As you say, Yddrass." The demon bowed, shifting his eyes right and left as he withdrew. Strange that he called me Warden. I wondered if I had met him in combat at some time. Perhaps that was why he disliked me so fiercely. I stepped to the doorway and watched his glimmering form move down the passageway, and just before he turned a corner . . . I blinked and squinted in the dim light. I would have sworn Raddoman's light flickered a different color . . . purple and blue with swirling gray-green mixed in. With dawning understanding, I watched him disappear. So I had been wrong to think I could identify every demon unerringly. Some were trickier than others. Some had a sense of humor and showed up in places they had no right to be—in an artist's soul or a Warden's dreams or in bodies that wore faces not their own. Some were clever deceivers.

"Many thanks, brother." Merryt stepped out of his hiding place, and shifted his wide shoulders uncomfortably. "Unfriendly brute. But if I'm right, and they've got wind of what I've done, life will get decidedly less comfortable by the hour. I'm at your mercy."

"What have you done?" I snapped, more curt than I intended as I switched my attention to the Ezzarian.

"I've told Denas that Vallyne and Vyx are looking to take command of the legion and that they plan to use you to open the gateway. I've seen naught of anger in my life beside his answer to that news! I'm afraid your life is no safer than mine. Denas swore to kill you before allowing a rival to use you."

"Told Denas? Gods of night—you traitorous—"

Merryt raised his hands high and backed away, his bronze skin blotched with red. "Hold, Exile. It's not what you think. Hear me out. Not more than an hour after that, I told Gennod that Denas was out to murder him and Rhadit and take you for himself. Gennod is less despicable than most demons, and it seemed only fair to tell him of Denas's threat. We can hope it will leave the villains in disarray for the moment. Give us time to get out and warn the Ezzarians. It was the only thing I could think of to do. But someone was lurking about the courtyard where I was talking to Gennod, and I'm sure I've been followed ever since. If we're ever going to leave this wicked place, we'd best get to it." Merryt was twitching like a mother sparrow guarding her hatchlings.

Dismayed beyond telling, seeing all possibility of caution ruined, our one bit of knowledge—our one advantage— given up before we even knew its worth, it was all I could do to contain my anger. "What kind of fool are you, Merryt?"

I understood his urgency. It would take me more than three hundred seventy years to forget the sting of demon vengeance. But I was not ready to leave the demon realm as yet. Thwarting Vyx and Vallyne and warning the Ezzarians was not enough. If there was hope for Blaise and my child . . . and the mystery of the Last Fortress ate at me. "We've too many questions. We need to know more about the demons' plans. More about Tyrrad Nor. You yourself told me we don't know who's behind Vyx and Vallyne. And you could have bloody well consulted me before putting my life at such risk."

He shrugged and poked his head out of my door. "Sorry to bring it down on you before you've had a chance to sort it all out, but secrets don't last long in this place. We need to get the warning out. We'll stop the slaughter of the Ezzarians and that's that. This 'danger' in Tyrrad Nor is no worry if we stop them opening the gateway, and your life's at no risk as long as you get out now and stay with me. What more is there to know?"

"You didn't tell anyone about the escape route when you were spewing information about?"

Merryt stepped into the passage. "Of course not. I know exactly what I'm doing. Stick with me and everything will work out for the best."

Which one of us was the bigger fool? Merryt for his simplistic view of matters, or me for trusting him at all?

Merryt beckoned me to follow. "It's worth my life what I've done, Exile. And they'll learn soon enough that you were a part of it. We need to be off."

Wishing that I could allow him to reap the consequences of his blundering without further compromising my own aims, I threw on my cloak. "All right then," I said. "Vallyne's not expecting me for a few hours yet. I'll get you away." No one was about when I followed him down the passage.

Merryt knew more twisting, convoluted paths than my head believed possible. I couldn't have said whether we were on the third level of the castle or five levels below ground, going in or out or sideways. But we passed no more than ten demons, and though I no longer trusted my recognition of them, all ten seemed to be strangers. We emerged from the castle by the same back door the Ezzarian had brought me through on the day of my rescue.

"Now where?" he said.

"Beyond the city." I pointed to the dark smudge on the horizon.

"This Aife, she's your wife?" We had trudged a long way toward the scattered lights of the Rudai settlements before Merryt started talking.

"No. This is someone else."

I suppose he must have gathered enough from my tone to know I had no wish to discuss it further, for he said nothing more until we stepped into the lee of a rocky outcropping and entered a long, low structure with a peaked roof. I had seen many of them in my rides with Vallyne. They were Rudai dwellings and workshops, nine-tenths buried beneath shifting layers of snow and ice and connected to each other by tunnels and passageways. "Nevai prefer to live above ground, not huddle like beasts in their dens," she had told me.

The turns of the passage were vaguely familiar, and indeed we soon found ourselves in Merryt's "hideaway," his little room packed with all manner of goods.

"We've no time for delays," I said as he began rummaging about in a flat-sided brass trunk. "It's a long way to the city." And I needed to get back before the lady started looking for me.

"I can't leave without this," he said, pulling a blue Warden's cloak from the trunk. "I always swore I'd wear it again when I went home. As for you, wearing those demon things . . . you'll need some clothes. Who knows what becomes of Rudai shapings when we go back to the mortal world?" He dragged out a black shirt and breeches and tossed them to me.

"I'll think about it later," I said. I wasn't ready to tell Merryt that I had no intention of going with him.

After a hurried passage through an underground warren of workshops and kitchens that stank of hot tar, rancid bacon, lamp oil, and cloying perfumes, we were outside again, fighting the snow and wind for an hour as we made our way to the far gate of the deserted city.

"Now where?" said Merryt, his excitement cutting through the blustering wind like a knife.

"To the left . . ." We were blasted with sleet as we trudged around the city perimeter, hardly able to see each other, much less pick out our destination. The hilly area beyond the city was broken by massive ice pinnacles, easy to mistake for a ruined tower in the storm. Twice I led us the wrong way, and we had to backtrack to the city wall lest we become completely disoriented. But my third guess took us up a snowy rise, and after some five hundred paces I pointed to the dark tower sitting on the ridge.

"By my boots!"

We slogged across the plains, up the snowy hillside, and half an hour later we stepped through the doorway. The storm fell away behind us like a dropped cloak.

I drew in my focus. "Aife!"

There was no answer. Of course, there was no reason to expect that she would be standing her vigil at any particular time, but I hoped she would come soon. Almost three hours had passed since I had checked the time vessel, and it would take me at least two to get back to the castle. I might have to send Merryt on his way alone. Merryt looked at me inquisitively, but I shook my head and settled onto the floor. "She weaves only an hour a day," I said. "We're going to have to wait."

"Gives me time to enjoy the thought of it." The cheerful Merryt put on his blue cloak and sat down on the pine bough bed, the image of the one I had slept on while Catrin nursed away my fever. Catrin . . .

"You'll need to be careful in the world," I said, the immensity of Merryt's journey striking me all at once. Almost four centuries. "Avoid cities and caravans, and any place where people are desperate enough to sell another man. Ezzarians attracted some unfortunate attention in the recent past, and, though we are safe and protected in Ezzaria itself, imperial law requires us to be enslaved."

"That explains your collection of marks. So much to learn. You'll have to guide me. Teach me. How things must have changed in so many years." He ran his wide fingers over his face like a blind man. "I'll start to grow old again. Do you think it a fair trade for sunlight and warmth?" He started chuckling to himself. "Everything is a bargain, is it not? Some better. Some worse. Some beyond imagining."

As we waited, I told him more of the world. Of the Empire. Of Ezzaria. Of history and politics, money and roads. "This Aife will tell you what you need to know, and who you need to talk to. My mentor would be the one to start with. She's on the Mentors—"

"She! A woman mentors Wardens? This Derzhi war must have left us worse off than you've told me."

"Don't misjudge her, Merryt. I did when she first took me on. If anyone can get—"

Warden?

I leaped to my feet, holding out a hand to tell Merryt that I was hearing something he could not. "I'm here, Aife. And I've brought a friend."

With no more words, the portal took shape in the gloom, and beyond it the dazzling light of a full moon. Merryt rose slowly to his feet, his eyes riveted on the wavering image.

"By the Nameless," he whispered, stumbling forward as I nudged him to hurry.

As he stepped through, he began to laugh, spreading his arms, spinning about in wonder, craning his head back to see stars and moon and open sky. He whooped and swirled the blue cloak about himself. I yearned to follow him. But I stepped only as far as the portal itself, the place where I could speak to Fiona easily without Merryt overhearing.

Hurry, Warden, she said. *We need you here.*

"Again, I cannot. There's more to do here. But this Merryt, the Warden I told you of, I've sent him through. He brings warning, Aife. He must go to Ezzaria and make the Queen listen. Do you—?"

You must come now, Warden. Something terrible has come about.

Why wouldn't the stubborn woman listen? "I can't. Not yet."

If you believe anything I say, Warden, then believe this: I'll send you back after, if you think you must. But we need your help now.

Her determination was like a parent's hand, gripping my arm and pulling me forward to a place I had no intent to go. "For an hour," I said. "No more." And after taking a moment to change into the silver-embroidered black tunic and gray breeches that had been wrought by human hands, I heaved a nervous sigh and stepped back into the world of light.

CHAPTER 30

"Never tasted anything so fine," said Merryt, sucking on the greasy bones of a roast duck. He wiped his hands on his damp blue breeches. "You can invite me to eat the remains of your supper any time at all."

I was still filling my lungs with the warm, humid night air, while Fiona checked on Balthar, who was snoring peacefully in the ruined temple. Merryt had gone from one thing to another in the half hour since we had emerged from the portal, plunging his fingers into the damp earth, yanking fistfuls of grass and showering them on his head, touching or smelling every plant, bush, and tree. He had dived headfirst into the river like an otter, his bellowing laughter echoing from the rocks as he splashed and flailed, then come back and stuffed himself with every morsel Fiona could provide. It was impossible not to smile at his glee, even as the passing time nagged at my patience. Vallyne would be waiting, yet every moment I breathed the air of the living world made it harder to consider going back.

Somewhere from the darkness came a mournful cry, some bird or beast giving depth to the night beyond our cheerful firelight, while releasing its own troubled spirit. I shivered, poking at the jasnyr-scented fire, though the air was warm. Jasnyr . . . now I knew why the smell was abhorrent to demons. It had been used in the rites that destroyed their lives, their last true physical sensation before they woke in the frigid desolation of Kir'Vagonoth.

"The old man will sleep for a while yet," said Fiona, coming back into the firelight. Were I to judge by the young woman's appearance, no time at all had passed since I last sat on the temple's broken steps. Her thin body was no softer, her face no less stubborn, her dark, straight hair still cut short, her man's clothing as worn and serviceable as ever. Only the fine-wrought lines about her eyes hinted at a passing time of care and worry.

"You've survived it," she had said on emerging from her Aife's trance, greeting me with a probing look that told me she had sensed the worst of where I had been. "I could find no way to reach you in the darkness."

"How long?"

"We're just upon the Wolf's Moon."

"Wolf's Moon . . ." The first full moon of autumn, when wolves howled in anticipation of winter kill. Three full seasons had passed. My son had seen his first birthday. He would be walking . . . laughing . . . saying his first words. Would they have shaved his head as they would a Manganar boy at his first year? Likely they wouldn't know how to perform the rites of naming as were done in Ezzaria. And I . . . I had languished in the pits of the mad Gastai for more than eight months. What friend or kin or lover had ever been so faithful as my adversary Fiona? "It was the thought of your stubborn heart that kept me alive," I said, dropping my eyes, unable to face the intensity of either her scrutiny or her apology. "Only you. But now I need to get—"

She pressed her hand to my mouth. "Don't say it yet. Let me feed your friend and check on the old man, then we need to talk." Before she walked away, she jerked her head at Merryt, who was sifting earth between his fingers. "He's been in the demon realm for a long time." I heard the question in her statement.

"He got me out of the pits—saved my life—and opened my eyes to some hard truth. You need to listen to him and help him on his way. But, yes, he was there a very long time. I've told him of the mosaic and my beliefs, but I've not told him my name or yours, or anything of Blaise or—"

"I need to show you something about the mosaic, then we need to get him out of the way for a while."

"I don't think he has any desire to sit still." Merryt had said he was anxious to get on the road home. Who could blame him?

*   *   *

While Merryt started gnawing on another leg of Fiona's duck, Fiona beckoned us over to the mosaic, where the gap in our understanding glared at us in accusation. Merryt showed no interest in the pictures, saying he had no desire to discover any kinship to demons. After a cursory glance, he said he preferred to eat and drink his way through Balthar's stores, and he returned to the fire.

Fiona folded her arms and cocked her head at me. "The hole in the mosaic . . . have you learned what was the cause?"

"No. I don't know what it means as yet."

"Then, you need to see this." She whispered a few words and motioned with one hand, and causing a pulse of enchantment to shiver the air. I glanced toward the floor, and sank slowly to my knees. The empty hole preceding the saga of the demon split was no longer completely empty.

"It was your mention of this Kir'Navarrin," said Fiona, kneeling at my side while I tried to unravel the meaning of the complex patterns of blue and red and yellow that lay before me. "When I repeated your words for Balthar, he came near climbing the pillars. 'Don't ask it,' he said. 'I don't know anything about it.' Well, he did know, of course."

"He hid this part from us."

"Something frightened him about it, and he still won't tell me everything. Evidently, among the words around the edge of the mosaic, it says 'Kir'Navarrin is forever forbidden' or locked or some such business. This"—She pointed to a figure kneeling beside a pond and holding her head—"is a Seer. Balthar recognized the symbol on this ring she wears. And these three squares seem to be her visions. You can see where a fourth one is still missing. I think Balthar knows of that one, too, but the old fool won't tell me any more. Can you understand the images?"

The first square depicted a battle, destruction, people who looked like Ezzarians weeping and running away. "This one is the First Battle of the Eddaic Prophecy," I said. "The one that was to leave Ezzarians defeated and weeping." And so it had, we thought, when the Derzhi crushed us in three short days.

"And this one . . . I suppose it's you and Prince Aleksander. And the demon-ruled world behind—the consequence if you had failed." She laid her finger on a winged warrior, glowing with light as he battled a monstrous demon.

The warrior did not look so much like me, save perhaps for the river of blood pouring out of him and the shredded wing that still gave me twinges when I thought of it. But the demon opponent . . . even as I brushed my own hand across the snarling face, I felt the cold evil I had known so intimately for three very long days of combat. "If I had seen this before I set out that day, I might never have gone," I said. But my attempt at lightness fell flat, and my eyes raced to the third square.

The scene was like many in the other parts of the mosaic. A portal. A man with bronze skin and straight dark hair was walking down a road toward it. He was carrying a key. Beyond the rectangular gateway lay the images I had come to believe represented Kir'Navarrin, the home of my ancestors when we were one with the demons. On a distant mountaintop, beyond the graceful dwellings and the magnificent trees and flowers and fountains that were the true reflection of Vallyne's garden, was a small dark blot. At first I thought it was a bird, a hawk or a vulture brooding on the rocky peak, ready to swoop down on its prey. But the scale was wrong. The object would be much larger than a bird. Brooding, yes. Waiting. A fortress, perhaps—and indeed I could see the dark outline settle into shape as I thought of it. A fortress holding truth that was locked away, truth too terrible to know, a danger from the beginning of the world. Other figures were on the road between the man and the portal. Tiny images of men and women who carried swords. Some were fighting. Some were standing across the road, as if to guard the way. Many of them were dying. Some already dead. The essential question, of course, was the key in the man's hand. Was it the key to unlock the portal itself—the gateway between the world I knew and Kir'Navarrin—or was it the key that would unleash the secret danger of that fortress? Was the key an artifact of steel or brass that would unlatch a physical hasp or was it some word or action that would unleash the brooding danger? What most disturbed me was that the man with the key had wings.

"You feel it, too?" said Fiona, pointing to the black smudge. "This is something vile and dangerous, and you're walking right toward it."

"Yes, but I'm not sure what it means. Prophecy is so convoluted . . . and this doesn't show the consequence of the action. Right or wrong . . . even if this is me, even if I carry the key, I don't think we can outguess it. We need to get on with things—see what we can learn."

I didn't know whether Fiona believed my offhand dismissal of the image. Of course I carried the key. But I could not talk about it as yet, because the implications were too monumental. Prophecies were cautionary tales, warnings to have a care when approaching the future. Possibilities. The image of prophecy wrought upon these broken pieces of stone had indeed given me an insight . . . the portal and the fortress were two different pieces of the puzzle. Opening one did not mean opening the other. And so, perhaps, if I was strong enough, if I could force myself to do what was needed. . . . My judgment was suspect, so I could not say the words aloud until I had dismissed my doubts. But to right so great a wrong as had been done to my people and the rest of the world was everything I had sworn to do with my life. And the possibility of an end to the demon war was so enticing, so consuming . . . I had lived a life of violence and craved an end to it. I devoutly wished I could see the fourth square.

While I argued with myself about motives and risks and terrifying possibilities—first on one side and then the other—Fiona saw to Merryt. After filling his belly, a review of local geography, and a gathering of supplies enough to see him on his way to Ezzaria, he was ready to set out. Fiona told him to head down to the river to dig out our boat from where she had buried it in the sand, load his supplies, and wait. She would row him downriver to the lake and set him on his way.

As soon as the big Ezzarian was gone, Fiona hefted a bag and a waterskin and motioned me to follow her out the back side of the ruin and up a steep path toward the rocky center of the island. "You've been very quiet the last hour. Are you going to tell me your little secrets?"

"There's too much to tell," I said. "Everything in Kir'Vagonoth is plotting and intrigue. For now I just need to get back before I'm missed. Someone's expecting me."

"She's a demon?"

"She is remarkable." I glanced at the wiry young woman, striding with such ferocity up the short, steep path. Still my watchdog. "But she left me in the darkness, thinking that if I was there long enough, she could force me to do as she wished. She has misjudged."

Fiona nodded and kept walking. To my surprise she asked me no more questions. Her preoccupation convinced me that something was indeed terribly wrong. I shoved aside my internal wrestling and followed her around an overhanging boulder. "Now are *you* going to tell me where we're going?"

She thrust aside a stand of tangled bushes to expose a dark opening into the heart of Fallatiel. A faint light shone from deep inside the cave. "I don't know what you can do about this, but I needed you to see. Maybe you've learned something that can help."

As I stepped inside, I heard the same mournful beast cry I had heard earlier. Only it was not a beast. It was Blaise.

The young outlaw was huddled in a corner of the cave, his knees drawn up, his hands in constant motion, rubbing the skin of his bare legs, his arms, his face, pulling his stringy hair, his fingers twining about themselves in unending agitation. His eyes were dark pits, their blue fire unmasked now and staring into some distance I could not fathom. Spittle ran down his jutting chin, and the hollows in his cheeks were deep, the skin stretched tight over his long bones. Beside him knelt the Ezzarian boy, Kyor, holding a cup to his lips. "Come on, then. A drink will make you feel better. You've had a hard day." Blaise's hand flailed in uncontrolled spasm, knocking the cup away.

"They arrived yesterday, just after I spoke to you," said Fiona quietly, setting down her bag beside the small fire. "The boy says he persuaded Blaise to hold off his change and come looking for you, thinking you might not be able

to help him once he was in beast shape. He says that if
Blaise doesn't change soon, he won't be able . . ."

". . . and he'll go mad like Saetha and the others," I
said. "Perhaps it's better to be a beast—even if you forget
everything of importance. Which would you choose?"

Fiona took a deep breath. "If that's true and we're to
help him, it seems it must be you to do it. I'm sure the
Council would allow you to fight this battle—"

"Fighting won't help him."

"Are you refusing to oppose this demon, Warden?"

"Stars of night, Fiona. Think of what we've learned.
Blaise has lived almost thirty years with his demon—in harmony and health. This is not a matter of possession and
demon madness."

All my remaining resistance to the plan I had conceived
was swept away by the sight of the strong young man re-
duced to such a state. What mysterious danger, what insubstantial prophecy, could persuade me to ignore the hopeless
horror that lay before me?

Kyor had patiently refilled the cup and was dribbling the
water into Blaise's slack mouth. "How does he fare?" I
said, ignoring Fiona's protests as I crossed the cave and
knelt beside the two. The time for consideration had run
out.

Kyor jerked around, and his dark eyes widened with in-
supportable hope. "Oh, it's fine to see you, sir. He tries
very hard. Don't you, Blaise? Do you see who's come to
help? It's Seyonne—just as he said he would. I told you
he'd come." The boy corralled Blaise's restless hands and
held them tight, which seemed to help focus the older
man's attention.

"He didn't want to come at first," said the boy, looking
up at me. "He was thinking to let the bird have him when
he couldn't hold out no more. But I told him what you'd
said and showed him the knife that I'd carried all these
months with nothing ill come from it. I told him that you
bore no grudge, else why would you say what you did. He
said he'd not been fair with you, and as he thought back
on all you'd said and done, he knew you meant us no harm.
There were a thousand times you could have turned us
over if you'd wanted. On the night it got so bad that he

gave over his sword and had Farrol take command of us, he said that maybe it was time to see if I was right or wrong about you."

Blaise's blue-black eyes roamed wildly over the cave until they came to rest on my face. And when I laid my hand on his head and met his gaze with my deep-seeing, a spark of despairing intelligence flared through his madness. His mouth began to work and his hands to shake, though Kyor gripped them tight. "Teach . . . me," said Blaise, fighting to form the words. The flicker of a smile crossed his ravaged face. "Anything."

"Listen to me," I said, taking his hands from Kyor, willing him to hear and understand. "Hold on just a little longer. I promise . . . I *promise* . . . I'll take you where you need to go. It is the place where we belong, where *you* belong, a land more beautiful than Ezzaria itself—and you know how we Ezzarians feel about our home." His eyes were riveted on my own, drinking in my words. "You'll have to stay there awhile, I think, until this time passes, but then you'll be able to come back and help put this world to rights. You and Aleksander. It is the price I ask for what I'm going to do. You must find a way to work with Aleksander. He bears the mark of the gods, Blaise. And whatever comes, he needs you to stand with him. Do you understand me? It is the only payment I require."

I could not tell if he heard me, for he began to shift just then. In a grotesque interweaving of bird and beast and man, his writhing body stretched and shrank, grew wings and claws and absorbed them again, sprouted fur and feathers, scales, then flesh again, and performed a bone-twisting reshaping of legs and arms and head. For moments that must have seemed like hours, he resisted the demands of his nature, until he cried out and collapsed in a human-shaped heap of choking misery. What sense might have remained in him was masked by sickness and pain.

"He'll come around after a bit. There's not much to do to help him." Kyor pulled a blanket over the outlaw's bare legs, then tried to maneuver the bigger man into a position where he wouldn't foul himself with vomit.

I gave the boy a hand, gathering the trembling Blaise into my arms, cradling his broad shoulders and supporting his head until his retching spasms ceased. Then I laid him back on his blankets and called up what paltry healing enchantments I knew that might ease him, while the boy dabbed at his crusted lips with a moistened rag.

"We need to get him south, Kyor. Quickly. Can you—?"

"I can find the ways like Blaise does."

"And can you take the others—Fiona and the old man and one other, a man I brought here tonight?"

"Aye. If they want."

"Good. Fiona will know your destination." I gripped the boy's shoulder and shook it. "Keep telling him what I said, Kyor. Help him hold on. I'll come as soon as I can and send him where he needs to go."

"We'll be ready for you."

"Where are we going?" demanded Fiona as we walked out of the cave and down the rocky path. The ruined temple glowed white in the moonlight, the pool a sheet of molten silver. "And where is it you think to send Blaise?"

"Blaise needs to go to Kir'Navarrin—the land beyond the portals shown in the mosaic. It's our home, the place where we were whole. When all this happened—this split with the demons—we locked ourselves out of it. The rai-kirah believe we stole it from them, and we did, in a way. We just stole it from ourselves, too."

"And what of the mosaic? The last piece?"

"It doesn't matter." I turned my back on the ancient artwork, on the empty fourth square—the fourth vision that would perhaps reveal the outcome of the winged man's deeds. "Whatever the right and wrong of things, whatever else comes, Kir'Navarrin must be reopened. Our ancestors made a mistake, and the result, the injury that we did ourselves, was so terrible, both for us and for the world, that it must be undone." After weighing everything, I had to believe that. To consider anything else was to condemn Blaise and Kyor and my child to madness, the demons to their frozen wasteland, and the Ezzarians to unending war. "Dasiet Homol is the gateway—the Place of the Pillars. You've got to get Blaise there as quickly as you can if we're going to save him. Tonight, if Kyor can do it. And you've got to get me there, too, which means you must persuade Balthar to go."

While Fiona prepared herself and Balthar to send me back to Kir'Vagonoth, I went down to the river for Merryt. "There's been a change of plan," I told him as we sat on a rock beside the slow-moving water. Merryt was idly pulling the soft hairy bark from a piece of driftwood. "There's a boy here who knows a shorter, safer route to Ezzaria."

I was not easy at sending Merryt on such an important errand, but I had no choices. "Be convincing, Merryt. Make them listen. The Aife will tell you how to approach the Queen and the Council—she's in their good graces as I am not."

"But you have your own friends . . . this woman mentor . . . and you said you had a wife. She'll hear you."

"I'm not coming with you."

"Not coming . . . gods' boots, you're going back to Kir'-Vagonoth!" A volcano could not have outmatched Merryt's eruption. "You're a cursed madman, Exile. What do you think to accomplish? When they find out what you've done, they'll have you in the pits again. The witch will have your soul out of you."

"I need to discover whatever I can about their plans," I said. "There's no assurance the Ezzarians will listen to the warning from either one of us. If I can stop the attack on Ezzaria or disrupt it by going back, then I've got to do so. Vallyne still believes she can control me, which leaves me room to work. When the time comes that I can do no more, believe me, I'll get out."

Merryt frowned and mumbled to himself. "But you need to stay with me. Together we'll give the warning, and together we'll go to the gateway to stop this business. We're brothers . . . partners." He twisted the rotted driftwood in his hands until it broke. "You don't know the cursed demons as I do. Think of the advantage you'll give Vallyne. You'll never be able to hide knowledge of this portal. Maybe I should go back with you, and we'll give the warning later."

"I already told you. I'm forbidden to enter Ezzaria. And if I'm to have a way out of Kir'Vagonoth, then the Aife has to stay with our sleeping friend up there in the temple.

There's no one else but you." As jasnyr-scented smoke drifted from the heights behind us, I pulled Merryt close and dropped my voice, as if Fiona might be listening. "Make them listen, Merryt. Convince them. They've got to be ready to defend themselves, but only . . . *only* . . . if the demons attack them." If my deeds were going to count for anything, then they might as well count for everything. "If they're not in danger themselves, then the Ezzarians must stand aside and let the demons through the portal. All of the rai-kirah are going to go mad if they don't get out of Kir'Vagonoth, and the human race will suffer for it—worse than we've ever seen. They think they'll do better in Kir'-Navarrin. I'm going to see they get there."

"You're going to see . . ." Merryt's voice fell quiet, too. He narrowed his eyes at me, but quickly widened them again. "Damn! I see it. You are a determined fellow . . . beyond imagination . . . Oh, my friend, songs will be made of this." He clasped my hands. "It's Gennod's going to win out, you know. He's the one you need to talk to. Less despicable than most of the devils. More powerful than others credit—and he is determined to command the legion himself. He'll be grateful for the warning we gave him. Just give him a hint of your plan, and he'll likely work a deal with you."

"Keep the Ezzarians out of it. That's all I ask."

"I'll do as you bid me. Indeed I will. But to convince them . . . You need to give me a name. I don't like asking, but how else will they believe me? For a matter so important . . . "

He was right, of course. The chances of the Ezzarians listening to him were slim enough, but if they believed that I couldn't trust him enough to give my name, then he was wasting his time. *"Lys na Seyonne,"* I said, trying to smile. "Use it carefully, Merryt. A fair number of Ezzarians think it the very name of corruption."

"Fair enough. I'll take care of our people, and you'll take care of the demons." I rose and started up the path to the temple and Fiona and the portal that would take me back to Kir'Vagonoth. Merryt called out, "My friend Seyonne," and bowed gracefully. "I'll see you again. No doubt of it.

Farewell!" I heard him laughing all my way up to the
temple.

Fiona stood beside the sleeping Balthar, slapping a slender branch impatiently against her knee. I gazed down at
the old man, his round cheeks sagging in sleep, his brow
wrinkled as if his dreams troubled him. "Give Balthar my
thanks, Fiona. And tell him . . . tell him I value his teaching.
Will you do that for me? Whether or not he chooses to
continue, I want him to know that."

I sat down cross-legged on the floor and began to clear
my mind. I wouldn't need much preparation this time, not
with the portal enchantment still woven in Balthar's sleeping head. But before I could immerse myself in ritual, Fiona
threw her stick into a pile of kindling, scattering twigs and
branches over the floor. "You're going to die, aren't you?"

"No. Not if I can help it."

Fiona kicked aside a clay water pitcher that was in her
way, so that it toppled over and rolled to a precarious perch
on the edge of the steps, then she snatched up the vial she
needed to anoint the sleeping man's forehead in preparation for the rite. Before she caused some other destruction,
I smiled up at her. "Whatever your reasons, Fiona, thank
you for caring one way or the other. I will come back. Just
as I said."

Of course she wasn't going to like it—any more than
I was.

The walk back to Denas's castle from Fiona's portal
would have taken me at least two hours. But I didn't walk.
I flew. The cold bit deep after the humid warmth of Fallatiel, and only with the greatest reluctance had I begun the
long slog through the deep snow, watching over my shoulder for mad Gastai and wishing I knew the secret of demon
traveling. That consideration led me to the matter of the
clothes and the weapons, and the relationship of the realm
of Kir'Vagonoth to the souls I walked as a Warden . . .
and so to my wings. Never had I made the change with
such ease. Little resistance. No pain. Just what I had always
wanted . . . until I had watched Blaise's face as he transformed. But I told myself that what I had was enough for

now, and truly, negotiating the violent winds of Kir'Vago-noth was considerable distraction.

I landed behind a hill, whispered away my wings, and walked the last bit, then slipped through Merryt's back door and took one shivering moment to glance into the time vessel. The water was swirling just above the last mark. An hour and a quarter, no more, until someone would come to fill the vessel and count another day gone. Time enough. I hurried up the winding stair and through the dim passageways to Gennod's rooms.

I would have given much for someone I could trust. Saving that, Gennod was the only name I had. I would not approach Denas with my proposal. He had made it clear how little use he had for my kind, and I did not doubt that he would rather kill me than allow another to use me. Kryddon and Nesfarro, the other two demons who had expressed a willingness to do this thing, were friends of Vallyne's. I would not put my life in her hands. I had no time to get to know all the demons and select the perfect one, like a Manganar matchmaker. Likely it would make no difference in the end. Speed was the important thing. And power.

I had at last begun to sense the true magnitude of my melydda. It was greater than I had ever imagined, manifesting itself fully, I thought, because of my existence in this place of demons. In the past when I had walked the Aife's portal, I had been able to shape wings and to perform feats of sorcery and endurance I could not match in normal life. Now I understood that it was not only experience and developing skill that had made me stronger the longer I fought, but the closeness to my own kind, as if the barriers between us were worn down by physical proximity. As Catrin had remarked, I'd spent more time beyond the portal in my last two years as a Warden than in my own world. Now that I was immersed in the life of our lost spirits—and awake to notice it—power thundered in my veins like the waterfalls from the highest glaciers of Azhakstan. This was but one more confirmation of my beliefs. Demons and Ezzarians belonged together.

*   *   *

Gennod was surprised to see me, to say the least. The demon stood in his doorway staring, his form shimmering red against the darkness behind him.

"Perhaps our meeting should be a little less public," I said. Not waiting for his permission, I squeezed past him and flattened my back to the wall of his chamber. "You'll have to excuse this intrusion. I have very little time. But I was told we had interests in common, unlikely as that seems. May I speak with you?"

"Unlike some of us, I have no objection to your company, ylad, but what possible common interest could I have with you?" Gennod's welcome was as spare as his room—a cold, barren hole, starkly empty of the cluttered furnishings of the rest of the castle. A few candles in plain-work sconces, steady-burning to stave off an oppressive darkness. A single table piled with rolled papers, books and drawings, and a map half buried beneath the other materials, all weighted down with stones. A freezing wind slipped through the shutters, threatening to scatter Gennod's business on the floor.

No use in attempting pleasantries. "Denas plans to put himself in command of the demon legion," I said, "which seems to require seeing Rhadit murdered along the way. Since Rhadit favors you for certain ventures, your own existence could be in danger."

"Indeed." The demon hissed and twitched his fingers, and the doorway behind me was shut and sealed. Unsettling, but not unexpected. "So I have been told. Though I must say I'm surprised that you know of it. Has Denas sent you to threaten me? Or perhaps to attempt the deed yourself?" He cocked his head and peered at my hands in polite wariness. "Perhaps you have weapons hidden somewhere as Merryt claims."

"On the contrary. I'm the one who told Merryt to warn you." Almost true. My lying had improved considerably over the past year.

Gennod folded his insubstantial arms in front of him and nodded slowly. "I wondered where the sneaking ylad had learned of the plot. And now you wish to claim some reward?"

"There are many things I wish, but here are the two

most important. First I want to convince your people and mine that we are two halves of the same beings, that out of monumental fear our ancestors split us apart—cheated you out of your bodies and us out of half of our souls—and that we must discover how to undo it. But—"

"Preposterous!" Except for a slight tremor with the outburst—the first unstudied emotion I had ever seen from him—Gennod's red light was steady and unchanging. Unfortunate, for the movement and intensity of a demon's light were far more expressive than the face he wore.

"—but that is a great deal to expect from those who have been at war for a thousand years."

He turned away from me and picked up a page of oddly formed characters from the table, rolling it up vigorously and stuffing the scroll in a stiff paper tube. But he was still listening. "And the second thing?"

"Failing the first, I want to call a truce between the rai-kirah and myself. I'll help you open the way to Kir'Navarrin on condition that the demon legion refrain from any assault on my people—the *pandye gash*. Once you are all safe in Kir'Navarrin, I'll take it upon myself to convince my people to end our war. If they won't listen, then at least we are no worse off than we have been."

Gennod was not as self-controlled as I thought. He whirled about, his light streaking and flashing, his form shifting from light to beast—a catlike being, breathing tongues of fire. Perhaps he didn't understand that I could recognize his excitement, for his voice was yet cool and steady. "Why would I make a bargain with you? And what makes you think I have enough influence to call a truce?"

"Because I'm offering you what you want. Why else? The rai-kirah wish to be in Kir'Navarrin and to be free of the *pandye gash*. You don't have to torture me or trick me or anything to get me to do it. I think that any Nevai who goes to the others and says he has arranged such a matter will be listened to. And you . . . you will find glory in it . . . and a body of your own. Which one of you would refuse such an offer?"

"How can I believe you would enter into such an arrangement with those you despise?"

And so the fish was hooked. "Because I also know that

despite your love for intrigue, rai-kirah keep their bargains. It is a fundamental trait that Wardens learn from earliest training: make a bargain in a demon battle, and it will always be kept. Even the Naghidda did so. He swore to yield all Khelid souls if bested in single combat. When I defeated him, he gave the command and the Khelid were free. If he, the most corrupt of you all, kept his bargain, then I believe it must be a fundamental part of your nature."

"You understand what this entails for you?"

For a few moments I permitted his examination—the cold probing of my mind and body to seek my intentions and my truth—then I gathered my melydda and pushed him away. "I do."

"Wait here while I consult others. The terms . . . we will need to clarify . . . but I think we can find common ground."

"There will be no negotiation, Gennod. The bargain will be as I have stated or nothing. And I can't wait here while you persuade your fellows. I am expected elsewhere. When I'm ready to proceed—say two hours from now—I'll meet you . . . where?"

"In the courtyard beside the gates." From his quick response, I didn't think there was going to be much discussion with the others.

"Agreed. No delays. No trickery. If you're not there when I come, I'll find someone else."

"Indeed. Indeed. We'll be ready." He waved his unseen hand, and the doorway reappeared in the wall. I left him standing in the middle of his room, his light pulsing like a beating heart. For my own part . . . I wanted to be sick.

There was no time for self-indulgence. Everything depended on speed. On keeping them off-balance. I had to remain in control. So I hurried back through the shifting geography of the castle to Vallyne's "resting" room. One small thing I had to do before proceeding.

Demons had no need for bedchambers, as they had no need to sleep. But they remembered the desire for sleep, so each of them had a private place to which they retired alone for part of the day. Vallyne had pointed out such rooms as she took me about the castle, but until that day she had never invited me to her own. I took a deep breath and knocked on the door.

"Exile!"

I had come expecting a war, and indeed Vallyne was waiting for me in full battle dress. She stood at her door arrayed in midnight blue, a simple gown of woven air that hid only enough of her physical form to set my imagination on fire. Her pale shoulders were bare, and she wore no jewels save the emerald depths of her eyes. "You're early, Exile, but I'm glad of it." With a smile so radiant I wondered it did not make the dismal castle gleam, she took my hand and led me onto the battlefield.

Her room was hung with filmy veils of silver, a soft and delicate draping that hid the overabundant furnishings and glowed with candlelight. A small table was laid for two, wine poured in crystal goblets, a silver bowl of sugared cherries set between. Where had she learned of my favorite sweet? Beyond the table was a very large and very comfortable-looking bed. I reviewed the sincerity of my intents . . . and cursed Fiona and her tower one more time.

"In the city of the Rudai you offered to be my teacher." The lady picked up the wineglasses and pressed one of them into my hand. "Have I passed beyond the first lesson or is there yet more to learn before we go on to the next?"

I took a sip of the wine . . . sour . . . wrong . . . and then I poured it out upon the gray tiles, watching the dark red liquid spread and splatter over Vallyne's bare feet. "It won't work, my lady. I'm free of you."

Indeed. My lying was considerably improved.

CHAPTER 31

Vallyne had succeeded in one of her purposes, at least. She had convinced me of the reasons. No matter what, I could not condemn the demons to an eternity in Kir'Vagonoth. She had shown me worth and beauty in her realm, and I could no more fault her for her ways than I could fault Aleksander for the ways he was born to. But for myself, I was a warrior who was accustomed to confronting my opponent and settling matters in the open. That's why I could not wait for rumor to inform Vallyne that she had lost her game. I had to tell her that I knew what she was doing, no matter that it led me into such temptation as I had never known.

"So what I've guessed is true," she said, setting her wineglass back upon the table. The hanging veils shifted softly in the silver light. "You've reclaimed what I've taken from you."

"I can never reclaim everything you've taken. All those months in the pits . . . I must believe you don't know what such things do to a human, else I could not stand here and say I'm sorry I cannot continue with our playacting." I set my empty wineglass beside Vallyne's. "You took away the memory of my child, Vallyne. Days when I could have been imagining what he was like as he grew. Yet even as I say it, I grieve for you . . . knowing how it must pain you to hear such things."

"Exile . . ."

"Shall I tell you what you want to know? My name is Seyonne. You can bring out your friend Vyx—or is it Raddoman—or is it the unnamed guardsman who kept me with your other mindless animals—and tell him, too. None of this was necessary. I came here to learn. To help. To right the wrong that sent you here, even though I didn't know what it was. I would have told you my name and helped you do what you want."

No one could argue with Vallyne's persistence. Her physical form vanished, and only her silver radiance remained. She stepped closer. Her face shone with insistent perfection. "But how could we know?" Her enveloping fire began to sear my skin and my resolution.

I walked to the window and threw open the shutters, hoping that the cold wind and the sight of the pitiless wasteland would cool my fever. "You could have listened to me," I said. "Neither love nor trust nor friendship can grow without that one step. All you had to do was ask."

By the time I felt steady enough to face her, she had shifted yet again. She sat at her table, the candlelight reflecting on her lovely face—the older, wiser, more beautiful face I had seen only once before. And Vyx had shown himself. He was standing behind Vallyne protectively, though he didn't touch her. Rai-kirah never touched one another.

"When one lives a hundred lifetimes in Kir'Vagonoth, one has little experience of trust or friendship," said Vyx. "You are one of the *pandye gash*—an yddrass. We had no reason to believe you would consent."

"Be honest, Vyxagallanxchi," said Vallyne, softly chiding. "You told me he was trustworthy. I would not credit you." She lifted her chin. "It was I who chose to leave you with the mad ones. I wanted your power, your soul, and your body. I had no use for your mind. Perhaps if I had known you. . . ." As her words faded away, there came a great release, and I lifted my hands and stared at them as if I might see manacles falling away for the second time in my life. And then I shivered and heightened my vision, for the light had dimmed and the bitter cold bit into me as when a winter sun slips below the horizon.

"What's done is done," I said, my voice echoing in the void left by the loss of my mad desire. "I'll take my leave now."

"Stay, Exile . . . Seyonne . . . will you not hear us out?" Vallyne remained seated. Only her voice reached out to me now. "Have you not seen value here? If not in us, then in what we've shown you? If you were willing without our deception . . . then what of now? Our need is no less than if we'd been honest." No. One could not fault Vallyne for determination. And yet I was surprised. She did not try to bind me with my name.

"I've seen what you want me to see. And I'm going to do what you want me to do. I'm just not going to let you control the way it happens." I started toward the doorway. "You'll be able to go back to Kir'Navarrin, and perhaps once you're there, you won't be forced to do the vile things you do. But my people will also live, and someday they and you will understand what we are and what we've done to each other."

"We protected you," said Vyx. "You cannot know how many times you came near death from those jealous of your body or bent on vengeance. One or the other of us have been with you almost every moment."

"You nearly destroyed me."

"Vallyne allowed you to heal. All those days in her courtyard . . . did you not wonder at them? We had no healing medicines, but she gave you time and peace to mend your body."

"You stole my will." I fought my way through the draping veils, yet I seemed to make no progress. I ripped down a filmy trailer of white and spotted the door ten paces away.

Both of them called out. "Wait!" But it was Vyx who vanished, reappearing between me and the door, his light flickering blue-green and purple as he took physical shape again. "One word with you, Exile. I dare not ask whose advice you plan to follow in this venture; I doubt you know enough of the real issues here to make a wise choice. No, no, don't yell at me that I've given you no opportunity to make a choice. Indeed you've conveyed that message very clearly. And we repent. Indeed we do. But if you are the man you claim, the one we have judged you to be, are you not the least bit curious about my warning? Have you no mote of misgiving that perhaps you enter into a game where you do not know the stakes?"

There it was. Of course he would touch upon the stone in my boot. I did not want to listen. I had made my decision as best I could, and I needed to be off. "I understand everything I need to. I'll open the way because it's right, and I would not condemn any other of my people to do it. I will do my best not to unlock Tyrrad Nor. Whatever comes after, whatever is the 'danger without a name' that exists in the fortress, you will have to deal with it."

"Then, I will say only this, Exile. Everything depends on the one you choose. Everything—the safety of your people, of your child, of all of us. We need an ylad of immense power—you—to open the way to Kir'Navarrin. We are lost otherwise. But you must know the risk. We have no name for what waits for us in Tyrrad Nor; we know only that it means the destruction of your kind and ours. Sooner or later, it will strike. There are those who share this intent, who rejoice in the thought of chaos and destruction and revenge. They are the same who wish to destroy the *pandye gash* and go first into Kir'Navarrin, so they can seek out the danger. Wake it. Serve it. I can tell you more . . ."

I told myself I should not listen to Vyx. He and Vallyne had found it needful that I lie in a pool of my own blood believing I had no arms, that I weep in despair as I felt my mind disintegrate, that I forget the woman I had promised to love until I died and the child who seemed to be the single thing I had ever touched that was not death. Yet I found myself wanting to believe them. "I need to go." But my feet did not move.

Then Vyx made a mistake. "Tell me one thing only, Exile. Where is the other ylad?"

I did not expect this question, and it reversed my weakening resolve. The two of them were playing games with me again, and I would not permit it. "What business is it of yours?" I said, pushing the slight demon aside. "Were you thinking to destroy what little you left him? Or do you plan to do the same for me—strip me of power because I won't yield it to you and mutilate my body because you have none of your own?" Vyx's warnings had no meaning. He admitted their lies and deceptions. I needed to be gone from that place where Vallyne and candlelight, anger and wounded pride were confusing my judgment.

"What we left . . . ? Ah. So Merryt has told you his story of the feasting—how the terrible rai-kirah cut off his fingers and stole his great magic. You see, Vallyne, I told you we should have caged the vermin when we had the chance."

I touched the brass snake that was the door handle, but yanked my hand away. It was so hot I thought it might sear the imprint of the viper in my palm. "Easy to mock a captive." I invoked my melydda and touched the snake again. This time I did not feel the heat, and I pulled open the door.

"Shall I show you how it was done, Exile?" said Vyx, pelting me with words. "Shall I tell you why he came to our feasting? And what he did while he was there?"

"No," said Vallyne, her voice distraught. "I forbid it. Vyx. . . ."

"He needs to learn before he makes his choice."

"No," I said. "I've learned enough."

As I strode down the passageway, away from treachery and temptation, Vyx called out after me unrelenting. "Think, Yddrass. How has Merryt survived in Kir'Vagonoth when no other ylad ever has? Where does he get his human clothing and his weapons? Ask him who it is he mourns at his altar—and it is surely not his wife, whom he blames for his captivity, or his people, whom he blames for his failures, nor the rai-kirah, his captors, whom he blames for everything else and who are going mad here in Kir'Vagonoth. Ask him why he has sworn before every one of us to destroy the yddrass who can change form; any rai-kirah can tell you of his vow."

I would not listen. They were out to ruin my mind again, just when I had found some resolution. I hurried to my room, lit a candle, and ate a chunk of hard, sour bread left from some long-forgotten meal. The food did not quiet the gnawing in my stomach. My back itched with sweat. Beyond the rug stuffed in my window, the wind bellowed like a drunken god, but I ripped the dusty wad of carpet away, yanked open the shutters, and leaned through the rectangular opening, taking great gulps of the frigid air as if it might settle my jangled nerves. Why had I set a two-hour delay before my meeting with Gennod? Had I thought to bed Vallyne before . . . oh, gods, what was I doing?

Viciously I shoved the glass-shelved cabinet out of my way. As cups and jewelry and pots bumped and clattered to the floor, each article shattering into a thousand bits, I fell on my bed and buried my face in the coverings. I couldn't bear to think. The wind howled, fluttering the pages of a book that lay beside my ear. The god stories. What had I been trying to remember . . . about Verdonne and Valdis and the myth of the first Ezzarians? Our race had sprung from the uniting of gods and mortals, so we had been told. And the god had gone mad from jealousy and vengeance. When Valdis stripped the angry god of his power, he had locked him away in a magical fortress and pronounced a warning to all the peoples of the forest . . . a warning . . . because he had taken away his father's name . . . What was the truth and what was wishing—recreating the world to fit our desire, the attempt to shape our formless midnight fears and mask them with the protection of a benevolent god?

A man-high candlestick toppled when a gust from the window pushed the crumpled rug against it. All the candles were snuffed out. I jumped up and threw on my cloak, then raced down the shifting passageways to the back door Merryt had shown me. Once outside in the gloom, I triggered the change that gave me wings and fought my way through the raging storm to the Rudai settlement.

Only a few passing demons gave me a glance as I strode down the winding corridors of gray-lit stone. No one noticed me push open the door of Merryt's secret room; though my shoulders were still tingling, my wings were hidden again. The Ezzarian had sworn that no one knew of this place.

I poked around the bins and baskets of his little hoard, fingering gemstones and combs, cups and pens, a packet of needles, and bits of cloth and thread. Then, disgusted with my cowardly dawdling, I dropped to my knees in front of the brassbound trunk from which Merryt had taken his Warden's cloak. I would find nothing. The demons were master deceivers and were only trying to make me doubt myself. The lock was sealed with enchantment. I had no patience to unravel it, so instead I burst the hinges and ripped the lid away.

What story can be told by a heap of rags? I had once

seen rags piled higher than a roof, and they had spoken o
mortal suffering and grief—the garments of a town o
plague victims ready to be burned. Ysanne had tucke
away a small stack of fine-woven cloth in the bottom o
our clothes chest, deep down under the winter cloaks w
seldom needed in Ezzaria. I had found the little pile—th
ritual garments she had made for our child's naming day—
when hunting a clean shirt on the day of my trial befor
the Council. In my blind and cruel anger, I had left then
in a wadded heap on the floor for her to see. The rags i
Merryt's chest had a story, too.

One by one I pulled them out. A Warden's cloak rippe
and half burned. Another Warden's cloak with gaping hole
in it, the cloth eaten away by whatever acrid substanc
had made the stiff, splotchy green stains. A shredded tuni
embroidered with the intertwined symbols of Warden an
Aife, and husband and wife, the fine stitching telling a stor
of love and partnership. A single scuffed boot with th
name Dyadd scratched inside. A sweat-crusted shirt, size
for a giant of a man, with a jagged rent in the back of i
edged with rusty brown. One after the other I examine
them. Merryt had worn the ones he could repair. Thes
that were left—the garments of no fewer than fifteen War
dens—were too ruined, but evidently he could not brin
himself to destroy them. I pulled out one shirt that was i
fairly good condition. A little blood. A few rips, easil
mended. But, of course, he could not have worn that on
while I still lived. It was the shirt I had bought in Passil
on my journey with Fiona. I tried to persuade myself tha
Merryt had kept the clothes in honored memory of thos
he could not save . . . but the testimony of my own shi
proved otherwise. On the second day of my captivity in th
pits of the mad Gastai, that garment had been strippe
from me by a soft-voiced man who had taught my jaile
how to inflict obscene indignity—a human man.

I twisted the coarse fabric into a knot about my fist an
hammered the wall. *Fool. Cursed, blind fool.*

"We should have told you about him."

I didn't even jump when Vyx spoke from behind me.
was numb to surprises. "I should have seen it," I said.

"You wanted a friend in this terrible place. And he told you a story . . ."

Yes. A story. The residents of Kir'Vagonoth were all quite proficient at their lies.

"I can tell you another version of that story, though Vallyne commands me not."

"I don't want anything from you." Nothing that would tell me the magnitude of my misjudgment.

"But we need you to see . . ." Vyx moved quickly. As he had done as Raddoman, when he told me the tale of his terrible waking in Kir'Vagonoth, Vyx clamped his hand across my face and in a fleeting moment—*my body shuddering with power . . . my head swelled with wine, my belly and my loins engorged . . . my hands thrumming with a god's mastery, life and death within my grasp . . . fading glimpses of women and men naked on the grass . . . bleeding . . . dead . . . We'd had a jolly hunt such as the world had never known; across the hills and through my grandsire's woodland we had chased the pitiful villagers, some screaming, some in the desperate silence that was so pleasing . . . my besotted friends laughing with me*—he took me into his memory.

The grotesque images . . . the false memories . . . they fade at last, the tastes lingering longest . . . vile, wretched fodder . . . Where is the ylad? He came in just behind the Gastai. What business has he here? Cursed gluttonous fool, why did I not stop him then? No, I had to eat . . . such foulness . . . gross villainy . . . This one lived in depravity so despicable—hunting other humans for sport—I would rather starve than partake. So easy to say after, when you know what it is you have consumed; so difficult to say when your being cries for sustenance. For life. "Maybe this time it will be something marvelous," you say. "Maybe this time it will be like those you travel when you brave the outer world." So why did you not refuse it, knowing that so little of what the Gastai bring is fit? Because, despite what you say, you would not rather starve. And now the ylad has violated this last privacy. The privacy of gluttony. Of sin. Of starvation so foully satisfied. Before I sleep like these others, fallen on

*the floor like dead things—I must find out what wickedness
the ylad brings to our depraved festival.*

*There he is . . . in the corner beyond the dead fountains
and the dwindling smoke and screams of shameful
visions . . . where Denas lies, succumbed to the dead sleep
of bloating. My lord would not partake if he were not so
driven. Some would. Some have come to relish what is given
us. But the ylad has crept over there beyond Denas. What
is it he carries? Silver . . . Such horror the shape of it brings
to me . . . what is it? If I could do anything but crawl over
these others like a groveling beast, trapped in this foul body,
tainted by its lingering pleasures, I could get there faster
to see . . . Ah, no! Not good Zelaz! The last who knew
the danger . . .*

Murder. Merryt had crept into the aftermath of demon
feasting, when the rai-kirah had fallen helpless to the floor
in the exhaustion of satiety after starvation, and with him
he had brought a silver Warden's knife and a Luthen mirror. Vyx had watched Merryt murder Zelaz as he lay insensible. And just next to Zelaz, so close that the blood of the
dying body soaked her white gown, lay Vallyne, stirring
groggily . . . frowning . . . her heavy-lidded eyes widening
in confusion and dismay as Merryt ripped her blood-soaked
clothes away and sated his own depraved desires with the
body she wore.

"We could prove nothing," said Vyx, moving away from
where I sat, the last of the alien memory draining from my
head. He propped his backside against a table, gripping the
edge with his hands. "It is impossible to stay sensible after,
and by the time we rose, Zelaz was gone. As you well
know, Yddrass, nothing remains of our true being when
we're dead."

"And so you destroyed Merryt." I spoke defensively, trying to bury my disgust. Ezzarians and demons had been at
war for a thousand years. I was not guiltless, nor were the
rai-kirah who feasted on the nightmares of human souls.
And yet there was a difference in murdering and raping
those who lay helpless.

"I claim no innocence. We have none. Don't you see?
Why do you think Merryt yet lives?" Vyx slumped into a

chair and kicked at the well-turned legs of the table with short, fierce thrusts of his black boots. "We searched his rooms and took away his weapons—we didn't know about this little hiding place—and we made known among the circles that he had murdered Zelaz." He kicked the table again. "We accused him only of the murder. Not the other. Yes, we punished him, though we did not take his fingers or toes. He had already made his partnership with the mad Gastai. It was in trying to get another weapon from a captive yddrass that Merryt was damaged. We thought it fitting. As for his power . . . why do you think he had so much to begin with? You've only his word for it. No one of us has ever seen evidence of it."

"It's not true. You're trying to blame him so I'll trust you again. It won't work." I stood up and went to the door, my thick head still swearing to me that if I left that room, I could forget everything revealed there. "You have your justice. The Rudai Meet. You could have brought him before your judges if he had done such things." But I remembered Merryt's claims of "opportunities" and needs that only he could satisfy. And I remembered how Vilgor, the purple-clad Rudai who had taken me from the pits, had disappeared just after insulting the big Ezzarian. And I remembered our venture on the night of the demon feasting—when Merryt had found it necessary to kill the demons trying to capture me. Perhaps his vile deed was not purposed to save my life, but to prevent my discovering his complicity in their attempt. With a Warden's weapons, Merryt could arrange matters as he pleased.

Vyx leaned forward on the table and continued as if my protests had been but another blast of wind. "We could do nothing openly. Without his weapons Merryt had no strength to harm us, but he had a very powerful friend who used him and protected him. The same one who charged him to kill Zelaz."

"Who?" I demanded, still unwilling to admit that there was anything Vyx could say that would change my mind. I had sworn not to stand immobilized by my fear of what needed to be done, and so I had chosen to entrust my soul to someone else's hand. Between Merryt—a flawed man of my own race, my own training, my own sympathies, one I

believed had saved my life and my reason—and Vallyne—
a demon who had left me in torment to destroy my mind
and turned my head inside out with deception—I thought
I had made the only reasonable choice. And now Vyx was
trying to convince me that I had chosen wrongly. What
man can accept such a thing easily?

"Haven't you guessed it? His name was Tasgeddyr. You
know him as the Naghidda—he who tried to gain control
of your world to feed his purposes, to open Kir'Navarrin
and release the danger that is bound in Tyrrad Nor."

"What is this danger?" I yelled at him in frustration.
"The Lord of Demons is dead. I killed him. Of all the
bloody deeds I have done in my life, that's one I don't
regret. What has you so frightened?" And our ancestors
who had tried to destroy our memory of it.

"We don't know, Exile. The knowledge was taken from
us when we were sent here. You saw my own recollection.
That's all I have. Only a few of us remembered more, and
for a very long time they refused to talk about it, for fear
that some might use the knowledge wrongly. Zelaz was
one. Tasgeddyr also knew something of what lies in the
fortress. Tasgeddyr claimed that there was no danger waiting for us. Only power, he said, power that wore no name
because it was waiting for its rightful claimant. Tasgeddyr
said that the *pandye gash* had thrown us out of Kir'Navarrin because they saw that we were becoming more powerful
than humans and would someday control the human world
as well as our own. Merryt and Tasgeddyr were great
friends. The ylad told Tasgeddyr of the prizes to be won
in your world, and how the power he could gain would
enable him to destroy the *pandye gash* and open the gateway to reclaim our rightful place. And so Tasgeddyr began
to call himself the Naghidda, promising the Nevai unlimited
power, the Rudai unlimited materials for their shaping, the
Gastai unlimited hunting, and all of us unlimited vengeance
on the *pandye gash*."

Vyx picked up one of the pitiful rags and ran his luminous fingers along the bloody rent in it. The fabric wove
itself together again, but the rusty stain remained. "When
they saw what was happening with the Gastai—this madness growing worse by the hour—Zelaz and the others were

in a terrible dilemma. They agreed that we had to return to Kir'Navarrin or go to ruin, but Tasgeddyr was exactly what they had always feared. Secretly they began to speak to a few of the Nevai, warning them that, whatever the price, they must not allow Tasgeddyr or his followers to enter Kir'Navarrin first. A certain fortress must be secured immediately, or we risked war and destruction that would leave us all—both human and rai-kirah—in dark times worse than we had known. Before Zelaz could tell us more, he and all those who knew the truth vanished . . . dead, most certainly. All but Tasgeddyr. Do you see it now, my friend? You know very well of Tasgeddyr's quest for power—spurred on by Merryt's teaching. After you destroyed Tasgeddyr, Merryt was half mad with it."

I flattened my back against the wall. Truth weighs heavy, like a fruit full of juice, and pulp outweighs those dried up past use. And if these things were true, then what in Verdonne's name had I done setting Merryt free . . . sending him to Ezzaria? *Idiot.* What man had ever let himself be made such a fool by everyone he encountered? No wonder the Aifes and the Weavers and the Queens of Ezzaria were women and not warriors. I rubbed my face with my hands, wishing I would wake, wishing I could trust someone, afraid to believe Vyx, and afraid—terrified—not to believe him.

"Is Merryt joined? Can he open the way himself?"

"No. His sorcery is too little. Not even the Naghidda could have made him strong enough to do it, though Merryt boasts to the Gastai that such was Tasgeddyr's plan. We didn't take his power from him. His own weakness got him captured, and he yielded his name the first day. Magyalla, his Rudai captor, would not keep him after she tasted what he had to give her. And after Merryt took up with Tasgeddyr, Magyalla was never seen again in all of Kir'Vagonoth." Vyx gave a rueful smile. "We never even had a chance to learn what secrets Merryt told her."

And so I had sent a murdering liar, a craven robber of the dead and dying, a servant of the Naghidda, to warn the Ezzarians of the demon legion. I had sent him in company with Blaise and Kyor and Balthar and Fiona—my only hope ever to see the world of light. *Damned, cursed fool.* Again I was forced to put faith in my adversary Fiona and pray that she could keep herself and the others safe. Now I could afford no delays. If it had not all been so dreadfully serious, I would have had a good laugh at my pitiful plotting.

"I'm supposed to meet Gennod in the courtyard within the hour," I said. "And you're going to tell me that he, too, was a servant of the Naghidda—a partner with Merryt. And clearly the servants of the Naghidda are the ones who want to open Tyrrad Nor, whereas you and Vallyne are the ones I need to trust."

"Yes to most of that. Since you first came, Gennod has been working to get control of you, though Merryt is not his partner. They share similar goals, but Merryt partners only with himself. Gennod can't abide the man any more than the rest of us." Vyx jumped up and smiled, the blue fire in his eyes flaring brightly. Kind, one might describe it. Sympathetic. Victorious. "Now, if you would tell me of your plan . . ."

I told him of my agreement with Gennod, and how Merryt had a head start on us thanks to my pigheaded folly.

"No matter. Merryt would have found a way to follow you out and do as he wished anyway. But we can provide an alternative to Gennod. We have someone waiting. Someone worthy of you, Exile"—his grin fell away—"worthy of the yddrass you are."

I didn't want to hear the word yddrass—to be reminded of my oath. I shut off my thinking. "Let's just get it done. The sooner the better. As I told you, my name is Seyonne. Do with it as you will."

Vyx gave a quick laugh . . . embarrassed, I would have called it. "Oh, my friend. It is not I. I'm honored . . . but I have not the knowledge. Nor the grace to give up what I know of life." Gently he pushed me through the door and into the corridor. "And we can't do it here. It must be done in front of the legion. They have to see you agree; otherwise they'll never follow. That's why Gennod wants you in the courtyard. You can be sure he has summoned the host of Kir'Vagonoth to watch you yield."

CHAPTER 32

I had never imagined there were so many rai-kirah. Lights of every color the mind could grasp flickered, writhed, and glimmered like ropes of lightning tangled together in a massive brilliance, illuminating the front of Denas's castle. From my position in the shadowed arch of the jackal gate, I could see the vast courtyard jammed with demons, glimpses of faces and limbs turning in and out of my view as more arrived and they pushed together. And on the edges, in blots of seething darkness were the hunters. The Gastai. I smelled them. Tasted them. Felt the air turn colder whenever my eye crossed their presence.

Across the sprawl of the courtyard was the main entrance to the castle, towering pillars carved in the shape of stylized trees, thick-boled with a fringe of leafy growth where the pillar met the rectangular block of the massive lintel. In a place of honor at the front of the crowd stood Denas's gyossi—his "castle guests," the Nevai who lived in this sprawling ice palace by his invitation or his sufferance. A few of them were standing between the pillars on the sweeping curve of the castle's twenty steps. The pulsing red form was Gennod, craning his neck, glancing over his shoulder, waiting. Waiting for me.

I pressed my back against the cold stone, my breathing ragged, my skin alternately burning and freezing.

"Rhadit was supposed to lead the great venture, but he's gone missing," said Vyx in my ear. "Denas had hoped to profit from Rhadit's undoing, but it seems Gennod has out-maneuvered him. No doubt our wily friend Gennod plans to humbly accept Rhadit's place at the head of the legion when he presents you as his prize."

Four or five demons were clustered to one side of Gennod. A glowering Denas was one of them, gleaming gold, no imperfect physical body to mute his glory. Beside him stood Denkkar, the elderly dancer, and Tovall, the dark-skinned Nevai with the magnificent laugh. Kaarat, the Rudai judge, stood stiffly to the other side.

In the book-room assignation, Denas's co-conspirator had mentioned three rai-kirah who were willing to join with a human to open the gateway. Gennod was one. Another of them was the demon who stood alone on the fifth step, just beyond the torchlight, his hands clasped easily behind his back—Kryddon, a quiet, well-spoken Rudai who had come to many of Vallyne's reading sessions. He had once asked Vallyne if she would permit the "savage ylad" to read a book about sea creatures. He was fascinated with the idea of oceans and the world that existed beneath the surface of them. Nesfarro was the third. He was the stringy, wild-haired Rudai gesticulating vigorously as he spoke to a laughing Tovall. He fancied himself an artist, and had, indeed, created the color galleries. When he heard Vallyne had shown me his work, he had taken great offense. He vowed to slay any ylad who viewed his creation ever again.

Merryt had claimed that a demon joining accomplished in Kir'Vagonoth was indissoluble. If he was right, then one of the ten demons on the steps was to occupy my soul for the rest of my life. I wanted to bury my head in the gray stones behind me or grow my wings and let the storm carry me far from that place.

"Gennod will ask you some questions. Answer them truly, save for the most important one." Vyx grinned up at me. "You know which one?"

"My name."

"That's it. When he demands your name, step back from him and make room, for several of us will surround you, and the legion must be able to see what transpires. One of us will ask you if you yield. Speak your answer clearly—whatever it may be—and, if you are still willing to walk this path, touch the hand that is offered and say your name in the same breath. It must be quick, my friend, or Gennod will have you. He'll be prepared for just such a move."

"It seems a courtesy to tell me who it will be."

Vyx smiled a little sadly. "You underestimate your own

strength, Exile. It matters not in the least which of our kind takes this step, save that it not be Gennod or one of his sympathies."

I wasn't sure what he meant by that, and I didn't want to think about it.

"Now go, friend Seyonne. And may your gods care for you better than they have thus far." He grinned and gave me a nudge forward. "We may yet have time to see something of the world together."

My feet didn't want to move. "You're sure it isn't you?" I could use a dose of his optimism and good humor. At least I had shared more than five words with him.

Vyx threw his head back laughing. "It would be my privilege, but you have troubles enough without adding mine. I can't seem to stay in anyone's good graces for more than an hour's passing. We can't risk anyone knowing our players until the deed is done." He waved a hand toward the steps. "It will be well, Exile. It will be well." Then he shoved me forward into the crowd of demons, crying out in a voice much larger than his slender frame, "Make way! Our rescuer comes!"

Much of that hour was a blur. A blur of light as I walked through the sea of demons, fighting to ignore the stench as they opened a way to let me pass. A blur of sound—babbling, murmuring, demon words of anger and hope, and gut-twisting music that wailed and writhed and set my bones quivering with memory and dread. Events carried me along without thought or conscious agreement, as if my only choice had been made on the night I wrapped my arms about my wife and discovered she no longer carried a child, the night I tumbled down a well of darkness and could find no purchase to stop my fall.

But inevitably I found myself standing on the steps of Denas's castle, sleet stinging my face and Gennod's pulsing red light grating at the edge of my spirit. "The terms of truce are agreed to as you stated, Yddrass," Gennod said quietly when I climbed the steps to stand beside him. "In return for your agreement to open the gateway to Kir'Navarrin, the legion will not attack the *pandye gash*. Now that I am to assume command of the legion, you can be sure of it. Only if we are prevented from traveling the gateway will we fight your people, and once safe within our homeland, we will allow you to negotiate in peace. The entire host of Kir'Vagonoth will be bound by these words. Is that satisfactory?"

"Satisfactory," I said. But of course I already knew how things would fall out. The rai-kirah might not attack the Ezzarians, but Merryt was seeing to it that the Ezzarians would be in the fight. He would create chaos between humans and demons so that he could get through the gate first. What possibility of escape from this fate I might ever have possessed, I had squandered when I sent Merryt through the portal. I could not warn the Ezzarians away from the confrontation. If they believed the demon legion was coming to destroy them—possess their own souls or those of others—they would be ready. They would send in every student, every scholar, every person with any trace of melydda, and they would be slaughtered. So I had to prevent Merryt from passing through the portal, and I had to have the power to force the demons to leave whatever hosts they used without fighting. That meant I had to both control the gateway and command the legion. I. No one else. Even then I didn't know if it would be enough.

Demons gave speeches lamenting the missing Rhadit, glorifying his determination to lead the demon legion into the human world, and praising Gennod's nobility to risk all for a new life in Kir'Navarrin. Others gave exhortations for courage and pleas for unity and thanks to those who planned to take their places in the vanguard. Gennod was not highly regarded. The speeches seemed hollow, the cheering thin, but Gennod came nearer a smile than I had ever seen him. When it was his turn to speak, the red-glimmering demon was brief. "We will take what we want. No longer will we beg or steal."

That got the demon legion enthusiastic—especially the fringes of the crowd where the hunters lurked. As one of the things he wanted, I felt distinctly nauseated. Acrid smoke billowed from torches mounted on the tall pillars, burning my eyes.

Then they turned to me. "This ylad—an yddrass of many battles—has come to us in our need," said one of Gennod's followers, a slight lisp marring his high, clear voice. The growling from the Gastai had me shuddering; I would have sworn I heard Jack-Willow's voice among them. "This ylad has been punished for his crimes and has offered us his true repentance. We have judged him sufficient to do what must be done." More words. None yet that had meaning, but those would come soon, and I was not sure what I was going to do. A thousand plans flitted through my head like the winged seeds of the yvarra tree, all of them dismissed as useless before they could settle and take root.

And then it was time.

"Yddrass, is it your intent to help us on our way to Kir'-Navarrin?" Gennod now questioned me.

"Yes." Such a deep hush fell over the babbling crowd that even my half-strangled reply resounded clearly. A blast of wind flapped my cloak, and I drew it tight.

"And you will accept freely the one of us who offers to join you in this enterprise?"

"Yes."

"And you will abide by the agreements we have made and forsake the war you have waged upon our kind?"

Bile burned in my throat. "Yes."

Gennod leaned toward me and whispered, "There is one more thing we require of you . . . because of your history . . . because so many of our kind have suffered at your hand, they'll not believe that you submit unless you kneel."

"Kneel . . . no. I will not." How foolish to rebel at such a small matter, when I was violating every law I had sworn to uphold, betraying every Ezzarian who had lived and fought and died for a thousand years. Yet every fiber of my body revolted at such blatant humiliation . . . such abject surrender. I might be renouncing my people, but I would not humble them. "Impossible."

Even the wind fell still. Gennod sneered, still keeping his tight voice low. "Then, you have no intent to accomplish this deed. Your claims of sincerity are false. What does appearance matter when you have already said you will yield?"

The crowd was stirring uneasily; those on the steps were leaning closer. Vyx now stood with the group of Nevai, his head cocked to the side, the blue flame of his eyes sharply

focused. What would Gennod do if I refused? I shifted my
senses and looked deep into the red light, and the answer
was unmistakable. He would try to force me. Along with
all my other misjudgments . . . what if I had misjudged his
power? I knew nothing of what was to come, and I could
not allow him to gain any advantage. I had gone far enough
along this path . . . what if he won?

"When I give you my name, I will not kneel, but I will
bow," I said. "A very deep, formal bow, as one honorable
warrior to another, as a local king gives to our Emperor.
If that is not enough, you can find someone else." Some
things just could not be.

Gennod stared at me, assessing my intent. Evidently he
was satisfied that he had gotten all he could get. He smiled.
"We will do very well," he said. "I could not live a coward." He continued, louder again. "And this choice you
make freely, witnessed by this host before you?"

"Yes."

As one the crowd leaned forward. I darted my eyes about
looking for Vallyne, but she was nowhere I could see.

"Speak your name, ylad."

I forced myself to smile at Gennod, then jerked my head
at his friends who were crowding close, almost touching my
shoulders. Gennod waved his hand, and his friends moved
aside. At the same time, I stepped back, and as I grasped
the edges of my cloak and spread them wide, pointing one
foot and dipping my head low over my knee in the most
formal of courtly bows, I felt others move up close behind
me, a circle of demons at my back. When I came up, I
spun on my heels to face them as if I were surprised. Tovall
and Denkkar were to my right and my left. In between
them were Nesfarro and Kryddon, a slyly smiling Vyx, and
Kaarat, the Rudai judge.

"The name, ylad, the name." Gennod was at my shoulder, waving at the others. "You—Vyx, Tovall, the rest of
you—move back."

Kryddon spoke the question. Not loud, but very clear.
As inescapable as a trumpet call on the battlefield. "Do
you yield or not, ylad? Answer Gennod's question."

My breathing stopped. And yet there was one moment
of relief when I saw it was Kryddon. *Not horrid . . . not*

crude or sly . . . forever . . . oh, gods, have mercy . . . The wind blasted sleet into my eyes and made the torchlight dance wildly.

"The name, ylad." Gennod was angry. Closer.

I closed my eyes and envisioned my son, grown into a sturdy child, his cheeks of rosy gold, his straight black hair, his coal-black eyes, laughing with kind Elinor and Gordain back in the world of light. It was the image I wanted to take with me—my purpose. A Warden can accomplish nothing without a purpose, so I had taught my students a lifetime ago. This purpose is the framework of his honor, the foundation of his strength, the standard to which he can attach everything he needs to remember.

"I yield," I said. "I, Seyonne . . ." . . . *son of Gareth and Joelle of the line of Ezraelle, husband of Ysanne, father of Evan-diargh, Warden of Ezzaria.* Though I dared not speak the names aloud, I invoked them under my breath to ensure I did not forget. Then I opened my eyes, touched the hand that reached for mine . . . and looked up into the bitter, golden eyes of Denas.

CHAPTER 33

I burn. Blazing torment . . . blinding . . . devouring. I am lost . . . lost . . . how could I think this possible? All ending . . . all desire . . . undone . . . This other . . . this vile, murderous other . . . setting me afire . . . Flames shoot from me in every direction . . . A crushing weight of otherness . . . destroying, burning . . . to leave everything I am behind . . . passing into nothing . . . to live in unending horror . . . such darkness . . . such pain . . . I am and have ever been a creature of fire, shaped from flame, forged, scarred, marked . . . If I could but remember . . .

The blacksmith's thick-fingered hand wields the iron rod, the foul implement, the end of it shaped into figures of the falcon and the lion—graceful shapes turned to horror and evil purpose. Glowing red . . . the iron heat comes closer . . . closer . . . Oh, powers of night, it burns . . . through my flesh, through my mind, through my being . . . the mark of degradation, of bondage, of everlasting ruin . . .

Wait . . . don't go . . . I need to remember . . . even ruin . . .

"Comes the time for the change, my son."

"I am not prepared enough, Father. Please, can I not wait a while . . . practice more? I'll listen better. Please, Father, I cannot breathe. It burns when I try, as if I've fallen into the heart of Vesuk'na, where the rock itself boils. Who could bear it?" He will not hear me. Not when the time has come. Father says it is my heritage, and shame awaits the laggard. So do. Easy . . . easy . . . first shape your arms . . . as you were taught . . . as you know better than you know the sunrise . . . then your body . . . The priest claimed it would go easy for you, but when did Mopryl ever know easy? "The

*burning will end when it is done," he always says, "when
you are changed." Why must it burn so? But strength is
all . . . and so shape the legs, and then the head, the most
difficult . . . I will not cry out. Only a little while burning,
then I will be as I am meant to be . . .*

*Wait . . . I need to see . . . did I pass this test? I can't
remember . . .*

*"So long have I waited, my darling . . . to see you crowned
in autumn leaves and hear you speak the words of forever
loving. How blessed is life! What love holds faith beyond
death and corruption? In the years of bondage, of despair,
of pain and forgetting, I never dared dream of this day . . .
the burning sun kissing my face, and the forest itself . . . the
trees arrayed in flaming golds and reds, spreading a carpet
of glory beneath your feet . . ."*

*Wait . . . I need to hear the words . . . to taste again the
fiery liquor of joy and loving . . . come back . . .*

*She abides in the gamarand wood, Keyzzor told me, and
if true, it is a wonder. I did see the girl run into the wood,
but abide there? She is cleverness itself, and beauty, and I
admire such boldness, but no one must live in so holy a
place and one so fraught with danger. Who could believe
such a matter without looking? All perish who go to the
gamarand wood, so the tales say—the wood of power that
surrounds the dread fortress, protecting us, shielding us from
its wickedness. But there is no danger for me in the gamarands, though it has been far too long since I walked its
glades. Keyzzor vows that half the gamarand forest is dead
from the touch of the fortress . . . rotted, burned . . . the
rarest wood known, and he does not even know the precious
source of its rarity. Ah, dearest Mother, I miss you so. To
think of your beauteous wood destroyed . . . But the girl
who ran in . . . I'll see her out before she brings harm to it.
List! What is that screaming . . . weeping? The gamarands
are burning . . . and there, hanging from the tree . . . oh,
hideous . . . charred . . . no longer screaming . . .*

Wait . . . it is the danger . . . I need to remember . . .

*   *   *

"No!" Several voices yelled it, and one of them was
surely mine. "Treachery!"

Hands of flesh clawed at my arms, while invading, unseen
hands grappled for my mind, ripping me apart. *Lost . . .
forever lost . . . ruin . . . horror . . .* Images exploded like
bursting stars behind my eyes, blooming huge and vivid
then fading in painful brilliance against a background of
midnight: landscapes, faces, writing, pictures. Snips of
music, singing, chanted prayers, battle . . . unending battle,
blood, and death, unending cold and darkness. Smells and
sounds and sensations, grieving and mourning, joy and
lovemaking—all of them, one after the other coming and
going. Every finger's breadth of my body burned, and my
mind was stretched, twisted, seared beyond bearing as I
struggled to escape what I had chosen. The flames that shot
from my chest and from my arms and hands blinded me
as if the snow and sleet and choking smoke from snuffed
torches had not done enough. I was on fire . . . so many
images of burning . . . As each one dwindled into nothing—even those so terrible no man could wish to own them,
even those that must have come from stories, for they were
none of my experience—I cried out to summon its return,
terrified that I was losing all I knew of life.

Denas . . . Only the fleeting glimpse . . . the knowledge
of my last misjudgment. No time to speculate, for I was
going mad, and I would not waste my last sane moment
on my own stupidity. I was a Warden of Ezzaria . . . a
warrior . . . and I needed to be in control. Even if I had
yielded my soul to the most powerful of the Nevai, the most
deadly, the one filled with bitterness, cruelty, and hatred for
everything that I was, I would fight to hold sway. My
son . . . my people . . . were depending on me. *My purpose
must sustain me.* And then came the burning and the explo-
sions of memory in my head, and I could scarce stand up
for the brutal result of them. He was devouring me.

Have care, Yddrass. Gennod comes . . . The sharp warning pierced the tumult.

I felt a new attacker, using my vulnerability to claw at
my purpose, loosing worms to burrow through my head,
probing for names, for talents and weaknesses, for information that could be used against the *pandye gash*. But the

moment's warning gave me time to gather my melydda and repel the assault, to build a barricade that would split my skull and release a holocaust were it breached. *You'll not use me to destroy them, Denas. I'll not permit it.* Anger was my sword.

Not Denas, ylad fool. This is Gennod's touch. He must be controlled quickly.

"Vyx, is that you? I'm blind." Because of my inner chaos . . . blazing tumult . . . invasion . . . violation . . . I could not see what was happening around me on the castle steps. Jostling. Stumbling. Cries heard only faintly beyond the raging in my head. Fear so palpable it must be sitting on the steps by my feet, laughing. I staggered, ready to crumple under the weight of horror and darkness and unending confusion, but my anger and my purpose held me up and kept me from being pulled apart.

The voice whispered in my ear again. *This way. Stay behind the others, away from Gennod. Then to the center of the top step. Raise your arms and speak the words I tell you.*

My feet moved without me telling them, taking me up a step and forward. I came near falling on my face. "Who's there?" I said. "I can't see." My body and soul were on fire, and someone wanted me to speak. I flung my hands out wildly, but felt no one near. How could I reassure anyone, when I was going to be ash in less time than a hummingbird lights on firephlox?

You must reassure them. They don't understand what's happened. They couldn't see. My mentor was very tense. On the verge of screaming himself. *Will you simply display some care for them? By the Nameless, hurry. I can't think. You're killing me.*

"Warriors of Kir'Vagonoth, my brothers and sisters of the Nevai, honorable kin of the Rudai Circle, glorious hunters who have sustained us in our trials, our venture will go forth." It was my tongue that spoke the words. My lips that shaped them. But they were not my words, nor was it my will that drove them past the barriers of madness. "I could not stand by and let this mission be diverted. Our first and only goal is Kir'Navarrin. Nothing else. Not vengeance. Not the resurrection of evil legend. Not power over anything

but our own fate." Wavering lights, floating on ocean of
fire. The dark shapes of the jackal gates took vague form,
scarcely visible behind the walls of flame. My back was
straight, my arms spread as if to embrace the storm-
wracked world. I wanted to cry out for help, but instead I
kept on speaking to the surging lights. "In this ylad's form
I will lead you to your home. When the time vessel is emptied once again, Tovall and Denkkar will dispatch the
Nevai, and Kryddon and Nesfarro the Rudai, into the
human lands. All is prepared for us. Our hosts approach
the gateway. I praise noble Gennod, our brother, for relinquishing this duty to one of greater strength and experience, and I exhort and command him to hold the Gastai
here, ready to come when the signal is given. To war, if
the *pandye gash* choose war. Home, if the *pandye gash*
choose to let us pass. I will meet all of you at the gateway,
and I will hold the way open until every one of you is
home."

As the last word fell from my tongue, the host of demons
cheered in wild madness. "Denas! To Kir'Navarrin!" Then
they began to disperse, winking out like stars obscured by
cloud. Kryddon and Tovall, Denkkar and Kaarat remained
close behind me, and Vyx was at my elbow.

Gennod knew he was outmatched. I batted away his invisible hand that was reaching for my throat. My own hand
twisted in the air, and I came near vomiting with the words
that my tongue spoke—a binding that would hold him in
physical form, imprisoned in the pits until I loosed him.

"You will rue this hour, Denas!" Gennod called out to
me from beyond my protective circle, even as three of
Kaarat's Rudai came to deliver him to the mad Gastai. "A
fine trickery. You had all of us fooled into thinking you
saw the truth of this vile universe. But we will have him
out—our master who will lead us to greatness without these
bestial humans. And you will be trapped with this one outside, for I'll see that you never walk Kir'Navarrin. May you
enjoy dying. May it be slow—" The Rudai guards spoke
their own words, and the red light flared and vanished.

My feet were released from the will that had moved them
to the center of the steps, and I backed away from the
small circle of demons who stood staring at me—in awe, in

thinly disguised disgust, in anger, in sympathy. Who were they looking at? The man . . . or the thing that now lived inside of him? Inside of me?

I flattened my back against a pillar and wiped at my mouth with my clammy hand. I had not spoken. Though the words had come from my mouth, I'd had no hand in shaping them. Hand . . . I wanted to laugh. I extended my hand in front of me, flexing my fingers, feeling the cold rough flesh, scraping my fingertips on the scars of twenty years of battle and slavery. For every one there was a story, and each story sped through my awareness like fluttering pages in a book. I found myself staring in curiosity at the calloused ridge around my wrist where bands of steel had held my chains for sixteen years—as if I had never noticed it before. But there was more. About the edges of my fingers and my palm flickered golden light, and when I curled the fingers into a fist, the light grew brighter, fiercer. I was revolted. *Crude flesh* . . . No! Why did I think that? It was the light that horrified me—the garish gold light that did not belong with human hands. Was it I—Seyonne, son of Gareth and Joelle—who felt this creeping sickness? Or was it the other? How would I ever know? I wanted to strip off my flesh, rip open my head to release the presence that had taken control of my speech, whose visions and memories—yes, now I understood it—were obscuring my own, whose scraping, abrading invasion had set my flesh and spirit on fire.

"Come, my friend, are you well?" Vyx motioned the others away. "Is it done fairly?"

"Which one do you address?" I said harshly, choking on the very words. "We may have differing opinions."

"You are only one."

I knew better. Everything was changed. The cold wind had a new edge to it, a honed razor that scraped at my skin. The pelting sleet sounded like hail drumming on the paving stones. I could hear each frozen droplet cracking, splitting as it struck each other one. Vyx's soft voice snapped sharply at its edges like a sheet hung in the wind. I could hear the creaking of the ice crystals buried in the castle stones, the ring of boots as some demon wearing a body raced across the tile floors inside the doors, the faint trickle of water passing through the time vessel, marking the passing moments since the changing of the world. My head was about to shatter. *So loud . . . all these sounds . . . so clear . . . like knives they pierce . . . We've got to get out of Kir'Vagonoth. There's so much to do. You've no idea what is needed.* Anger, resentment, and bitterness welled from my depths. My feet started to move again.

"Stop it," I yelled, holding my ears as the whispering began again. "Leave me alone." My heart was hammering at my chest. My blood was liquid fire, racing through my veins, threatening to burst through my skin like spewing geysers. I turned my back to Denkkar, Tovall, Kaarat, and Vyx, and pressed my head against the pillar, forcing my feet to obey me and be still, forcing aside the anger that was not my own. How had I ever believed this could be the way of things? How had I come to think I was strong enough to manage it? "He wants to destroy me."

"For a time it will seem so," said Vyx. "Denas was a very powerful being, as are you. And he desired to relinquish control of his existence no more than you. But he is one with you now. There will come a day when you can no longer tell the difference."

I would not believe that. I could not. "I hear his voice."

"We believe that when you step into Kir'Navarrin, that too will end." Even in my frenzy I could hear Vyx grieving . . . for Denas, his friend and honored lord, the one who had loved his darling Vallyne for a thousand years, though neither could remember if he had even known her before the dark times. The three who had plotted my downfall.

"You will remember, Vyxagallanxchi?" Only the movement of my lips told me I had spoken . . . softly and with as much gentleness as pain and unbounded fury would allow.

The slender demon gazed at me with blue fire in his eyes. "Aye. I will remember. We will all of us remember." Then he motioned me toward the castle doors, held open by two gaping Rudai. "Come. Time is fleeting. You need an hour's peace before we begin."

I could see no prospect of peace ever again.

*   *   *

I sat rigid in the dimness of my room . . . Denas's cold and barren room . . . staring at a miserable fire, trying to resist the urge to plunge my hand into it to remember what it felt like. Vyx had shooed everyone away, then made me promise not to do anything but sit and try to come to some balance within myself. "Free yourself of anger and fear, and things will look very different," he said. "You have done what you believed right—as did the rest of us. It is all any one of us can do. I'm sorry we had to keep this secret, that we could give you no time to learn more of Denas, but you know . . . now you know . . . that it was necessary. You possess a great deal of knowledge that you didn't before, but you must allow yourself to see it."

I didn't want to see. I wanted my own memories, my own knowledge and understanding. Nothing else. I buried my head in my arms and forced myself to take slow breaths. "The fire will burn worse than what I . . . we . . . felt earlier," I said through clenched teeth. "I will not put my hand in it. I may have use for a hand later, and I can't grow another one." Madness. But the urge faded quickly.

The semidarkness was soothing—quiet. For once the cold was welcome. My shirt was drenched with sweat. I blotted my forehead on my cloak.

We need to be on our way. There is much to be done. My body began to rise from the chair.

But I put it back again and held my seat firm. "I will go when I'm ready."

When you feel you are in control and can do only what you wish. That will never happen. I am not your slave.

"Nor am I yours." I stared into the darkest corner of the room, trying to make my eyes relax. They felt like glowing coals. And I needed to slow my heart before it burst, and settle my jangled head, or I was going to start screaming. Desperate for some kind of balance, I rose and began the first exercise of the kyanar.

Cursed ylad! Why did you do this if you care nothing for the outcome? There are preparations . . . and we must have the gateway ready to open when the hosts arrive. I must learn to work this damned flesh to get it done. Gennod may be stopped, but the vile ylad that you sent ahead is not— what blind stupidity. He plans to enter Kir'Navarrin before

*any of us and do whatever he thinks will bring this chaos . . .
the danger. He despises humans and rai-kirah equally. Have
you no sense?*

I spun and lunged forward, then drew back and curved
my arms into the second movement, struggling to put aside
my fear and horror, knowing that it was not possible, yet
finding comfort in the attempt itself. For the few moments
that I was lost in familiar practice, concentrating everything
upon the precise working of body and mind, I could pretend I was as I had always been.

*Have you gone mad? We thought you had strength of
mind. We thought you shared our purpose in your limited
human way. I did not give up my existence to dance. Powers
of earth, will you not listen? We have no time for this
jousting.*

I pressed outward with my arms, and pulled my foot back
slowly, deliberately, folding myself inward. One by one I
forced my body through the moves, pulling the charred
rubble of my soul into some semblance of order, shutting
out the anger and resentment blaring inside my ears, fighting his insistence that jerked at my limbs and demanded
my feet do other than I told them. I would hear him. I had
no choice. But only when I was ready.

After a time he fell silent, and soon the furious resistance
moderated. He was tired, too. "This is what I do to prepare
for battle," I said as I shifted into the tenth movement. "It
has served me well since I was a youth. Body and mind
must work in harmony to do the work I do." I began to
laugh as a man can do only when he is freed from fear
because his worst nightmare has come to pass. "Body and
mind, and *mind* will be more difficult."

Half an hour later, I knelt upon the cold floor in the
silence, my mind quiet, though my body was quivering like
a newborn lamb on a cold spring morning. "Now tell me
what I need to do."

CHAPTER 34

"You what?" I almost lost the delicate balance I had fought so hard to build. "Rebellion in the Empire! Verdonne's child, do you have any idea what that means in the human world?"

"We cannot exist in the human realm without bodies," said Kryddon, patiently. "We need a great number of them all at once. We need them . . . susceptible . . . to our entry. And we need them at the gateway. It was not our design. The Naghidda put it in place long ago, though he was planning to use these Khelid that you won free and do many other things that you would possibly find even more unpleasant. We looked for humans who were restless . . . greedy . . . all those things that cause human upheavals, and we decided to use what we found. We didn't know what else to do."

This was perhaps the most bizarre conversation I had ever held, more ridiculous than discussing surrender terms with a three-headed snake, more awkward than listening to the curses emanating from a dragon while held in its mouth and stabbing its tongue with an enchanted knife. Vyx was perched on the wide stone mantelpiece over Denas's hearth. Kryddon, Tovall, and Denkkar were settled on chairs in front of me, looking distinctly uncomfortable at my outburst, and Denas . . . Denas, of course, was in my head, exposing the details of the demon venture to retake Kir'Navarrin and scoffing at my "cowardly" reaction. *Humans are always at war or murdering one another. All we had to do was make sure it happened in the place we needed.*

"Once the gateway is open, we'll be gone, and the humans can settle their differences," said Vyx, his face wrin-

kled like a dried grape. His puzzled expression would have
been amusing if the matter had not been so appalling.

"So it's Rudai 'scouts' who have been driving the wedge
between the Derzhi nobles and the Emperor," I said, "trying to incite a battle that will just happen to take place at
Dasiet Homol. And you think to go merrily upon your way
into Kir'Navarrin, leaving us to say, 'Oh, sorry. I didn't
mean to hack you to pieces or burn your children in their
beds. It was an itch in my head, and now it's gone, let's be
brothers again? The world doesn't work that way. The Derzhi don't work that way. This will take years . . . murderous,
destructive, terrible years . . . to get over." If ever. And
Aleksander would reap the bloody harvest.

"Tell us another way, ylad," said Denkkar, his courtly
gentleman appearance everything of reason as we spoke of
thousands of deaths, years of tumult, and unending hatred
and vengeance. "All we want is to get to Kir'Navarrin."

I rested my head in my hands and tried to decide
whether to laugh or weep. Now it wasn't only one war I
had to stop. It was two.

*Why do you take this upon yourself? What do you care
for these people who are not your own? It's foolish. Pay
attention to matters of importance.*

"I seem to have made a bad habit of such foolishness of
late," I said. "Interfering in problems that are not my
own."

This is not the same. The pandye gash *caused our destruction, so it is only right that you help us recover from it.
These humans have caused their own problems.*

"You know nothing of humans. We—"

Those seated around me looked at me strangely, and I
realized what I was doing. They were privy only to half of
this discourse.

I'd hoped to see the world better, I said silently. Carrying
on these conversations in my head was exhausting. *And
Aleksander is the key. You should be able to figure it out.*
If Denas had access to my memories, then there was no
need for me to tell him everything.

*You are holding your memories very tightly. If you want
me to know, then you need to let go of them.*

Let go . . . exactly what I was afraid to do.

As I said. A coward. I should have expected it.

A slave is allowed no privacy. No modesty. On the day
Aleksander bought me from a slave merchant in Capharna,
I had been required to hobble across that cosmopolitan city
in chains, naked in the freezing weather and tethered to
the back of a horse. I had thought then that a man could
be no more exposed. But my thoughts had always—even
on that day—been my own. No more. Never again.

"Do any of you have an idea how far it's gone?" I said,
forcing my attention to the events at hand. "How close are
the rebels or the Emperor's men to the Place of the
Pillars?"

"One of my circle has just returned with word that a
human army approaches the gateway," said Tovall, her rich
voice as well suited to serious business as to laughter. "I
don't know which one. It is enough to begin, once the gateway is open."

"I've got to go now," I said, rising from my chair. "I've
got to stop this madness. I suppose I'll see the rest of you
at the gateway."

Not yet. The legion is not ready.

"What does it matter? You seem to forget there is a
body involved now. I have to go my own way. I assume
the legion knows how to get where they need to go."

*I must lead my gyossi from this castle to the legion. I
cannot sneak away like a murdering ylad, abandoning those
who have been faithful to me—or those who have not. They
will not arrive at the mustering point like miserable Gastai
who have forgotten their circle.*

"Within the hour or we leave them."

I didn't want to wait an hour. Nor a minute. Every minute gave Merryt time to work. It had been some twelve
hours since I had sent him on his way. The Place of the
Pillars was only two days' journey from my home . . . from
Ysanne and Catrin and the young Wardens. And those who
could weave threads of enchantment from the lands of the
Derzhi to Aifes waiting in Ezzaria certainly would have no
difficulty contacting the most remote settlements in our
land. The Ezzarians would come, and they would come
quickly.

I gave the orders that those who lived in the castle must

make ready to join the legion as soon as possible. The voice in my head had been impatient while I came to grips with what I had done. Now it was my turn to chafe as the complex protocols of the demon aristocracy took their course. Each gyos had to be notified in person by one of the Nevai captains—Tovall or Denkkar—and be given a dignified time to respond. Each had to decide—now that the time for the great venture had come—whether to stay or go. Most were going, of course. A few were afraid, and wanted to wait until they saw what fortune awaited in Kir'Navarrin. A few had made accommodations with Kir'Vagonoth and saw no reason to change. They wished to stay in the familiar castle until the last Gastai stopped hunting. A few had agreed to stay behind and make sure the mad Gastai were not let loose until provision was made for them in Kir'Navarrin. No decision was irrevocable, and, in many cases, a decision was made, only to be reversed as soon as the next gyos was notified and made his or her choice. And that, of course, took more time.

"If Myddluk is staying, then I, Flyynot, might as well go, for I'll never be raised in rank. Better to be in Kir'Navarrin as Denas's gyos, than here as Myddluk's."

"I'll not leave Wanevyl here alone. He cannot shape himself at all properly. And who knows what waits? Perhaps we'll begin to die."

"I have waited since the dark times to see Kir'Navarrin again, but if Grat is willing to hold the pits, then I will stay alongside. We'll come as soon as the word is given. Tell Denas . . . this ylad—what do we call him?—to make it soon."

It took forever. Fifty times I strode down the broad staircase to the vaulted atrium ready to set out, and fifty times I returned to my rooms ready to break furniture and tear down walls. I saw Aeno, a Rudai servant, refilling the wine vessel, and only half of Denas's gyossi were notified. While the messengers came and went, Vyx brought me a request that I visit one of the Rudai encampments. "Kryddon says his people are nervous and need to see you and hear your words again. It would give you something to do besides break things." Indeed there were piles of twisted papers, broken candles, bent spoons, and unraveled cloth scattered everywhere in my chambers. I could not keep my hands still. "Go on," he said. "I'll bring word when things are ready here."

I was glad to move. Though I desired nothing more than to proceed straight to Fiona's tower, I understood the need to reassure the circles. They remembered the dark times. The horror. We could not have that again. We would not.

As I walked out of the castle and bade farewell to a few gyossi who planned to remain in Kir'Vagonoth, my eye caught a glimmer of silver on a high, windswept balcony. Golden hair gleamed like a touch of sunlight in the murk. She would stay in Kir'Vagonoth. I knew it for a certainty . . . even as the consideration and every emotion it raised were cut off as swiftly and decisively as a Derzhi executioner removes a head. Vallyne had made no appearance since I'd left her in the candlelight of her resting room, yet I could no more summon a thought of her than I could sleep. I did not try to force the matter. I understood enough and guessed much more about why the lady had tried to destroy whatever of Seyonne might interfere with the one who took up residence in my soul. It had nothing to do with me. But as I turned away, she raised her hand and mine went up in reply. I was not privy to the communication that took place. He would not permit it. I turned and walked down the steps into the courtyard.

A horse was brought to me, but I said I would not need it.

You will do what? It is disgusting to shape flesh. I won't . . .

Only when he was fighting in the practice arena had I ever seen Denas assume a physical body. I understood his reluctance, his pride, but this body was mine, and I would not let him rule it. I had scarcely begun to summon the enchantment, when my extremities grew warm and flushed with such pleasurable tingling as if I had just drunk a barrel of summer ale. Then came the onslaught . . . a surge of glorious melydda that nearly stopped my heart . . . and my wings unfolded as swiftly and easily as the sunlight spreads at dawn.

Oh, storm of darkness . . . how is this possible?

I had never known anything like. Not in myself. I had seen such exhilaration once—on a young man's face in the

Makai Narrows, as he transformed himself and set off to save the lives of his outlaw band. I soared into the driving wind, not fighting it awkward and graceless, but sensing every whisper, every eddy, every nuance of the storm, and knowing how to glide through it, under it, using it, shaping it to serve my need, to bear me up. For that moment the two minds who lived in my body were one in awe at what we made together.

We could have made a thousand other shapes—a wolf to run swiftly, a dragon to breathe such fire that would melt the snows of that wasteland. We could have become a horse finer than Aleksander's prizes, or found warmth and comfort and monumental strength in the thick fur of a Makhara bear. But I was made for wings, and there was nothing more I could desire. Every moment of that brief flight was completion.

My pleasure was short-lived. I circled the flickering lights of the Rudai encampment, and by the time I touched my feet to the snowy plains, every demon eye was on me. My skin burning, I pushed my way into the crowd, as if I could hide among the light-drawn shapes. The flat roof of the dark low buildings offered a venue from which to exhort the crowd as I had done from the castle steps. But instead I found myself speaking to each one alone. They crowded close, their luminous faces fearful, tentative, flickering on the edge of hope and terror. Some of them touched my skin that glowed golden in the darkness.

"To Kir'Navarrin," I said. "Home. It is the first step." I didn't know what would come after. We would learn that when we had made the passage safely. "Be easy on the vessel that you choose," I told a broad-shouldered youth whose essence was deepest green. "You are only borrowing the body, and the host will be frightened and in pain." A thick, rugged fist gripped my hand, and I turned to meet the bold eye of blue fire. "You must not use that fear and pain, for it is not yours. You have no right to it." A haggard woman brushed her fingers on my cloak. "You deserve your own life, not one that is borrowed or stolen. We'll find it in Kir'Navarrin."

The visit took much longer than I had intended, and I lost track of the time. But I was just speaking to the last of them when a messenger appeared at my side. "Your gyossi are prepared, and Vyx told them to come ahead. They'll meet you on the way. No need for you to go all the way back to the castle."

I walked into the stormy darkness beyond the perimeter of the Rudai camp toward the castle, trying to think how I would proceed once I stepped into the world of light. Try to see Ysanne? Try to find Aleksander? Open the gateway? There was no way to know how long that might take, and someone had to make sure that Merryt was kept out until this mysterious fortress—the fortress beyond the gamarand wood, the source of corruption that caused the rare and beautiful forest to smolder from the inside out—was secured. And the human war had to be stopped before there was irrevocable bloodshed—which meant Aleksander had to have something other than a sword's point to give his rebellious nobles, something that would not demean him to yield.

My steps slowed as the magnitude of the tasks weighed heavy. I stood at the crest of a snowy rise, waiting and thinking, my attention focused inward . . . until I looked up and saw my gyossi mounted on their illusory beasts, riding out of my castle. Luminous, tall, magnificently beautiful. Proud, as well they should be. They had survived horror, made what bargains and compromises were necessary with what they had been left, and shaped beauty from nothing. They had learned to dance again, and to laugh.

I waited for them to come to me. They did not need a lord to lead them into the wilderness. Each one of them should rightly hold that place of honor. Vyx led my own horse, decked out in trappings of black and silver, and when they had traversed their winding way through the snowy hillocks to my position, the column slowed and waited for me to mount. Vyx handed me the reins, looking at me strangely. It was only after I had thrown my leg over the saddle and kicked the beast into movement that I understood my friend's expression. I had seen it all before: the column of shimmering demons riding over the arched bridge . . . the howling wind . . . the riderless horse . . . the one arrayed in black and silver waiting for them in the stormy darkness . . . The demon. The doom of the world. Me.

CHAPTER 35

"What am I?" I shoved Vyx's slender frame against the gray stone wall, calling up the power that would prevent his shifting into light and out of my grasp. "What else do you plan for me to do?"

I had led the column of riders to the Nevai camp that adjoined Kryddon's Rudai, dismissed them into Tovall's temporary command, then grabbed Vyx and dragged him to this shadowed corner of two snow-draped shelters. Horror, fury, dread . . . I was beside myself. My dream was so vivid I could not bear to consider it. Before I went one more step down this terrible path, I had to understand.

"I don't know," said Vyx, the first time I had ever seen him worried. "I sent the visioning, yes. I held a tether to your spirit all that time, hoping to draw you here. You had the strength and power that we needed so desperately, and I believed that fortune or gods or fate or whatever might rule such matters had at last smiled upon us in our desperate hour. Denas had already chosen to go. He is . . . was . . . my friend and brother as much as any one of us can be, and I would have none but a human of honor and purpose to join with him. But this part of the image . . . the one who waits . . . the destroyer . . . I didn't—"

"The destroyer. Gods of night, what am I going to do?"

"I cannot see the future, ylad. My talents are not so great as that. I showed you our sorrow—this horror that is Kir'Vagonoth. I showed you our form, so that perhaps you would not be afraid. I touched you with the hunger to come here and the warning that danger was waiting if you did not come. But I never gave that danger a shape. I swear to you that this portion of the image was not of my doing.

I believed it was a creation of your own fears adding to what I had wrought. I can tell you nothing more."

"You tried to destroy my mind. How can I believe you?"

"We have entrusted our fate to you." He raised his hands over his head helplessly. "If you believe that any rai-kirah can make you do what you are unwilling to do, then you've not looked at your own power. Tell me who speaks right now. Tell me who it is holds me here most uncomfortably against this wall. It is not Denas, who would never touch me ill."

I held him pinned for a time, searching his demon eyes, seeking answers, lies, truth . . . But there was nothing but his words and what sincerity a face could express while centered with demon fire. Snowflakes blown from the roof behind him dusted his curling hair. I released the enchantment, and shoved Vyx away, pulling my cloak tight with bloodless hands.

"If you have changed your mind, friend Seyonne, please tell us now."

There was nothing else to do, of course. I had made the only possible choice. Those I loved were depending on me. But no matter what the truth of Ezzarian origins, I did not feel whole. I felt diseased.

Your child . . . a son . . . is joined . . . and this other, too . . . joined, not taken . . . Born and nurtured in the human realm. How is this possible?

I wanted him silent. "Leave me alone. I need to get to the gateway. It may already be too late to prevent disaster." But, of course, no matter how I tried to keep my focus strictly on events, the story of my son and Blaise unfolded in my mind. No secrets. Ever.

I flew to Fiona's tower, and even such a wonder as the shaping of my wings could not ease my dread. "Aife!" I called.

I never thought to invoke that name.

"I never thought to walk a portal bearing a demon." Our bitterness pushed against each other like the two giants of legend—Night and Day—who grappled throughout eternity, so equally matched that the sky settled to rest upon their backs. When Night took a slight advantage, it became winter, and Day's advantage brought spring, but if one or the other was to prevail . . . There the story gave me pause. If either was ever to prevail, the sky would fall.

Warden! Verdonne's child, I was so afraid . . . The gray doorway took form in the frigid air, and beyond it the dawn, the first flush of pink ravishing the lingering night. Without a backward glance, I . . . we . . . stepped through the portal.

I gasped at the touch of warm air on my skin. Indeed I fought the temptation to remove my clothes so as to feel it on every part of me. I told myself I would fry my skin— even my dusky Ezzarian skin—with too much sunlight after so long without. I looked like the belly of a worm. And sight . . . how was I going to take my eyes from the sun, whose fiery edge was teasing at the horizon? A few moments too long, and it would be the last thing I ever saw. Yet if one were to be blind, what better way than gazing at the sunrise after a thousand years of twilight?

Life was awakening around me. A twittering grassbird streaked through the air by my ear, its hunting song mimicking the melodious rasp of a locust. A desert lark whistled its morning plaint. A brown rabbit twitched its whiskers, waiting to see what I would do before making the next move in its morning's rituals. Red streaks shot from the brown edge of the world, the sere and rocky grasslands of southwestern Manganar. I recognized them. For eight days I had walked and run over those rolling hills, waiting for Aleksander.

I whirled about, and in the distance, blushing with the color of the morning, stood the lines of pillars stretching north in ancient majesty toward the deserts of Azhakstan and south to the mountains, the border of Ezzaria. The gateway. Waiting. Instructions scribed on each pillar: the words to be spoken, the patterns to be drawn, the magic to be wrought . . . the seals at each pair to be unlocked. The last of the passages between the two worlds, blocked and barricaded, yet left unbroken as if, even in those dark times, someone suspected that it might be needed once again. Was it a lapse of caution or a gamble taken willingly? Or was it so difficult to unlock that it hadn't been worth the pain to destroy it? I had no idea how long it might take to do the deed, even assuming the inscriptions had not been erased by a millennium of wind-driven sand and rain.

But though my thoughts were already trying to unravel the puzzle waiting in the pillars, my eyes did not linger on the gateway, but fell to the white-robed young woman kneeling in the grass beside a snoring round-faced man.

The Aife. One Aife of many . . . We were never sure there was more than one.

They were tucked into a shallow depression in the land, shaded by a roof of tall-growing weeds. Beside them burned a small fire, and as a wisp of its scented smoke found its way to my nose, I gagged and felt a sudden oppression of nauseating, soul-darkening dread. I wanted to run . . . to escape . . . to hold off the horror that was sure to follow . . . and I found myself recoiling from the woman and her stinking fire. Jasnyr. Even as I identified the scent and understood that my moment's distress was only someone else's thousand-year memory, a blight fell upon my own spirit. Only rai-kirah were sickened by jasnyr.

Fiona sighed and rubbed her arms, then lifted her head to look for me. Quickly I pulled up the hood of my cloak . . . a knot tying itself in my stomach. I could not let her see. Not yet.

"Warden!" She jumped to her feet and her thin face brightened, then clouded again as I backed away from her. "Are you all right?"

"I'm well. Fine. The others? Where—"

"Down the hill by the spring. I didn't want them stumbling over us."

"And Merryt?"

"I've not seen him since we arrived here night before last. He was off right away. Said he'd have the warning delivered before we could get to sleep." She leaned her head to the side and stepped closer again. "What's wrong?"

I tried not to back away so obviously as the first time. "Everything's wrong. Merryt . . . I misjudged him. He's not going to warn the Ezzarians; he's going to bring them here to get them slaughtered. For vengeance. We've got to keep them away, Fiona, and we've got to keep Merryt out of Kir'Navarrin. And two Derzhi armies are close by, planning

to destroy each other, and we're all going to be caught in
the middle of it if we don't—"

"I mean, what's wrong with you? I felt it when I wove
the portal yesterday, and again today. Are you ill? Why is
your face covered?"

"It's the sun. After so long without . . . all these months.
When I was with you in the temple, it was night." As I
made my limp excuses, I held onto my hood lest the determined young woman decide to rip it away. "We've got to
move fast. Does Merryt know where you are?"

"No. He left us at the pillars, saying he'd be back to help
once he gave your message. I couldn't grasp why you
trusted him. I never let go of my knife when he was around.
He kept looking at me . . . unseemly. When he was gone,
we moved down here to stay private. You never told me
what was going to happen here, and I had no intention of
being in the middle of it. A little more explanation would
be useful."

"Ah, gods, Fiona . . . I'm sorry . . ." But I stopped
myself. I was not yet ready to tell everything. "I've no time
right now. Just stay hidden. I can help Blaise as soon as
the gateway's open. How is he?"

"I'll show you." With a quick look of skepticism and a
brief examination of the snoring Balthar, she led me down
the hill to a rocky cleft, hidden behind a thick stand of
gray, spiny buckthorns. Between the cleft and the trees was
a spring, the shallow depression filled with lush green grass.
A flurry of pipits and grassbirds fluttered upward from the
grass as we approached, twittering in protest at the
disturbance.

Kyor was sleeping in the stone-like dedication of youth,
curled up on bare ground, his smooth bronze cheek resting
on one arm. He lay across a shaded notch in the rock,
making it difficult for anyone to get in or out of it without
stepping on him. In the shadows of the cleft huddled Blaise,
the blue fire of his eyes lending a morbid cast to his haggard face. He sat unmoving, staring into nothingness. Trem-
ors rippled unceasingly through his body. With each one, a
portion of his body would shift slightly, a finger into a claw,
ears into those of a wolf, skin into feathers or scales. With

the next tremor, that part would revert to itself again while another part changed.

I stepped carefully around the sleeping Kyor—which had the boy up with his knife blade ready. I stayed his hand before he could slash the veins in my thigh. "It's all right, Kyor."

"Master Seyonne? Is it time? He needs—"

"Not yet. Soon." I crouched in front of Blaise, laying a hand on his head, wishing I knew what might ease him.

The passing rite. He needs to bathe in the Naiori Fonte, or he'll never retake himself. His true being screams. I didn't credit your beliefs about him . . . joined since birth . . .

Indeed I could hear Blaise's silent agony tearing at my inner hearing. "The Naori Fonte . . . the Well of the Spirits," I said. "I'll get you there—I promise—and this torment will end."

"What's that?" Fiona spoke from behind Kyor.

"It's a pool in Kir'Navarrin. He needs to find it . . . bathe in it. It will ease this madness. Reverse it, if it's possible, while the land itself does its work with him."

The knowledge of it was unfolding within me, accompanied by a disbelieving whisper. *Joined since birth . . . whole . . . Not possible. We are not part of you. I won't believe it.*

"The time of passing is different for every person," I went on, trying to sort the fragments of memory from the raging denial. "It comes to some as young as twelve, some as old as fifty. For some it lasts a day; for some many years. It is the time of choice . . . when you decide what is the shape of your desire, the one written in your body and your power, the one you will spend the rest of your life exploring and perfecting. Until your passing time, you can change into many things, but afterward, only the one. It is the part of our melydda that comes from our true homeland, bound up in it, just as the melydda you know is bound up in the trees and grass of Ezzaria."

I felt Fiona's stare burning a hole in my back. "You've learned a great deal in a day and a half."

It had been more like the space of a heartbeat. "I've got to go up to the ruin now," I said. "Have him ready, Kyor. As soon as it's dark, get him to the southern end of the pillars. When the time comes, we'll have to be fast." I laid my hand on the Ezzarian boy's slim shoulder, then walked into the growing sunlight away from Fiona. I embraced the air and light, the scents and sounds of the sweet morning: the smell of the dry grass, wild hyssop, and sage, their pungent scents released by the touch of warmth, the rasp of bees and the chitter of the knackees, the tiny rodents burrowing under the tufted wheat grass.

"You're going to do this thing . . . unlock the darkness that we saw in the mosaic." Fiona had followed me.

"I'm going to unlock the portal to Kir'Navarrin, yes. But the evil . . . Whatever it is, it's also locked away. The blot we saw in the mosaic is a fortress beyond the gateway, and I'm going to do my best to keep it secure. Merryt wishes otherwise, and that's why we can't let him in."

"Before you do it, I have to show you something," said Fiona. "It fell out of Balthar's pocket yesterday when I put him to sleep." From her own tunic she withdrew a wad of dirty cloth just larger than her hand. As she pulled away the cloth to expose its contents, she looked toward me, as if to ask whether I understood what it was. Three shards of chipped stone, flat on the back, colored very simply. Fiona had arranged the three pieces to fit together along the interior breaks, forming a painted square outlined in red.

"The fourth square. The fourth vision of the Seer."

Fiona nodded and continued to hold it steady as I sought the meaning. In truth, its puzzle was the simplest to unravel of all the mosaic. The interior of the square was completely black, a midnight ebony that might have been a shaft penetrating the bowels of the earth or the sky behind the glimmering stars. I touched the broken tile and felt the blood leave my face—my guilt-marked face still hidden behind the shadows of my hood. I had lived in that darkness, the remnant of overriding nothingness where the mad Gastai had shaped a prison to their liking. Fiona, in maintaining her connection with me through my time of torment, had touched it, too, and I felt her quivering revulsion as she gazed upon the square. But what I had survived and she had touched was only a small part of what was to come.

"What is it? Is it the place where you were? It feels the same. Is this what you call Kir'Navarrin?"

"All this is but legend," said Balthar, who had come up behind Fiona. "Seeings are not truth, not in the way we think of truth. They are only possibilities." The old man's arms were wrapped around his belly, and his eyes were fixed on the chips of stone. He was near weeping. "It could all be wrong."

I laid a hand on Balthar's arm, trying to comfort him, even as the words rose up from the depths of my memory. "Woe to the man who unlocks the prison of the Nameless God, for there will be such a wrath of fire and destruction laid upon the earth as no mortal being can imagine. And it will be called the Day of Ending, the last day of the world."

"That's from the story of Verdonne and Valdis," said Fiona, puzzled. "What does that have to do with anything?"

"I don't know." My theories were too vague and ill formed to speak of as yet. But as I looked upon the tile and ran my fingers around the red border, the ancient artifact became familiar, as if I had played a role in its shaping. It was with conviction that I continued. "Fazzia envisioned the winged man unlocking the gateway—remember that he was on the *outside* of the gateway with the key—and she envisioned this dreadful ending. But one vision does not follow from the other. Balthar is right that prophecies are only possibilities. Warnings. I believe that this results only if the fortress itself is unlocked. Remember they had lived alongside the fortress for a long time. The mosaic shows that they moved freely between this world and Kir'Navarrin." I tapped my finger on the black tile. "This does not mean that I'll do the deed, or that I'm wrong to try to heal the wound we caused."

Fiona shook her head. "But these elders would know such things about prophecy. If it was only a warning . . . unlikely to happen . . . then why would they destroy themselves?"

"Think of it, Fiona. A Seer has these visions . . . a woman well-known for the accuracy and wisdom of her insights. Imagine how the elders felt . . . that one of their own could be the cause of such horror as this. So how do they make the world safe? Remove the ability to shift, and you will never have a man with wings to unlock anything."

Balthar nodded slightly. "And destroy all records of the place, eradicate every memory of it, and no one will ever try to go back and take the risk. It is far easier to hide from a disaster than to decide how to prevent it or to remedy it."

"Exactly. Only we didn't count on the result," I said. "The great flaw in our plan. The piece of ourselves we ripped away didn't die. Thus the demon war and our responsibility to fight it. Us alone. And without understanding, lest we cause the very thing we set out to prevent." I shook my head with the irony of it. "You can't hide from true prophecy. With all their work, their pain, their terrible choices . . . we stand at this place anyway. All we can do is try to put things right." Such a surge of longing came over me that I could scarcely speak. "We remember, and we want to go home. We must go back."

"Go home? Go back? So you're not just opening the gateway for Blaise." Slowly Fiona folded the dirty kerchief over the artifact, fixing her eyes upon it as she did so. " 'We remember . . . We want . . .' We."

The round-faced old man gaped at me. "Fazzia! How did you know the Seer's name? I only discovered it a few weeks ago. It was not in any of our lore. All these years we thought the Seer was called Eddaus, but I found out he was only the scribe. Your interpretation does make sense. Of course it would be the elders of the people who would decide on such a drastic course of action. I've hidden this tile all these months. It was too terrible to think about. And then this girl tells me that you are the one with wings and were speaking of 'opening a gateway.' I came near prostration with it. All this you've discovered . . . was it from the demons that you learned it? Can it be believed?"

Balthar's prattling might have continued forever. But I wasn't listening. Rather, I was watching Fiona. A warm wind caught a few strands of her dark hair and whipped them in her face—her grave, still face with lips pressed tightly together. She tied the string around the bundle and gave it to Balthar, then raised her eyes to me. "Take off your cloak, Seyonne. It's autumn in southern Manganar.

Why would you need it?" Her voice was quiet. Expressionless.

I had known she would not be put off. Whatever dogged question had kept her with me all these months would be answered the moment I lowered my hood. I had not Blaise's skill to mask what I had become. She would name me Abomination—the ultimate corruption of a Warden—and she would leave. I hated the thought of it. But I could not lie to one who had held faithful for so long. "I didn't want to disturb you with things that cannot be undone."

"Disturb me or disgust me?"

Balthar looked from one to the other of us as if trying to discover where he had lost track of the conversation.

"It's the only way, Fiona. Believe me when I say this: with everything I have been, I wish the answer could have been other. But I have to do what I believe right, what is necessary . . ."

" . . . no matter who it destroys." Her composure was like a silken garment, fitted so tightly that I could see her fury ready to burst through. "You're going to take the demons through this portal."

"I hope that there will be a great deal more saving than destruction. That's the whole idea."

"Show me."

"As you wish." I lowered my hood and faced her only long enough to glimpse her thin face redrawn by shock and revulsion . . . then I closed my eyes, folded my arms upon my chest, and transformed.

From the first day I had shaped my wings beyond the portal, when I was a cocky young Warden of eighteen, my most profound desire had been to take flight into a brilliant morning of the human world. Yet I could take no joy from it on that bright morning in Manganar. Not when I looked down and saw Fiona turn her head away, and Kyor restraining Blaise as the mad outlaw cried out after me in agonized yearning. Only Balthar the Villain stood gaping and grinning, his sin at last eclipsed by someone else's.

No point in going back. Kyor would keep Blaise where he was until time to move him to the gateway. Fiona would run back to the Ezzarians and tell them of corruption fulfilled. Best to get on with the impossibilities of the day.

I flew high above the arid grassland that was scarred so strangely with the double white line of the pillars, looking to see how much time I had to work on the gateway. Not long. Twelve leagues west of the pillars was a rolling cloud of dust, a sizable force—perhaps seven hundred mounted warriors. Three banners. At least three Derzhi houses in rebellion. It was inconceivable. Ten leagues northeast was a smaller cloud of dust—perhaps five hundred . . . but the banners told me they were Aleksander's prize troops, and the Prince's own pennant flapped boldly at the front. They would all be in place by nightfall, when the restless fears and angers of battle's eve would give the demon legion the opening they had planned. It was tempting to fly south to seek signs of the Ezzarian passage through the mountains, but it was more important to unravel the enchantments of the gate. Not all of them. Just enough that I could finish the job quickly when the time came. I had no idea what I was going to do about the Ezzarians as yet.

I touched earth at the southernmost pair of pillars. Sixty such pairs of pillars stretched before me for a quarter of a league across the rolling sea of golden, knee-high grass. To unravel the enchantments binding this vast forest of stone was a daunting prospect, especially as I had not the least idea how to begin.

For each pair there is a spell-pattern buried in the writing. Each pattern must be realized precisely, threaded with power, then joined with each other one to form a spell-working that is the key to open the gateway.

I should have known the answer would come. It was the reason I had done the unthinkable. I walked to the first pillar and examined the band of characters carved into the white stone. It was gibberish.

Let me see it.

"You have my eyes. Use them. Tell me what it means."

You must allow it. Must I beg? Grovel?

I closed my eyes and wrestled with anger, forcing away the memory of Fiona's horror, trying not to imagine what it was she had seen: pale blue fire in my eye sockets where there should be Ezzarian black. Did she smell me, too? Had she heard the soul-devouring music lapping at the edges of my words? Seen gut-twisting gold light at the edges of my body?

Enough. You settled this long hours ago. What's done is done. What's not done is waiting only on you. So do it.

I forced my eyes to relax. To let go. With conscious will I relinquished my hands and my tongue and the melydda that I had carried with me since I first breathed the air of the world. I gave them all up to service the work I had chosen, and when I opened my eyes again, the words and symbols scribed on the pillar made perfect sense.

CHAPTER 36

The shadows were long on the brown hills the next time I looked out from the line of pillars, and my mind was awash in enchantment. Never had I imagined the kind of complexity used to seal the Kir'Navarrin gateway: tangled intricacies of words and gestures, senses and abstractions, mental acrobatics so strenuous that demon combat seemed tame. I had to cast fragile lines of magical commands into the teeming ocean of enchantments that comprise the natural world, wait until I felt a response no easier to notice than the pressure of a snowflake landing on my hair, then snatch it in before a gnat could twitch its eye, and weave the answer into the key that I was building.

Of course, it is easy to say that I was the one who did all this, but, in truth, it was the demon. He wielded my sight and hearing, my touch and taste and smell in this combat of sorcery as a Derzhi warrior uses his sword, his horse, his body, knife, and whip to define and encompass the art of war. Though I brought my own mind and experience to bear upon the problems we had to solve, I neither moved nor spoke without his bidding, and the farther we progressed through the sixty pairs of pillars, the more completely I was forced to rely upon his instruction. If ever a being was born to ride a horse or rule an empire, I believed it was Aleksander; but if ever one was born to wield melydda, it was Denas.

Enough. We'll not open the last pair until they come. The ylad lurks somewhere nearby, waiting to get through the gate before anyone can stop him, but Vyx must go through first.

"Vyx?"

Vyx is not the fool he appears . . . He said no more than this. Articulated words were becoming less necessary as the hours of our joining accumulated. A single thought from either of us would open up the associated portion of memory, understanding, and knowledge to the other. With this brief reference to the mischievous architect of my corruption, I learned that Vyx could have accomplished the work we had just done in half the time it had taken us, and that if any being, mortal or immortal, could prevent the breach of the fortress, it was the slender, teasing demon. The easy acquisition of such understanding did not preclude astonishment at the revelation.

I was mortally tired. I could not remember when I had last slept. My head was swimming with the enchantments I had learned in the past hours, a level of complexity the finest Ezzarian scholars had never imagined. And my stomach was gnawing on itself, having had nothing in it for far too long. But before trying to deal with hunger and steal some rest, I needed to see how the landscape of disaster had changed in the hours I had worked.

There were too many eyes about to consider my usual form, so I searched out what new knowledge I might have of shapeshifting. My demon partner did not deign to speak—his disdain of flesh was doubled for beastflesh. But after a number of false starts and considerable discomfort, I managed to conjure myself the body of a falcon . . . and instantly believed I'd made a terrible mistake. I came near choking with the panicked suffocation of close confinement. But it was only for a moment, until I experienced the efficiencies of a body shaped for flight and the usefulness of eyes designed to see the small creatures scuttering through the dry grass far below—creatures that quickly satisfied the cravings of my empty stomach. I smiled inside my feathered head. Soldiers' eyes would be turned to the sky, watching for omens. Seeing a falcon, the symbol of Aleksander's house, might give the rebels pause.

The royal encampment and the rebels were situated a short distance east of the line of pillars, separated from each other only by a line of low hills. The rebels had the superior position, a wide plateau pushed up when some upheaval fractured the earth around it. To reach them, the Prince's troops would have to climb a short escarpment. They would be vulnerable the moment they came over the edge. If the rebels had good bowmen, a great number of Aleksander's men would die.

I swooped low toward a small forest of fluttering standards on the barren summit of a hill halfway between the two camps. A cluster of men stood posturing at each other, airing their grievances, no doubt, making demands, stating terms. I passed very quickly near them, only long enough to glimpse angry faces and to hear indecipherable snatches of their bellicose rumblings. One man strode away from the group to the crest of the hill, the sunlight glinting off his red hair and the gold trappings of his rank. I circled and cried out to him, the harsh screech echoing from the hills. He stood, arms folded tightly across his breast, his anger rising like the heat shimmers from the dry ground. *Hold, my Prince. Hold. This is not real. You are meant for better things.*

I continued to circle until the negotiations broke off. The rebels mounted and rode away first, an inconceivable insult to the Emperor's son. Aleksander threw himself onto his horse and spurred the beast furiously down the hill to the north. He was seeing blood, no doubt, yet I didn't believe he would fight that night. Derzhi valued their horses too much to drive them on a long journey, then risk injuring them in the dark. Dawn would bring the killing. And the night . . . they had no idea. The night would bring the demons.

It was difficult to abandon my watch on the encampments. However sure I was of Derzhi custom, who knew what to expect when festering resentments had been manipulated by rai-kirah? I needed to meet with Aleksander, but he would be busy for the next few hours, planning for the assault—I had not the least hope that any other solution would present itself—and I needed him alone. To get him to listen to me would take some persuading, and to allow his subjects to observe the process would be unwise. I just prayed I could think of some way to convince him to forego this battle.

Despite my anxiety, I had to give up my vigil at last. My mind was turning to porridge.

Sleep . . . it is like death, I think. Why do we yearn for it so?

I was too tired to attempt an answer. I flew back to Dasiet Homol, grabbed my discarded cloak, and sprawled out in the shade of the first pillar, unable to worry or plan or weigh the future. For a nervous moment I wondered what dreams might infest a demon's night, but, in truth, I slept like a dead man.

I believed it was a lamp shining in my face that woke me, or perhaps a demon who had shaped a single round bright eye, but then waking memory struck, and the world settled into its proper shape . . . and I recognized a gloriously beautiful full moon hanging huge on the dark edge of the east. With newborn awe I examined the silver-edged shadows and the transformation of the stark landscape into luminous mystery, so different from the day's brilliance just fading into the west. Every rock and scrubby tree, every blade of grass, even my own hand was made clean and new when washed in silver. The pillars towered above me in eerie majesty.

But there was no time to contemplate the scene. Though I had slept no more than two hours, something had changed. As I sat in the shadows of the Kir'Navarrin gateway, I felt an uneasy pulse in the veins of the world. I needed to get to Aleksander. The demons were coming . . . and the Ezzarians would soon follow . . . and I had no solution for any of them.

Sometimes a seemingly impenetrable wall is so precariously built that to move but a single pebble will cause it to crumble. So it was with the first of my dilemmas. A simple, fleeting image gave me the solution for Aleksander. Before setting out to find the Prince, I took stock of the enchantment I had constructed, to make sure that no unseen hand had intruded on its fragile perfection while I slept. The key, glinting silver, hung in the dark center of my mind like a sword of light. Yvor Lukash . . . Like a dying star, the name blazed through my consciousness. Of course. Aleksander needed something to give his rebellious nobles, and I had just the right thing for him to offer.

Soon I was in the air, in the bird shape again, gliding northeast through the warm, heavy air into the heart of the Derzhi royal camp. I perched on one ridgepole of Alek-

sander's tent, and contemplated the two heavily armed
Derzhi who stood beside the door flap.

Lure them away. You have many other forms.

But I was too impatient to learn another form; it required
more concentration than I wanted to spend. Instead, I used
a less sophisticated tactic. I spread my wings and flew right
into their faces, one and then the other, screeching loudly,
flapping wings in their eyes, and catching their braids in my
claws. Only a moment's assault, then I flew to the top of
an adjacent tent, leaving the two cursing and flailing. I
didn't give them time to think, but flew at them again.
Noisier. More vicious. I raked their faces with my talons.
The third time, they came after me. I led them a short
distance into a crowded row of tents, so that they were
crashing over men's legs and weapons, stumbling through
the watch fires, and kicking over the supper pots, then left
them explaining to their fellows what they were hunting,
while I circled back to Aleksander's tent. With one thought,
I returned to my own form. With one gesture I snuffed the
blazing torches. And with one look over my shoulder, I
slipped quietly into the royal tent.

A single candle flame cast its soft glow over the thick,
richly colored rug spread throughout the small enclosure.
This rug was the only luxury Aleksander allowed himself
when riding to war. He refused to be slowed by wagons
filled with the vast tent, gold dishes, and elaborate furnishings available to the Emperor's son, but he hated sleeping
on bare ground. The Prince was brooding, sitting with his
back against his war saddle, his long arms propped on his
knees, one soft boot tapping furiously on the blue and red
rug like a woodpecker on a dead oak.

I held still, wrapping my dark cloak about my face and
sitting in the deepest shadow of the corner by the door
until his guards begged entry and reported that the commotion outside had only been a mad bird. "A demon bird,
Your Highness. I've never seen the like, attacking a man."

"I hope you were victorious. If you can't wring a bird's
neck, how will you gut a traitor?"

"We will destroy the insolent Hamraschi, my lord." The
guard didn't mention that the bird had escaped him—or

that the vicious bird was Aleksander's own symbol. Wringing its neck would have been the worst of omens.

Aleksander dismissed the man with a jerk of his hand, then drew his knife, laid it on the rug beside him, and stretched out on his back as if to sleep. I moved quickly. Before any harm could be done, I had a firm grip on his wrist, making sure his gleaming blade was nowhere near my vital parts.

"A sneaking rebel assassin!" Despite my tight hold, he twisted in my grasp and aimed a knee at my gut, but before he could get any leverage, I had him in a less comfortable position—on his face with my knee in his back and both of his arms pinned behind him. He didn't like it in the least, and it took more force than I wanted to use to persuade him to lay still. He still refused to give in. "Hamraschi bastards! First you turn on your rightful Emperor, and now you stoop to cowardly murder. Your hands should be cut off for touching your anointed Prince. How can you claim to be Derzhi warriors? May your fathers and grandfathers rot—"

"I wish you no harm, my lord. Listen to my voice. I am not your enemy." We were never going to get anywhere if he didn't listen.

"Bloody Athos . . . " I tried to convince myself that there was some hint of relief or pleasure in his surprised recognition, but, if so, it was quickly dismissed. Though he no longer fought me, his flesh was rigid. "So you've joined the rebellious vermin. Were the pitiful outlaws not followers enough?" His disgust swelled into monumental fury. "By my father's head, if you've had a hand in this, I'll enslave every last Ezzarian that breathes. I'll—"

"Please, my lord, I need you to listen."

"I warned you—"

"Neither the Ezzarians nor I have violated your commands, my lord, and I care only for your good. All I ask right now is that you hear me out." I kicked his knife well away, then let go of him, retreating to my shadowed corner of the tent while he sat up, rubbing his wrists. I motioned him backward to lean against his saddle again. I kept my hood drawn up, and hoped he remembered enough of my warrior's skills not to test me further.

Though his face was scarlet, he remained well behaved, folding his knotted arms across his chest, as if daring me to breach the wall between us.

"I've come to help you out of your dilemma."

"Ah, you're going to 'serve me' again! Will you lead Hamrasch and his traitors into battle? Kill a few of my warriors, steal a few more of my horses, put these villains in control of my father's throne? Such service as yours, an empire could do without."

"This battle must not happen."

"Your outlaw rabble has held quiet these past weeks. I'd think you needed more excitement."

I wondered yet again if there was any man born more stubborn than Aleksander. "Tell me, my lord, what would it take to send these nobles on their way without bloodshed and without dishonor to you or themselves?"

"If you've turned craven at your treachery, you should have considered asking such a question a bit earlier."

I tried to hold patience. "Leave your pride behind for just one moment, my lord. Think back to the Khelid, to the things we experienced and the things we learned together. As vast and powerful as your empire is, the universe is much larger, and its right ordering is far more important. When we last spoke, I was searching for answers to some of the questions the universe had presented to me . . . and I've found a number of them. Not all. Far from all. But I'll swear on the blood I shed for you, on the lives of my wife and my son and my people, that this conflict is not of human making. These nobles have been goaded into action against you. Yes, they have grievances with you and your father, and I have no doubt that injuries have been done on both sides that seem irreconcilable, but you must believe me that only evil purpose will be served by bloodshed."

"You think you can explain away treachery with more of your demon stories? These rebels have insulted their Emperor. Disobeyed him. They will die for it."

So onward to my only play. "If you gave them the Yvor Lukash, my lord, and said that you had put down the outlaw raiders and that your nobles would be bothered with them no more . . . would that be enough?"

"You are vile." He spat toward my feet. "Have you no honor, even with outlaws?"

"I am not betraying them. Rather, I'm going to convince my friends that there are larger issues facing us, and that humans do nothing but set back their goals by pecking each other into frenzy. I'm going to convince them of *your* honor, my lord, and that you're looking for ways to make the world better. I believe I can make them listen. Will that help you?"

"You think you can persuade your 'friends' to give up their leader to Derzhi barons? If you're not the thieving traitor I've named you, then you are a fool and a madman."

"I promise you'll have someone to give them. Someone who fits the description of the Yvor Lukash in a most convincing manner. The activities of the outlaws—those that violate your trust and prevent your working for good—will cease. I swear it."

The flush of anger on Aleksander's face cooled instantly. He peered into the darkness that I had drawn deeper about myself. "You. You're saying you'll give yourself up to stop a Derzhi war . . ."—his curiosity unsatisfied, he settled back against the saddle—"and then escape, no doubt. Work some sorcery to stab me in the back." But he didn't say it as if he believed it. I had breached the wall.

"Think back to a few moments ago, my lord. I've no need to work sorcery to stab you in the back."

I had thought his skin could get no brighter red. "What kind of warrior sneaks up on a sleeping man?"

I could not help but grin at his grumbling. "I've a number of other things I must do tonight. But if you can find a way to convince your unhappy countrymen that you've resolved their grievances as you always said you would and that you'll give them their enemy to prove it, I'll come back at midday tomorrow and do whatever you ask of me."

"They'll cut out your heart."

"There are things worse, my lord. They can't put it back and do it over."

The legion comes!

The hairs on my arms rose and fingers of dread brushed my spine. Darkness crept underneath the door flap, and my mind was filled with whisperings . . . searching . . .

hunting . . . fearful . . . From the deep quiet of the sleeping
war camp came a muffled cry of terror . . . and then another
and another.

"Druya's horns, what's happening?" Aleksander leaped
to his feet, poised to run out of the tent if the alarm was
called. He rubbed his bare arms as if the wind of Kir'Vagonoth had penetrated the canvas walls. "I've not felt anything like since . . ." He turned wide eyes to me. " . . . since
Parnifour . . . ." Since our encounter with the Naghidda, the
Lord of Demons.

"Your Highness! Message!" The urgent call came quietly
from beyond the door curtain.

Glaring sideways at me—fiercely, as if daring me to stop
him—the Prince stuck his head out of the door curtain and
spoke with the guards.

*We must get to the gate. Vyx will be with Tovall at the
head of the legion. Be done with this human folly. He is a
stubborn brute who will not be satisfied until blood is shed.*

Soon, I said, trying to fend off the demands in my head
and restrain my feet that were trying to take me away without my consent. *Learn of him.*

When Aleksander returned a few moments later, he was
altogether more ready to listen to what I had to say. "It's
not the Hamraschi attacking, is it?"

"No, my lord. As I told you."

"Sovari sends word the Thrid mercenaries are about to
desert, claiming our venture is ill omened. They've never
seen so many evil spirits on the night before a battle. Their
shaman is bleeding at the eyes from trying to banish them.
One of Gezza's warriors has fallen on his sword from unnamed terror, and everyone is complaining of nightmares.
Evil spirits . . . demons." He pointed to his patterned rug.
"Sit down here and tell me what's happening, Seyonne."

Even as he tried to draw me from my hiding place, I
shrank back farther. Aleksander had lived a horror no man
should ever experience, when the Lord of Demons had
gnawed away half his soul to make a dwelling place, then
taken up residence there. If the Prince saw what I was, I
would never get him to believe me. "I've no time to explain
it all, my lord, but you must reassure your warriors. There's
no threat—"

"No threat? But you said the conflict was not of human making." I thought Aleksander might pull down his tent poles in exasperation.

"Exactly so—but the purposes of this onslaught have nothing to do with human grievance. I beg you trust me. I've learned a great deal since I first taught you of rai-kirah. Don't sleep tonight. Go out and reassure your men. Send word to the rebel leaders to do the same. Tell them that this unsettled night is but the work of the Yvor Lukash and will be finished with the morrow, for you will hand him over to show that you keep your promises." I breathed a silent prayer that Vyx was correct when he assured me that it would only take one night for the demons to pass the gateway. Certainly my own work would be finished by then, for good or ill. "Before midday tomorrow I'll come back here, and you can do with me as you will. Your barons will not want to cross a man who can bring such a night to a peaceful end."

He thought about it so long, I wanted to shake him. "You'll not betray me again?" he said at last.

"You bear the light of destiny within you, my lord. Even if I cared nothing for you, I'm sworn to protect you. But you read the hearts of men better than any sorcerer, so you already know the truth of mine."

He walked slowly to the door of the tent. "Midday tomorrow, Seyonne. Don't be late." It was a command and a warning. But it was also a plea. He was asking me . . . willing me . . . to be what he wanted and not what he feared. I would not fail him.

I pulled aside the curtained door and watched the Prince give orders to his guard captain Sovari, then head toward three soldiers who were standing guard duty by cowering in the corner of the horse pen, their drawn weapons shaking. When the Prince approached and spoke to them, the men jumped up, their backs straight. I had to trust him to do what was needed. Aleksander was undiplomatic, unsympathetic, and ignorant when it came to most concerns of ordinary people, but he knew how to deal with his warriors.

Now can we leave this useless babbling and get back to the gateway? We must start the legion moving through before the pandye gash *arrive.*

A number of warriors' legends were born that night. With Denas's urgency driving me to hurry, I stood hidden in the shadowed doorway and shaped wings, then called the wind and shot upward into the moonlight. Only when I heard a "bloody Athos, save us" far below me, did I realize that I had forgotten to use the form of a bird.

CHAPTER 37

I streaked for the ruin, speeding westward through the moonlight toward the pillars. The campfires of the Derzhi lay behind me, so it was with apprehension that I noted the new lights flickering in the distance to my left. From the south—the mountains. Ezzarians were two hours away, three at most. I prayed that Vyx had arrived, and that the last pattern of the enchantment was no worse than I had judged. Half an hour more, perhaps.

Vyx had not yet come, but Kyor was coaxing a stumbling Blaise up the last steep pitch of the path to the ruin. I touched feet to earth and ignored the silent protests of my demon partner as I went to help the boy, taking a part of the bigger man's weight to get him up the hill. Kyor stared at me for a moment, then wrenched his eyes away and urged Blaise to another step.

"You must persuade him to walk the whole length of the gateway," I said. "Once we've got him through, I need you to get a message to Farrol. Listen well . . . and you, too, Blaise, if you can hear me. There must be no more raids for a while. I've made a start at getting what you want . . ." As we climbed the gentle slope, I told the two of them about Aleksander. About the promise I'd seen in him when I lived under his yoke, and about the bargain I'd made with him in the hour past. "He will do as he says as long as I meet him at the time we agreed. None of you will be harmed. But you must hold back and learn of him. He'll protect you, he'll learn from you, and he will change the world. Do you understand, Kyor?"

"I'll tell Farrol to hold off. I'll convince him."

A shudder rippled through Blaise and left his head bobbing. I rubbed his head and laughed. "So you hear me, too. Is that it? We will do this. We will."

We crested the hill, and I shifted Blaise's weight back to the youth. "I hate to leave you, but by the time you get him to the northern end, I'll have it open. Someone should be there to help him on the other side of it."

"I'll take him through myself." The boy blew a strand of dark hair out of his own face and took firmer hold of the slumping Blaise.

"Are you sure, Kyor? We don't know—"

"I told him I'd do as you bade me. As soon as we find this Well of the Spirits, I'll get back to Farrol. You can depend on it."

I smiled at the boy. "You're going to save him. The world will thank you for it."

As he urged Blaise onward, Kyor called softly over his shoulder. "I hope it doesn't pain you overmuch . . . what you've done."

"It's no matter," I said. "Keep Blaise alive and remind him of my price. He must learn to work with Prince Aleksander; it will be even more important when this is over. Don't let him forget."

The boy nodded, and the two of them staggered southward, the boy talking softly and constantly to the failing man.

I flew to the northernmost pillars and decided I couldn't wait for Vyx. We needed to be ready, so I buried myself in enchantment once again. The last pattern was terrifically complex, and though I tried to stay aware of any threat from my surroundings, I could not afford any slip of concentration.

The moon had risen high over the pillars by the time the shining key was complete, perfect in its outline, the silver surface hard, smooth, flawless . . . ready. Before me wavered a portal, not the rectangular doorway of an Aife's weaving, but a new pair of pillars, identical in every respect to the sixty pairs beside and behind me. Between the pillars was nothing. Beyond them was nothing. Entry was still locked, barred, sealed with ancient power, and though I held the enchanted key in my mind, I had no idea how to use it.

"Tell me, demon. We've come this far. You must know what's next."

You're still holding back. As long as we work separately, the deed is impossible. It must be our combined will that wields the key.

"My will . . ." The only thing I'd not yet yielded. He wanted everything.

This is not some trick to service my desire. It is the only way.

I had done the unthinkable, mutilated myself, made myself anathema. And now he was demanding that I take the final step—and trust a demon's word that I would ever again be able to utter a word or perform an act of my own choosing.

Do you wish to open the gateway or not? It is a simple question with a simple answer. If you refuse . . . the legion will have no choice but to remain in its hosts until someone else is joined with one of us to do all of this again. So choose. You needn't fear me.

Was it his bitterness or my own that shriveled my tongue? None of it mattered, of course. Once he posed the question, he knew my answer. "Do with me as you will."

And he did. Like a Suzaini woman shoved out of her family's councils when her son's new wife is brought into the household, I receded into a corner of my mind with nothing to do but watch Denas work. Deftly he wove a pattern of light between the two new pillars and used my melydda to infuse the pattern with power. As he held the structure in mind, it reformed itself—whirling, surging, coiling upon its center, shaping an empty slot, a void as starkly incomplete as an empty eye socket. Then carefully, precisely, Denas retrieved his shining key from the depths of our mind and positioned it in the slot, and with our hands and our voice and our will, he drew down lightning to seal it there.

I had never felt such power as that which poured out of me in that hour. From body and mind, voice and hand it came in a thundering river, until I thought my very soul would be sucked out along with it. My heart seized in my chest. I could get no breath. As the nothingness in the reflected portal resolved into a night sky and an alien earth,

into trees and hills and a dusty road turned white by moonlight, the demon's triumph raged through me like fire con-
sumes a dry forest.

"Gods of night . . . breathe!" I slipped to my knees, and
my vision failed, and the giant's hand gripping my chest
squeezed out the last of life. "Help me . . ." I had no will
to help myself. Whether he took note of my cry or discovered my distress on his own, the air quickly began flowing
again. I gasped and coughed, and my hands clawed at my
chest as the bloodless stricture eased. I was so drained of
melydda, I could not have conjured a dust mote.

It is done.

And indeed it was. Like the reflection in a pond of perfect stillness, the entire line of pillars was now doubled in
its length, stretching into a moonlit nightscape of grassy
hills and silvered ponds. The scent of wildflowers drifted
through the square gateway that was formed by the last
two pillars of the world I walked and the first two pillars
of Kir'Navarrin. A magnificent buck with antlers as wide
as my arm span raised his head from a small pool in languid
curiosity, and two does wandered down a hill to drink beside him. Myriad bright stars struggled to outshine a
double-sized moon, stars laid in patterns that were familiar,
though they were not the patterns I had studied as a boy
in Ezzaria. The gateway would stand open until the dawn
closed it again.

Ah, Vallyne. To see this wonder with you. The vision of
our homeland so close flooded my mind with remembrance
of her bright music and her beautiful face, alight with intelligence and wit. I came near crying out with the piercing
torment of desire: unable all these years to touch her in a
way that could give her pleasure or to satisfy my own need
without causing her grief. Beyond this gateway was the
truth of her; was she my wife or lover as I had always
believed, or was she a stranger I had never known until I
found her in the dark winds of Kir'Vagonoth, laughing in
defiance of her fate? A perilous journey to learn the
truth . . . for once through the gateway, I would no longer
be myself. I would be lost in the ylad, drowned in flesh and
soul, and so I—the one who had loved her for a thousand
years—would never know the answer, or if I knew it, would

never be able to act upon it. *What justice in this cruel universe condemns a being to such bitter ending?*

Confused, astonished, I shied away from these shattering images, shaking my head as if to confuse them or obscure them with the other debris floating in my head. These grieving torments were not mine—not Seyonne's. My own longings for Vallyne had been but the products of enchantment, fed by loneliness and longing for a touch of beauty amid the desolation of my life. Yet even as I averted my inner eyes from Denas's raw and gaping wound, I realized that it was my own will that I do so. I had choices again.

I told you not to fear me.

"I never wanted to know these things. I have no right."

What matter now or an hour from now? Sooner or later you would have discovered that you are the master here. Vyx told you truthfully. It didn't matter in the least which one of us you chose to join. It is not your bodies that give you humans power, it is your souls. And you've left us none. We are but shadows, and no matter how long we exist within you, we never own you. Most of you are just too stupid to see it. Unfortunately for me, you are not.

"I'm sorry."

I do not want your pity. The only thing of importance is to get the legion through the gateway. Where is the cursed Vyx? We've only until dawn, or we'll have to open the blasted thing again.

I tried to forget what I had seen and felt—my own violation of a realm where I had no place. Behind my back waited the dangerous world that I had shut out while I worked enchantment. And when I turned around to reenter it, I grinned. Kyor, his dark hair plastered to his face in a sheen of sweat, was no more than fifty paces behind me. He was breathless with exertion—Blaise was little more than dead-weight upon the slight youth's shoulders—but Kyor's dark eyes were fixed upon the gateway, shining with hope and excitement.

I hurried toward the pair and was some ten paces away when Kyor halted abruptly, his eyes widened in surprise, and he opened his mouth as if to speak. But no words came out. Only dark blood—bubbling from his lips and trickling down his chin. He took another step, tugging on Blaise, but the bigger man slipped out of the boy's grasp and slumped to the ground. Young Kyor shook his head, then pitched forward on top of Blaise, a dagger hilt protruding from the boy's slim back.

"No!" My bellow might have crumbled a lesser structure than Dasiet Homol. I ran toward the two of them, spinning as I moved, peering into the shadows of the pillars, trying to see what murderous devil had so violated an innocent youth. "Oh, gods of the universe, no!" I dropped to my knees and laid hands on Kyor, but felt no beat of life. Only warm wetness. Blood. Everywhere. Frantically I worked the knife from his back and gently rolled the boy into my arms. Nothing to be done. Nothing. Not even time to chant his death song. "I will sing for you, child. On the soul of my own son, I will."

Hurriedly . . . brutally . . . I shoved the boy aside and examined Blaise. Though his shirt, too, was soaked with blood, he was still breathing. I could see no wounding, but before I could check him for injury, a razor-sharp blade pricked the vein on my neck, and a deadly steel point appeared in dangerous proximity to my right eye. My least twitch would drive one or the other of them home. My captor was behind me and quickly pinned my legs between his as I knelt on the hard ground, catching me in a leg-hold that felt like a giant vise was going to snap my limbs at any moment. A Warden's hold.

"You didn't take my advice, did you, lad?" he said from behind my rigid shoulders. "You had to go and do something mischievous, get yourself tangled up with Denas . . . of all the proud devils. I never trusted him no matter what loyalties he spouted. Of course, unlike some fools, I never trusted any of them."

I might have known. A man who could rob a dying brother Warden, who could help a captor refine his torturing, was certainly a man who could stab an innocent boy in the back. "Merryt."

"Aye, and so it is. Back from lovely Ezzaria after delivering your message . . . or something like." He chuckled. "Here you've tried to let the devils take their passage, and you've kept Gennod and his Gastai out of the fight . . . but it's not going to work. I couldn't make my passage without making sure you knew."

I quickly assessed my chances of surviving a change of form and decided they were too slim to take the risk. Even if I hadn't just used up every scrap of my melydda to open the gateway, I was not experienced enough to shape-shift out of danger. One instant's delay in removing my neck or my eye from the vicinity of his knives would leave me bleeding or blind. "You'll not get through the gateway, Merryt. I won't let you through."

"Did you think to send this boy and his mad friend in before me? Or the witch Vallyne? Or Vyx the fool? Too late, lad. No one will go through the gate before me. I'll have no one else take the glory of releasing the Nameless from his prison. I've looked for the way to pay you and the rest of them for your proud ways: oh, yes, I saw how you looked at me. Just like my wife. Just like the devils. All thinking that you were more powerful, more clever, stronger than Merryt who lost a few battles and became a serving man for vermin. I'll show you all." Merryt's body was tightly wound. Though the night was cool, his deadly embrace was sweaty, and he stank with nervous excitement. His heart drummed like summer thunder against my back.

"You plan to destroy the world."

"If that's what comes, so be it. As long as neither Ezzarian nor rai-kirah survives. But I'd guess the Nameless has his own plan. Likely he'll be grateful to the one bold enough to set him free."

"So you're going to be a god, are you?"

He didn't like it when I mocked him, and he pressed the knife blade ever so delicately against my neck until I felt the skin pop, leaving a thread of fire across my throat. "That's not your concern. For you see, I've brought some here as won't be happy with what you've done to yourself. I told them I'd come secure you, and make sure none of the other devils were here to interfere. You can keep each other busy while I'm off to seek my fortune. That way I won't have you nor the other devils chasing me. Interfering." He saw himself supremely clever.

"And you felt it necessary to do murder on the way?

What kind of cowardly bastard god stabs a child in the back?"

"Me? Murder this poor boy? Nay, lad. There's no blood on me, and who is it holds the killing knife?" Merryt's gleeful whisper slipped into my ear like poison. Then he called louder, over my head. "Over here, my lady. If you have ever believed in true corruption, it waits here to scar your sight. Drop the knife, demon!"

Lights swam into view beyond the fallen outlaws—not lanterns or torches, but clear white lights such as sorcerers cast for their nighttime journeying. The host of Ezzaria. And I was kneeling in a child's blood with the fouled weapon just fallen from my bloody hand and betrayal glaring from my eyes.

A thousand words skittered through my head: pleas for hearing, protestations of my innocence—innocence of murder at least—threats of doom, warnings of how they had been deceived, prayers for them to kill me quickly so I could not think of the consequences of my misjudgments. But when the line of men and women emerged from the darkness, all plans and words failed me. I saw only one among them—the slender, dark-haired woman standing rigid in the center, a thin circlet of gold banding her brow—and my lips formed only three words. "Forgive me, beloved."

She could not possibly have heard my whispered plea. And the offenses for which I craved her absolution were so insignificant beside the consequences of this night's actions, she could likely not remember them: my cruel anger, my refusal to listen to her, to trust her, to consider that her pain and her dilemma had been of so much deeper wounding than my injured pride and shattered hopes. That I had blamed her that my slave's dreams of returning to a life of beauty and meaning and all-consuming love were impossible to realize. That I had blamed her for my own soul-sickness.

As if moving in a dream world, where sounds were muted by the beating of one's own heart and actions were slowed to the pace of drifting clouds, I watched my wife's bloodless face turn away, and her hands fly up between us as if to block the sight she could not bear to look on. Hands reached out to sustain her: from hard-lipped Catrin, her own dear face shattered, from cold Talar, nodding in fulfilled expectation, from rosy-cheeked Maire, crying out to the heavens in devastated fury, and from one other . . . Though I had no reason to expect otherwise, it was still a blow to see Fiona standing with the other women, her hard eyes fixed on the fallen Kyor. She, too, offered her support to her Queen, but she did not look at me. She had already seen.

Ysanne pushed their hands away, and with a motion of her own, summoned others from the crowd. "Nevya, see to the injured. The rest of you, do as I instructed you. Quickly." Not the slightest tremor marred her precise command.

The short, plump healing woman hurried to Blaise. She called for help and had him carried gently away from me—a small comfort to know that he, at least, must still be breathing. But I could see nothing more, for a crowd of others bustled toward Merryt and me, blocking my view. Five of them wore the badges of temple guards, and Caddoc and Kenehyr followed them, wreathed in powerful enchantment . . . so familiar . . . Searcher and Comforter. Gods have mercy . . . they were going to try to take the demon out of me!

"You can't do it," I cried, trying to reach Ysanne wherever she was. I couldn't see her. "You mustn't—" Merryt's knife pressed deeper into my throat, the drips of warm blood from the stinging cut now a constant trickle. "I was joined in the demon realm, full-consenting"—the point of his second knife grazed my eyeball—"no going back."

"Hold, Warden," said Ysanne, stepping into view just beside me, Fiona and Talar and Catrin still flanking her. Her command allowed for no misinterpretation. "I told you not to harm this victim. Only to hold him incapable of harming others." Victim. Not friend, not lover, not husband. Yet she was refusing to see the truth, and I could not permit that.

"I'm not a victim. It's impossible—"

"This perverted creature is dangerous beyond telling, lady," said Merryt, his hand trembling, scarcely controlled, which left me well paralyzed. "In only one way does he speak truth. You cannot get this demon out of him. Joinings forged beyond the portal cannot be undone. Seyonne had hoped he could hold out when the devils came after him, but he wasn't strong enough. Look at what they made him do here. The young Aife there can tell you how he prized these two as his friends, and now he's slaughtered them like beasts."

Ysanne looked to Fiona, and the young woman nodded. "As I told you, my lady. He was determined to discover how to help them. It drove him to this."

"We care nothing for his 'reasons,'" said Talar, her tongue laced with venom. "There is no reason save corruption. Abomination." Talar saw it clearly. Her proud hatred did not waver when I glared at her.

Merryt burst in again, his feigned grief quite convincing. "The man you know is lost, my honored Queen, buried in this devil's cloak, in torment everlasting. I've told you of the horrors they had waiting for him. Only swift death will release him from this dread captivity. Let me do it, then we can set up the blockade to keep the devils out of this place. It was what Seyonne wanted. What he gave everything for you to do. Even as he fought this madness, his intent was to prevent the devils from getting through this passage."

Was any man so clever as the vile Merryt? I had expected he would run to Ysanne claiming my longtime corruption and dealings with the demons, but instead he had made me some kind of mad hero . . . with Fiona to witness my deterioration . . . and my own deeds to weigh in evidence. The cursed villain had recognized Ysanne as a woman who could kill her own child to save her people . . . a woman who could murder her own husband to release him from torment. "Beloved, don't—"

A fiery wash of blood stung my eye and dribbled down my face as Merryt ripped my eyelid with the point of his knife. "Be silent, devil, if you value this body you have stolen from our friend. I'll not allow your twisted words to harm our Queen."

"Warden, cease! I command you again not to harm him. Though I thank you for your concerns, we will proceed as I have spoken in this case."

For once I blessed my wife's royal stubbornness. Now, what in the name of sense was I to do?

The guards were uncoiling ropes, and white-haired Kenehyr was pouring liquid from one very large vial to another, shaking the resulting mixture: vammidia, in the quantity he was mixing a sleeping draught strong enough to fell a horse. Ysanne was still addressing Merryt. "Since I must deal with this victim, you will direct my kafydda how to set up the blockade as we agreed. If the rai-kirah are as close as you claimed, we have little time. Kafydda!" She motioned to someone behind her.

Kafydda . . . not a name, but a title—the "one who waits," the Queen's successor. I'd had no idea Ysanne had chosen a successor; she was young to be thinking of it. Even more astonishing was the identity of the one who stepped forward. Fiona.

So much explained. I would have laughed if it were possible. No wonder she was so dogged in her attentions. Test the young kafydda by setting her to watch the present Queen's husband. Who would be more diligent, more excruciatingly correct? She could show no leniency, or Ysanne would see it and believe her weak. She could not be overzealous or it would show lack of balance or too much eagerness to claim her future position. I was a challenge. A risk. A training ground. I had been her mentor, but not in the way I mentored student Wardens or even Aleksander. I had taught Fiona of corruption, of subtle evils, of flawed and foolish judgments. To protect the safety of Ezzaria, she had to understand what I was. I had retained some small belief that Fiona had learned something of truth in our travels together, but when I heard that she was to be Queen of Ezzaria, that misbegotten hope went on the scrap heap with all the rest.

Look to your left, Exile. The new voice intruded on my thoughts, sharper than the pain in my eye. While two of the Temple Guards carried Kyor away, another man knelt down beside me with ropes ready to bind my hands. I glanced at his face, and it was not the blood blurring my vision that caused a slight smear of blue and purple light to flicker around his hands. Slyly he glanced up at me and grinned, a faint blue glimmer in his eyes. *Only a little late.*

His words were as clear in my head as those of Denas. *To move the circles and admonish them fully as you required was not a trivial matter, Exile.*

Someone behind me was trying to bind my feet, and I took a moment to test my melydda. To hear the sprizzle of burning rope and a yelp was satisfying, but I could not have split a thicker rope. I would have to rely on other skills for a while longer.

If you, my friend, can keep this Merryt engaged for a time, prevent his venture into the gate, I could perhaps get the legion moving more quickly. Perhaps before your fellows can disrupt the working and cause us all a great deal of trouble and unhappiness.

Keep him engaged . . . Indeed I would. Keep him or kill him. *Get them through,* I said. *Go.*

My hand crept into the pocket of my cloak, where I had stuffed one of the Warden's rags from Merryt's hoard. Quickly I wound the cloth around and around my hand to make a thick padding. When it was done, I closed my unbloodied eye, envisioned the precise positions of Merryt's two knife blades, then, wishing I had the power to create a true distraction, I let loose a ferocious bellow. Merryt was a trained Warden, and though it had been a long time since he had used his skills, they were far from dead. The knife blades wavered not at all at my noisy surprise, but I was quick and gripped the blade at my eye with my protected hand, while bringing up my left hand inside his arm to catch his wrist and push the second blade away from my neck. Once free of his immediate threat, I broke his leg-hold, kicked away the grabbing hands of the temple guards, and bashed my head backward into Merryt's face. Hoping the villain was dizzied from the blow, I let go of his hands, then ducked under the knives that were now aimed to smash into my chest, and rolled to the side. My heart racing, I scrambled to my feet and crouched low, waiting for the snarling Warden to come at me.

"We'll take you, devil," said Merryt, a bloody bruise centered on his forehead.

"As you murdered this boy? Will you put a knife in my back, too, before I can tell these people what you are?"

"They can see which one of us has blood on his hands,

laddie, and they can see which one of us bears a demon. You are the abomination."

He was right, of course. What a damnable predicament. I wanted to keep talking, to convince Ysanne and the others of my truth. I wanted to take Merryt by the throat and destroy him for what he had done and what he planned to do. But as the traitorous Warden and I circled like warring kayeets, I knew that wasn't the answer. Ysanne saw a demon, not a man. And there were so many Ezzarians. Unless I transformed and flew away in less than a minute—impossible at present with my depleted melydda—they were going to take me down with sheer numbers, using sorcery and ropes and weapons and potions. In either case, Merryt would walk away. They would never let me kill him. Once I was gone or disabled, the Ezzarians would block the gateway, and the demons would have to force their Derzhi hosts to dislodge the annoying interlopers. Slaughter. And Merryt would have all the time he needed to unlock the danger in Tyrrad Nor.

No. Proof of my "innocence" was not important. Timing was the key—delaying and disrupting Ysanne's plan. Perhaps they would need her power to set their blockade—even with so many of them, it would take considerable melydda to pull them together and stop the demons' passing. But if I forced her to attend to me and made sure Merryt wanted to be in on it . . . It seemed a flimsy plan, but it was all I could devise.

"You're a weakling, Merryt," I said. "Word in Kir'Vagonoth had it that you yielded to the Rudai on the second day of your captivity. Was it the first lash discomforted you? Or was it sleeping in the dark? Such hardship for a Warden used to easy battles . . . and there was no Merryt to teach your captors how to torture a captive Warden. Perhaps I should teach you what you could have faced." I leaped onto Merryt, vented a bit of my anger by a few choice blows to his jaw and his gut, then held back and let him dump me off of him. I rolled to the side and popped back onto my feet, snatching up the bloody knife blade I had pulled from Kyor's back. "Will you not fight me, weakling? Or is it you're afraid to fight without a woman to blame when you lose? Your wife. Your Aife. It was all her fault, wasn't it?"

"Silence, vermin. Don't you dare speak of my wife with your demon-infested tongue."

For a while the Ezzarians held back. Perhaps they were afraid of my demon. Perhaps they were afraid of my melydda and my training. I preferred to think they found it difficult to believe Merryt's story when they saw me in the flesh. I was the one they had known for so long, the one who had taken them back to Ezzaria, the Queen's husband, and friend or student, teacher or brother to so many of them. But that wasn't going to last long once they glimpsed my eyes for themselves and listened to the demon music, once they realized that I couldn't fry them with lightning if they touched me. Even as I circled again, a few men started to move forward and I held ready. But it was Merryt who waved them off. "Stay back. I'll take the devil myself."

"The great Merryt, the lost Warden. So sure of himself," I said. "Is the archivist here? Tell me the tales of the ancient hero Merryt. Surely I missed them in my education."

We exchanged more taunts and scrapped like nasty boys—while a ring of Ezzarians stood protectively between us and Ysanne. But as we circled and ducked and rolled and fought, the crowd shifted, and I watched for an opening. No possibility of getting close to Ysanne, but the others . . . The time came, and, in the space of a gnat's breath, I had Fiona in my grasp, with the bloody knife at her breast.

"Oh, my good and faithful watchdog, you're going to be Queen," I growled into her ear. "Why in the name of sense didn't you tell me? Did you think I would kill you for it?"

I pulled the slight figure farther away from the crowd, keeping a snarling Merryt well in view.

"Seyonne, don't do this." Fiona spoke through clenched teeth and tried to wrench her arms from my grasp.

"Here"—I tightened my grip on the wriggling young woman, hoping to give her pause before the others drew near enough to overhear—"be still and listen. Whatever you think of me . . . however you abhor what I've done . . . what I am . . . I beg you have mercy on Blaise. For the

love of the world, for all you profess, get him through the
gateway. You've let your eyes deceive you, Fiona. I thought
perhaps . . . Your mind knows so much of truth. Think.
Gods, if you would but think."

"I am not deceived. I know exactly what I see." She said
it loud enough that all could hear.

Maybe someday she would sort it all out, but clearly it
was nothing I could count on happening very soon. Her
head was harder than the stone pillars. With a silent apology to Blaise, I proceeded with my plan.

"Now perhaps we can speak on equal terms for one moment," I said, as everyone held rigid in shock. "We're getting nowhere with this little scrap. You wish to set up
obstacles to my friends' passage through this gateway—a
sorely misguided venture—and some of you think to salvage this human soul I have taken. I warn you now that if
you persist, you will bring the wrath of the rai-kirah down
upon you." Nothing like a bit of the truth to sound convincing. "No doubt your scouts noted the Derzhi encampment
not half a league from this place. Send a runner and discover what ill infests Aleksander's legions this night. If you
set this blockade, I will tell the Derzhi legion who is responsible for their horrors. You know, my Queen, that Aleksander will believe one who appears to him in this body.
And so you can be sure that whatever forbearance has been
shown you will end quickly. The Ezzarian people will cease
to exist. I would prefer to avoid such messy business, and
prevent your interference in matters you don't understand."

Ysanne pushed her guards aside and walked toward me,
pale and regal. No softness. "Are you offering us a bargain, demon?"

I almost could not speak for her closeness. Her violet
eyes stared at me boldly . . . contemptuous . . . filled with
loathing. What in the name of the gods was I doing . . .
standing before the Queen of Ezzaria—the love of my
life—with a knife to a woman's breast and threatening the
end of the world? Had any man ever become so thoroughly
the very object of his nightmares? Yet my lips kept on
speaking. Time was so short. "If you hold back and let the
rai-kirah pass to their own homeland, I'll not tell the Derzhi

you have caused their troubles, and I will allow this human Seyonne to choose his own fate. It's as simple as that."

She did not even hesitate. "There is no bargain here. Demons have no passage through the souls of this world—my people are sworn to prevent it—and you cannot bribe me with one life, no matter whose it may be. The one you've taken understands that better than anyone in any world."

"Indeed he does," I said softly. I had not expected her to relent. "Then I'll be off to visit Prince Aleksander. You cannot destroy me. I know your names. I know your secrets. You have no one who can challenge me. I will live, no matter what you do to this body, and I will see that Ezzaria never knows another moment's peace. Ask this woman to tell you of Balthar's mosaic. Ask her who holds the key to the end of the world." I shoved Fiona back toward the Ezzarians and invited Merryt to continue our engagement. "Come, coward, let us finish our discussion."

Even as I voiced these dreadful threats, three streaks of colored light flicked into view near the gateway . . . and slowly . . . majestically . . . moved through it. No human eye could have seen them. *Oh, gods of night and day . . .* It was all I could do to resist running off to join them. But I still had my role to play.

"I'll take him, Lady Queen," said Merryt, spitting at my feet. "He will die by my hand and no other." And we began to wrestle again. *Engage, separate, not too much. Let him win a point. Give him confidence.* How long would it take Ysanne's fellows to be ready?

Not long. I sensed Caddoc and Kenehyr working behind me. Even distracted as I was, I could feel their power growing. Before too long my feet began to drag; my arms might have been lead. A loop of rope snared one arm, and I could scarcely summon the power to snap it apart. Another threatened to snag my feet until I set it aflame. My efforts were pitiful.

"You are a sneaking thief, Merryt," I said, "a violator of the helpless and a murderer of children. You're afraid to face a true warrior. Afraid to face a rai-kirah. And I am your worst nightmare, for I am both at once." I stumbled to my knees, feeling the heavy mantle of enchantment envelop me. Hands grabbed my head and shoulders from behind, bent my head back, and forced a river of sticky, bitter liquid down my throat.

As I choked and gagged on the potion, Merryt stood glaring down at me, his hands trembling as they gripped his two bloody knives. "Abomination."

I considered using my last sensible words to ask that someone please prevent his cutting my throat, but instead I forced out my last play of the game. "Do not send your child Wardens to try me, Catrin. I'll eat them for breakfast and spit their bones back at you while picking their balls from my teeth. Too bad you have no one to send who dares face an opponent rather than sneaking up from the back. Too bad you've only children and mewling cowards." A loop of rope tightened about my chest and pulled me onto my back. Like hungry spiders they wrapped me in ropes and spells, and the bitter-tasting vammidia spread throughout my veins like rivers of mud. "This 'Warden' has used you. Lied to you. He has lain with a demon woman . . . told us his name . . . begged us to take his soul . . . to give him power. We would not have him. Not even rai-kirah." I could scarcely speak. "Try him . . . see if he will do a Warden's duty or tries to sneak away."

Faces hovered over me: a stunned Catrin, Ysanne, clear-eyed and cold, Merryt grinning. Fiona shoved her way in front of them and knelt beside me, testing my bonds.

"We've no time to waste," said Ysanne, turning away. "Fiona will see to the blockade while I take care of this matter. Merryt, tell her what is necessary to block the demon passage. Talar, you will take the right. Maire the left. Gansard . . ." She walked away, giving an unending stream of orders.

Of course Ysanne would be the one to weave. She was the most powerful of Aifes, and she knew me better than anyone in the world, so she could weave the portal quickly, making it strong and unyielding. Would I feel her inside me? *Beloved* . . .

Someone kindly closed my uninjured eyelid, for I was staring up into blazing torchlight and blurred faces and could not close it for myself. I think it was Fiona. The last thing I saw before the darkness came was the reflection of my face in her hard black eyes: the purple slave mark on my left cheekbone, my torn and bloodied eye, the blue fire . . . Abomination.

CHAPTER 38

Gold lightning ripped the darkness. The air was close and sultry, and stank like a refuse pit that had been burned to kill the rats. Rain. It needed to rain. I shifted in my sleep . . . only to realize that, although my eyes were closed, I was not sleeping. My face was buried in my arms, which were wrapped in some kind of heavy scratchy cloth, therefore the gold flashes were not lightning, but in my head. Something wrong with my eyes, perhaps, or the remnant of an unpleasant dream. I didn't want to think about it. What had waked me—summoned me from the realm of sleep? Summoned . . .

There was rock all around me—a cave, cramped and stuffy and dark as pitch, save for the glimmering gold streaks that had not stopped when I opened my eyes. I uncurled myself, which seemed to take an inordinately long time, as I kept bumping into the walls and ceiling of the cave. And the stench . . . My head swam in the nauseous closeness. Which way was up and which way was down? Ahead of me was a smudge of gray light, and I gave up trying to sit, and instead began to crawl toward the light.

"I am the Warden, sent by the Aife, the Scourge of Demons, to challenge you for this vessel. Hyssad! Begone. It is not yours." The words rang out clearly from beyond the smudge of light—outside the cave. The words . . . terrible words that scraped my skin raw, that blared in my ears like a discordant trumpet, that caused my intestines to clench in disgust . . . in rage. *Insolent beggar . . . Summoning me . . .*

Wrong. This was all wrong. I hesitated just short of the smudge of light. Why did those particular words infuriate me . . . pain me . . . so sorely? They belonged to me. They were written in my soul with fire and blood. Yet the voice was so young, so brave, and I did not feel at all brave and certainly not young. I felt sick. The stink . . . the gold light that confused my vision. I wanted to rub my eyes that felt as gritty as if I'd just walked across the Azhaki desert without blinking. But as I reached for my eyes, I saw something move along the ground in front of me . . . a claw, huge, deadly, razor-sharp talons just visible in the light from the cave mouth. Quickly I drew back and held still, hoping to stay invisible, and the wind sighed outside the cave, carrying the scent of ashes.

"Do not hide from me, beast. This place is not for you. This life of strength and honor and duty is not yours. Hyssad!"

I bellowed at the hurtful word, and the attacker must have discovered my hiding place at the same moment, for just as I cried out, the cave was filled with flame. I lunged for the opening, and was at last able to untangle myself . . . only to discover that I was not what I expected. Wings . . . monstrous, leather-covered fingers of bone . . . and the talons . . . mine, too, not hands, but feet ready to lift boulders and drop them on unwary heads, sharpened on stone and ready to slit the bellies of cattle or deer or puling human warriors. I stretched my shoulders and my long neck, and bellowed again. Flame shot from my mouth, leaving pools of fire in the ashy desolation.

Before I was even sure what body parts I had, someone tried to remove one of them. I felt a piercing sting in my right side. With injured fury I swept my right wing forward so hard it made the air whistle. Something small scuttered out from under the blow and took shelter behind a rock, and without thinking I blasted the rock with fire.

If you have no intent to kill this yddrass, then I'd suggest you control yourself. This exasperated voice came from inside me, and I would have blasted it, too, if I could have. I roared in annoyance and clawed at the desolate earth. *I tried to make you immune to injury, not immune to intelligence. I knew they would come after you quickly, and their villainy had you tangled up so sorely in mind and body, I surmised you might not be able to move when attacked. If they kill this body, we are both dead. Do you understand? Can you comprehend?*

Another stabbing pain, this time from the left. I reached for the scrambling creature with my claws, but missed as it ducked and disappeared.

Fly, fool. Get off the ground until you can think.

This seemed the first sensible suggestion. Everything was so confusing. I swept the heavy wings through the hot air and pushed off, lumbering into flight with all the grace of a goose carrying a pig. It was cooler in the thin gray clouds, and the stench less vile. I circled, reluctant to leave the cave, drawn to the ugly, uncomfortable place, though I could not explain why.

It's the summons. You've used it hundreds of times. You know its effects. We can't resist it, and it locks us to the place of combat chosen by the yddrass. I never understood why, and thought it was the most bitter irony that the pandye gash *had discovered some magical word that we could not escape, when we didn't even know it ourselves. But you . . . your theories . . . if we are two parts of a whole, then it isn't magic at all. Perhaps we hear the summons of a human spirit . . . the voice of our own selves, one might say . . . and that is what we can't resist. I don't like the thought that I am nothing but a discarded scrap of something else.*

Gradually, as the one-sided conversation continued, the cool wind of the upper airs began to clear my head. I looked down on charred desolation. An endless forest of blackened trees, gaunt, brittle, broken, some fallen, many still upright, pointing accusingly at the gray sky. No leaf, no blade of grass, no hint of green relieved the palette of gray and black. The earth was deep in ash, the protruding stones like a dirty skeleton in a grave, smudged and stained with its own disintegrated flesh. A gaping scar creased the land between two hills, the seared bed of a dead river, its smaller tributaries like the dried wrinkles in an old desert woman's face. Even the sky was the same dismal gray. A dreadful place.

Not to push, but you're going to have to decide soon what to do about these yddrassi. There are at least three of them. The matter-of-fact tone belied the urgency of the message.

I tried to think. *Yddrassi . . . Wardens. Summoning. Why*

would I worry about three Wardens? I looked down at the ruined landscape that had no relation to any geography I knew, and the first piece fell into place. I was beyond a portal. How in the name of sense had someone gotten me beyond a portal without my knowing it? Vague memories of a nighttime confrontation, of ropes, enchantments, potions . . . *Gods of night! What am I? Where am I? Dreaming? Oh, sweet Verdonne, let me be dreaming.*

Rai-kirah do not dream. Did you know that? The inner voice twined itself in my thoughts like a snake.

Denas.

That name no longer has meaning. Not that it ever did. Only a convenience. It's very awkward to exist for a thousand years without a name. Are you beginning to comprehend?

Again I surveyed the smoke-stained sky and the charred forest. *This is my own soul.*

And they've sent not one, but three warriors to slay the rai-kirah who dwells here . . .

. . . who is myself . . .

. . . and if they succeed, you/I/we will be dead. There is no possibility of separation. As you see.

Even after everything, I had not really believed we were inseparable. One being. Inside, outside, now and forever . . . as long as forever was going to last with Ysanne bent on ripping us apart. I had assumed that Denas would be the one to fight this battle, using my knowledge and skill. He was the demon. The invader. In my deepest self had lingered the faint hope that somehow, someday, this nightmare would be done with, and I would go back to being only Seyonne. After all, I had survived the death of hope that was slavery when it seemed impossible, and surely this was something the same. I was a warrior who had surrendered only for the moment, believing that somehow I would strike down my enemy and win free. But once I knew myself as my own demon, there was no possibility of self-deception. As had happened each time I thought I had discovered the true depth of despair, I turned another corner and found the way still pointed downward. *Gods have mercy . . . what have I done?*

I circled one more time and landed atop the rocky prominence that sheltered the cave where Denas had hidden me, and with a thought, I shed the dragon shape and took my own winged form.

"Three Wardens, you say." I shook off the chill of such a massive change in size and tried to regain my inner balance. "And is one of them Merry?" If I was to be this horror, then at least let my flimsy ruse succeed.

That I do not know. We will hope so. A strange plan you've devised.

"Begone, rai-kirah. You take human form—a familiar form—but I will not be deceived. Come fight me or abandon this place. Hyssad!" A tall young man with light brown hair and wearing a red cloak had climbed up the rocks beside me and stood brandishing his sword. Tegyr. The boy had always been a bit pompous. Had I not taught him to stay silent once the summons had drawn the demon? Perhaps he was just nervous at facing a demon who happened to know his habits and his weaknesses.

I wondered for a moment how a demon produced its weapons . . . considered what I would choose . . . and instantly found a broadsword in my hand. No. That was wrong. Too likely to produce serious damage. I only wanted to tire the boy and scare him away. To use up time. The weapon shifted form. Better. I whipped the slender blade a bit to get its feel, adjusted its balance with a thought, then tried again. Good enough.

"Go away, Tegyr."

The youth turned pale at my voicing of his name, but he did not retreat. His sword was at the ready. "I'll not listen to your treacherous tongue, demon. Fight me, and we'll see who survives."

"I don't want to hurt you. I have more important things to do."

"More important than survival? Because I plan to kill you. Hyssad! Begone!"

I sighed and stepped up, and in less time than he could blink, I had ripped a long tear in his shirt. Not his skin. Only the shirt. Then I stepped back again. "Are you sure you want to fight?"

Perhaps the lesson brought his other lessons back. He wasn't supposed to chatter with a demon. And he didn't anymore. He attacked. I furled my wings tightly and responded.

Tegyr thought he was doing well, for he remained the aggressor. I did not attack, even when he left me an opening. Instead I kept my guard low and let him come after me, leading him across the rocks, making sure he had to go up and down a thousand times, testing his footing and balance, while I stayed on reasonably level ground. He had improved in his year of warding—obvious, since he was still alive—and he was young and very strong. But his eagerness would be his downfall—he made five strokes for every one of mine—and I had taught him his most sophisticated moves, so I could counter them almost before he began. He wasn't going to make much progress before he got very tired. As soon as that happened, I would bash him in the head and send him home.

But my plan was complicated by his companions. I had hoped Denas was wrong about there being three. I wanted only Merryt. A slight movement to my left caught the corner of my eye, and I leaped backward. A young Warden from southern Ezzaria had sneaked up the steepest side of the little ridge and almost caught me in the back.

"Welcome, Emrys." A wiry, coarse-skinned young man tossed his short dark hair out of his eyes and slashed hard at my legs. I skipped out of the way, and he struck rock. Probably numbed his elbow with the power of his blow. "So the two of you are going to take me together? Have you ever practiced it?" I parried Emrys's next cut, then whirled and kicked Tegyr's descending sword out of the way. It made things a little more complicated, but soon I had them stumbling over each other. Tegyr drew first blood—not mine, but Emrys's. Once they realized what I was doing—and what they were doing—at least they were intelligent enough to adjust. They would alternate, and make sure they weren't coming at me from opposite directions, where I could step out of the way and let them hurt each other. It kept me busy, but it was manageable. I still took fewer steps than either of them. So when would I see the third?

Fortunately for me, a tired Emrys stumbled off a rock and broke his leg before the third Warden found us. The snap of bone was unmistakable. I circled until Tegyr was between me and his fallen comrade. The light-haired youth, heaving in great gulps of air, dropped to his knees to make sure Emrys was living. He never took his eyes from me for more than a second, but his sword point was wavering.

"Take him out," I said. "Tell Mistress Catrin to send men instead of boys."

"We're not finished here yet," he said. Brave, but stupid. I could have walked up to him and cut his throat.

"Never be so foolhardy with a real rai-kirah," I said, then turned to greet the third Warden who had slipped up the promontory almost unnoticed. Almost. Drych, dark-eyed and sturdy, a nasty scar across one cheek hinting of hard experience, slashed at me with a long-sword. I quickly switched my own weapon and adjusted my grip to counter his heavy blow, discovering that Catrin's most promising student had indeed come into his prime. I forced his weapon back, but, unlike sparring with Tegyr and Emrys, it took a great deal of effort.

"I don't want to hurt you, Drych. Step away." Damn the coward Merryt—letting these boys fight this battle for him, while he was off into the gateway, no doubt. Damn my own foolish self to risk everything on this kind of stupid game. Surely I could have thought of something else.

Drych did not step away. He kept coming. Doggedly. Furiously, keeping his blade close, his movements tight and efficient. Drych would not be so easy to tire. I led him across the rocks, but he had better judgment than the others and picked his positions, letting up on his attack rather than pursuing over unsteady ground. But he did not relent. He just slipped around the obstacles and came at me from another direction. I gathered in my concentration. I could not afford to take this young man anything but seriously.

"You've progressed fairly, lad. I knew you would." I led him down a steep hillside, leaving him stumbling and off balance while I used my wings instead of feet. But he compensated well and left a bloody streak on one of my shoulders. If I hadn't been quick, he would have severed my arm. Every once in a while, I pressed him hard, to show him that I could—left him a few cuts that could have been more severe—and then I let off again. "I won't kill you,"

I said. "But you need to get out of here before we do something we'll both regret."

After several more engagements, I considered stopping the fight altogether—taking wing perhaps—and trying to explain to him what I had done and why, trying to salvage something from this debacle. But Drych was trained not to listen even to the most reasonable blandishments of a raikirah, and I had no reason to believe his discipline in that area was any less mature than his fighting skills. I had to stay focused. "I won't let you kill me, either. I have a number of things I need to do. We could have a very long night, and I can't let you use up all my time."

"You've taken my teacher." His scarred face—so very young—was sculpted of steel. "I'll have you out of him."

"You have no idea how it cheers him to hear that," I said, smiling. "But it's truly not possible. I've just come to see it clearly for myself."

I needed to stop Drych before I got too tired, just in case some sudden realignment of the stars brought Merryt to face me. So I began to drive the young man hard, through ankle-deep ash, down into the dry riverbed, on and on until his movements became erratic. I slashed and cut, changing stances often to keep him off balance, pushing him harder until he was staggering and fell backward onto a charred stump, his heavy sword jarred from his hands. Yet even when I pressed the edge of my weapon to his throat in position to take his life, he glared at me in defiance.

"You remember my lessons well," I said. "Never forget the victim. I thank you and bless you for that, Drych. Now remember another lesson I taught you. I once killed a demon and the victim together, and I told you it was a mistake. Some Ezzarians don't believe a Warden could regret such a mistake; they don't understand caring for another human that is not kin or friend. But you know I did care—even though that victim was a horror who should have been executed for his crimes. I'll not allow you to make a similar mistake. If you kill me, you'll kill the one you're trying to save. Believe me, I wish it could be different." Then I whacked the boy in the head with the hilt of my sword and hefted him in my arms.

Tegyr was shoving the grimacing Emrys through a portal. At the sight of me, he dropped his friend and raised his weapon.

I dumped Drych in front of him, then took wing. "Take them back, Tegyr. I won't fight children. Tell the Queen to send someone else. Tell her that I'm waiting, and that the one she's trying to save suffers more every minute she refuses to send the murderous coward Merryt." *Tell her that I love her more than life, but I'll not allow her to destroy her people. Any of them. Even the ones she does not know.*

Astonished, disbelieving, the nervous, exhausted youth dragged his fellows through the portal. I circled the desolate hill as the gray rectangle faded into the gloom. Then the sky began to spin and the charred forest to dissolve, and I unshaped my wings and fell into the darkness.

"Seyonne?" The whisper from behind my back reverberated in my aching head like a bull's bellowing.

The only answer I could seem to come up with was a moan. Perhaps because my lips were numb. Or maybe they were bound with spell-wrapped ropes like every other finger's breadth of my person. I had been laid on my side, my head on a bundled cloth, and it was a race to see which was going to make me return to oblivion sooner: the pain in my head or the burning laceration in my right eye. Every breath I took was like an earthquake, threatening to crumble the world. I was drooling, and it was such a grotesquely difficult endeavor to breath, I would have sworn the pillars of Dasiet Homol lay across my ribs.

"Can he hear me, Nevya?"

"Unlikely. They've put enough spells on him and in him, he'll never wake up. I'm just trying to ease the pain of his eye. Can't bear to see it left, no matter they said not to heal him." Nevya, the healer, was spreading some cold, thick substance on my eye.

I couldn't quite place the other woman's voice. "They'll be ready for him again soon," she said softly.

"That's hardly time enough . . . and he's still bleeding from this cut in his throat. I ought to stop the bleeding at least." The old woman's hands were gentle as she pressed a folded cloth to my face.

"They don't want the rai-kirah to have time to recover in between. They want to beat down the cursed demon. Destroy it."

"Well, I hope they get it done this time. Master Seyonne was a kind man. A good man. The young Wardens had such strange tales of their experiences. Tell me, Kafydda, what will happen if they cannot get the demon out of him?"

"We'll have to kill him. The Queen knows the law." Kafydda—Fiona. My watchdog was still watching.

The second time I came to awareness in the cave, I knew where I was. Denas had taken the liberty of making me a dragon again. He seemed to have the freedom to do as he willed with my shape while my soul was being manipulated by Ezzarian sorcery.

" . . . Hyssad! Begone! It is not yours . . . and it will not survive this day." The last echoes of the challenge still echoed from the rocks. The hateful words drew me inexorably toward the mouth of the cave. I understood well why the demons despised them so. But I would have gone out anyway. The challenger was Merryt.

Fury and power surged in my veins. There was only one thing I needed to know before I began. "How much time do we need?"

Some have crossed. Many have not. There are still a number of hours remaining to this night.

"And Vyx?"

I cannot tell. To make this passage fast and secret as he asked, he has to force the legion from its hosts sooner than they would like. For many, this is their first experience of life since the dark times, so they're likely hard to dislodge. The pandye gash *have put up some kind of barrier, and I don't know if any more will be able to pass the gateway. Merryt must not get through until Vyx tells us the fortress is secure. You should kill the vile* ylad.

But if I killed Merryt right away, Ysanne would believe that I—Seyonne—was unsalvageable. She would kill me and be free to reinforce the blockade. Until the demons passed through the gate or until I was sure that they couldn't, I had to hold. It might not work, but it was all I could do. "I'll hold him," I said. And then I would kill him.

I couldn't see Merryt when I emerged from the cave.
Likely Tegyr had told him about the dragon form, and he
was waiting to see what shape I would choose. As before,
I reverted to my own shape. I knew more about fighting in
my own body, and I really had no desire to roast Merryt . . .
not right away at least. We needed to have a nice long
chase. I didn't want to discourage him, lest he decide to
leave me and go on about his business.

"Ah, the abomination." Merryt stood atop the promontory, looking down on me with such hatred as I had never
felt in all my demon combats. "How does it feel to be on
the wrong side of this battle? To hear the words and know
that the chants and rituals are all aimed at you? And you,
Denas, to know that you will remain trapped in this human
flesh . . . until I kill it, and you disappear into the void.
There is no afterlife for a demon." He jumped down in
front of me, landing lightly on the balls of his feet, as if he
were twenty-seven instead of three hundred and seventy
years old. He twirled the Warden's knife in his fingers.
"Tell me, abomination, how did you do it?"

"Do what?" I approached carefully, ready for any treachery, choosing a springy, fine-edged blade for my weapon.

"How did you lay the filthy spell to keep me out?"

"Spell?" I expected to hear more of his ranting, but without another word, he pounced, knocking me off balance
with a ferocious attack, followed by a boot in the chest,
then spinning around with a dagger blade slashing at my
throat. I caught his arm and was tempted to break it in my
surprise, but instead I flipped him onto his back and kicked
him over the break in the slope, letting him slide and bump
to a stop before coming on him again. No rushing. And no
more distractions. This was not a child.

His weapon had bounced out of his hand. I kicked it
toward him. "I'm not finished with you yet," I said. Warily
I stepped close to where the Ezzarian lay on his back.

With remarkable quickness, he scrambled to his feet and
laid into me, the knife changed to a broadsword. "Nor am
I finished with you, demon. You will tell me what I want
to know if I have to carve your polluted flesh into ribbons."

We ranged all over that rocky knob, then took our duel
down into the dry riverbed and traversed the length of it.

He was good. Better than I had expected. He wanted me
dead, but only after he had mastered me. I was better. I
just couldn't afford to show it. I had to keep him believing
he could win. Yet if we went too long, it might not matter
who was better. I hoped Vyx was getting about his business
smartly. It had been a very long two days.

Merryt did not speak, save for his constant mouthings
that I had set some spell and he needed the word to break
it. I couldn't imagine what he wanted. He could not mean
the gateway. Until the first light of dawn, it lay open to
any who walked through it.

Once, Merryt lost his weapon and took off running. But
moments later, as I searched for him, trying to decide how
to get him armed again, he jumped down on my back
laughing merrily and came near slicing off one of my wings.
He had brought more than one Warden's knife. The second
time he lost a weapon, I knew to be careful, and indeed,
he came up with a third.

We had been at it for nearly an hour when my left thigh
seized with a cramp. I stirred up a cloud of ash with my
wings, then used the cover to slip down into a thick stand of
burned trees. Flattening my back against a charred trunk, I
stretched out the cramp and forced my hard breathing shallow so as not to inhale too much of the choking dust. Merryt was somewhere to my left and up. I could hear him
coughing. I'd left a gash in one of his legs, and it looked
like he'd torn something in his left shoulder. Neither injury
was debilitating. Just painful enough to make him angry.
He had left a shallow cut across the middle of my back.
Not serious, but it kept breaking open every time I moved,
and there was no way to bind it up. I bent over and leaned
my hands on my knees. I was getting tired. Well, so was
Merryt.

"Where are you, demon?" he called, still coughing. "The
blood on my sword is getting dry. I need to freshen it. But
first . . . perhaps I need a different weapon . . . Aife!"

I started up the opposite slope, planning to come around
behind him, but as I did so the sky dimmed from gray to
black, as if the torch of day had been snuffed out.

I heard him running for the portal, and in less time than
a gnat's breath, the ground crumbled beneath my feet, and

my belly heaved with the now familiar nausea of nothingness.

Wake up, Exile. Curse it all, will you wake up? Someone is already in the cave, and I didn't have time to change your form.

My head felt like new-forged iron: pulsing, hammered, hot, and soft. I was trying to figure out who was working so hard at waking me, when I glimpsed a flash of silver in the darkness, and my training saved my life. I could not consciously have come up with the plan to roll out of the way and bring an arm around like a battering ram to take out my attacker. I connected with a body, but I couldn't see where it had landed or what was its condition, so I backed away and hit a stone wall. Ash and soot sprinkled on my head like dry rain. I was back in that other place again . . . inside my own soul . . . mind . . . whatever was the truth of the landscape the Aife wove.

I struggled to remember what had happened since Merryt ran for the portal, but could come up with nothing. Sickness. Falling. I felt the back of my shirt and found it wet with blood. My leg still ached from my cramp. The bruises from my battle with Merryt were still fresh. I had not regenerated. Ysanne must not have shut down the portal as she had after Tegyr, Emrys, and Drych had gone back. To hold the portal open between battles was tiring for the Aife, but worse for me. I felt like I had rolled down a mountain in an avalanche. The toll of the long days and nights, the sorcery I had worked, the combat, the fear of my change . . . all of it dogged my feet like iron shackles.

Another flash of silver. I dodged it and ran outside the cave. It was Drych who came after me, his face still serious . . . and far too fresh and rested for my taste. How long was this taking? For the first time in forever, I thought of Aleksander. How in the name of sense was I going to get to him in time? If I was fighting here too long . . . captive . . . he would think I had betrayed him again.

I had little time to worry about it. At least three Wardens were present. Maybe more. Perhaps the Ezzarians had sensed the demons slipping past their barrier and realized that they needed to be done with me. Perhaps they guessed that I was reaching the end of my endurance. Although the Aife could not see what occurred on the battleground, she could sense the changes in the Wardens and the demon. If Ysanne was still the Aife—and of course she was, for only Ysanne was skilled enough to bring more than one Warden at a time beyond a portal—she would read every change in me as an author reads his own book.

I took to the air to escape Drych and surveyed the desolation until I caught sight of Merryt. I had to kill him before I got too tired. Merryt and Tegyr were together, creeping through a region thick with charred trees that backed up to a sheer cliff. I touched earth and took them on.

Merryt still thought to gain his prize. After a brief flurry, I misjudged the angle of the cliff and got myself trapped in a wide, angular notch. With only one opponent, I would have been out quickly. But Merryt pressed me backward, while Tegyr guarded his left flank and prevented my slipping past. "The word, devil," growled Merryt, grinning with such evil that I kept glancing over my shoulder. "Tell me the word or you will pay a price you've not yet counted."

"I have no word to give you, save the tally of your faults, Merryt—murderer, thief, violator."

"Perhaps I can prime your memory," he said. "Here, boy, let's switch sides. I want to test his strong side." Merryt retreated a few steps so Tegyr could pass in front of him, but before the youth could take up his position, Merryt grabbed the startled young Warden and put a blade to his throat. "The word, devil. Give me the spell to open the gateway or I'll carve a hole in this young neck."

Stunned, horrified, I scanned Merryt's face to find some evidence that he was bluffing, even as my feet crept forward ever so slightly to get within range of a knife throw. "There is no—"

Before I could so much as get out my protest, Merryt left a gaping bloody gash across Tegyr's throat and shoved the tall young body to the ground. "I'll have the word. You'll not keep me from my destiny."

"Murdering bastard!" I went after him with everything I had left, anger and indignation giving new life to my sword arm. Blow after blow I laid on him, blood madness blurring my vision and leaving me heedless of my own safety and good sense. Before a quarter hour more, I had him running for his life . . . exactly the wrong thing to do, for he ran straight to the top of a barren hill—where he found Nestayo, a cocky youth who could not have been fighting for a month.

"Nestayo! Keep away from him," I yelled when I saw Merryt wrap his arm paternally around the unsuspecting young Warden's shoulder. The knife was in position before Nestayo could turn to see me. "Verdonne's child, Merryt, don't do it."

"Then tell me the word," he yelled down from his hilltop. "You've sealed the gateway to human flesh, and I *will* pass. I will free the Nameless God to take his vengeance on those who have imprisoned him since time's beginning. I will do it. Not you. Not Vyx. Not—"

"There is no word, Merryt." I flew to the hilltop and touched earth only a few paces from him. "No spell. The gateway's open. Gods of night, let this boy go. He's done noth—"

"You lie, demon." And Nestayo, too, was dead, his blood soaking the gray ash.

Beside myself with helpless fury, I would have slain Merryt then. But no sooner had Nestayo fallen, than Drych came running up the far side of the hill and caught sight of Nestayo's body and me hacking at a staggering Merryt. "Keep away," I screamed. "This wretch has murdered the others. For your life, Drych, for everything, stay away from him."

My moment's distraction had Merryt scrambling down into a dry gully that split the hillside. He was bleeding from wounds in his belly and a bone-deep laceration in his leg, off balance, reeling, his flat face dark with rage. I jumped down the steep slope, sliding and skidding on the gravel, ready to meet him at the bottom to finish him. One blow and I would rid the world of his evil. But Drych took a long leap and landed on his fresher legs between Merryt and me, his sword puncturing the flesh between my ribs before he had fairly landed. I pulled away quickly. For a moment I thought my lung was pierced. I tried to shape the wind to take me upward, so I could pounce on the squirming, growling Merryt from the other side; but Drych was too close, his dark eyes blazing and his sword hammering at me with fury. "Murdering demon!" he swore. "You've killed them all."

The stubborn boy wouldn't budge, so I had to push him back. My arms were like lead. My pierced side was burning. And then came an explosion of cold fire in my back as a spear point buried itself just beside my spine.

"We'll die together, devil," panted the fallen Merryt, hatred boiling from him like the blood from his mouth.

I backed away from the two of them, stumbling, trying to stay on my feet as I reached over my shoulder and around my side to reach the spear. Threatening to rip its own bloody way out, it was doing more damage every second. Drych looked from one to the other of us, evidently trying to decide whether to finish me or help the other Warden. "Keep away from him," I said, grunting as I wrenched the steel point from my back and felt a river of blood wash down my back. "In the name of all the gods, believe me, Drych. He's killed your friends and mine. For nothing. Nothing." I tried to raise my sword again, but could not lift it.

Drych hurried over to Merryt, dropped his weapon, and fell to his knees. "I'll get you out, brother. Are you badly—?"

As the boy bent over the wounded man, Merryt laid a hand on Drych's sword and transformed it into a forearm-long dagger.

"Watch out!" I yelled . . . too late.

The snarling man shoved the blade into the young Warden's belly, then pushed the limp body off himself and rolled to his side in the ash. "I'll take what vengeance I can, friend Seyonne. The world will reap the harvest of this night for a thousand years. Your wife will bleed you for this, and the rai-kirah will have their way with the rest of the Ezzarians." Merryt started laughing, blood spurting from his lips in company with gasping, grotesque guffaws. "You've opened the way. Someday soon the Nameless will be free. He will rewrite the story of the world in terror, and he will bring its end in blood and fire and madness." He pointed a shaking finger at me. "And no one will ever know the truth. They will name you Abomination forever."

I willed enough blood to stay in my body to move three steps, raise my sword, and cut off Merryt's grinning head. Then I fell to my knees beside the fallen Drych, woozy, breathless, the world spinning and pulsing, my hands and feet already numb. The boy was still.

Ah, sweet Verdonne. So many things left undone. There was no help for most of them, but one . . . one duty I could not ignore were the beasts of the netherworld devouring my flesh. With every breath I could summon, I began to sing the Ezzarian death chant, raising my voice—no, it was Denas's voice, for it was clear and melodious, speaking everything of sorrow that I had never had the words or music to shape—for Kyor and Drych and Tegyr and Nestayo, and for Blaise who lay in madness and my son and the others who would follow him . . . and for Ysanne, who would now know that her Wardens were dead. I sang every word of it. Even Fiona could not have faulted me.

"I'm so sorry, Drych. So sorry," I whispered when I had done. Then I lay my nerveless hand on the boy and rolled him to his back . . . and found him still breathing. Shallow. Painful. His dark eyes were open, begging life not to desert him here on the brink of the abyss

"Gods of earth and sky! Stubborn . . . to hold on while I sing you into the afterlife."

With the slightest movement of his lips and the slightest bit of apprehension in his face, Drych whispered a profound question. "Master?"

"I'm here, Drych," I said, trying to smile with lips that were numb. "Indeed I am. And if you can hold on a bit more, then so can I. Here . . ." I laid his flaccid arm about my shoulders and considered the immense problem of getting to my feet. I fumbled for the dropped spear, still stained with my own blood, and transformed it into a wooden post. Using it for leverage, I eased upward, hoping the rent muscles in my back would hold together long enough to get the boy up.

"You must call the Aife," I gasped, heaving him to his feet, both of us swaying dangerously. "I can't do it. Tell her . . . just say, 'Aife, *gyat*.' She'll understand it." *Gyat* meant "get the portal as close to me as you can possibly make it." Ysanne and I had made up our own language for hard times.

Drych managed to get out the words before he slipped into insensibility. But he wasn't dead when the portal appeared . . . not quite. "Go safely," I said after dragging him the few steps to the opening. "Heal well. Live." I shoved him gently through the wavering doorway, then fell to my knees, fighting for a last breath as the world and I dissolved together.

CHAPTER 39

*Verdonne ruled the sweet forest lands until she grew
tired, for her body was mortal. But Valdis honored her
and made her immortal, and even unto this day she
rules the forests of the earth and he remains her strong
right arm.*

*Valdis built a magic fortress, a prison furnished with
beauty and comfort. Because Valdis would not be a
father-slayer, he locked his immortal father away in
that fortress. And the young god took his father's name
from him and destroyed it, so that no man or woman
could invoke it ever again. But woe to the man who
unlocks the prison of the Nameless God, for there will
be such a wrath of fire and destruction laid upon the
earth as no mortal being can imagine. And it will be
called the Day of Ending, the last day of the world.*
*—The story of Verdonne and Valdis as told to the First
of the Ezzarians when they came to the lands of trees*

Once an Aife's portal is closed down, the possessed victim
does not retain the wounds his demon suffered in the
demon combat. The spear hole in my back, the sword
wound between my ribs, and the other results of my night
of combat were gone when I came to awareness on a morning that was gray and still. I was, however, exhausted to the
point of desperation. And as before, my head felt exactly as
one might expect—as though a war had been fought within
its bony confines. My bandaged eye throbbed, and my
shriveled heart grieved for what had happened and what
was to come. My wife was going to kill me. And there was
nothing I could do about it.

Ezzarians were cowards when it came to meting out judg-

ments on their own. While finding it easy to say "live" or
"die" or "go mad" to those demon victims we sought out
in the world, we had a difficult time in condemning ourselves to necessary death. The children like my son, born
possessed, were laid out naked in the forest near the haunts
of wolves. If the gods meant for them to live, we said, they
would live. But the gods had created wolves to devour such
tasty morsels of flesh, and when we found the tiny, red-
stained bones, we claimed it was the gods who killed our
children, not us. A possessed Warden was another such
dilemma. If he could not be healed, then what was the
Queen to do? He could not be allowed to live, for he carried secrets that could endanger our existence. He was a
powerful sorcerer and a powerful fighter who could afflict
other humans with his demon madness. He, too, had to die,
but what Ezzarian, sworn to protect life, could wield the
ax or rope to do it?

And so another way had been devised. Immobilize the
abomination with spells and potions and bindings, lay him
out well guarded so that no one could come to his rescue,
and cut him. Not the large veins that would surely kill him
quickly, but in other places—arms or legs or back—or perhaps put a knife in the belly. If the gods wished him to
live, he would live. But the gods had meant a man to have
blood in him, and so when the man's heart had nothing
more to pump, it was the gods who had executed him,
not us.

Drych was not dead. But neither was he conscious, able
to give some small evidence that perhaps I had not slain
two young Wardens and one very old one, as well as the
young Ezzarian stranger. The demon fire still burned blue
in my unbandaged eye, and that was evidence enough.

I lay on my belly, my arms and legs spread out and tied
to stakes driven very firmly into the ground. They had built
a circle of small fires around me and thrown enough jasnyr
in each one to stuff a pillow. The smoke hung thick and
choking, making my nerves thrum painfully with demon
memories. The air was heavy. Oppressive. Still. A storm
was coming.

"Will you not allow him to tell his story, my lady?" said
Kenehyr. "To bleed a man without defense . . . ." The white-

haired Comforter sat leaning against one of the pillars a
few paces away from me.

"Three Wardens and one youth lie dead," spat Talar.
"In Nevya's tent another victim lies lost in hopeless madness, no doubt afflicted by this same demon. This Warden's
soul is destroyed. What more evidence is needed?"

My bandaged eye blocked any glimpse of those who
stood over me. Ysanne, Fiona, Maire, Talar, and Caddoc
were unbodied voices. Waves of helpless rage washed
through me as they spoke across my back as if I were already dead.

As always, Caddoc added his voice to Talar's. "We have
seen his corruption and his villainy. Fiona says our barrier
has held firm, and the gateway has disappeared with the
dawn. We need to be done here and get home before these
possessed Derzhi pounce. Who knows what this devil has
told them? Who knows what will happen with the
demons now?"

Lightning ripped the blackening sky behind the pillar,
and a muted rumble lagged only briefly. Not far. The
storms in this wild land were ferocious. My skin was
clammy with the stifling stillness, and the vessels in my
head throbbed with warning. I tried again to move. If I
could only uproot one of the stakes to get a hand or foot
free . . . but either their spells and potions were too potent
or I had reached the end of my strength.

"But Emrys claims that Seyonne did not slay him or
Tegyr when he had the chance," said Kenehyr. "Does that
not seem strange?"

"It was clear that this demon held a grudge against poor
Merryt and wanted to save his power to crush the older
man." Maire. Even the Weaver had been deceived by the
old Ezzarian. "Tegyr now lies dead, and Emrys admits he
was confused."

"But Fiona's reports of Seyonne's ideas . . . What if . . . ?
I think we should wait for Drych to waken."

"These reports are but evidence of madness and corruption," said Talar. "And Catrin says it could be weeks before we even know if the boy will survive."

Kenehyr would not leave it. "Fiona, tell us again. Why

did Seyonne go to the demons? What is this madness about
splitting ourselves apart?"

"It makes no difference," said my watchdog fiercely.
"The Queen has decided." I recognized that tone of voice,
and I pitied whoever had to deal with Fiona in the next
hours. Nothing was going to please her.

"But—"

If I could have spoken, I would have begged Kenehyr to
stop. The dear old man was going to get himself into trouble, and indeed, there was nothing to be done. Vyx had
not come. The demons had not yet slaughtered the Ezzarians, but if they had not been allowed through the gateway, it was going to happen soon. And if they had gotten
through . . . Merryt was dead, but there were others like
Gennod. If Vyx had not secured the fortress, then I had
unleashed the darkness. Blaise lay in madness, and his time
had likely run out. I could not determine the hour, but I
was not going to make my rendezvous with Aleksander.
What comes, comes. Let it be done with. Let the storm break.

Caddoc forced himself calm. "My lady, we should be on
our way home. Our spies tell of these dreadful disturbances
in the Derzhi camps all night . . . just as this one threatened.
The warriors are in frenzy."

"Enough," said Ysanne, her voice like ice. "All of you,
leave me alone here."

"But, my—"

"Leave me or I'll have you spread out with him,
Caddoc."

The others withdrew. For a while, all I glimpsed was the
tail of Ysanne's green gown swirling in agitation. She was
angry. When she was troubled, she sat still; when she was
angry, she paced. At last she came to kneel beside me, so
close I could smell her hair and the sweetness of her skin.

I could neither move nor speak. Their potions and enchantments had seen to that. But with every shred of my
being, I begged time to run backward and Ysanne to hear
all I wanted to tell her of love and memory and desire. *Let
me take you in my arms once more, beloved, and let me
brush my hands over the swelling form of our son. Let me
whisper to you again of the joy we know and the joy to
come when our love takes life. You are my heart, my peace,*

the breath of my being. Make me forget everything that's come between us, my love. Help me forget. My tongue held the words shaped by my longing, but there they died unspoken. My cheek was pressed against the hard ground, my good eye half-closed. A few cold spatters tickled my face. Rain. Not Ysanne's tears. When she spoke at last, it was not with regret or longing.

"Damn you, Seyonne! Damn you. I thought you loved me. I betrayed my oath for you—letting the demon child live. I was ready to come with you as soon as Fiona was prepared. I would have given up everything for you, but you wouldn't wait. You, in your infernal stubbornness and pride . . . you wouldn't trust me. Then you went and destroyed yourself and left me nothing. You get to die, but I'll have to see you this way forever and know what I did. What love is that?"

I heard the slip of a knife pulled from a sheath, and at the same time, something dropped to the dirt in front of my eye. Small, round . . . gleaming dully in the storm-laden air . . . ah, gods of night . . . the token I had given her on our wedding day: a gold ring, delicate, graven with roses and wrapped with enchantments of protection and loving memory. I was staring so intently at the abandoned ring that I didn't even notice the movement of her hand, only the ripping fire when she buried the knife deep in my right side.

She stood up and spoke to someone who approached her from behind me. "Let no one succor him. Send word when he's dead." And as the storm broke, lashing the hills of Dasiet Homol with bitter rain, she walked away.

It was a long day dying. The cold rain that battered my bare back pooled beneath me, and a constant warm tide leaked into it from the dull ache in my side. Thunder and lightning rampaged across the hillsides; soft hail tried to hammer me into the ground and had the two guards softly cursing. I supposed they kept so quiet because they were afraid the demon might invade them once my physical existence was done with. I, the demon.

I did not close my unbandaged eye. I could not bear to be alone in darkness with my thoughts, with Denas, whose voice was mercifully silent, though I felt his anger raging deep within like a subterranean river. Better to keep focused on some dull object: the smooth white roundness of a pillar, the ant struggling to get around a melting hailstone, the dirt clod dissolving into the wet ground. *Fill your senses with the ordinariness of it—its color and shape and texture and smell—and soon there will be no room for other, more uncomfortable sensations.* Galadon had taught me the technique so a healer could stitch my wounds without giving me any pain-dulling medicament. A Warden could not afford to drink such potions. Too much of them left a man muddled in the head. And now when I would have given much to be so muddled, the Ezzarians had filled me with this useless mess that kept me paralyzed and powerless, but left every pain of body and mind excruciatingly vivid. Bad enough to be required to lie in the cold rain dying. One shouldn't have to think about it.

Lightning shattered the gloom, so close I could smell it, and the belch of thunder followed so soon after, the storm must be just on top of me. Perhaps it was the storm that weighed so heavy on my back. Raindrops rolled down my face. I was parched, but could lure few of them onto my tongue. Periodically someone would jam a thick, warm finger onto my neck, then tiptoe away, whispering "stubborn devil."

Stubborn . . . if I could have made it go faster, I would have done so. I was pleased when I began to shiver, for it meant I'd lost enough blood to make a difference. When my vision began to blur and my breath to labor, I tried to make my peace with life. I had done my best. But what had come of all the pain and grief and blood? That was the worst part of the whole business—to die believing I had accomplished nothing.

Soon I could no longer focus my attention, and all my unwanted memories were set loose to play havoc in my head: childhood, training, demon battles, slavery . . . So many faces accusing me of treachery and blindness and insufficiency: Aleksander and Blaise, my son and Kyor and Drych, all the dead demons, all those, human and demon, who were going to be dead in the next hours and years. . . . And throughout everything was Ysanne, the threads of our

lives binding everything else together. From the moment
of our first meeting, I had never passed a day without loving her. On the day of my freedom and homecoming, I had
believed that no man had ever been so blessed as to see
the living substance of his dreaming. And she . . . she had
said she was ready to give up the throne for me . . . but
my anger had driven me away. What wretched fool had
ever destroyed himself so perfectly?

All this was terrible enough . . . but as the cold rain fell
and the blood leaked out, hard memory abandoned me to
wilder visions . . .

*Riding in the desert . . . splashes of purple and gold sand
billowing behind us and Aleksander laughing. He gloried in
the desert. What was so beautiful as watching a human being
reveling in his purest joy? The gold circlet on his head glittered in the sunlight . . . he drew the sunlight with him like
a mantle of health and laughter across the shadowed world.
But there . . . across the dunes lay a shadow . . . nothing
visible to cast it, but even Aleksander's golden mantle did
not illuminate it. Yet he kept riding, and though he tried to
stay astride his mount, bony hands reached up from the
shadow and pulled him down . . . tearing him apart piece
by bloody piece . . .*

*And all I could do was watch from the hot, bare courtyard
where I knelt beside the bloodstained block. They gave me
no hood to hide the terrible view, and so I saw my hope
ripped apart, and I saw the headsman's ax begin to fall . . .*

"No! No! This prisoner will not die this day. I have de-
creed it."

Oh, but he would. And soon. *Please, whatever god there
is to hear me, let it be soon.*

*Soaring in the brilliance of the day with my companion . . .
such delight. The brown and white bird showed me the ways
of beauty, leading me through the dappled forest and out
over the highland meadows. So gloriously lovely, but the
sun burned my naked back; my lash marks throbbed and
ached in the heat. So we dipped down into the cool and
shady rift, following the stream as it cut down into the pale*

white stone. There at the curve, the turquoise water swirled around upon itself and joined a smaller stream of deepest green. Together they'd made a round basin . . . such gem-like color as artists can only dream of. We plunged into the water, deep, cleansing, healing . . . but now to breathe . . . Which way is up? Not this way . . . it is darker . . . much darker and so cold . . . the wrong way . . . downward . . . but the water is too heavy on my back, and I can't breathe . . .

Only a moment's jarring wakening, as if I were falling. Mud was splashing in my eye, but I could not close it. *Soon. Soon.*

Flying again . . . gliding above the gold-touched hills of Ezzaria. How beautiful it was . . . serene . . . the splashes of red and blue from the firephlox and larkspur . . . the babbling of tiny brooks crossing the meadows. Magnificent trees . . . yellow trunks intertwined . . . Gamarands? So this was not Ezzaria . . . not my home . . .

"Go away, intruder, or be silent if you cannot leave me. Let me do my dying alone at least. Let me choose my visions." But he wouldn't go. The silent sharer of my soul drove me beyond the forest of yellow trees to the place where the trees were burned and ash lay deep on the ground . . . No, no. I've been here. This is a terrible place. I live in this place, and I cannot bear it any longer. There is no sustenance here.

Soon. Soon. The thunder was very far away. The ground beneath my cheek had lost its gritty texture. As in the pits of the Gastai, I could not feel the edges of my physical being. I sank deeper . . .

I flew upward, seeking the blue sky, craving sunlight. But every turn took me toward the darkness, this dreadful blot that obscured my sight—Tyrrad Nor. Gray stone, carved from the cliff in graceful spires and arches, but grown terrible, overlaid with deadness. Corruption. Fly away. Stay away. It is not meant for mortal beings to walk here. Yet still I flew, drawn there, knowing that I needed to see. I circled closer to the walls, overgrown with vines as thick as my fingers, bearing thorns like small scythes. And there in the thick wall was a breach . . . a jagged chasm of darkness broken out of the wall . . . and warm blood, so darkly red it was almost black, flowed out of the breach and down the rocky precipice into the gamarand wood. The burning, blighted wood.

Someone came running down the road below me . . . a brilliant light of purple and blue and swirling gray-green. "Late. Always late." Laughter . . . charming, mischievous laughter . . . relieved the oppressive darkness of the stone. "Just my size, don't you think? Until the next breach, of course, but someone else will have to deal with that. Sorry we had no time to see the world together." And with a laughing spin, the light dissolved, flowed into the breach, and sealed it . . .

No! A last, weak burst of impotent rage pulled me out of my visions. Rain had pooled beside my face, and the water did not move with my breath. *Vyxagallanxchi!* Was it truth, what I had dreamed? Had he done what he intended and died in the accomplishment? It was not fair that I was never to know. *So leave it fool. Everyone is mad or dead . . . or going to be so very shortly. Enough is enough.* I reached for oblivion, and it was just at my fingertips . . . but I could not yet escape . . .

The fortress . . . the bloody breach in the wall . . . the spinning blue and purple light flowing into the breach and sealing it . . . protecting us all from the leaking river of death and fire . . . But that was not the end of the tale. From the fortress came a bellow of rage . . . of vengeance . . . of madness. I circled high like an eagle seeking a new eyrie in the midnight crags. The sun paled and sagged below the mountains with the prisoner's curses, and in the protection of oncoming night, I circled closer. Once I had dreamed of a frozen castle, and it had been a hard lesson that I needed to learn . . . and now this, too. I needed to understand . . . to see the face of my Nameless enemy, the one who would destroy the world . . .

He was standing on the windy heights of his prison, a dark shape against the gray rock and the black sky. The night had fallen silent as the rising moon went dark and the cowardly stars retreated behind boiling clouds. Closer. Circle, and open the senses. Devouring darkness . . . so familiar. I knew this evil. I wanted to fly away, but as the Warden's summons draws the demon to the place of battle, so the truth of the fortress beckoned me. He turned as I approached, and his robes fluttered in the rising wind . . . robes of black, trimmed with silver. Blue fire colder than the winds of Kir'-Vagonoth burned in his face. His face . . . scarred with the mark of bondage . . . and when he spread his arms wide to test the wind, I saw that he had wings . . .

No! I will not! It is not me!

The cold darkness crept inside me and began to eat its way out . . .

"Let me through. I'm commanded to see if he's dead." The clear voice was scarcely audible against the steady downpour.

"No one is to touch him but myself, madam. The gods will have him soon. There's a lake of blood on the other side of him."

"Do you know who I am, guardsman? I bear the Queen's mandate. We want to be sure." Of course. The watchdog would want to know when her watch was over. Fiona.

"My apologies, Kafydda. Be quick and hold your protections carefully. The demon will be free soon."

Someone breathing close by. A slender cold finger on my neck and the soft press of a hand on my back. A hunting bird's cry. A fluttering of wings.

The vultures are here, I thought. *A bony, bloodless meal for both bird and woman. Too bad.*

I wasn't shivering anymore, and as the puddle of water lapped against my staring eye, the world was drowned in murk.

"Damnation. Did she have to gut you?"

One would have thought the speaker herself was doing exactly that, for she stuck something extremely sharp right into the place where I hurt the most. I was surprised to hear a man screaming and even more so to discover it was me. I was surprised to hear anything. I thought I was dead. I wanted to be dead. The tugging, stinging aftermath of the stabbing pain seemed benign compared to the first sticking. Or the next. Or the next. Only the novelty of it all kept me from passing out.

"I'm sorry. All right. I'm sorry." The mumbling apology came somewhere from behind me.

I was still on my face. My arms and legs were still bound, though with rags instead of ropes, and it was still raining, just not directly on me. My head lay on something soft and dry, though every other part of me was soggy.

"I've got to get it closed up, or you're going to lose what little blood's left inside you. The cursed closina won't let your blood clot, and I don't have any of the right things. If we'd had more time, we could have taken you to someone who knew what she was doing. Damned stupid woman, why didn't you learn these things when you had the chance?"

From the course of the conversation, I realized that the speaker was actually addressing herself, even if some of the words happened to be aimed at me. And since the speaker was Fiona, I knew she had no intention of me hearing her. Just as well. The only responses I could come up with were the pitiful wavering scream and a few abject groans. By the time she finished with her sewing exercise—I finally figured out what it was she was doing—I was quivering wreckage.

To my continuing surprise, as soon as she had wrapped a dry bandage about my middle, she unbound my hands and feet—not that I was going anywhere. I stayed spread out like a starfish in a tide pool, because I had no strength to move. Through my churning head drifted the vague presumption that Ysanne had decided to pretend she was a Gastai—kill me, heal me, then have the pleasure of killing me again.

"Now to get something in your stomach."

When Fiona pulled my arms and legs together and attempted to roll me onto my back, I was lost again. My death dreams—my visions of failure and destiny and horror—continued to plague me with far more vivid reality than the young Aife and her mysterious activities. But still I did not die.

Sometime much later I seemed to be in the rain again. Drowning. But it was only Fiona trying to pour water down my throat at the same time as I was trying to fight off the vision of my infamy. "I will not!" I shouted—my voice harsh and weak—choking and gasping as I inhaled the water. "I will not. It is not me." Even when my one usable eye came open, all I could see was darkness . . . the end of the world resting in my hand.

"Here, be still. You're going to tear yourself apart." Firm hands held me down until I could wake up, catch a breath, and fall limp against whatever lumpy pillow supported me half sitting. I was covered by a cloak that stretched only between my neck and my knees, which meant it was likely Fiona's. Just beside my feet was a tiny fire—a sorcerer's fire, for it put out a great deal more heat than its size would lead one to expect. While she proceeded to pour more water down my parched throat, I got a blurred glimpse of our surroundings—a grove of thin trees, some rocks behind our backs, tall grass trampled by no more than three or four sets of boots, an immensity of silence, and infinite damp darkness. We were nowhere near the Ezzarian camp. I could make no sense of it.

"Did the Queen command you to try drowning next?" I said. "Just be done with it. And quickly, please." I rolled to the side, drew up my knees against the tearing pain in my side, and dug the heel of my hand into my eye, vainly trying to erase my seeing. No matter how I denied its legitimacy, no matter the platitudes about prophecy and possibility . . . had not the vision of my first dream come true? I had become my enemy. I had led a demon legion into my world, bringing death and ruin. No rains could ever cleanse the blood from my hands.

A hand lay on my shoulder. "You need water."

"I need to be dead. Why am I not dead?"

"It isn't time for you to die yet."

"Is there someone else I need to kill first? Some other war to start or make worse? Some other stupid mistake I need to make? My wife has judged me abomination. She is always right. She warned me."

"You're very sure of your guilt."

"Tell me of someone I did not fail."

"First you must drink and eat a bit. Then I'll tell you." I didn't argue with her. I assumed that dying prisoners being

guarded by the future Queen of Ezzaria had few options.
Fiona proceeded to fill a cup from a small pot that was
steaming beside her fire. "Here. Try this and see if it set-
tles." I reached for the cup, but my hand was so unsteady,
Fiona bypassed it and took the cup straight to my mouth.
Broth . . . rabbit or gorse-hen . . . strong and hot. The very
smell of it gave me a hint of how monstrously hungry I
was . . . and how sick. I pushed away the cup and vomited
up most of the water. My side felt like Ysanne's knife was
still within.

The sickness left my head muddled, and soon I was flying
again, across the river of blood to take my destined place
in the fortress of darkness. Images and words were laid one
upon the other until I could no longer distinguish vision
from reality . . .

*Circle . . . observe . . . You have no home but this . . .
truth awaits . . . magnificence . . . glory . . . peace . . . It is
your place. Your birthright.*

"I thought you'd never get back, old man. What of the
Derzhi? Any sign?"

"Nothing. No movement."

*I soared and swooped like a homing vulture. No, Vyx,
don't do it. I need you to tell me what is this place. What
am I? As I touched my feet to the gray battlement, an arrow
of fire pierced my side, shot from an unseen bow, and a
spear of ice pierced my back. I could not stop the
bleeding . . .*

"Damned if I know if it's done right. Looks wretched.
Fifty colors of purple. I've never sewn flesh . . . and so
deep a wound . . ."

*The winged figure began to turn so I would see his face,
but I buried my eyes. No! No! Please. Oh, gods of the universe, let it not be me. Blood dripped from my hands . . .
cries of torment . . . death everywhere . . .*

"We'll just have to wait and see. The trouble is we can't
move him far enough . . . and he's so weak . . ."

"The young Warden yet lives, but Searchers have sensed
the demon. They're coming fast . . ."

The young Warden . . . Drych, don't die on me . . . oh,

*sweet Verdonne, let him live. One life, however brief . . . let
there be one life not held to my account.*

I was bound again . . . no, just held tight, my shoulders
burning, my chest on fire. It was only determined hands
holding me still. I could not breathe for my despair. Could
not think. "Tell me the story, Fiona. Tell me something
of life."

"Come, Seyonne . . . we've got to move. The Queen is
coming to retrieve you." Fiona's face took blurry shape in
front of me, and behind her a line of white lights, strewn
through the darkness like a string of glowing pearls.

A small, bulky figure was huffing and puffing as he
stuffed pots and cups in a pack and kicked the fire to ashes.
Balthar. "Sorry I couldn't give you more warning. Just
couldn't move these old bones fast enough. They had scouts
out and about moments after you got away. I thought you
were going farther."

Fiona stuck her arm beneath my shoulders. "We didn't
have time. It took too long to get through the guards. Curse
it all, what are we to do?"

"No more than a quarter hour 'til she's here."

Stunning clarity at last penetrated my clouded mind. As
Fiona eased me to sitting, I stared at the young woman in
disbelieving wonder. "Fiona, what have you done?"

"Stop babbling. Save your strength to move. Balthar,
help me get him up the rocks."

"Up there? Woman, are you mad?"

"He needs to be where his friends can find him. Come
on, old man. He doesn't weigh anything. He has no blood
in him."

Before I could blink away the rest of my confusion, Fiona
had her bony shoulders under one of my arms, and Balthar
had his soft, round ones under the other. For someone who
didn't weigh anything, I gave them a great deal of trouble.
I could scarcely see the ground, much less place my feet
on it to any purpose. They half carried, half dragged me
up a steep, gravel-strewn path that led to the top of the
little rock prominence that sheltered the niche and the
spring. Then, as the world spun drunkenly, they lowered
me to the ground in an untidy heap.

"Stay quiet and stay low. Balthar, don't let him fall off the cliff." Light footsteps scrambled back down the path.

For a while I had my head bent over my knees, dizzy and nauseous, unable to speak for the pain in my side and the weakness of my head—unable to ask the thousand questions to which Fiona's actions gave birth. The old man mumbled sympathetically, but soon crept away from me toward the edge of the rocks.

"Kafydda!" Ysanne's command rang out through the night. "What do you imagine you're doing?"

"I'm going to prevent my Queen from murdering her husband, lady." The strong young voice showed no signs of the speedy climb and descent.

"Seyonne is already dead."

"He has more of life in him than the entire Ezzarian race, my lady. More of grace. More of honor. I will not let him die." *Foolish Fiona. Never argue with your Queen.* I mustered a scrap of strength and lifted my head enough to see the line of sorcerers emerging from the grove. Their white lights burned steady like small droplets of moonlight. I could not see Fiona, who must have been standing just below me at the base of the rocks.

"Do you understand the consequences of your actions, Fiona? All your preparation . . . your testing . . . your skills . . . wasted. To let a demon corrupt you . . . You were to be Queen of Ezzaria."

"Everything we live is a lie, lady. I believed that if I came and told you the story as this man has revealed it to me, you would see the truth. I thought that anyone he loved so deeply must be capable of hearing his message, and that anyone privileged to know him so intimately must certainly trust it. But you persist in your blindness . . . even to the most precious thing you possess."

"How dare you speak of these things to me?"

"Keep your throne, madam. Keep your war. I'm done with all of it."

"Corruption!" Talar called the verdict, and in that moment Fiona disappeared from the sight of the Ezzarians. Their eyes went out of focus, denying her existence, and their minds shut out all memory of her, and their tongues forgot her name. I well knew the devastating loneliness that would sweep through the young Aife as the Ezzarians turned and walked away. But I did not doubt her strength. Her straight back would not bend under the weight of their shunning.

"Find the demon," commanded Ysanne angrily. "He can't be far. Bleed him until he's dead."

No one could mistake the finality of Ysanne's words. No matter if I were transformed into Valdis himself in front of her . . . my life with Ysanne was done with. A tomb of ice could be no colder an ending. Such pain would take a lifetime to ease, assuming a man had a lifetime to spend on it. And yet Fiona had done what I had begged for her to do. I rested my head in my hot, damp palm and smiled. Someone knew the truth and would find a way to carry on. How had I ever doubted her?

"Curse the everlasting pomposity of Ezzarians," growled Balthar from above me. "They're on their way up here. What am I to do with you?"

"Leave," I whispered. "You've no friends among the Ezzarians. You'll be dead before morning." The night was not going to hide me. The Searchers had sensed my demon presence all the way from Dasiet Homol. The small matter of a steep hillside was not going to slow them down. "After all this is over, find Fiona and help her."

"But—"

"Go, Balthar. Hurry. And my thanks and Verdonne's care go with you."

"The gods preserve you, Warden. You are in their hands." He touched my shoulder kindly, then hefted the pack onto his back and ran.

I could hear the drumming of hooves from my left, the easiest way up for horses. They would find me long before Fiona could climb the hill again . . . and even if I had the strength to move, there was nowhere to go. I would have transformed, but could not remember how. And so I stayed on my knees and wrapped my arms around my middle, trying to hold myself together and my head upright. I did not want to shame Fiona.

The shouts came quickly. "There at the cliff edge!"

"Careful! Keep your distance!"

They needn't have worried. Waves of shivering nausea

swept over me, and my heart was racing faster than the Ezzarian hooves.

Three different loops of rope fell over my shoulders and pulled tight, straightening my back and tearing at the inexpert stitches in my side. I closed my eyes and buried my cry. I had not screamed for the Gastai. I would not scream for Ysanne.

I expected to be dragged away, or bound and drugged and cut again right there at the top of the hill. But things quickly became very confusing. In an instant's blur of noise and darkness and strong enchantment, there came harsh screeching from above my head, then shouts and curses and a brief clash of steel. Abruptly the cruel ropes fell slack, and I would have toppled over save for a man who slid gracefully from his horse and caught me in his arms before I fell. "By Athos's head, you'd best not be dead, my guardian. It's one thing to miss an appointment with a prince, but it's a damned impertinence to die without his leave."

"We'd best hurry if you wish to keep your identity secret, my lord." The softly accented voice came from above me. "The Ezzarians are getting their nerve back and will be on us in moments."

As my mind still grappled with the whimsical belief that it was Aleksander who was lifting me from the ground, my eyes took in another wonder. Swimming into view alongside the red-haired prince was a second worried face—a lean Ezzarian face with an arched nose and dark angled eyes and a healthy peace that I could only guess was that of Kir'Navarrin. Blaise.

The two of them lifted me to Aleksander's saddle, the Prince threw himself on behind me, and Blaise leaped onto another beast where Fiona was already perched. In a moment's magic we were gone from that place . . . traveling . . . a few steps, fifty, a hundred leagues, I could not have said, for the world went spinning off its axis and took my head along with it.

CHAPTER 40

Ezzarian stories would likely have little to say about the demon-led villains who snatched away the Abomination before he could be properly executed. How would they explain it? A huge brown and white bird had threatened to tear out their eyes; then an unknown Ezzarian and a red-haired Derzhi warrior appeared out of nowhere and fought like wild men to release the vile traitor that had just been recaptured. And then the three—for of course they could not mention the woman who no longer existed—rode off in the moonlit night, vanishing as they took a path no human man could discover.

Two days went by before I could verify my own view of what had happened, that indeed it was Blaise, Fiona, and Aleksander who had contrived to save my life. They took me to a stone hut Blaise knew of, high in the mountains bordering Ezzaria, and there swathed me in dry blankets and plied me with all the food and drink and medicines that Aleksander could command and Blaise could transport through his hidden pathways. They stayed close by my side until a confused Derzhi physician, similarly transported to and fro, persuaded them that all I needed was rest and nourishment. Even then I was forced to come to my senses, just to avoid drowning in their care.

Only bit by bit did I learn the full story. Fiona was ferocious about keeping me undisturbed, though in my muddled, mumbling way I tried to tell her how desperately I needed to know. She told me that she had managed to "get Blaise to the gateway," where he had let go of his struggle and transformed. She had watched him fly off into the strange land beyond the pillared gate, knowing nothing of his prospects or his fate. But because I had kept Ysanne occupied with the struggles beyond the portal, Fiona herself had a chance to "suborn the Ezzarian blockade." In essence she had made sure the massive Ezzarian enchantment could not possibly work. The demons could pass easily—indeed Aleksander confirmed that the demon disturbances in the Derzhi camps had ended with the dawn as I had rashly promised. And instead, Fiona had devised a Weaver's block aimed directly at Merryt, frustrating his attempts to pass through the gateway. As the blockade was Merryt's own working, the rest of the Ezzarians could only think it was his own mistake. But Fiona had not been able to come up with any way to get me out of my predicament until the miracle of Blaise's return after only a few hours in Kir'Navarrin. Together the two of them snatched me from Ysanne's guards. As Blaise had heard my commands to Kyor and was determined to make my rendezvous with Aleksander, he had no time to take me too far from the Ezzarians. And so it had been a long afternoon for Fiona, waiting for Blaise to return and trying to keep me alive when I wouldn't stop bleeding. The rest I mostly remembered for myself.

Fiona tended me kindly, feeding me, washing me, poking the physician's remedies down my throat or smearing them on the ugly wound in my side. She even helped me with more private necessities when Blaise or Aleksander was not available, showing much less embarrassment than I felt at such an extension of our partnership. The three of them took turns watching when a mild fever sent me very low, and laughed in satisfaction when I mumbled that I was feeling much better, if they would but stop breathing in my face.

I should have been content. From what we could tell, the demons had passed safely into Kir'Navarrin, the Ezzarians had returned to the forests beyond the mountains, and the Derzhi had not killed each other or anyone else. Though I had no evidence but visions, I believed that Vyx had accomplished what he set out to do . . . at the ultimate cost to himself. I slept like the earth. It was only when I was awake that I dreamed, and therein lay the problem. The disturbance of my death visions lingered like the taste of

musty wine, like the telltale cough that signals the disease
yet lurks within the lungs. I was not done with the dark
fortress in Kir'Navarrin. Someday I would have to confront
the fearful questions Tyrrad Nor presented, if for nothing
but to sort out the relationship of legend and truth and
destiny. But first I had to find some way to live each day
with what I had done, and I could not see how that would
ever be possible.

On the morning of the fifth day, Aleksander came to
take his turn sitting with me and also to say good-bye. He
needed to get his warriors back to Zhagad before new trouble broke out. It was my first day sitting up, and Fiona
kindly left us alone for a while with the door of the hut
propped open to let in the warm air. The Prince sat on the
floor beside my pallet, his long arms propped on his knees,
the angled sunbeams from the window lying across his
knee-high boots and glinting off his golden arm rings.

"So all this has fallen out well for you?" I said.

"For the moment. That night of madness, birds flying in
and out of my tent and attacking my guards, nightmares,
visions, things that were not men looking out of other warriors' eyes . . . who knows what rumor will be saying? Some
men swear they saw a man with wings flying over our
camp." He waggled his eyebrows in question, but I shook
my head, and he went on. "I wasn't sure how it would go
when this Blaise came instead of you. I was a bit . . .
perturbed . . . as you might expect." In fact Blaise had told
me that Aleksander had come very near removing his heart
until Blaise had got out the story of my captivity.

"But your barons were convinced to leave without a
fight?"

"I told them that during the night's disturbances, I had
rooted out the Yvor Lukash and defeated him in single
combat. The night was so confused, no one could dispute
it. And so, I said, the sorcerer himself would kneel before
me and yield his sword, swearing fealty to my father with
all of them to witness it, and that would have to do. They
truly don't like the thought of an emperor who yields to
his barons' whims. So they complained, but were happy at
the same time." He sighed wearily and tugged absently at

his braid. "Of course, they'll never trust me completely, and I'll never trust them. I'll have to take their sons and daughters as hostages, arrange unhappy marriages into loyal hegeds, and the like. They know that, and so the peace won't last forever. But it is enough for today. As long as this Blaise keeps his word."

"He didn't have to come, my lord. He has every right to despise both Derzhi and Ezzarian; we've done our best to destroy him and his family. Yet he was willing to die for us, just after reclaiming his own life. He saved both your people and mine."

Aleksander leaned back on the stone wall, his wry smile bringing light to his eyes. "Ah, no, my guardian. We three know who saved everyone—you, who carry a part of all of us within you: Derzhi and Ezzarian"—his face grew somber—"and now rai-kirah." He inhaled deeply and shook his head, as he always did when broaching a subject that made him uncomfortable. "I want to hear the whole story from you someday." His amber gaze touched my face, then bounced away quickly. "The woman has told me what you believe about the Ezzarians and the demons, but I can't grasp it yet. I can't believe that the demon who lived in me two years ago was ever a part of something good. I need to know what this change feels like for you, because I can't bear to think it is as dreadful as—"

"Look at me, my lord."

"I've looked." He shifted uncomfortably as he avoided doing that very thing.

"Please. I need you to do this. I've no one else to ask, because these other two don't know me as you do."

"What do you want of me?"

"Look at me and tell me what you see." I was afraid for him to do it, but I didn't know when I would have another chance. The years ahead, as he found his way to the destiny scribed in his soul with light, were going to be busy and difficult.

Aleksander nodded and raised his eyes, examining me with the hard assessment he used for allies and horses. He possessed nothing of sorcery, only clear seeing and intelligence and the natural wisdom he kept hidden beneath his youthful carelessness and pride. He winced when he studied my eyes, but he did not turn away. Only after a long time did he speak. "You are the man I know."

I heaved a deep breath. "Thank you." I didn't quite believe him, but it gave me heart.

He leaped to his feet and pulled on thin leather gloves. "I would chase these Ezzarians into the wilderness for you, Seyonne. Cut off their hands for touching you ill. You know that."

"They will reap punishment enough, my lord. Truth is much harder to bear than injury. Leave them be."

"Be well, my guardian."

"Go in safety, my Prince."

I saw very little of Blaise. He, too, had responsibilities. As soon as Aleksander's physician pronounced me unlikely to die, the young outlaw had hurried off to Farrol to command him not to lead any more raids. He returned two days later, just after Aleksander had gone, and stayed only a few hours. "They were a bit surprised to see me fit," he said, laughing with an extra-reddish cast to his bronze cheeks. "Saetha kept tickling my cheek and saying, 'not mad, not mad, not mad.' "

I now owned Denas's fragmented memory of the maturing process Blaise and those like him required—and of the unchangeable consequences of its interruption. "We can't undo what's already done, even in Kir'Navarrin," I said. "You probably know that better than I now."

As always, joy balanced the sorrow in Blaise's expression. "I know. But I was able to tell Saetha and Gallitar and the others about Kir'Navarrin and the Well, and how this terrible thing that happened to them will never happen to anyone else. I thought they would never stop laughing. And for Farrol and Gorrid and Brynna and all the rest . . . think what it means for them . . ." He smiled. "I've sent word to everyone who might be interested."

"I'll make sure you know how to open the gateway." With time and teaching, Blaise would be able to unravel the enchantments of Dasiet Homol. The gateway was a part of his heritage like shape-shifting and walking the ways. He had not yet touched the beginnings of his power.

"I told Farrol he should stay in command, but he seemed

anxious to turn things back to me. Winter's coming on, and we need to see everyone safe. This isn't easy for them; we have to rethink what we're about. But I told them how the wonders I had seen demanded that we reconsider our course. Do you know which part of my story they agreed was the most marvelous?" He grinned slyly.

"I can't imagine."

"A prince of the Derzhi serving a wounded Ezzarian with his own hands. You may not be the lowest of his subjects, but what I saw in him as he came for you and tended you . . . it is enough to make me listen before I strike again."

"You won't regret it." Well, he probably would a number of times . . . but not in the end. Not if he came to know Aleksander as I did.

"I hope. As for now . . . I can't stay any longer, although . . . you and I have a great deal to talk about. I need to tell you about Kir'Navarrin. And I have so much to learn."

"When this determined young woman allows me to get back on my feet, I'll find you," I said. "I need . . ." I could not say what it was I needed. With three such friends, I felt guilty at my continued malaise. But I could think of no better place to find a little peace than in Blaise's shadow.

"I'll come back for you a week from today," he said, laying his hand upon my shoulder. "You should be fit to travel by then." With a smile and a soft brush of joyous enchantment, he transformed, and I watched him flutter through the door of the hut and soar into the morning.

Once Blaise and Aleksander were gone, Fiona and I settled into quiet days of sleeping, eating, and sitting outside to soak up the last days of autumn warmth. A little walking, leaning on her sturdy shoulder when my knees agreed to hold me up. Fiona had been extraordinarily quiet since they had brought me from Dasiet Homol, avoiding any mention of her personal predicament. I did not press her, knowing well how much introspection was involved when one took steps that could never be revoked. But as my slow days of healing passed and she stayed so quiet, I feared that her own healing did not progress. I decided the time had come for her to talk. "So what are you going to do?" I said, one evening as she gave me a bowl of soupy porridge that was still the stoutest food my damaged stomach could abide. "I'm sure Blaise would welcome—"

"I'm not brooding, if that's what you're thinking," she said, poking up the fire against the cooling air. Through the door I could see the last pale glow of day fading in the west, and a soft, fragrant wind had come up, whispering of the changing season. "You needn't worry about me."

"It's no burden to worry about you, Fiona. You saved my life a thousand times over. And so much more than that . . . more than you will ever understand. I truly want to know what you plan to do. I'm trying to figure out the same thing for myself."

"I thought you were going to Blaise." She seemed genuinely surprised.

"For a while. I'm hoping he can help me learn how not to loathe myself." I had not meant to say it so bluntly. I wasn't sure I'd ever voiced it so clearly in my mind. I was facing the most difficult battle of my life, and I needed something . . . some small hope that the struggle would be worthwhile. "But other than that, I don't know. The one who lives in me has been silent since I came so close to dying. I've no idea what that means. Vyx claimed that once I step into Kir'Navarrin, Denas will be silent forever and we will be indistinguishable. Every part of me desires to go to Kir'Navarrin, but first I must decide if I can live with the consequences, whatever they may be, or if it will be better to stay as I am, whatever that is."

"And what of your son?"

"I hope to see him. But Blaise is his guardian, and we'll decide together whether that's wise. I will not be an instrument of my child's destruction."

"Destruction?" She threw her stick in the fire, showering sparks all through the darkening hut. "Gods, is there any man alive so blind as you?"

"I've lived a life of violence, Fiona. Everywhere I've walked, I've brought death. It's not a happy consideration."

"I never told you who it was I killed at the Gasserva Fountain," she said. She stood up and walked over to the door of the hut, the line of her back saying a great deal more about the intensity of this telling than her calm, even voice.

"You don't have to—"

But she didn't pause for me. "I was six when the Derzhi conquered Ezzaria. My story was little different than that of a thousand other children. I saw my father hung up by his feet and his belly slit open while he screamed and gibbered like a mindless animal. And I saw my mother violated by a Derzhi warrior who wore the symbol of a kayeet on his breast. He took her right in front of my father, and when he was done he had his serving man put her in shackles and throw her across a packhorse. 'Get the witchery out of her,' he said, 'and she'll make a passable whore.'"

Fiona turned toward me, far enough away that I could see nothing but the dark wells of her eyes. The dying flame of sunset left a gold corona about her, as if she had taken on her own demon.

"I was hiding in the trees that day—the same tree where they hung my father and cut him open. For two days I stayed there, afraid to climb down because I would have to touch him, and because I thought there were Derzhi still looking for us. But I promised my father's spirit that I would find my mother and save her—a child knows nothing of corruption. So . . . you know well enough how we lived in those next years. Though our lives were hard, Talar taught me everything of discipline and history and law, and she found that I had talent, so I began to train as an Aife . . ."

"But you also worked as a gleaner, so you could go out into the cities and find your mother. That's why you went to Zhagad. You traced the kayeet crest—the Fontezhi heged."

"It took me nine years, but I found her. I told myself that my father's spirit would cleanse her corruption. A kitchen slave recognized my race and was willing to tell me that the woman named Carryn was still living in the house. I begged the slave to take a message, and she agreed. When she came back, she told me that Carryn would be occupied all evening in the master's courtyards, but would meet me at midnight at the Gasserva Fountain. I couldn't wait. I climbed up on the courtyard walls and examined every person who passed through, hoping to see her. The Fontezhi

lord was having a feast that night . . . hundreds of guests,
hundreds of slaves waiting on them. I couldn't see my
mother. But the lord's family was there: his first wife—the
Derzhi wife, a haughty woman, ignored by everyone—and
then his second wife came in, not Derzhi, but dressed in
silks and jewels, and she sat down at his side smiling . . .
and their children, three of them, clean and well-fed and
dressed in fine clothes . . ."

It was simple to fill in the story between her sparse
words. "He had married her, and she had borne him children. She seemed happy. You thought you had seen the
truest meaning of corruption."

It was no more possible to interrupt the flow of her
words than to turn back the rising tide. "When she came
to the Gasserva Fountain that night, I was sitting on one
of the stone benches. I had worn a veil to cover my face,
but when I saw her step down from her litter, I took off
the veil to make sure that she recognized me."

"And did she?"

"Oh, yes. She stopped ten paces away and fell to her
knees, holding her hands to her mouth and weeping and
laughing. *'Tienoch havedd, dallyya,'* she said to me. 'Greet-
ings of my heart, my precious girl.' "

"And you . . ." I didn't want to hear it—such private
pain that I could do nothing to ease.

"I stood up and walked away as if she didn't exist. I
made sure to pass close beside her, so that she knew there
was no mistake."

"Ah, Fiona . . . It is very hard, but it is not murder. Now
you've experienced it yourself and survived it."

But Fiona was not finished with her telling. "On the next
day I went to spy on her once more, to view the image of
corruption so I would never forget. The house was draped
in mourning banners. She was dead."

"You don't know . . ."

Fiona came to sit beside me and held a cup of water
for me to take a sip. "I know very well, Seyonne. I saw
her face."

"No wonder you hated me."

A girl of fifteen had convinced herself that it was the
corruption of slavery that had killed her mother, and not

her own cruelty. And then her queen's husband was welcomed back from half a lifetime of slavery, with people claiming he was the fulfillment of prophecy. She had been forced to hear me teach that slavery could not corrupt, because it was the character of your soul, not the experiences of your life, that made the difference.

"I tried to hate you. For a year, I worked hard at it, as you know. I followed you across the Derzhi Empire to find the evidence, sure that if I watched and listened long enough, I would learn of the depths of sin and corruption and masterful deception, and thus justify what I had done. But instead you have taught me everything of compassion, everything of forgiveness, everything of honor. You showed me my own guilt, and at the same time set me free of it. These are not the gifts of a man of violence."

"Fiona—"

"Whatever else you've done or will do, we three—Blaise, the Prince, and myself—are your handiwork—forever changed because of you."

I had no words.

Fiona saw it, and nodded in satisfaction. "Now. Lie down and go to sleep."

I did as she bid. The choice to do otherwise did not seem available. But there was one more thing before I let a pleasant tiredness and full heart take me to oblivion. "You never answered my question, Fiona. What are you going to do now?"

She threw another blanket over me and set the enchantment to hold the fire steady. "My mentor has made himself a demon because he believed it was necessary to put the world in order. I will go everywhere, read everything, ask everyone—do whatever I need to do—to find out if he's right. Is that answer enough, Master Seyonne?"

I smiled and sank into the soft pillows. "Enough."